Dear Reader,

We've all done it: fallen blissfully in love and thought This Is THE ONE ... until you meet the family and want to run a mile. If it's not the gimlet-eyed mother who blatantly dismisses you as not good enough for Her Precious, it's the weird uncle who's always standing that bit too close. Or maybe the evil sibling who keeps mentioning your partner's ex, and how hilarious and cool they were (i.e. you are neither).

Of course, none of my in-laws are like this (Hi, by the way, if you're reading this. You are all SO GREAT) but there is something scarily random about the way you are thrown in with your partner's family once you start a relationship.

I thought it would be fun to write a novel about three brothers – the Mr Joneses of the title – and the women who fall in love with them, who are then absorbed into the Jones family. It felt like rich pickings for an author: so much scope for rivalry, drama and explosive arguments, yet also great potential for humour, unlikely friendships and love.

I hope you enjoy *Me and Mr Jones* as much as I enjoyed writing it. And do tweet me your own tales of family joy or woe @LDiamondAuthor with the hashtag #MrJones.

Love

Lucy Diamond

x

Lucy Diamond

ME AND MR JONES

PAN BOOKS

First published 2013 by Macmillan

This edition published 2013 by Pan Books
an imprint of Pan Macmillan, a division of Macmillan Publishers Limited
Pan Macmillan, 20 New Wharf Road, London N1 9RR
Basingstoke and Oxford
Associated companies throughout the world
www.panmacmillan.com

ISBN 978-1-4472-0866-2

A CIP catalogue record for this book is available from the British Library.

Typeset by SetSystems Ltd, Saffron Walden, Essex
Printed and bound by CPI Group (UK) Ltd, Croydon, CR0 4YY

Visit www.panmacmillan.com to read more about all our books
and to buy them. You will also find features, author interviews and
news of any author events, and you can sign up for e-newsletters
so that you're always first to hear about our new releases.

For Hannah, Tom and Holly,
with lots of love

Acknowledgements

Enormous thanks to my family, who put up with me while I was writing this book: my husband Martin, and my children Hannah, Tom and Holly. You are all brilliant and lovely people, and I am lucky to have you.

Thanks to the fabulous Lizzy Kremer, my agent, for pep talks, 'compliment sandwiches' and all your help. I'm so glad to have you on my side. And thank you, gorgeous Rowan Coleman for introducing us in the first place! The rest of the team at David Higham are wonderful too – thank you, Laura, Ania, Tine and Harriet for all your work on my behalf. I appreciate every single bit of it.

Thank you to my fantastic publishers, Pan Macmillan, in particular Jenny Geras for your wise and perceptive editorial input (and lovely lunches). I'd also like to thank Natasha, Ali, Chloe, Isolde, Jeremy, Geoff and Matt – what a brilliant team. It's an absolute pleasure to work with you all.

Thanks to everyone at the Bay Hotel in Lyme Regis, which is where I finished writing the last chapters and finally discovered how the story was going to end (thank goodness! It was touch and go at times). Your eggs Benedict breakfast is amazing – every author should start the day with one.

Thanks to the genius children (who wish to remain unnamed) for letting me pinch their carefully crafted Scooby-Doo lyrics, which weren't at all annoying when sung repeatedly on long car journeys at top volume. I'm certain you all have glittering song-writing careers ahead of you. Or perhaps as foghorns?

Thanks to everyone who has emailed or tweeted me to say they've enjoyed my books, or has come to a book signing and told me in person. Your support makes all the hard slog worthwhile. Thank you so much.

Last but definitely not least, a million thanks to Mum, Dad, Phil, Ellie, Fiona, Saba and Ian. You all rock.

Welcome to the website of
MULBERRY HOUSE!

Set in the picturesque village of Loveday, with easy
access to Lyme Regis, Charmouth and Axminster,
MULBERRY HOUSE is a friendly and welcoming
family-run guest house. Built in the seventeenth century,
with generous-sized rooms, beautiful views and
a spacious garden, it is the perfect place
to enjoy a comfortable stay.

FEATURES INCLUDE:

Centrally heated bedrooms with
televisions and **hairdryers**

•

En-suite facilities in most bedrooms

•

Delicious **home-cooked breakfasts**
using local ingredients

•

Free parking

We look forward to seeing you soon!
Your cordial hosts, Lilian and Eddie Jones

No dogs or smokers. Thank you.

Chapter One

'So,' said Lilian, pushing her glasses up her nose and addressing her husband with the kind of look that generally made his heart sink. 'The question is: what are we going to do with the house?'

Eddie still hadn't managed to conquer the dread that always churned inside him whenever his wife asked this sort of loaded question. She was particularly adept at them; would have been a shoo-in for an interrogation job with the Special Forces. *Are we going to get married or what, Edward Jones?* she'd demanded nearly forty-five years ago, one hand on her hip. *Only I'm getting fed up waiting for you to ask me, that's all.* He could picture her now, wearing the red polyester tabard she had to suffer as part of her Woolworths uniform, her glorious mane of chestnut hair up in a ponytail, those blazing blue eyes fiercely expectant.

He swallowed, just as he'd done back then. 'Well,' he said, after a moment's careful deliberation. 'I suppose we should see if one of the boys wants to take on the business first.'

She arched an eyebrow. God help him. Lilian's eyebrows – skinny, plucked and with a beautiful arch to them, even now – could speak volumes with a single brisk twitch. This one, unfortunately, was screaming WRONG ANSWER at one hundred and twenty decibels. 'I don't think it's quite as straightforward as *that*, dear,' she said, a muscle flashing in her cheek. 'If we simply *ask* do any of them want to run Mulberry House, then…' She gave a theatrical, damning shrug. 'Then the wrong one might end up with it. I mean, what if *Charlie* put himself forward, for instance? What would we say then? *Oh – sorry, darling. When we asked if anyone wanted the house, we were rather hoping it wouldn't be you.*'

Eddie felt hurt on behalf of his youngest son. 'Why shouldn't Charlie run the business?' he asked. 'Out of the three, he's the one who could do with a lucky break. And you never know, it could be the making of him. A bit of responsibility might be just what he needs.'

Lilian pushed out her lips in a small, tense moue of disagreement. 'He's too much of a risk,' she stated. 'And we both know he's hopeless with money. No, Eddie. Handing over the house to Charlie would be an unmitigated disaster. We might as well give it to a complete stranger. Or burn the place down!'

Eddie sighed. There was no mistaking the firm set of his wife's jaw, the flint in her eyes. Thirty-seven-year-old Charlie wasn't a bad lad – he didn't have a malicious bone in his body. He was just one of those kids who'd always drifted along haplessly without any signs of a master plan whirring elsewhere in his brain. Nothing wrong with that, though, was there? Eddie could relate to such an approach, having plodded aimlessly through life himself. And okay, so Charlie might have been unlucky with work in the past – and money, and women, come to that – but he was still a good boy.

'Who did you have in mind, then?' he asked after a moment, not having the energy to wade into an argument right now. He'd learned to pick his battles with care. 'Hugh?'

Hugh was their eldest son – the undisputed leader of the pack. At the age of forty-two he was a strapping man, just on the edge of portly, who had worked solidly all his life, and now had the job and family life to show for it. Hugh had gone to university – Oxford, no less (my word, *that* had been a proud day) – where he'd studied hard, joined the rugby team and met his wife, Alicia, with whom he'd been ever since. Twenty years down the line they had three children and lived very comfortably in a large Victorian house in Axminster, five or so miles away. He worked as a manager of a midsized engineering works and they enjoyed holidays abroad every summer, as well as piano lessons for the children and an Ocado delivery pass.

Lilian wrinkled her nose. 'But would Hugh and Alicia

want the house?' she wondered. 'Do they need the business? I can't see either of them giving up their jobs in a hurry, can you? Hugh's just been promoted, after all, and Alicia's . . . well, she's doing her own thing, isn't she?' There was an edge to her voice. Alicia taught biology in a nearby second-ary school and had recently been made head of department. She was so thoroughly *nice* and well-mannered that she had never once flaunted her first-class degree or career successes at anyone, but Lilian was still braced for it, all these years on, and stored a few digs about working mothers up her sleeve, just in case. There was such a thing as being 'too clever', whatever Eddie said.

'They might want to buy it as a family home,' Eddie suggested, although privately he had his doubts. Hugh and Alicia were happy where they were, he knew that. Their road was a safe, friendly one, where the children played out on bikes and scooters, and the neighbours organized street parties with home-made bunting and cupcakes. He wasn't sure they'd want the upheaval of leaving that behind.

Of course, Hugh had grown up here in Mulberry House, as had Charlie and David, back when the building was the Jones family home. The place had rung with boys' shouts and wrestling matches, the thwack of cricket balls on willow, the swishing of shuttlecocks over the washing line and, later, the thump of music and slammed bedroom doors during the teenage years. When the boys had all, finally, left home (it had taken Charlie a number of aborted attempts), Lilian and Eddie had felt the space was too large for the two of them, and began letting out the rooms to paying guests.

Fifteen years on, Mulberry House was a three-star B&B and was booked up for months in advance. 'A charming, family-run establishment with good facilities' as the AA put it, back in 2003. It had kept them well, this house, Eddie thought fondly, stroking the faded arm of the red velvet sofa as if caressing the head of a beloved child. The guests appreciated it too, if their repeat bookings were anything to go by. Jack and Doreen Willis hadn't missed a Whit weekend yet, and the Dalgliesh family always came down from Aberdeen, regular as clockwork, for their week in July.

Lately, Eddie had felt weary of the hard work, though. Because it *was* hard work, make no mistake, having a house full of guests to tend to. Lilian managed the laundry and cooking, and they had Mrs Daniels, the cleaner, who helped out during the summer season when they were busy as loons. He, meanwhile, kept the gardens tidy, did the accounts, answered calls and organized bookings, as well as undertaking all the hundred and one maintenance jobs that needed doing at any one time in order to keep the place looking shipshape. He'd always liked being busy, and relished the satisfaction of making people's holidays that extra bit more pleasant, but over the last year the relentless slog of work had begun to weigh heavy on his bones. He'd hurt his back putting up a new shower rail. There had been that bad cough right through the winter that he simply couldn't shake off. And was it his imagination, or were people getting . . . well, *ruder*, these days? More demanding? Time was, folks were satisfied with a Teasmade and a hairdryer in their room. Not any more. He'd lost count of the guests who'd complained about there not being satellite television, or Wi-Fi, whatever that was. He felt tired, tired of it all.

As well as the hard graft, he'd never been entirely comfortable having other people coming and going from his home, either. Although the back of the house had been converted to their own private quarters, off-limits to guests, it was still discomfiting, sitting in your favourite armchair in the evening, trying to watch *Gardeners' World* while hearing complete strangers through the wall – singing in the shower, watching a different channel, even having noisy, eye-popping sex without a thought for anybody else in the building. There were some things about running a bed and breakfast that Eddie would *not* miss, that was for sure. Whereas the thought of having their own little cottage, just the two of them, and not needing to get up and make twelve cooked breakfasts every morning of the week . . . it was becoming more appealing by the day.

'Which just leaves David,' Lilian concluded, steepling her fingers together and eyeing Eddie over the top of her spectacles.

Eddie blinked, having momentarily lost himself, imagining the peace of retirement. He was particularly looking forward to not having to be polite to anyone if he didn't feel like it. 'David,' he repeated, adding, 'and Emma,' after a second. He liked David's wife, Emma. She was quite feisty and spirited, the sort of girl Lilian had once been, in fact. Not that he'd ever dared voice this comparison to either his wife or his daughter-in-law, of course. Heavens, no. He had the feeling both would be horrified.

'Mmm,' Lilian said. 'You'd think they'd be keen to move out of Bristol and live a quieter life by now, especially after their recent run of bad luck. And I've all but given up asking when Emma is planning on having any kiddies, but she's not getting any younger, is she?'

There was a degree of tartness in this last comment and Eddie lowered his gaze. 'Well, we can certainly see if they'd like to take over the business,' he replied. 'But David always seems so happy in Bristol with their friends and...' He could feel his wife's eyes boring into him and broke off with a small cough, not daring to remind her that Emma worked in the city too. 'No harm in asking, though. Chances are, we'll have to sell up, but we can cross that bridge when we come to it.'

Lilian didn't speak for a moment, as if unable to bear even contemplating the idea of selling. Mulberry House had been their life for more than forty years after all. 'Yes,' she said finally. 'I've invited them all down for our anniversary lunch next month anyway. We'll put it to them then.'

One thing was certain. They both knew that their beloved home and business wouldn't slip out of the Joneses' hands without a fight.

Chapter Two

Alicia Jones was having a wobble, and not just on her thighs. Up until now she had felt herself blessed in all aspects of life, propelled from one unexpected triumph to another. Born lucky, her dad used to say proudly. At the age of eighteen she'd aced her A-levels and won a place at Oxford University, not only the first member of her family ever to achieve such a feat, but also the first person from her entire comprehensive school. There, enveloped in the blissful world of academia, she met Hugh, who was two years older than her – sensible, kind, dependable Hugh – and they had married the summer she graduated, both still virgins on their wedding night. And here they were now, with their nineteenth wedding anniversary due this August, three lovely children and a big house in Dorset to show for themselves. Perfect.

Although . . . Well, without wanting to sound ungrateful, things didn't feel quite so perfect these days. Lately, she'd been thrown into doubt and turmoil because of a certain date on the calendar that loomed horribly on the April page, just two short months away. Alicia Jones was going to be forty, and it was freaking her out big time.

Forty. FORTY! It sounded so old and middle-aged, so over-the-best-years. Her twenties had centred on her relationship with Hugh, their blossoming life together, their new-found careers. Her thirties had been consumed by the children, by family Christmases and birthdays and seaside holidays. But what on earth did she have to look forward to in her forties, apart from new wrinkles and a double chin?

'I feel like I'm getting old,' she moaned one evening on the phone to her sister Sandra, who lived in Cheltenham and ran a dog-training school.

'You've always been old,' Sandra said spitefully. 'Even when you were thirteen you were middle-aged, Al.' She followed this by a snorting laugh, so as to make it sound like a joke, but Alicia wasn't fooled. The words stayed in her head for days, stinging her whenever she thought about them.

Had she really been middle-aged at the age of thirteen? Admittedly, she had been a sensible and, some might say, swotty child (she hated that word), but she knew how to have fun too, of course she did! Just because she listened to choral music rather than the Top 40, it didn't make her dull, merely different. Her own person. That was good, wasn't it? And just because her sister had gone off the rails and dabbled with drugs and what-have-you, just because *she'd* dropped out of school as soon as possible, and shacked up with a police line-up's worth of unsavoury types over the years without ever settling down, just because Sandra was still the spoilt, vivacious, attention-seeking baby of the family, it didn't mean Alicia always had to be marked up as 'the boring one'.

Rationally she knew this, but nonetheless, with the dreaded 4-0 approaching, she was starting to wonder if she'd got it wrong the whole time. What if Sandra was right? What if Alicia had wasted her entire youth being prematurely middle-aged, therefore missing out on the so-called fun years; fun years that she could never get back?

'Hugh, do you think I'm middle-aged?' she asked in bed one night.

Hugh looked up from his Stalingrad book in surprise. 'Middle-aged? Well, technically, I suppose...' he began, until he realized she was wilting with dismay. 'Of course not!' he amended hastily. 'Isn't forty-five when middle age begins? We're still classed as young, I think. Aren't we?'

She shrugged. Not the best answer, Hugh. Not the most reassuring words ever spoken. Who cared about 'technically'? She wasn't talking about 'technically'. She meant, did he think she was a boring old frump? Did he think she was mutton dressed as mutton? Judging by the way he hadn't leapt to shout down the question as being absurd — *of COURSE you're not middle-aged, darling!* — she was depressingly certain that she knew the answer.

Yes, Alicia. You're an old fart. You're past it.

Worst of all, in just two months she'd be even more past it. 'Technically' past it, so to speak. No longer a thirty-something with the world at her feet, everything to play for. She would cross a line into the next decade, while youth and fun slipped permanently away through her fingers. Unless she acted pretty damn quickly, that was.

If only she had Christine to talk to. Her twin sister had been on her mind more often than usual recently. Alicia was originally part of a set, you see; a double act that had been torn in half far too early.

The sisters had shared the mutual intimacy of their mother's womb for thirty-five weeks before the merest whisper of time together in the real world. Unfortunately, poor tiny Christine had died from heart complications when she was just three days old, and that had been that. Alicia wished she had some memory — even the tiniest flicker of recollection — but there was nothing left of her sister, save a tiny headstone in a Cotswold cemetery. *An Angel Returned to Heaven,* the engraved letters read. Growing up, Alicia had imagined her small deceased sister with angel wings, a long white nightie and a chubby cherubic face. *Oh,*

Christine, she'd been thinking lately, *we should have been in this together.*

Hugh had once suggested that you couldn't miss someone you'd never known, but Alicia couldn't have disagreed more. She still ached for the *idea* of her sister, her lost other half. She couldn't help worrying that there was something missing in her, which only her twin could have completed.

In her bleakest moments she blamed herself for having lived when her sister hadn't made it. Survivor guilt, they called it, the long nights of torturous self-questioning, the recurring 'Why me?' In the dark, pulsing space of their mother's womb, had she somehow consumed more of the nutrition they both needed to thrive and develop? Had Alicia's greed inadvertently caused Christine's death? Such agony was the jump-start that galvanized her to work doubly hard at everything. No girl could have crammed more for her GCSEs, or practised harder for her violin lessons. Alicia was determined to live life for the two of them, her and Christine, so that nobody could ever think she was a disappointment or a let-down. Nobody would be allowed to say the wrong twin had survived.

Only now . . . had it been enough? If Christine had lived, would she have made better choices, led a more interesting life?

Don't torture yourself. You'll never know. Agonizing over what might have been can only lead to madness.

Oh, Christine. If only they could go into the next decade hand-in-hand, laughing together at whatever adventures their forties might bring. The thought just made Alicia feel lonelier than ever.

Enough hand-wringing, she decided one night. It was Thursday evening and the house was quiet; the children in bed, and Hugh at the gym. Alicia poured herself a glass of wine while she waited for their ageing PC to crank up, then opened a brand-new document. Now then. How could she shake up her life a bit, drip some excitement into the mix before it was too late?

THE TURNING-40 ACTION PLAN, she typed at the top, then leaned back in her chair, considering. If she could have her time again, start from scratch, what would she like to have achieved by now? She shut her eyes, imagining different versions of herself: a brave, intrepid Alicia, who strode through jungles and dived in warm oceans with frolicking dolphins. An Alicia who taught abroad or volunteered in decrepit orphanages in Third World countries, lavishing hollow-eyed babies and children with love and compassion. Another Alicia might have continued her studies, perhaps even conducted a scientific breakthrough, written important papers to be studied by generations to come.

She pictured a theatrical Alicia too, one who'd followed

her heart and taken A-level drama, rather than allowing her parents to steer her into straight science and maths. 'There'll be plenty of time for acting later on,' they'd said, but it hadn't really worked out like that. Once at Oxford, she'd been too scared to join the Footlights gang, even though she longed to take part; they all seemed so much louder and more confident than her. But there was an am-dram society in Lyme, wasn't there? It was never too late to try.

Explore a new country, she typed. *Volunteer for something. Undertake a research project. Act!*

Simply seeing the words on the screen made her feel excited, as if new possibilities were opening up before her eyes. So what else?

She curled a tendril of hair around her finger while she thought, and a more trivial option occurred to her. Her hair! She'd worn her hair in the same style for the last twenty years or so: long and layered, falling either side of her forehead in a centre parting. She barely thought about it most days, shoving it up in a hasty ponytail for school, and only really bothering to condition or blow-dry it during the holidays. How boring was that? And why hadn't it crossed her mind to experiment before now? Over the years she'd seen friends crimp, curl and crop their hair; she'd complimented new fringes, glossy extensions and daring colour schemes, while she'd trudged along throughout, with the same drab brown curtains framing her face. Sometimes, if she was particularly hard up for time, she'd even taken the scissors to her locks herself.

Hair, she typed, imagining walking into the staffroom with an attractive new style to a chorus of compliments. Maybe she could overhaul her entire look while she was at it. She thought of Sandra, who always appeared groomed, with silk scarves and look-at-me jewellery choices, who wore perfume and lipstick even when putting wilful Jack Russells through their paces. She thought of her sister-in-law Emma, who wore daring bright colours and clashing patterns with pretty clips or flowers in her hair. Alicia, by contrast, always lumbered about in scruffy jeans and an old fleece.

Hell, her list couldn't entirely consist of massive challenges – there had to be a few frivolous ones too. And sometimes it was the tiny things that made the biggest difference. *Wear lipstick!* she typed, draining the last of her wine.

The phone rang, jerking her out of her daydream of self-improvement. It was Sandra. 'I was just thinking about you,' Alicia said cheerfully.

'Oh yeah?' Her sister immediately sounded suspicious.

'In a nice way,' Alicia assured her. 'Just how good you always look – how you make an effort with your appearance. I'm going to start doing the same.'

There was a pause. 'Are you drunk?' Sandra asked.

Alicia giggled. 'No – well, a bit tipsy, maybe,' she replied.

'I was having a flap about turning forty, that's all. I'm trying to think of some exciting things I should do while I'm still a thirty-something.'

She could hear Sandra puffing on a cigarette. 'And making an effort with your appearance counts as an "exciting thing"?' she asked dubiously.

'Well, no, that was more of a general—'

'Go on then, what's your most exciting one? How are you planning to live it up before you're officially over-the-hill?'

Alicia pulled a face at the telephone. There was a phrase she'd heard on television recently: 'harshing my mellow'. Sandra was *definitely* harshing her mellow, spoiling things like she always did. 'Well...' She scrolled back through her list. 'Travel to a new country,' she said triumphantly. 'Join an acting group. Volunteer for something.'

So there, Sandra. Put that lot in your pipe and smoke it.

'Hmmm.' Annoyingly, her sister didn't sound impressed. 'What about the fun stuff? What about an adventure?'

Alicia's shoulders slumped. She wished she hadn't picked up the phone now. 'That *is* fun stuff to me,' she protested. 'And I was feeling really good about it until I spoke to you. What are you phoning about anyway?'

If Sandra noticed the irritation in Alicia's voice, she didn't offer any kind of apology. She didn't even answer the question. 'Tell you what, *I'll* give you a few challenges to get your teeth into, Al,' she said. 'Things every woman should do before she hits forty.'

'Like what?' Alicia rolled her eyes. When would Sandra get it into her head that she was actually the *younger* sister in the family? She'd always been patronizing to Alicia, but now she seemed to be casting herself as some kind of woman-of-the-world role model. Even more annoying was the way Sandra insisted on calling her 'Al'. It made Alicia think of Paul Simon, which was not how she liked to see herself.

'I'll email you a list,' Sandra said, and chuckled to herself.

A weariness descended on Alicia. 'Thanks,' she managed to say through gritted teeth. *I won't bother even reading it*, she vowed as she put down the phone.

The following morning was taken up by a double lesson on homeostasis with the Year Tens, but as soon as it was breaktime Alicia leapt into action and called up the nicest hairdresser's in town, as opposed to her usual perms-and-pensioners salon, largely staffed by girls who'd dropped out of school early and still called her 'Miss'. As luck would have it, they had a cancellation for eleven o'clock on Saturday, so she gratefully booked herself in, completely forgetting until she'd put the phone down that this would clash with her daughter Matilda's ballet lesson.

Any chance u can take M to/from ballet tomorrow? she texted Hugh from the staffroom. *Have got hair appt at 11.*

He replied just before the bell rang to signal the end of break. *Sorry, no can do. Boys' cricket match in Blandford.*

She sighed. Typical, she thought dismally. Fallen at the first hurdle. She was just about to resign herself to cancelling her amazing new haircut – it was probably for the best; people like Sandra would only mock her for it anyway – when her phone buzzed with another text. *Will see if Charlie's free to do it. Love Hugh x.*

It felt like a sign. Alicia, you *shall* go to the ball. Well, she'd go to Waves for a cut and blow-dry anyway. Every long journey started with a single step, after all.

Sandra's list arrived via email that afternoon.

Challenge Alicia!, the subject line read jauntily, and Alicia felt her nerve falter. She clicked open the message, wishing for the twentieth time that she hadn't let slip her turning-forty plans in the first place. If she was going to tell anyone about it, she should have told Hugh, rather than her sneering sister. For some reason, after her conversation with Sandra, she hadn't been able to confide in him when he returned from the gym that evening, red-faced and dishevelled. What if he laughed at her too? She'd end up feeling like the biggest thirty-nine-year-old joke ever.

Oh, what the hell. Looking at Sandra's suggestions did not mean she actually had to *do* them, she reassured herself, glancing around the empty classroom where she was sitting with a pile of marking. She began to read.

Hey Al,

So here goes: Twenty Things a Woman Should Experience Before Forty. And yes, I have done most of them, if you were wondering. Let me know how you get on — we can compare notes!

S x

1. *Ride a motorbike*
2. *See the Pyramids*
3. *Bungee jump*
4. *Do something your friends (and sister!!!) wouldn't approve of*
5. *Have an affair*
6. *Buy expensive lingerie. Like,* really *expensive. Marks & Sparks pants do not qualify*
7. *Have dirty sex in Paris*
8. *Go shopping in New York*
9. *Skinny-dip in the ocean. Preferably a warm ocean. Coogee Beach in Australia was good for me (the English Channel doesn't count, by the way. Nor does the North Sea)*
10. *Buy a sex toy (and USE IT!!!)*
11. *Break the speed limit, just for fun*

12. *Travel alone. This doesn't mean popping to Tesco for the weekly shop*
13. *Buy expensive face cream*
14. *Try anal sex . . .*

Alicia closed down the browser the instant she saw the word 'anal', her hand shaking. For goodness' sake! Why did her sister have to be so . . . disgusting? Why was she so obsessed with sex and buying things? It was the most tawdry collection of ideas Alicia had ever seen; she felt tarnished just reading them.

Well, if Sandra thought she was warped enough to abandon her morals and lower herself to that sort of depraved, sleazy behaviour, then she jolly well had another think coming. Dirty sex in Paris, indeed. Sex toys and lingerie. Honestly! As for number fourteen . . . she couldn't even bring herself to repeat the words in her head. No, never, not in a million years.

Still, there was at least one positive to take from her sister's list: it made her own ideas for self-improvement appear a lot less daunting. Who cared what Sandra had to say about the whole thing anyway?

Within the next twenty-four hours two miracles had occurred. Small ones, admittedly, but miracles all the same. For one, Hugh's brother Charlie had willingly taken Matilda to her ballet class, actually picking her up on time and everything. Even more astonishingly, he'd offered to do the same again the following Saturday when he brought her home. 'Nice to spend a bit of time with my niece,' he said.

Alicia wasn't usually that keen on Charlie – he'd proved to be shockingly unreliable in the past, the complete opposite of solid, steady Hugh – but on this occasion he'd come up trumps. 'Thank you, and yes please,' she said in delight.

'Nice hair, by the way,' he added with a grin, and wolf-whistled her there and then in her kitchen, sending a blush sweeping right up to her newly conditioned roots.

That was the other miracle. Not the wolf-whistle (although it was pretty much a first in Alicia's life, admittedly), not the compliment either (again quite rare, if she was honest), but the haircut itself. The best haircut *ever*, in fact. Alicia couldn't stop admiring herself in the mirror, turning from side to side, examining the beauty of its shape, the way the longer front strands fell so prettily around her face, framing it perfectly in a swingy, chin-length bob. The back was shorter and layered to reveal the nape of her neck, and she kept stroking it absent-mindedly, thinking how much lighter her head felt with so much hair lopped off.

Alicia had left a massive tip for the hairdresser – she'd wanted to hug her, actually, and only just managed to restrain herself – and walked out of the salon on air. So *this* was what people called a 'good hair day'. It felt amazing. So amazing, in fact, that she found herself picking up a string of purple glass beads and a new bag too, in Wishes, her favourite boutique. Forget shopping in New York, forget filth in Paris. Right now, this felt like the high life to Alicia.

Charlie wasn't the only one to appreciate her new look. 'Ooh, Mummy!' Matilda squealed. 'You actually look really pretty now.'

It wasn't the exact phrasing Alicia would have wished for – she'd have left out the 'actually' and the 'now', for starters – but there was no disguising the genuine enthusiasm in her daughter's voice. 'Thanks, darling,' she said, hugging her. 'How was ballet?'

'Oh, it was fine,' she replied. 'Well, apart from when Uncle Charlie—'

Charlie coughed quickly. 'I'd better get going, ladies,' he said, retreating towards the door.

'Are you sure?' Alicia asked. 'You're welcome to stay for a coffee, or lunch. Hugh will be back with the boys in half an hour or so.'

'Sorry, better run,' he said. 'People to see, things to do, all that malarkey.'

So he'd gone, and Matilda never got to finish her sentence, distracted as she was by spotting Alicia's new necklace in the next moment. 'Ooh! That's nice! Can I borrow it for Florence's party tomorrow?'

'Thank you, and definitely not,' Alicia said, patting the beads as they lay gleaming in the hollow of her throat. Humming to herself, she made a cafetiere of steaming coffee just for her, a luxury she'd never usually bother to indulge in. Perhaps this self-improvement thing was going to be fun after all.

Chapter Three

Izzy Allerton had been living in Lyme Regis for precisely four weeks, and still couldn't believe her luck. Manchester seemed a million miles away already. She was not going to look back.

Funny how things left their mark on you, wasn't it? She'd come down here just once before, for a precious holiday when she was seven, and had clung to the memory ever since, clutched it close like a talisman, a reminder that life didn't always have to be shit. Because, frankly, the rest of her childhood had been far from idyllic. As a baby she was put in foster care because her mum was a schizophrenic and couldn't look after her, then she went to live with her granny from the age of four. Those years had been happier at least: she'd felt safe and wanted and looked-after, with a vest under her school uniform, clean shoes on her feet and a hot bath every other night.

But one winter, when Izzy was twelve and her mind was filled with such pressing concerns as pimples, whether or not she'd ever grow breasts, and what it would feel like to kiss a boy, her granny developed pleurisy and died before either of them realized quite how ill she was. A tired-faced social worker came to meet Izzy at school later that week, and said she couldn't stay alone in the flat any more. It was as if the door was slammed shut on her childhood, never to open again.

The teenage years saw an unhappy succession of foster placements, care homes and running away, before, at the age of sixteen, Izzy was deemed capable of standing on her own two feet and left to get on with things herself. 'Have a nice life,' the care worker said, without any apparent irony, as she handed Izzy a bin liner to pack her stuff in, and twenty quid. By then, her mum was dead too, of an overdose. As for her dad . . . Izzy didn't even know who he was.

The one holiday she'd had in Lyme remained in her mind throughout all of this, like a beacon of light, a golden spell of happiness shining out from the surrounding turbulence. It had been the first time she'd seen the sea, the first time she'd been on a beach. She'd loved the light, floaty feeling of freedom, which had fizzed inside her for the whole week. Sandcastles with paper flags. Paddling in her knickers and sun hat. Fish and chips for tea. Granny snoring in the small room they'd shared at the B&B. *When I'm a grown-up*, she vowed, *I'm going to come back and live here.*

Twenty-one years later, she had actually done it: she'd

escaped from her crap life, past and present, and made a break for a brighter future with her two daughters in tow. The light, floaty feeling had returned the moment she drove onto the southbound M6, the boot crammed with their belongings, both girls wide-eyed on the back seat. 'Where are we going, Mum?'

We're going to live better lives, love. We're going somewhere Gary won't find us. We're going to be free.

'We're going to the nicest place in the whole world,' she replied, hoping her memory hadn't let her down.

Freedom had been quite scary at first. Rocking up on the south coast with only the number of a women's refuge in her pocket, and the half-promise of a job . . . Yeah, it had been a risk. A massive risk. But when you were desperate, sometimes you had to gamble, didn't you? You had to throw the dice and hope your number came up. Four weeks later, although she daren't count any chickens, she had a faint, excited feeling that she might just have rolled a double six.

Because look at her now! Living in one of the prettiest, loveliest parts of the country, the girls having started at the nearest school and made friends, and her, with two new jobs keeping her busy – teaching ballet classes on Saturdays and one evening a week, and a lunchtime shift in a tea shop on Broad Street. Best of all, there was no Gary.

She didn't plan to get involved with anybody else for a

long, long while, that was for sure. She was happy serving her old ladies cream teas and milky coffees, and teaching her leotard-clad juniors jetés and glissades in the dusty church hall; happy to tuck her daughters in bed every night and know they were safe. Just the three of them now, and it was a proper way to live, a vast improvement on before. She could not believe life could feel so sweet.

Fate was a bugger sometimes, though, wasn't it? Because the very next Saturday she was halfway through her long morning of ballet classes when in walked a scruffy unshaven man with needing-a-cut golden hair (like a lion, she thought absent-mindedly) and the naughtiest blue eyes Izzy had ever seen. He wasn't her type at all – he had stone-washed jeans on, for heaven's sake – but there was something about him that made her look twice. What was more, he looked right back.

Their gazes locked for a long, slow beat of mutual fascination, and something strange happened: a sudden bolt of warmth gushed through her body and her heart seemed to stutter. Eventually she managed to pull her gaze away, hot with embarrassment and confusion. *Izzy Allerton, don't you ever learn?* she scolded herself, wheeling round to check on Hazel and Willow, who were at the second-hand clothes table, taking money for the leotards and dance skirts on sale there.

'That will be seven pounds fifty, please,' nine-year-old Willow was saying, with so much solemnity and assurance that Izzy swelled with pride. They were good girls, her two; they were survivors, like her. And now she was going to make sure that nothing ever rocked their little worlds again. Especially not a bloke.

'If we're all ready to begin...' she said pointedly to her class, hands on her hips, steadfastly ignoring the sexy blond man, even though she could feel him trying to catch her eye again.

There was a series of excited squeaks and rushing movements from her pupils as they tugged on ballet shoes and fastened ponytails, then hurried to stand next to their best friends in the hall. Izzy was strict about not letting parents stay and watch – too distracting for the children – and made a point of waiting until they had all left for the small anteroom nearby before she began. She'd been so lucky landing these classes as maternity cover for a friend of Monique, a fellow dance teacher in Manchester, and she was determined to do everything by the book.

The blond man didn't seem to know the etiquette and sat down expectantly on a chair at the side of the hall. 'I'm afraid I don't allow parents to sit in on my classes,' Izzy told him. 'We put on a show at the end of each term, which you are welcome to—'

'Ah, but I'm not a parent,' he interrupted teasingly and her skin prickled. 'What about uncles, do we get to stay and watch?'

'Uncle *Charlie*,' one of the girls hissed, her pale freckly face becoming suffused with scarlet embarrassment. 'You're meant to wait in *there*. Didn't Mum *say*?'

Izzy maintained a poker face. 'I'm afraid there is no preferential treatment for uncles,' she said. 'Willow, would you mind showing this gentleman where he can wait? Thank you.'

Everyone was staring at him, apart from his niece, who looked as if she wished he'd fall through a trapdoor and disappear, right now, please. Izzy turned to the class and smiled. 'Good morning, everyone!' she said, as Willow led the man down the back of the hall and away. 'Let's begin our warm-up.'

It wasn't as simple as she'd hoped, putting 'Uncle Charlie' in his place. He sought her out at the end of the lesson, elbowing aside all the nicely spoken mums who wanted to find out how little Annabel's pliés were coming along, and whether or not Izzy had any tips vis-à-vis Rosie's audition piece for the Marine Theatre youth group.

'I was wondering if you'd like to come out for a drink with me some time,' he said, bold as brass, and the mum-clamour instantly dropped away to silence.

She flushed at his brazen approach. Who the hell did he think he was, asking her out in front of all these parents, making a fool of her *and* himself in the same breath? Worse, she could feel Willow's questioning gaze on her. He might have sparked the merest flicker of attraction and intrigue earlier, but the wary light in her daughter's eyes was enough to stamp it out immediately.

Gritting her teeth, she went on discussing Rosie's *pas de chat*, as if he hadn't uttered a word. Cheeky bastard. She could feel him grinning at her as if this was a shared joke between them. It was not.

He didn't give up easily, though. He waited until the cluster of parents had finally all peeled away, then approached her again, with his niece, Matilda, mutely cringing beside him.

'Just a drink,' he wheedled. 'Go on. I think we'd get on really well, me and you.'

'Mum, can *I* have a drink?' Hazel asked, interrupting the moment, thank goodness.

'Yes, love, of course, the water bottle's in my bag,' Izzy replied. Then she gave the man one of her looks, the sort she reserved for difficult pre-schoolers. 'Look, mate, I'll just say this once: I'm not interested,' she told him flatly. 'Not in you, not in any bloke. Now, if you don't mind, I'm busy here, all right? I'm working. Goodbye, Matilda, see you next week.'

That was Matilda's cue to start dragging him away and, bless her, she tried. Unfortunately he didn't budge. 'But I'm not just any bloke,' he replied, deadpan. 'I'm Charlie Jones. And you're . . . gorgeous.'

From anyone else's lips the words might have sounded cocky. But somehow he said it in a way that made his confidence stunningly attractive. Judging by the collective raised eyebrows and hushed attention of the ballet mums in the vicinity, they thought so too.

'Sorry,' she said firmly, meeting his blue eyes full-on. She might look like a wisp of a ballerina, but he needed to know that she was pure northern steel underneath her leotard; more than a match for a Dorset boy. Then she swivelled her gaze briskly away and smiled at Bella Hardcastle's mum, as if that was the end of it. 'Mrs Hardcastle, did you want to speak to me?'

It turned out that Charlie Jones wasn't the sort of person who took kindly to the word 'no'. He appeared the following week as well, this time with a bunch of red tulips, which he proffered at the start of the lesson. 'I promise I'm not a freak,' he said, his eyes crinkling at the edges as he smiled. 'And I'm not a dodgy stalker type, either. I just have this feeling about me and you. That we're meant to be.'

'Oh, Uncle Charlie, please stop it, you're embarrassing

me!' Matilda cried in mortification, pulling a face at her friend.

'You're not the only one,' Izzy told her drily, ignoring both the flowers and the glint in his eye.

He was back at the end of the lesson with a punnet of strawberries, like an offering of bright jewels. 'Just in case you're hungry,' he'd said, handing them to her with a flourish. 'And if you happen to be thirsty as well, then maybe . . .'

'Here we go again,' she heard one of the mums mutter. This was turning into a soap opera.

She accepted the strawberries. 'Thank you,' she said, trying to keep her composure.

'Ooh, yummy,' Hazel said at once, selecting the plumpest and cramming it into her mouth.

'And if you're thirsty . . .' Charlie repeated, raising one eyebrow meaningfully.

'I'm not thirsty,' she said. 'Sorry.'

He pantomimed exaggerated despair, his shoulders flattening, his head falling. God, he really was attractive. She couldn't help a flutter of desire.

Matilda tugged at his hand. 'Come *on*, Uncle Charlie, stop it, or I'll tell Mum.'

'But . . .' Izzy said before she could help herself. Damn it. He'd got to her after all. 'I might be later on. And so might my daughters.'

She flung in the mention of the girls like an explosive, watching his face carefully for his reaction. He grinned. 'Sounds like a party to me,' he said.

'No,' she replied, shaking her head. 'Not a party. Just a quick drink at the Pilot Boat, before I take the girls home for tea. Take it or leave it.'

'I'll take it,' he said instantly.

'I'll see you there at five o'clock then,' she said, hoping she wouldn't live to regret it. Nothing could happen at five o'clock in the afternoon, could it? Surely it would be safe: broad daylight, plenty of people around, the girls as her chaperones. Besides, she didn't have anyone to babysit for a drink later on without them. Mrs Murray from the flat next door kept an eye on the girls while she took her Adult Beginners class on Wednesday evenings, but that was work — the sort of thing that her neighbour, a retired nurse, understood and appreciated. Izzy wasn't sure if she could ask the same thing in order to go for a drink with this strangely persistent man. Mrs Murray had already taken a nosey interest in any prospective 'gentlemen callers' Izzy might have, making it quite clear that they were not to be tolerated. 'Fine by me,' Izzy had said, meaning every word.

This was just a drink. Nothing was going to happen. Nothing whatsoever.

*

'Why are we going out now?' Willow wanted to know later that afternoon as they prepared to head to the pub. 'Isn't it, like, teatime soon?'

'Are we going to the beach?' seven-year-old Hazel asked hopefully. She'd fallen in love with the beach from the moment she'd clapped eyes on it, and was a total surfer girl in the making. She was already angling for her own wetsuit so that she could swim whatever the weather, and had filled in most of the *I-Spy at the Seaside* book that Izzy had picked up from one of the charity shops, eagerly pointing out herring gulls, hermit crabs and sandworms whenever she spotted them.

'No, we're not going to the beach,' Izzy replied carefully. 'And yes, it'll be teatime when we get back,' she added to Willow, who was anxious about everything happening exactly as it should do. 'We're just popping out for half an hour or so to meet a new friend.'

'Oh *God*,' Hazel groaned in disgust, even though Izzy had told her plenty of times not to say that. 'We're going to meet that man, aren't we, the one who brought the strawberries today? He is like *so* embarrassing.'

'Oh, Mum, we're not, are we?' Willow's voice went up three notes, and her eyes burned into Izzy, dark pools of worry.

Izzy hesitated. Strawberries, tulips and that crooked smile . . . So much for being made of steel, so much for never again. She was a bloody pushover. 'It's just one drink,' she said awkwardly. 'Hey, what do you think you'll choose? Lemonade or fizzy orange?'

'Orange,' Hazel said, perking up with astonishing speed. 'Do you think he'll bring us some more strawberries? They were yummy.'

'I'm not having a drink,' Willow said mutinously, turning away and folding her arms. 'Because I'm not going. I've got a tummy ache.'

Izzy crouched down in front of her. 'Listen, chick,' she said, taking Willow's hands in hers. 'We're being polite, that's all. If he's really boring and we don't like him, we'll say sorry, bye, and we'll come back home, just the three of us. And do you know what we'll do then?'

'What?' asked Hazel breathlessly. 'Make chocolate krispies again?'

'Even better than chocolate krispies,' Izzy said, thinking quickly. Willow was listening – she had to make this good. 'When we get back here, us three are going to have . . . the best ever pyjama party. We'll put on our pyjamas and get the duvets off the beds, and cuddle up under them together on the sofa while we watch a film. I'll even make popcorn. And do you know what we'll do after that?'

'What?' both girls said now.

'PILLOW FIGHT!' shouted Izzy, grabbing Hazel and ruffling her hair.

Hazel squealed and giggled. 'Yay!'

Even Willow was smiling a little bit. 'We could just stay here and do that now,' she suggested.

'YEAH!' cried Hazel, bouncing up and down. 'Pillow fight! Pillow fight!'

'No, let's go, because I did promise, and you know I never break promises,' Izzy said quickly, before Hazel became too hyper. 'We'll give him a chance, this Charlie fella, all right? But if he's boring or annoys us, then the code word is "pyjamas", got it? And as soon as one of us says "pyjamas", then we'll come back and have our party. Yeah?'

'Yeah,' the girls chorused.

Izzy smiled, loving them so much it hurt. She was well aware of the damage Gary had done. Willow was wary of strangers, and tended to stay on the sidelines of any group, casting suspicious glances around her until she was completely sure it was okay to join in. Hazel, by contrast, was eager to be everybody's best friend, all too willing to please. From now on, Izzy wanted them to have the best ever childhood, one of fresh air and giggles and bear hugs, one where fun and innocence reigned for as long as possible. She would not let them down.

'Come on, then,' she said. 'Let's go.'

Willow stayed glued to Izzy's side as they walked into the pub garden. Charlie had bagged a table in a sunny spot and waved them over. 'Evening, all,' he said, then made a point of smiling at the girls. 'Hello, ladies, my name is Charlie. What are you called?'

Hazel beamed. 'Hazel,' she said. 'Hello. We're having a party later on, just for girls.'

Izzy stiffened, hoping Charlie wouldn't do anything so naff as to try and invite himself along. He didn't.

'Cool,' he said gravely. 'And you must be . . . ?' he added, looking straight at Willow.

Hazel hadn't finished yet, though. 'It's a certain *type* of party,' she said mysteriously, 'but I'm not really allowed to say any more, otherwise I might not get my fizzy orange. But it's a party where you wear something funny.' She tapped her nose beguilingly.

'Aha,' Charlie replied. '*That* sort of party. Sounds brilliant.' He smiled at Willow. 'Hello,' he said, considering her carefully. 'You look to me as if you're a bit older than my niece, Matilda. Let me guess: are you . . . ten?'

Willow shook her head, still on her guard.

'Sorry,' Charlie said cheerfully. 'Rubbish at guessing ages. If you're not ten, you must be . . . thirteen?'

Willow shook her head again, although Izzy was sure she detected a tiny uplift of her mouth at the corners, as if privately thrilled to be thought a teenager.

'Twenty-nine?' Charlie guessed. 'You're never *thirty*?'

Hazel giggled. 'She's *nine*,' she said. 'And I'm seven.'

'Shut up, Hazel,' Willow muttered, glaring again.

'Girls, that's enough,' Izzy said. 'I've not managed to get a word in yet. Hello, Charlie. This is Willow and this is Hazel. Nice to see you.'

He grinned. 'You too. You look even better out of your leotard,' he said, indicating the denim skirt and pink T-shirt she'd pulled on. 'I mean . . .' He blushed.

His awkwardness made her like him a little bit more. 'Thank you,' she said. 'So, what are you drinking?'

'No, I'll get these, it was my idea,' he said at once. Phew. She only had a fiver in her purse, but her pride would never have let her admit as much.

'Thank you,' she said. 'I'd like a small glass of red wine, please, and the girls would like . . . what was it? One fizzy orange and one lemonade?'

'Correctamundo,' Hazel beamed. Willow was staring pointedly away.

'Coming right up,' Charlie said, and vanished off to the bar.

'Pyjamas, pyjamas, pyjamas,' Willow said, as soon as he was out of earshot.

'Come on, babe,' Izzy said, putting an arm around her. 'Let's sit down. He's all right.'

'But you said—'

'I know, but we haven't given him a chance yet. We've only been here two minutes – we can't walk out now.'

Hazel had already sat down and was swinging her legs happily. 'He's funny,' she said. 'I like him.'

'Well, I don't,' Willow said.

'Give him a chance,' Izzy said again. 'And, before you know it, we'll be back home in our jim-jams. Tell you what, Willow, if you're really good, you can choose the film, okay?'

Willow nodded. 'That's my girl,' said Izzy.

As it happened, there was no need for anyone to throw the word 'pyjamas' into the conversation from then on. Charlie turned out to be the best fun any of them had had in ages. He taught the girls how to flip beer mats and catch them. He made them all laugh with stories of his naughty boyhood. And he even charmed Willow, by producing a fossil he'd found that afternoon on Charmouth beach. 'Have you been fossil-hunting down there yet?' he asked, and looked appalled when they shook their heads. 'No? Oh, you'll love it, you can get some cool ammonites,' he said. 'Tell you what, I've still got the little fossil hammer that I had when I was about your age. I can lend it to you, if you want.'

'Will you come with us?' Hazel asked immediately, her big brown eyes beseeching.

Charlie glanced up at Izzy. 'Maybe, if it's all right with your mum.'

'Can we, Mum? Can we?' chorused both girls with such excitement and enthusiasm that Izzy was powerless to refuse.

'I should think so,' she managed to say eventually, keeping it vague. Much as she liked Charlie, she knew she had to tread carefully. Baby steps, she needed to take, nothing bigger, nothing faster. 'Girls, we'd better be getting home now,' she said soon afterwards.

They were both completely under his spell already though, even Willow, who'd just been taught to make her cheek 'pop' using her finger. (Even better, Hazel couldn't do it; only Willow. A triumph indeed.) 'Ohhh, do we have to?' she complained.

'We do,' Izzy affirmed. Boundaries, boundaries, she intoned in her head. If she'd learned anything in life so far, it was the importance of self-preservation. 'Thanks, Charlie,' she said briskly, rising to her feet.

'And . . . maybe another time?' he asked, his gaze hopeful.

The girls looked up at her with similar eagerness. 'That would be nice,' she said, determined not to be pinned down until she'd had time to think about it. 'Thanks again. We'll see you around.'

And that was as much as she would give him. For now.

Chapter Four

OH BABY! *website — for helpful, friendly advice on*
CONCEPTION, PREGNANCY *and* MOTHERHOOD
Members' forum > Trying to conceive > New thread
Subject: New member
Posted by: EmmaJ35

Hello everyone,

  *I'm new to the forum so I thought I'd introduce myself. I'm
Emma, and have been trying to conceive for nine months. I am
starting to feel obsessed with sperm counts and am pouncing on
my husband as soon as I hit my ovulation window, but nothing's
happened yet.*

  *I'm 35 and aware that the clock is ticking. I can't help
wondering if we've left it too late, or if there is something wrong
with me/him. STRESS!*

  *Friends with babies keep saying unhelpful things like 'Just
relax! As soon as you stop thinking about it, you'll get pregnant!'
but I CAN'T stop thinking about it, and I can't relax — it's not*

as easy as that. Work is a nightmare and, since my husband lost
his job two months ago (yes, just before Christmas — great
timing!), I am the only breadwinner and feel under massive
pressure. I work as an interior designer and used to love it, but
recently have found myself getting increasingly impatient with
customers dithering over a light switch or a paint shade. A light
switch, for heaven's sake!! It all seems so trivial when my mind is
taken over by baby-making.

ALSO, before my husband lost his job, we were meant to be
moving to a really lovely house — perfect for a family! — but at
the very last minute (we were packed and everything) the vendors
upped the price. I was all for coughing up — I LOVED that
house — but then he was made redundant, so we had to pull out.

We went ahead with the sale of our house anyway, as it
seemed a good idea at the time, but are now living in a tiny
rented flat with all our stuff still piled up in boxes and, believe
me, it's not remotely conducive to getting pregnant. David, my
husband, is fed up because he can't find another job and is now
saying we can't afford a baby anyway. HEEEEEELP.

Emma stopped typing and read back what she'd written.
Then she frowned and deleted almost all of it. If she posted
such a long rambling rant on the forum, the other women
would think she was a fruit loop. Maybe they'd be right.

I have been pregnant once before, she began typing again, more
slowly this time, *but—*

'What are you doing?' David asked just then. He was lying at full stretch on the sofa, watching the football and slagging off the referee's atrocious decision-making.

Emma jumped. She'd almost forgotten he was in the same room. Hot colour surged into her face and she swiftly backspaced the sentence she had begun. Had she seriously been on the verge of sharing her darkest secret with an online forum of strangers, when her husband had absolutely no idea of its existence? 'Nothing,' she replied, editing her post right down to the barest introductory sentences and sending it off.

She scrolled through some of the other topics on the discussion board, unwilling to leave this world of women like her just yet. *Ovulation charts — do they work? Polycystic ovaries. Fertility diet.* Someone had started a thread with the heading GOOD NEWS!!!! and Emma clicked it open to reveal some nameless woman — BroodyMama37 — announcing that, after four years of trying, including three rounds of IVF, she was pregnant with twins, whoop-whoop. There then followed a long list of congratulatory comments, but almost all of them failed to disguise the writer's envy or self-obsession each time.

LilMiss: So pleased 4 u — hope it's me next time. Period due next week — am crossing fingers that I have news like yours 2 share!

Me and Mr Jones

NicNac: Well done! Any tips???? *hopeful face*

BiddyWren: LUCKY YOU! How are you feeling? We have decided to go down the IVF route too now — wish us luck!

For some reason Emma felt compelled to write as well, as if by *not* congratulating the woman she might jinx her own chances. *Congrats!* she typed. *What lovely news. Well done!*

'Well done' indeed. Like there was some special art of procreation that BroodyMama37 had fortuitously hit upon. Like there was any particular skill involved, any incredible talent. Luck — that was all it was. Luck and good genes and having youth on your side. None of which seemed to apply to Emma and David right now. They seemed to be getting more decrepit and unlucky and genetically cursed by the day.

'Moan, moan, moan,' she muttered to herself, turning off the computer. She hated feeling like this — so glum, so despondent. It just wasn't her. Five years ago, when she and David had got married, she'd been Fun Emma, throwing parties, dancing until dawn with her friends, cavorting around the bedroom with David at the drop of a hat. Now look at her: whinging on to anonymous people online, getting sucked into a forum of other unhappy women obsessed with their wombs. Every time she saw a pregnant woman in the street she wanted to cry with envy.

47

'And he SCORES! Get in!' crowed David, punching the air. He lifted the beer to his lips and swallowed triumphantly. 'Watch this, Em. Amazing passing.'

'Mmm,' she said dully. The screen showed a bunch of jubilant men hugging each other and the crowd going wild. *Don't worry, David,* she felt like saying. *You sit there and watch the amazing passing. I'll just agonize about our finances, if we'll ever be able to afford another mortgage, if you'll ever find another job, if we'll ever have a baby. But you enjoy the match, won't you?*

Emma woke up at six o'clock the next morning, even though it was Saturday and there was no need to move for hours yet. Rolling over, she was on the verge of slipping back into a dream when a thought pinged into her head, a message from brain to body. Alert! Alert! Ovulation peak time has now begun! Prepare for imminent shagathon!

Sleep was instantly forgotten. It was like waking on Christmas morning when you just knew something special was in the air. Her cells felt primed for action, her womb was all a-tremble with anticipation (well, you know, *probably*; if such a thing was physically possible) and she felt a thrilling thump of joy as she imagined that brand-new egg inside her waiting to be brought to life. *Hello, little egg. I know you're there. Please turn into a baby. A nice, fat, beaming, toothy baby. Please.*

She wrapped her arms around her body, resisting the

urge to molest her husband there and then. All in good time, she told herself. No point waking him too early; he'd be grouchy and not in the mood. She had to time it all perfectly.

Slipping out of bed silently to go to the loo, she noticed when passing the chest of drawers that a red light was flashing on her phone to indicate a new text. She paused outside the bathroom to open it, and saw it was from Sally, her closest friend from uni, who now lived across town with her husband Paul and baby Violet. The text had been sent at five-thirty: ouch. Violet was still not a good sleeper, by all accounts.

Hi hon, the text read. *Are we seeing you later for V's party?*

Emma sighed. Violet's first birthday party. She had been putting off replying because she wasn't sure what to say. Had it really been a whole year since Violet was born, and Emma and Sally had been immediately cast into different universes? In some ways it seemed longer. Emma had *tried* to be delirious with happiness for her friend – she truly had – showering her with treats and goodies, hoping to paper over the gulf that had suddenly widened between them, with hand-stitched baby shoes for Violet and Jo Malone bath oil for poor shattered Sally, but it hadn't been enough. Sally had crossed to the other side – the side of breastfeeding and birth horror stories, the side of broken nights and teething and nappy-bags, her life now completely dominated by the tiny pink-faced tyrant who always seemed to be crying or smelling or wanting something.

It wasn't just Sally who'd defected. Almost all their friends were doing it. Bellies were swelling, phone calls frequently began with the portentous 'We've got some news . . .', beautiful announcement cards showing teeny baby feet plopped through the door, heralding the safe arrival of Flora or Alfie or Lola. Wild sweaty club nights and wall-shaking house parties with the old gang were a thing of the past. Nowadays she was more likely to be invited to a baby's christening or a toddler-infested Sunday lunch than anything outrageous or fun. Their friends had joined the National Trust en masse and went for buggy-pushing walks in the leafy grounds of stately homes; they ordered packages from Mini Boden and compared notes on breast-pumps or washable nappies. Emma felt the mutual ground between them was crumbling away. She had become sidelined, left behind. Was she a bad friend, an evil person, for feeling so damn jealous?

'You're so *lucky*, still being able to wear skinny jeans/lie-in at the weekends/go on nice holidays,' various friends had sighed over the last few months. 'I would kill to lose this last stone/have a single good night's sleep/go abroad again.'

Emma didn't feel lucky, though. Not the slightest bit. She wouldn't care about sleep or having a post-pregnancy muffin-top or never getting on another aeroplane for the rest of her life, if she could just hold her own baby, feel that soft new body against her skin, nuzzle into his or her fragile, sweet-smelling head. Her friends were the lucky ones, not her. She hadn't even gone to visit the most recent arrival – baby Poppy, daughter of their friends Mike and Sara – because she was scared that if she had to hold and coo over little Poppy, she might cry actual tears onto the baby's face.

When would it happen for her and David? When?

She sniffled, trying to stay positive. Come on, Emma. This could be the weekend where it all turned around. In a matter of weeks they might be rejoining the gang with their own breathless good-news phone calls. *I've got something to tell you!* Months from now they might be posting out their own announcement cards and asking for advice about prams. They could do it. They *would* do it.

Sorry, Sal, she texted back eventually. *Feeling a bit ropey today, so had better not bring my germs to the party! Hope V has a lovely time, and you too. Must catch up properly soon. Love Em xxx.*

There. Sent. The guilt lurked around the edges of her mind for a few minutes until she reassured herself that one day she'd be able to apologize to Sally for not being beside her this year, for letting their friendship drift. *Sorry I was so crap while Violet was tiny,* she'd say. *I was just jealous that you had something I wanted too.*

And Sally would give her a hug (because Sally was the lovely, forgiving sort) and say, *Don't worry about it, hon. I understand. I'd have been the same.* Then they'd both look over at their brood with adoration (multiple babies and toddlers, Emma imagined, crossing her fingers), and back at each other with renewed affection, and it would be okay.

It would all be okay.

After a cup of tea in the living room, watching the sun rise above the city streets, Emma crept back into bed. Seven-thirty. Let the shagathon commence!

She lay on her side, feeling jittery and excited as she looked at her husband sleeping soundly nearby. He was going to be such a great dad, she knew it already. He was an outdoorsy type, David, tall and strong, built for hunting and gathering. She could already imagine him carrying a tot – their tot! – on his broad shoulders, swinging round a giggling toddler, playing noisy games of football in the garden, helping to make paint-splattery Mother's Day cards and breakfast in bed.

She watched his eyelids flicker mid-dream and smiled. Look at him there, so golden and strong and handsome. It was unusual to see him at rest; he was the most energetic person she'd ever met, always wanting to be out and about doing something. She'd never let on as much, but secretly he reminded her of a bouncy, boisterous dog in the way that he needed to be out every day, if not being taken for walk on a lead, then exerting himself physically: pounding around Victoria Park, playing five-a-side football with his mates every Thursday evening, swimming a ferocious, splashy butterfly in the pool on Dean Lane...

Lately, though, he'd even seemed disinterested in exercise. A torpor had settled upon him since he had lost his job; an inertia that leached him of energy and enthusiasm and kept him in the flat, watching daytime television. This was not a good thing. She was worried he was becoming depressed.

Feeling a pang of sympathy, she rolled closer and put an arm around his warm, sleeping form. He'd had a tough few months in all. Being made redundant had dented his pride, sending him into a downward spiral. It was hardly surprising he was self-absorbed, withdrawn into his shell. She had to keep making the effort to lift his spirits, to remind him that she still loved and wanted him, even if the architecture world didn't right now.

She ran a hand lightly down his chest, gently caressed his nipples, snuggled closer into his body. *Brace yourself, little egg. Prepare to be invaded.*

He stirred and muttered something. Encouraged, she slipped her hand along his side and down to his hip. Then he jerked irritably and his eyes snapped open. 'F'fuck's sake, Emma, I'm asleep,' he grunted, pushing her hand away and rolling over.

The breath seemed to catch in her throat; her eyes suddenly filled with tears. She retreated to her own side of the bed and listened to the tick of the clock, the traffic grumbling outside, her own heartbeat slowing with disappointment.

He didn't even want *her* any more. How could she draw him back in from the cold?

She gazed helplessly at his dozing body. This was peak ovulation time. This was their chance. She couldn't let another month slip by with an empty womb, and her soul silting over with numbness. *I'm not beaten yet*, she told herself fiercely. *Not by a long chalk.*

'Sorry about earlier,' he said an hour later when he finally emerged from the duvet. His skin was etched with pillow-creases, his hair stood on end and there was something adorably vulnerable about him. Then he scratched his balls, which rather killed the moment. 'I didn't sleep very well.'

'No worries,' she said lightly. *Mustn't turn it into An Issue.* According to the Oh Baby! forum, bleating incessantly about conception often turned husbands right off sex. 'Want some coffee?'

'Ta.' There was a pause while she poured and stirred, and he leaned against the doorjamb. 'I'm a bit worried about what Dad's going to say tomorrow, you know.'

'What do you mean?' She passed him the steaming mug. 'Here.'

'He sounded so odd on the phone the other night. He

said he had something to tell me. I can't help wondering...'
The pause that followed said everything. It said: cancer,
heart disease, months to live. It said: blood tests, hospital,
goodbye.

'I'm sure they're fine,' Emma said. 'Fit as fiddles, both of
them.' This was true. David's parents still seemed so robust
and active, running their bed and breakfast around the
calendar with barely any help, still with it, still uber-
competent. She thought wistfully of her own parents, now
up in Scotland, who'd slumped into old age as if defeated,
their lives a pale, shrunken version of before, revolving
around the twin focal points of their boggle-eyed spaniel
and the television viewing guide.

He ran his hand through his hair. 'I hope so,' he said. 'I
don't think I could take any more bad news right now, Em.'

She went over, gently removed the coffee mug and set it
on the table, then wrapped her arms around him. 'Don't
worry,' she said into his chest. He was still warm from the
bed. 'We're on the way up again, I just know it.'

Mulberry House was a large sprawling farmhouse in a quiet
corner of Loveday village, down in Dorset. Back when
David and his brothers had been growing up, the Joneses
had kept chickens, a couple of ponies and a goat, and there
had been a large and well-tended vegetable plot, according
to David. There was an orchard and a paddock, and

incredible scenery all around – luscious green hills, woodland and the garden itself, Eddie's pride and joy, which was a riot of colour throughout the year.

It had once been a comfortable, warm family home, if the old photos were anything to go by, but in more recent years the house had become rather battered around the edges. The paint was flaking on the window frames, you could see missing slates on the roof, and the ivy that swamped the front of the house had caused the brickwork to become damp and waterlogged. Inside, it never felt truly warm, even on a summer's day, and there was a permanent dankness about the front rooms, which clung to your clothes after an hour or so. As an interior designer, Emma had often cringed at the dark-painted walls and mean windows that didn't let in enough light, and at the ageing carpets everywhere, which were no doubt covering beautiful old floorboards. There were enough style crimes in Mulberry House to warrant a citizen's arrest, in her opinion, although only someone with a death-wish would dare voice any criticisms of Lilian's home turf to her face.

You had to feel sorry for paying guests, though. If Emma and David were staying over for the weekend, Lilian always tried to set aside the best room for them: the one that caught the sun setting over the hills, with just a faint streak of sparkling sea visible on the horizon – but on occasions when this hadn't been possible, they'd slept in one of the less attractive guest rooms, complete with thin, scratchy covers on the bed and the prickliest towels Emma had ever used. The Four Seasons Hotel it was not.

Outside, Eddie did his best with his garden, but he wasn't as fit as he used to be, and the weeds were creeping in. The farm animals had long since departed, but there was still a stable-block and various outbuildings, all in differing states of chaos, which Charlie had been helping him do up for the last two years. The aim had been to turn them into 'holiday chalets', but so far the going had been painfully slow. This was no surprise to anyone. Charlie wasn't exactly Captain Reliable.

They pulled up now in the small parking area next to Hugh and Alicia's car, and David turned off the engine. Emma was always struck by the absolute silence of Mulberry House, after the bustle of city life. The house was set right back from the road, so you never heard the traffic, just the gentle peeping of little birds or an occasional seagull screech.

Talking of screeches . . . There was Lilian opening the front door and standing on the step with her arms folded over the apron that proclaimed 'Mother Knows Best!' It wouldn't have surprised Emma if Lilian actually slept in that sodding apron; it was a permanent fixture on her tall, trim body. 'Oh, *here* they are,' she was saying, then called over her shoulder. 'Eddie! David's here!'

Emma got out of the car, steeling herself. She had tried

her hardest to like her mother-in-law, she really had. She'd been polite and friendly, she washed up after Sunday dinner, she smiled in the right places and bit her tongue whenever the subject of politics arose. For all her best efforts, though, the charm offensive had not been enough. In fact, when Emma and David told his parents one Christmas that David had proposed and they were going to get married, Lilian hadn't even tried to fake pleasure. 'Why would you want to do a thing like that?' she'd said.

David had laughed it off. 'Because we love each other, of course!' he'd said.

Emma hadn't been able to laugh. The words stung even now, hurting like a running sore that wouldn't heal. It was almost as bad as the 'When am I going to have some more grandchildren?' line, which she must have been asked at least seven hundred times by now. Lilian seemed to think it was her divine right, as matriarch, to make pronouncements about other people's relationships and harass them about their fertility. Well, hello? Newsflash! It wasn't okay, not remotely.

In contrast, Emma's parents never badgered her about children in the same way, although this was partly because they'd always been more interested in her brother Neil, and partly because she rarely got to see them since their retirement. She didn't get to speak to them much either, unless she made a point of phoning. Her mum remained convinced that the phone calls from Scotland to England came under 'foreign rate', however many times Emma had tried to convince her otherwise.

She glanced now at the woman on the doorstep – the white-haired gatekeeper to the Jones brothers, she who must be obeyed. The devil in Emma bristled, flexing his muscles. She would make things work with David because she loved him, she thought, but also because it would give her the satisfaction of proving Lilian wrong about the two of them. Hell, yes. *You can't get rid of me that easily*, she thought, slamming the passenger door shut.

Chapter Five

Lilian had known deep down that something wasn't right for a while, but didn't want to look it full in the eye, for fear of having her shadowy dread brought sharply into focus. Instead, she'd told herself that everything was fine, that everyone got a bit forgetful as they became older, that Eddie had just had a lot on his mind lately.

They both had, let's face it. Over the last week their guests had included Mr and Mrs Phelan from the Wirral, who'd complained about absolutely everything – the view from their window (as if she could do anything about *that*!), the food, the facilities in their room, the *weather* even, for heaven's sake. Hard on their heels came Mr Castle and Ms Farthing from London, with their grizzling little baby, who sobbed and snivelled from dawn till dusk. Lilian thought she'd heard Ms Farthing crying one night too – gasping tears of exhaustion, as if she'd been broken. *Try having three boys, dear,* she'd thought, putting the pillow over her head in an attempt to block out the sound. *Then you'll know the meaning of tired.*

Finally they'd had the McPhersons, down from Glasgow, whom Eddie had managed to offend repeatedly by calling them the McDonalds, about five times in all. They'd smiled initially, as if he was joking, but gradually the smiles became wintrier, thinner-lipped and more glare-like with each repetition. 'Has he never *met* a Scottish person before?' Mr McPherson sniffed after the third time. 'Is this meant to be a joke?' Mrs McPherson demanded after the fourth. It got to the point where Lilian had to physically shoo her husband away whenever the poor pair appeared in the breakfast room, for fear of one of them leaping up and stabbing him with a fork.

It was a relief when the McPhersons finally left and she could let her breath out again. Well, for about ten minutes anyway, before she had to stock up on food for the anniversary lunch, and clean the house from top to bottom. Still, better to be busy than bored, she supposed.

Eddie said he'd drive them both to Axminster as he wanted to pick up a bag of plaster from B&Q while she tackled the supermarket, so off they went. But they weren't even three miles out of Loveday when he suddenly dropped the speed and puttered to a halt, stopping the car right in the middle of the road. 'I . . .' he said, gazing through the windscreen. 'I . . .'

A silver Passat that had been buzzing along at 50 mph behind them beeped and swerved wildly to avoid cannoning straight into the back of them. Then it roared past, the driver gesticulating furiously.

'Eddie, what are you *doing*?' Lilian screeched, grabbing at his shirt sleeve. 'You can't just stop here!'

His eyes were misty and confused. 'I ... I can't remember where to go,' he said simply. 'Where do I go, Lilian?'

She stared at him, uncomprehending. He couldn't remember where to *go*? He'd lived here more than fifty years, and he couldn't remember the way to B&Q and Tesco? 'Don't be so silly,' she said, her voice shaking. 'It's straight along to the roundabout, then right, of course. Remember?'

He blinked. 'I ...'

Another car screamed past, making their little Ford shake on its wheels. 'Swap places,' she ordered, scared and alarmed by his behaviour. 'I'll drive. No – don't get out your side, Eddie!' Whatever was *wrong* with the man, trying to open his door when a Volvo was about to whizz by?

That was the big question, though. What *was* wrong with her husband?

The episode had sent a chill down her spine, a freezing anxiety that didn't let up, all the way to the supermarket car park. 'Here we are,' she said brightly as she pulled on the handbrake, her hands still trembly. 'Okay?'

He nodded and, in that moment, he was back to Eddie, *her* Eddie, just as normal. 'Sorry,' he said, shaking his head a little. 'My mind went blank. Most odd. Right — have you got that list, then? Let's go.'

Normality didn't last long. Something seemed to have unwound in his head. It was as if he was running on a different track from her now — a parallel, similar track, but one that no longer quite matched hers. He was quiet in the supermarket, trailing around after her, and spent a long time choosing the plaster he wanted once they got to the DIY store. Then, when they were safely back home, the groceries put away and the kettle boiling, he suddenly said, 'I think I'll catch up a bit in the garden this afternoon, love. I'll just pop round and see if I can borrow Tony's mower. Grass needs cutting.'

She swung round in surprise. 'Tony?' she echoed, staring at him.

'He's got that new one, hasn't he?' he said mildly. 'Much better than ours.'

'Eddie . . .' Oh Lord. Where to begin? 'Tony's . . . gone. He moved away, years ago. Don't you—?' *Don't you remember?* she was about to say, but stopped herself. Her skin prickled. He'd made a mistake, that was all. He must have meant Barry, their neighbour who'd lived next door for more than twelve years. Eddie knew that. Didn't he?

He passed a hand over his head, frowned unseeingly.

There was that terrifying blankness in his eyes once more and she leaned against the worktop, feeling unsteady. 'Eddie, love, sit down,' she said. Fear was jolting through her. What did all of this mean? What was happening? 'Let me make you a drink. The grass doesn't even need cutting – look.'

He let himself be guided to a chair. 'He had a good mower, didn't he? Tony?' he said, sagging into the seat.

Lilian swallowed. 'He did,' she said faintly, still holding on to him. Time seemed to stop and everything felt magnified: the slow sliding tick of the clock, his soft cotton shirt beneath her fingers, the perfumed scent of the blue hyacinths on the window ledge, her own racing heartbeat – boom, boom, boom. 'Yes, love, he did.'

Chapter Six

Self-reinvention or not, there was nothing like Sunday lunch at the in-laws' to bring you back down to earth with a bump, thought Alicia. And in the twenty or so years she'd been with Hugh, she'd racked up a good number of those, a veritable parade of gravy boats and roast potatoes, of cracker snaps and terrible jokes, of clinked glasses and slurred voices.

Funny to think that the very first time she'd come here, she, David and Charlie had all been teenagers. David had been in the midst of A-levels and was pale and stressed, like a plant that hadn't seen the sun for ages, while Charlie had white-bleached hair and acne, and wore ripped jeans and grungy T-shirts. It seemed just days ago in some respects, yet a whole generation had rolled by in the meantime. She could chart the progress like a procession of snapshots flicking through her head. David starting at Swansea uni and returning with a girlfriend from the Valleys – Angela, with the dirtiest laugh you ever heard. Charlie vanishing down to Cornwall, then London, then Goa, then Bourne-mouth, returning each time with his tail between his legs, having run up enormous debts. Her, with her sapphire engagement ring sparkling in the Christmas photos. David moving to Bristol and landing a great job, Charlie made redundant and refusing to come downstairs one Christmas Day. Hugh getting a promotion and cracking open champagne. Her again, with her gold wedding band and flushed cheeks, a bump, a babe-in-arms, a toddler, another baby...

The Christmas turkey getting bigger by the year. A long line of girlfriends for Charlie, then Emma appearing with David like an exotic bird from afar with her pea-green coat, the jangle of beads around her neck and glittery eyeshadow. Job news. House moves. New wallpaper. New curtains. The garden rising and falling, blooming and dying in the background.

Alicia didn't appear as much in the photos from then on; she was always tending to some child or other, or helping in the kitchen, steam sending her hair frizzy, a gulped glass of wine mottling her cheeks. If she did make it into a frame, she'd always be the last one still with a lopsided paper party hat on her head, the others all having removed theirs by the time the cheese plate came out. Typical of her.

Still, it didn't have to be like that, though, did it? Nobody was forcing her to blend into the background for the rest of her life. With this in mind, she'd sat at her dressing table that morning spritzing on perfume and styling her hair, then put on a pretty blouse and skirt and carefully applied her new lipstick. She looked at the woman in the reflection and smiled experimentally. Maybe, just for once, she'd sit back after the meal today and let Hugh help his mum with the fetching and carrying. Maybe David or Emma would offer to pour drinks or make coffee this time, so that she didn't have to. And maybe, instead of acting like a meek little skivvy, she'd be sparkling and witty, regaling others with funny stories and pithy quips.

'Alicia, where's my blue shirt? Have you ironed it?' came Hugh's voice just then.

She opened her mouth, helpfulness rising in her automatically. Then she caught the gaze of the woman in the mirror and thought again. 'Not a clue!' she called back gaily.

For the first time ever, they arrived late at Mulberry House. Unaccustomed to fending for himself, Hugh had hunted through all of the dirty washing and the entire ironing pile before eventually finding his blue shirt hanging pristine and crease-free in the wardrobe. 'Why didn't you just tell me it was there?' he demanded irritably, thrusting his arms into its sleeves.

'Sorry,' Alicia said lightly, as if such things were beneath her. 'Must have forgotten.'

This wasn't the only hold-up. Lucas, their eldest son,

who was eleven and seemed to be morphing into an adolescent slug, was loath to get dressed at all. Normally Alicia would have coaxed and wheedled, she might even have bribed him. Today she shrugged. 'Oh well. Wear your pyjamas then,' she'd said, without looking up from painting her fingernails.

Lucas hadn't been expecting this, and began to scowl and bluster. 'But . . . then I'll look like a dick.'

Clearly this was meant to push her into a comment about language, but was Alicia going to rise to it? Not today. 'Then look like a dick,' she replied airily. 'Your choice.'

He'd actually backed away, completely at a loss as to how to react. 'Oh, all *right*, so I'll get *dressed*,' he grumbled. *Slam* went his bedroom door.

Alicia's lips twitched. 'Your choice,' she repeated sweetly under her breath.

Finally, when they had assembled in the car – there was some jostling between Rafferty (nine) and Matilda (eight) for the least favoured middle seat, which Alicia chose to ignore – Hugh put the key in the ignition and started the engine.

'Oh. Wine,' he said suddenly. 'Have you got the wine?'

'Wine?' she echoed, deliberately blank.

'Did you not buy any?'

'Did you want me to? It wasn't on the shopping list.'

'No, but . . .' *No, but I assumed you'd get it, just like you always do, because you're the woman and you always remember these things.*

She waited, hands in her lap. As it happened, they did have two bottles of Oyster Bay in the utility room, if only he bothered to check. But as ever he'd expected her to look after the niceties, even though Lilian and Eddie were *his* parents. Something stopped her from mentioning any of this.

'Fine, we'll just stop somewhere on the way and I'll pick something up then,' he said grumpily.

'Okay,' she replied. A thrill of rebellion went through her.

Then the engine started and they were away.

It turned out that, despite their lateness, they were still the first to arrive by a long chalk. Lilian was having a paddy about the vegetables in the kitchen, but, against all her instincts of rushing to don an apron and help, Alicia poured herself a large glass of wine instead and went out into the garden with the children. Hopefully they'd burn off some energy before they were forced to sit down politely for the longest meal of the week.

Emma and David arrived – David looking somewhat pudgy about the face and in need of a decent shave, and Emma in a peacock-blue dress that had tiny purple flowers stitched around the neckline and hem. Her cropped hair shone coppery in the weak spring sunshine and showed off her lovely white neck.

'I love your dress,' Alicia said. 'Such a gorgeous colour.'

'Thanks,' Emma said. 'You've had your hair cut! It really suits you.'

Alicia positively glowed. She had always felt that her life must seem small and drab in contrast to Emma's cooler, sparklier existence. But maybe they weren't so different after all. They were both career women, there was common ground between them. It was time she stopped painting herself into the boring corner.

A tussle between the children had broken out, but she turned away. Hugh could deal with them for a change. 'How's work?' she asked Emma brightly.

Half an hour passed and still there was no sign of Charlie. This wasn't extraordinary in itself, of course: Charlie was always late to family gatherings; his world spun on Charlie-time rather than in sync with mere mortals. Normally, though, his doting mother would forgive him for this, and all his other bad habits, excusing every misdemeanour by dint of him being the youngest. The fact that he was now in his thirties and definitely an adult didn't seem to make any difference.

Today, however, there was no pandering or excusing, no

'We'll just give him another ten minutes'. Today, a line seemed to have been drawn in the sand. 'We can't wait any longer,' Lilian decided eventually, wheeling the food in on her hostess trolley. 'I'll put his share in the oven.'

Alicia felt positively riddled with guilt by now for not helping earlier. Lilian was usually completely in control – of herself as well as the entire family – yet today she seemed all over the place. Her hands shook as she dished up the meat then she knocked over a glass of water, which splashed Hugh's trousers. Eddie, meanwhile, appeared blank and unresponsive, a million miles away. Something, thought Alicia with a lurch, was definitely up.

Hugh had noticed too, and kept looking at his parents with a small frown between his eyebrows. 'Everything all right, Mum?' he asked.

'I'm fine!' she snapped. 'Why does everyone keep asking me that?'

Eddie blinked at the sharpness of her voice, before putting a calming hand on hers. 'We've got something we'd like to discuss with you after lunch,' he said. 'That's if Charlie ever turns up, mind.'

Oh dear. That didn't sound promising. Were they in financial trouble? Alicia wondered. Hugh occasionally helped out with their accounts and had said that bookings were considerably down recently.

'Has anyone actually heard from Charlie?' David asked,

getting out his phone. 'I'll text him, remind him that he's meant to be here.'

Lilian's lips were tight as everyone shook their heads; she was clearly hurt by Charlie's careless neglect.

Alicia felt sorry for her. 'Let's have a toast, to Lilian and Eddie,' she said, trying to salvage what was, after all, meant to be a celebratory occasion. 'Forty-five years' marriage is a wonderful achievement.'

'Absolutely,' Hugh said quickly. He raised his glass. 'To Mum and Dad!'

'Lilian and Eddie!'

'Grandma and Grandpa!'

Everyone clinked glasses and Lilian smiled thinly. Then David's phone beeped. 'Ah,' he said, reading the message. 'It's Charlie – he's on his way.'

The meal began and a feeling of jollity slowly spread across the table, with any previous tension ebbing away. Lilian was pink in the cheeks from the wine and the attention, and the food was unanimously declared a triumph. Lucas started telling Eddie some of the less-rude jokes he'd learned at school, and Raffy launched into a gruesome description of the dead fox they'd seen on the way over, in full technicoloured detail.

'Not now, darling,' Alicia tried saying, noticing Lilian's mouth pursing with disapproval. 'Raff! Enough gore, thank you.'

Thankfully David had a better tactic. 'Did your dad ever tell you about the fox cub he smuggled up to his bedroom when he was about your age?' he interrupted, grinning at Hugh.

'No WAY!' Raffy breathed, open-mouthed. 'Dead or alive?'

'Goodness, yes. It was most certainly alive,' Lilian said, shuddering at the memory. 'What a mess it made of the carpet, the wretched thing!'

David caught Alicia's eye and winked as the children immediately began bombarding Hugh and their grand-parents for details. 'Do you mean it actually, like, POOED on the carpet, Grandma?'

'What else did it do?'

'Was Dad in really massive trouble?'

Alicia smiled at David. 'Thanks,' she mouthed gratefully. She liked David a lot more than she did Charlie, always had done. He had come to visit when Lucas was a week old and she was in the absolute fog of new-motherhood, shattered with sleep-deprivation and wondering if she'd ever feel normal again. She remembered becoming increasingly flustered when Lucas wouldn't stop crying, despite her trying to feed him discreetly, and was embarrassed at having her big cow-boobs out with Hugh's brother there in the room, valiantly attempting to keep up a conversation.

After a while David had gone to make everyone coffees

and it wasn't until later on that Alicia realized that, as well as making the drinks, he'd done all the washing up that had been toweringly stacked by the sink and had even scrubbed the bottom of the washing-up bowl clean too. Tears had sprung to her eyes when she'd made the discovery. It was only a small kindness, a tiny helpful gesture, but at the time she'd been so pathetically grateful that she'd never forgotten it. If David and Emma ever had children, she'd be round there like a flash with her Marigolds and Ecover, just wait.

Halfway through the rhubarb and ginger crumble the doorbell rang. 'Ah, here he is,' Lilian said, rising from her seat in relief.

She went to let in Goldenboy – who was patently (and unfairly) the favourite son; something that had always irked Hugh – and the table fell silent as voices came from the hallway. Several voices, some of which were unfamiliar. 'Oh,' they heard Lilian say, her tone suddenly full of reproach. 'You could have *told* us you were bringing some other people. Honestly, Charlie!'

Her interest piqued, Alicia exchanged a glance with Hugh, and saw David and Emma giving each other similar looks. *Do you know what's going on? Not a clue. Do you?*

Lilian's voice became shriller than ever. 'Well, I suppose we can make room. We *were* just in the middle of dessert, though, Charlie. Really!'

'Oh, Mum, it's not a drama,' they heard him laugh. 'We'll stand in the garden if we're inconvenient.'

It must be nice being Charlie, Alicia had often thought. Born with a natural confidence and charm, he was one of those people liked by all, a Peter Pan figure who had never really had to grow up and fend for himself – yet. Why would he, when his devoted parents always bailed him out?

'What's happening, Mum?' asked Matilda, suddenly aware of the change in atmosphere.

'I'm not sure,' Alicia replied. 'Uncle Charlie's talking to Grandma about something.'

'But I thought I heard someone else,' Matilda said, leaning over Rafferty in her attempt to see round the open door.

Raffy pushed her. Matilda squealed. 'Stop it, you two,' Alicia hissed.

'Hello, everyone,' Charlie said just then. As ever, he burst into the room as if walking onto a stage. His skin was tanned, even though it was only just March, his eyes sparkled a light bright blue, he was unshaven (he was *always* unshaven) and there was a button missing from his shirt. Same old Charlie. 'Guys, this is Izzy. And these two young ladies are Willow and Hazel, Izzy's daughters.'

There were more exchanged glances. *Did you know he was seeing someone new? Not a clue. Did you?*

The only person whose expression showed joy was Matilda. 'Miss *Izzy!*' she cried in delight. 'What are *you* doing here?'

The penny dropped as Alicia too recognized the woman. *Oh, right,* she thought. *I see.* So *that* was why Charlie had been so willing to take Matilda to ballet lessons recently. She should have known there was more to it than plain old generosity.

'Hello!' she said, blushing slightly. She was almost certain that the pretty, elegant ballet teacher wouldn't recognize her; people never did. 'I'm Matilda's mum. From ballet. Alicia.'

'Hi, Alicia,' Izzy said. She had olive skin, a thick mane of glossy dark hair and cat-like green eyes, and seemed relieved that there were two familiar faces in the crowd at least. 'Nice to see you, Matilda.' She gazed around the room, her smile faltering. 'I'm so sorry, I didn't realize we'd be interrupting your lunch.'

Lilian gave one of her almighty sniffs. 'It's an anniversary lunch, actually,' she said, stiffening. 'A special occasion. Family only. Oh, Charlie, this is very rude of you, you know.'

Izzy – Alicia had to stop thinking of her as 'Miss Izzy', as the ballet girls called her – looked mortified. 'Sorry,' she said again. 'We're obviously intruding. Come on, girls, let's go.'

'No!' Charlie said. 'Honestly, there's no need. Right, Dad?'

Alicia felt for Eddie as he struggled for the correct reply. His face florid from the lunchtime wine, his eyes flicked from Lilian to Charlie to Izzy, before finally he said, 'Not to worry' and clapped his son on the back. 'We were just finishing.'

Izzy hovered, clearly wanting to make a break for it, but Charlie seemed immune to his mother's frostiness. 'Cool,' he beamed. 'All right, down there, kids?' he went on, waving at his niece and nephews. 'Izzy, this is David, Hugh and Emma. You know Alicia and Matilda, and those rascals are Lucas and Rafferty. And, of course, this is my mum and dad, Lils and Eddie, who have been married . . . er . . . forty-three . . . ?'

'Forty-five,' Lilian said through gritted teeth, looking as if she might explode. Charlie appeared to have been relegated to least-favourite son in a matter of minutes.

'Forty-five, even better!' Charlie corrected himself. 'Forty-five wonderful and happy years.'

'Congratulations,' Izzy said, still clutching her girls' hands. 'That's . . . lovely.'

Poor woman. Poor, poor, embarrassed woman. Talk about a farce.

'So, girls –' Charlie squatted on his haunches – 'would you like some orange squash and a biscuit?'

Lilian stiffened. 'I did *save* you some lunch, Charlie, but I'm afraid there's not enough for *everyone*—'

'Don't worry, Mum,' Charlie said, waving a hand. 'We had chips in Charmouth. Come on, girls, this way. Orange-squash hunt: go!'

Silence fell as they left the room. 'Well,' said Lilian tartly, the cords in her neck straining with ill-disguised fury. 'So. A single mother, eh?' She snatched up her spoon and attacked her crumble with unnecessary vigour. 'Not so sure how long *this* one will last. A fortnight? A whole month?'

Alicia cringed. Lilian's fury was completely misdirected, for Charlie was clearly the one in the wrong. How could he mess up so spectacularly? There wasn't just the special lunch to consider; there was this agonizing announcement that Eddie wanted to make too, now presumably put on hold.

'She's very nice,' she said in Izzy's defence. 'Although I must admit I had absolutely no idea anything was happening between them.' Honestly! Charlie could be so crass. They asked him for one single favour – after all the times she and Hugh had helped him – and he had to turn it into an opportunity to go on the pull.

'Uncle Charlie has been *so* embarrassing,' Matilda put in conspiratorially. 'He's always trying to ask her on a *date* and things, right in the middle of lessons!' She stirred her crumble and custard into a revolting-looking brown slop. 'Mind you, she is pretty,' she added.

'Hmmm,' said Lilian darkly.

'Are you okay, Dad?' David asked.

'Do you want us to have a word with him?' Hugh put in. Alicia knew how frustrated he'd been with Charlie's past misdemeanours; now he looked as if he'd like to punch him.

Eddie seemed far away. 'Eh? A word?' he asked.

'With Charlie,' Hugh prompted, still bristling.

Eddie blinked again. He really did seem preoccupied. 'Charlie's all right,' he mumbled after a while. 'Where is he, then?'

Hugh and David exchanged confused glances, and nobody replied for a moment. Then Emma jumped to her feet. 'I'll make coffee,' she suggested, and escaped with visible relief.

Alicia snatched up the crumble dish and went after her. The sooner this lunch limped to an end, the better.

Chapter Seven

Izzy hated surprises. One of her worst days ever had been her eighteenth birthday, when a friend had organized a surprise party for her. Not only that, but the plan had been for everyone to pretend they'd forgotten it was her birthday in the first place. She had spent the whole day feeling utterly despondent, thinking nobody cared about her, that all those friendships she'd warily built up through sixth-form college were actually just meaningless fluff. Eighteen years old and she felt as if her armour had been knocked askew to reveal a tender vulnerable patch of skin. It had hurt. She'd been looking forward to her eighteenth for so long as well. At last, her childhood would be officially over. At last, she'd be an adult in the eyes of the law, free from the interference of social workers, no longer a case in anybody's filing system.

It seemed that adulthood hurt just as much as childhood, though.

'Surprise!' they cheered that evening as she walked into

the flat she shared with a couple of other girls back then, a greasy hovel above a Chinese takeaway on the Albert Road.

She had burst into tears, feeling tricked and betrayed. And although they all laughed and hugged her, then took her to the Nag's Head in order to ply her with snakebite, nothing could shake off that tumultuous whirl of emotion she'd experienced during the day, nothing. She could still feel the pain of it now, ten years later.

It was being caught off-guard, that was what she hated. Being unprepared, unaware. Nowadays she'd rather know exactly what she was letting herself in for. She preferred to stay in control.

The thing was, being down in Dorset with the sea air and the dance classes and the friendly faces in the tea shop . . . it had been kind of unreal. Too nice for the likes of her. Too good almost to be true. She had started to relax, to let her shoulders slowly sink south instead of having them hunched up rigidly around her ears. That had been her first mistake.

They were down on the beach at Charmouth, the four of them, the girls squealing and laughing with excitement as Charlie chased after them pretending to be a dinosaur. She noticed the expressions of an elderly couple softening as they watched the spectacle, as if they were reminded of days gone by, perhaps charging around beaches with their own children. Seeing her daughters so carefree and joyful, their long hair streaming behind them both as they ran and dodged, filled her with a happiness so searing and raw that it almost felt like pain.

She and Charlie had met up twice more now, once for lunch in Lyme, just the two of them, where they had sat on the sea wall with tuna rolls and takeaway coffees from the bakery and chatted about this and that. Then they met for a drink after her Wednesday class and he'd told her funny stories about his childhood and his family. It all sounded so much fun, so idyllic. 'You'll love them,' he assured her, and she'd felt the pull of longing. She'd always envied friends with big families; she'd have given anything to be part of one herself.

And then today, Sunday, they had come here, to the beach, and it had been really fun. Charlie was such easy company; he was energetic, funny and breezily cheerful. There was no side to him whatsoever, and his laid-back nature couldn't be further from Gary's brooding intensity. Despite her determination to keep Charlie Jones at arm's length, she was already starting to feel that he might actually be the sort of man she could allow into her life, given time.

But then her phone buzzed with a new message and any warm, fuzzy feelings were swept away in an instant.

You can't get away from me that easy, Iz.

Shitting hell. It was Gary. He was the only one who ever called her Iz — a shortening she'd always disliked. How had he got hold of her new number? Only two people from Manchester knew it – Louise and Monique, good friends sworn to secrecy. Three people now, though, apparently. But what else did he know? Did he know where they were?

She stared at the message again, feeling cold all over, willing it to have been a misread, a mad brain-melt, where she'd got the wrong end of the stick. But they stayed the same, the words drumming around her head as she heard his voice say them. *You can't get away from me that easy, Iz.*

God. Getting away from him had been the most crucial thing she'd ever had to do, and definitely the most terrifying. She would never forget the way her heart had galloped as they'd sneaked away, her and the girls with their few measly possessions; how she had bundled the cases into the car – quick, quick, before he comes back! She should have known that Gary wasn't the kind of man to take such a slight without retribution.

Help. Now what should she do? Were they going to have to move again? Would they have to find another shelter to hide in? The refuge they'd first come to, in Dorchester, had been brilliantly helpful, but returning there would feel like a giant leap back. And what about the girls' school, what about work? She didn't want to have to unpick all the progress she had made, just for him.

'Everything all right?' Charlie had appeared by her side and she jumped. 'Izzy – are you okay?'

She must have been looking freaked out, because he sounded concerned, the usual jokiness stripped from his voice. 'Sure,' she replied briskly, avoiding his eye. She glanced at her watch, suddenly keen to be somewhere quieter, safer, less public. Somewhere she could slide across bolts and close the curtains. The frightened mice needed to scurry back to their mousehole and hide. 'We'd better push off now,' she said. 'GIRLS! Time to go!'

'Oh, but...' He sagged with disappointment. 'Really? Already? But it's only midday. I thought...' He scratched his head as Willow and Hazel galloped over, hair dishevelled, sand in their fingernails. 'How about I shout us chips and a pasty for lunch first?'

Sneaky. Like she could say no, when her daughters' eyes were already gleaming.

'Can we, Mum?'

'PLEASE?'

'Oh, all right then,' she said, trying to keep up a fake smile. Inside her mind was still ricocheting between potential dangers, and she forced herself to breathe deeply. *You're overreacting,* she told herself firmly. Gary couldn't possibly know where they were – there was no way Lou or Monique would have ratted on her.

No. Of course not. Get a grip, Izzy.

But what if Louise had let something slip? What if Gary had somehow got hold of an email or postcard Izzy had sent, with her new contact details? It could have happened – Gary was friends with Lou's boyfriend Ricky, and he might have gone on the snoop round at their place one evening. He'd got her new phone number, hadn't he? What else had he found out?

'Are you sure you're okay?' Charlie asked as they began walking towards the café. 'You've gone a bit pale.'

'I'm fine,' she said, hunching over her phone and deleting the text before he could see it. There. Gone. She stuffed the phone in her pocket, trying not to think about it any more. Salty chips and a strong coffee would take her mind off Gary, she told herself.

But they didn't.

She'd first met Gary when she was fourteen and put into a care home in Burnage. Before then, she'd had a foster placement with the McCreedys, Evangelical Christians who had turfed her out when they caught her smoking at the bottom of the garden. Which, in hindsight, hadn't exactly been Christian-spirited – throwing an unwanted child back to the wolves – but there you go. People were strange.

Angry and disempowered by yet another rejection, she'd lashed out at the world, pushing away everyone who tried to help her: her dance teacher, her social worker and Kirsty and Derek, the live-in carers at this particular home. She kept her distance, spending long hours hunched in her room, wrapped in the old leopard-spot coat, which was the only thing of her mother's that she'd ever owned. Once it had smelled of her (Shalimar, she came to discover, years later), and she'd gone to sleep many times breathing in that scent, imagining she was in her mother's embrace. Now the perfume had vanished and it just smelled of nothing, but slipping her arms into its cold, silky lining still proved a comfort.

Then she met Gary. He was in the home too, dogged by his own troubled past. His mum had been an alcoholic who had died months earlier, and his dad was completely off the scene. For some reason, he was the one person she could tolerate during those first few months, the one person who encouraged her out of the coat, and out of her shell.

Back then, he seemed lovely. Her soulmate, who understood what she'd been through, who could comfort her when the demons attacked. They clung to each other like sole survivors of an earthquake.

Admittedly, the warning signs were already there. He got into fights at school, sometimes drank too much, lunged too quickly into random acts of violence. Then he lost it and tried to burn down the school one night and was sent to a remand centre. They fell out of contact and didn't see each other for five long years. Everyone told Izzy it was for the best, but she felt as if her heart had been split open.

Just when she had turned her life into some kind of

order – living in Albert Road, studying for A-levels in between waitressing and cleaning jobs – he came back. He strolled into the café where she worked, and it was as if he'd never been away.

'I'll always be here for you, Iz,' he told her as they held each other after her shift that evening. 'Let's get married and be together for the rest of our lives. We'll be our own little family for ever and ever.'

It had seemed a good idea at the time.

After lunch, Charlie's phone beeped and she heard him swear under his breath as he read the text.

'Everything all right?' she asked, stuffing the chip papers into a bin.

'Yeah, sure,' he said. 'That was my brother – I just lost track of time. I was supposed to be at my parents' place by now.'

'Oh, right,' she said. She gazed around helplessly. They'd come in Charlie's car, and she'd been counting on a lift home later on. 'Well . . . we could get a bus from here, if you need to go.'

He waved her suggestion away. 'Don't be silly. I can take you back, unless . . .' He paused, making calculations in his head. 'Look, tell you what. Why don't you come with me, pop in there for a cup of tea. It's on the way to yours.'

'What, all of us?' She glanced at the girls, who were

crouched by some tussocky seagrass, whispering like explorers as they rummaged through its spikes. This was awkward. She didn't really want to meet his parents today. The girls looked like ragamuffins, their hair wild and tangled from the wind. She no doubt looked every bit as windswept herself, with no make-up and her scruffiest jeans, a hole in one knee. 'Actually, it's probably not the best time to—' she began, but he was already speaking.

'Yeah, course,' he said. 'No problemo. They'll love you guys.'

'LOOK! We got it – a sandhopper!' exclaimed Hazel just then, straightening up with her fingers curled around to form a cage. Her dimples flashed as she beamed. 'See him?'

She opened her palm and a sand-coloured insect immediately leapt to freedom, making her shriek. 'Oh no. Where did he go?'

Willow stood up too. 'What are we doing now?' she asked.

'Well, you can come and meet my family if you want,' Charlie said. 'There'll probably be some cake on offer...'

'Ooh, yes please,' Hazel said immediately, sandhopper forgotten. 'Can we, Mum?'

Right. This was where Izzy came up with a really good excuse for saying no, thank you, and goodbye . . . but her brain failed her. 'I suppose so,' she said weakly in the end. One cup of tea and a piece of cake with Charlie's apparently lovely parents, and then home again. How bad could it be, after all?

THIS BAD, was the answer, when they arrived at the Joneses' twenty minutes later. Badder than the baddest badness ever experienced before. Flaming heck, as her granny used to say. She'd had nicer welcomes from social services.

'You could have *told* us you were bringing some other people,' his mum glowered reproachfully on the doorstep, her eyes beady with dislike as she gave Izzy and her daughters the once-over. 'Other people' indeed, like they weren't just standing there. 'Honestly, Charlie!'

Izzy's fists tightened. She felt like spitting in this woman's face. How dare she make judgements about her and the girls, how dare she dismiss them with a single glance? She put her arms protectively around Willow and Hazel. Oh, why hadn't she followed her instincts and asked Charlie to take them home?

Once they'd been permitted over the threshold, things became even worse: there had been a whole room full of people around a dinner table, spoons in hand, all gawping at them in surprise. Matilda's mum — whatever her name was — stared dumbly, her gob hanging open in shock as she put two and two together. Probably didn't think a dance teacher was good enough for their precious Charlie, just like his cow of a mum. Awk-WARD, as Louise used to say.

Unnerved, Izzy followed Charlie into the kitchen, holding the girls' hands. 'I think we should go,' she hissed. 'They don't want us here.'

'It's cool,' he said cheerfully and she gritted her teeth. 'Orange squash all right, girls?'

But it wasn't cool, not in the slightest. The rejection she'd felt loud and clear from Charlie's family brought back a flood of old feelings, and all she wanted to do was escape. She was just about to make a dash for freedom with the girls when a woman in a blue dress came into the kitchen, her arms full of pudding bowls.

'Hi, Charlie,' she said, opening the dishwasher and stacking them inside. 'Hello, I'm Emma,' she added to Izzy, then gave an extra-big smile to the girls. 'I love your names,' she said. 'Willow and Hazel, right? Beautiful. So who's who?'

Willow introduced them shyly, gazing up at Emma through her eyelashes. Hazel beamed and butted in with their ages, their middle names and her favourite colour (lilac). 'We've been fossil-hunting,' she added proudly, 'but we didn't see any dinosaurs.'

'Maybe next time,' Emma said, then turned to Izzy. 'Sorry about the welcome you've had,' she added in a low voice. 'I promise we're not all like that.'

Before Izzy could reply, Matilda's mum walked in with a serving dish, closely followed by Lilian. Immediately the atmosphere changed.

'Charlie, I did *say* we were going to have a family talk later, don't you remember?' the witch snapped, giving Izzy a meaningful look, in case she was stupid as well as deaf.

'Yeah — sorry, Mum, it was just a spur-of-the-moment thing because . . . Well, I thought it would be nice for everyone to meet Izzy, Willow and Hazel, that's all.'

Nice? For whom? Izzy was starting to think Charlie was insane. 'Well,' she said, unable to keep quiet any longer. Time to abort this mission and bail out, she decided. 'It really has been an absolute *pleasure* to come here and receive such a friendly reception, but oh, gosh, is that the time?' Sarcasm dripped through her voice — it was impossible to stop it. 'Girls, you've got all that homework to do this afternoon, and I have a ton of ironing. We'd better go.'

'Ohhh!' Willow moaned. 'Homework? Can't we do that later, Mum?'

'We haven't even had a BISCUIT!' Hazel protested.

Charlie's expression was full of dismay. 'Already? Oh, but Iz—'

A shudder went through her, and it was like Gary was in the room, like he'd never really been away. 'Don't call me that,' she said, pulling her cardigan tight around her. 'Don't *ever* call me that.' She grabbed Willow by one hand and Hazel by the other. 'Come on, girls, we're off.'

Moments later they were out of the front door. 'Big mistake, Izzy,' she said to herself under her breath as she marched away. Huge mistake. Rule number one: do not get involved with a charmer. When would she ever learn?

'Wait!' Charlie yelled, running after them. 'I'm sorry – I didn't know it would be like that. Let me drive you home. Please!'

'No thank you,' she replied icily.

'But how are you going to get back? It's miles! Come on, don't be like this, let me give you a lift.'

'We'll walk,' she said, then rounded on him with venom in her eyes. 'Just sod off,' she hissed savagely. 'We don't need you. Not for anything!'

His shoulders sagged and she left him there, a pathetic figure alone in his parents' driveway. She couldn't have cared less.

'Are we really going to walk all the way home?' Willow asked in a whisper as they strode along together. The sun had gone in and a mean east wind was making the trees shiver.

Guilt swamped her. Here they were, stuck in the middle of bloody nowhere, with hardly any money and several miles from their flat. She didn't even know if buses ran on a Sunday around here. Some mother she was.

Swallowing hard, she forced an unnatural brightness into her voice. 'Don't worry,' she said, without a clue how she was going to get out of this. 'We can—'

Then she heard a car and Charlie pulled up alongside

them in his old Escort. 'Please,' he said humbly, leaning across the wheel to catch her eye. 'I can't let you walk.'

Nose in the air, Izzy opened the back door and the girls clambered in gratefully. She sat next to them and they drove in silence back to Lyme.

Lesson learned, she thought to herself. *Lesson bloody learned.*

Chapter Eight

God, Lilian could be a cow, Emma thought, as Izzy swirled out of the kitchen, dragging her two bewildered-looking children in tow. That poor woman – the way Lilian had spoken to her was absolutely unforgivable.

'Well, of all the . . .' Lilian spluttered now, as Charlie ran after them. You could hear raised voices from the hall and then the front door banging – not slammed, exactly, but certainly shut very firmly. And that was that.

'How *rude*,' Lilian fumed. 'Honestly! I don't know *where* Charlie finds these women, I really don't. None of them have ever had manners, not a single one.'

She stalked out, nose in the air, and Emma and Alicia were left staring at each other. 'What a total . . . bitch,' said Alicia.

It was the first time Emma had ever heard Alicia bad-mouth their mother-in-law, and she felt like punching the air. Thank you, God. Maybe she had found an ally among the Jones clan after all these years. 'I can't believe that just happened,' she agreed. 'It was like seeing a car crash in slow motion.'

'It was brutal,' Alicia said, aghast. 'Those poor little girls! What the hell was Charlie playing at, bringing them here? He must have known what would happen.'

'And of course he gets away with none of the blame, as usual,' muttered Emma before she could stop herself.

But Alicia was nodding in agreement. 'As bloody usual,' she echoed with surprising viciousness.

They caught each other's eyes and grinned like conspirators. There was something different about Alicia, Emma thought, and not just her swishy new hairdo and make-up. The two women had never had much to say to each other in the past; Alicia always seemed so preoccupied with her family and tended to let Hugh do the talking for them in any family get-togethers. She seemed feistier than usual today, though, as if she'd suddenly discovered her own backbone.

'Hey, do you know what this big talk's all about?' she asked, remembering David's anxiety on the subject.

'No idea,' Alicia replied. 'But I know Hugh's been worrying.'

'David too,' Emma said. 'Come on, let's make this coffee so that we can find out what the hell's going on.'

'The thing is,' Eddie began, with a sideways glance at his wife, 'we're not getting any younger, your mum and I.'

Charlie had returned looking chastened, and now the adults were all around the dining-room table, the children having been ensconced upstairs in the private living area in front of the television. The only guests currently booked in – a Mr and Mrs Ashburton from Devon – had gone out for a day trip to Dorchester and wouldn't be back for hours. *Here we go*, thought Emma warily, sipping her coffee as her father-in-law spoke.

'And . . . well, basically, we just feel that this place is becoming too much for us to keep going,' Eddie went on. You could have heard a pin drop every time he paused. 'So we were wondering . . . well . . .'

'We'd originally thought we could hand it on to one of you, keep it in the family,' Lilian said. 'Business is ticking along; there's no debt. But you know we've always tried to be as fair as we can with you boys, and we decided it would be wrong to give it to just one son.'

'So,' Eddie said with a heavy sigh, 'unless one of you wants to buy it from us, unfortunately we're going to have to sell up.'

Oh God. This was big. Not on a par with cancer or heart disease, as David had feared, thankfully, but still pretty seismic.

'Sell the house?' Charlie looked devastated. 'Oh no. But this is . . . this is *home*.'

'I know, son,' Eddie said. His mouth twisted downwards

unhappily. 'But it's a lot of work for us. We'd like to retire before long, and move somewhere smaller that doesn't take so much cleaning and looking after. A . . . what do you call them again? Those houses with no stairs. Little flat things.'

'A bungalow?' Hugh prompted.

'A bungalow – that's the chap.'

Nobody spoke for a moment. Emma couldn't tell what David was thinking, but his eyes were far-away. She knew how much he loved this house, steeped with so many childhood memories. The first time they'd come here he'd taken great delight in showing her the fireplace where they'd hung Christmas stockings as children, the hallway where he and Charlie had practised rollerskating on wet days (until Charlie had crashed into the front door and cut his head on the letterbox, and they'd since been banished to the drive). He'd pointed out where Eddie had built them a treehouse in the garden, and the low roof below his old bedroom window onto which he'd climbed out and jumped down from, in order to meet his mates, despite being grounded.

Poor David. He would be sad to see it go. He turned to her now and, instead of the dismay she'd expected, there was a flicker in his eye that she hadn't seen for a while, an almost tangible air of excitement. 'What do you think, Em?'

She hesitated, taken aback. 'Of what? Your parents moving out?'

'About us taking this place on. We could do it, couldn't

we?' His words tumbled out in a rush. 'I mean, you'd have to give up your job, but you hate it anyway – you're always saying. We could move down here and make a fresh start together, keep the B&B going. What do you reckon?'

She stared at him, incredulous. What did she reckon? She reckoned it was a terrible idea, that he must have lost the plot if he seriously thought otherwise. The last thing she wanted was to be stuck miles from civilization, cooking breakfasts for complete strangers and washing sheets every day. *No freaking way*, she thought with a shudder.

'Um . . . I don't . . .' she began, but stumbled, aware of everyone's eyes on her. Lilian's face in particular was alight with hope. *Forget it, love*, Emma wanted to say. *It's never going to happen.* She was sure they didn't have enough money to buy a house like this, for starters, however much David might want it. 'Well, we'd need to think about it,' she replied after a moment. 'This isn't something we can decide here and now, is it?'

'Of course,' Eddie said, but he seemed disappointed, as if he'd been hoping for closure by the time they'd finished coffee. 'Hugh? Alicia?' he prompted. 'You've been very quiet.'

Alicia hesitated and turned to Hugh. She didn't want this place either, Emma could tell a mile off, and yet the two of them were surely the only ones who'd be able to afford it.

'This is rather out of the blue,' Hugh blustered. 'And

with our jobs, and the children's school . . . Well, we're settled where we are, Dad.'

'I could do it,' Charlie offered.

An awkward silence greeted his words, no doubt because, like Emma, every single other person around the table thought that actually Charlie could *not* run a B&B, given his track record. He could barely manage his own life competently, let alone oversee a business. He wasn't exactly dripping with ready cash, either.

Lilian and Eddie exchanged a glance, then Eddie cleared his throat. 'That's kind of you,' he began diplomatically. 'But . . . well, it's a lot of work, day in, day out – that's all. Especially for one person.'

Hugh cleared his throat. 'No offence, Charlie, but have you got the money to buy out Mum and Dad?'

Charlie coloured. 'I could raise it,' he said. 'I could!'

Nobody spoke, but Emma could almost hear the pantomime-style chorus of 'Oh no, you couldn't!' that they were all thinking.

'Or we could pitch in and run the business between us,' he went on doggedly. 'This is a family, right? And families pull together. We can't have you two struggling along on your own. If we all lend a hand, then we can get this ship back on course.'

No one seemed to know how to respond to this display of magnanimity. Emma, for one, didn't believe him for a second. Charlie never did anything for anyone out of simple decency or family-feeling – it wasn't his style. Look at the pathetic progress on the so-called holiday chalets out the back! Besides, she didn't think Lilian and Eddie were asking for people to merely lend a hand – they had said, clear as day, that they wanted out.

There was an awkward silence. 'I could help out in the meantime,' Alicia offered with a somewhat resigned expression. The sparkle had vanished from her eyes. 'I could do some of the washing and ironing for you. And . . .'

Hugh interrupted before she roped herself in for any more chores. 'This is something we all need to think about,' he said rather pompously. You could so tell he was the eldest of the brothers; he could never resist taking the lead. She knew it got on David's nerves sometimes. 'Now that we know how you feel, Mum and Dad, we can pitch in during the short term, but longer-term we need to weigh everything up carefully. Emma's right, we can't rush into a decision today, however willing we are to save the family business. We need to take a more measured approach, think it all through. When, for example, would you like to move out, ideally?'

'I think we could manage one more summer,' Lilian said, steepling her fingers together. They were rough and gnarled, Emma noticed, dotted with liver spots, the skin almost translucent in places. Hard-working old-lady hands that had scrubbed and cleaned and polished year after year. Hands that were ready for a rest. 'Don't you, Eddie?'

Eddie nodded. 'We've already got lots of bookings for the summer, and it would be nice to say a proper goodbye to our guests,' he said. 'But come the autumn, we'd like to move on.'

'Yes,' Lilian agreed. 'One last summer – and that's our lot.'

Emma could feel David looking at her with the same eager, imploring face, and her heart sank. She took his hand and squeezed it, guilty that she didn't share his excitement, especially when he hadn't been so animated for weeks. But could he really not tell that the idea of them taking on the business left her completely cold?

'Well, that gives us a clear timetable at least,' Hugh said. 'I can carry on doing the books for you until the autumn, and Alicia's kindly offered to help with the laundry. Charlie, maybe if you could aim to have at least some of the holiday chalets completed in that time, and—'

'What I could do,' David put in, 'is help smarten the place up, while I'm out of work. Whenever rooms are empty, I could redecorate and get them looking their best. I can help Charlie with the holiday chalets too – and whatever else comes up.' He looked at Emma. 'It would be good to have something to do.'

Her heart turned over, knowing how miserable he'd

Lucy Diamond

found it being unemployed. Being active and busy again might be just what he needed. 'Great idea,' she agreed. 'And then if you two *do* decide to sell up after the summer,' she went on to his parents, 'at least the place will be looking wonderful. You'll certainly be able to get a better asking price if everything's been freshly painted and decorated.'

'Good, excellent,' Hugh said approvingly. 'How does all that sound?' he added, turning to his parents.

Eddie nodded. 'Very sensible,' he said. 'Thank you.'

'Yes, thank you,' Lilian said, pressing her lips together suddenly as if she felt emotional. 'That's an enormous weight off my mind, I can tell you.'

Charlie was the only one who didn't seem happy. Emma got the feeling he was sulking because nobody had taken seriously his initial offer of shouldering the business single-handedly. Even David talking enthusiastically to him about how they could transform the barns over the next few weeks didn't draw the youngest brother out of his pique.

Get used to it, Charlie, she found herself thinking unsympathetically. *You can't have everything your own way.*

Emma hadn't realized just how keen David was to get started with the paint rollers and dustsheets until he broke the news that she would be driving back to Bristol alone that evening.

'What . . . you're not coming back?' she asked in surprise.

'But ...' *But what about the shagathon?* she wanted to say, but the words stuck in her throat. Oh God, he'd forgotten that this was the crucial time for conceiving. Dare she remind him? What if he shrugged it off?

'You don't mind, do you? I just want to *do* something, Em. I want to feel useful again. Dad's got some spare painting overalls he can lend me, so I might as well get stuck in straight away.'

How could she say no, when he put it like that? How could she start nagging about ovulation windows and fertility, when he was cheerful for the first time in weeks? 'Of course I don't mind,' she said untruthfully, after a moment.

It was the right reply to give, but nevertheless there was a hollow ache inside her as she hugged him goodbye later on. And as she drove away, all on her own, waving over her shoulder, the tears were brimming before she'd even reached the main road.

There went another egg, wasted and unfertilized. And here came another long, miserable four-week wait racking up ahead of her. She was starting to get the feeling that maybe this was never going to happen. Perhaps she was destined to remain childless and barren for the rest of her life. Maybe it would serve her right for—

She gripped the steering wheel tighter than necessary. *Don't go there, Em.*

All the same, she wished she'd had the nous to persuade David to return with her now, wished she'd said, *Actually, why don't you come home tonight, pack a few things and then head back in the morning?* That was a perfectly reasonable request, wasn't it? And then she could have seduced him back at the flat; he'd have been up for a farewell shag, surely? She wouldn't even have had to say the word 'pregnant'.

Damn it. And now it was too late, and she would spend tonight alone, while her husband (and his sperm) was fifty miles away. Bloody Eddie and Lilian, she thought, banging her fist on the steering wheel. Wrecking everything, as usual! Did they want another effing grandchild or not, for heaven's sake!

The only tiny thing that comforted her, the only meagre crumb of solace that kept her going, was the knowledge that back at home, the Oh Baby! forum would be waiting for her on her computer. Those women would understand, even if her own husband didn't.

Chapter Nine

Alicia was already regretting her offer to muck in with the Mulberry House laundry. That very afternoon Lilian had loaded up their car with two bin liners full of sheets, duvets, pillowcases and towels, all of which needed washing and ironing. 'By Wednesday, if you can,' she added.

'Right,' Alicia said faintly, mentally kissing goodbye to all the marking she had planned for that evening, and the next, and the next.

Hugh hadn't come away empty-handed, either. Eddie had pressed on him a cardboard box full of files and folders, a stack of bills and the company bank accounts. Great, Alicia thought with an uncharacteristic attack of sourness as they drove home. So much for the Turning-40 Action Plan; in just a few hours it had been rudely shouldered aside by the Helping the In-Laws Chore List. And surprise, surprise, while she and Hugh were saddled with the dirty work, Charlie and David got to lark about with paint pots. How come it always turned out that way?

Still, in fairness, she only had herself to blame. The guilt reflex had inevitably kicked in and she'd ended up conforming to type after all, old Goody Two-Shoes sticking her hand up for more drudgery. Why couldn't she have thought of a more interesting contribution to make, though, like the others, instead of washing and flipping ironing?

It was time to go back to her Action Plan and step up her game, she decided, if only to shock the rest of the Joneses into realizing that there was more to Alicia Jones than laundry and home-making. Hell, yes!

She was prompted into action the very next day, during her lunch break in the staffroom. The morning had been spent invigilating a history mock-GCSE exam and she'd sat there watching all those young heads bent over their papers, brows crumpled with thought. What lay ahead for this group of bright-faced teenagers? she wondered. What were their dreams, their futures? She remembered so clearly sitting her own GCSEs, the gruelling revision timetable she'd drawn up with different coloured felt-tips for each subject, the butterflies she'd felt every morning the instant her Snoopy alarm clock went off, the solemnity of her teachers' voices as they intoned, 'You may now turn over your papers . . . and begin.'

Little had she known that she'd be saying those very same words to her own students, twenty-three years later.

And if she *had* known, would the thought have filled her with pride at the achievement . . . or a twinge of disappointment? Might she have thought: Is that *it*? She gazed out across the hall unseeingly. Did I do enough, Christine? she wondered. What would you have done differently?

Afterwards, in the staffroom for morning coffee, she happened to tune into a conversation taking place behind her, and her ears pricked up.

'Oh, you should come along next week! It's such fun. Martine and I were in hysterics the whole time, honestly. And you don't have to be super-fit to do it, either, it's just a laugh. Something different, you know.'

Alicia's interest was caught. *Such fun. Just a laugh. Something different.* Wasn't this exactly what she had been hankering after?

She turned, coffee in hand, to see Juliet Cannock, one of the music teachers, talking to Wendy Turner, who taught IT. 'What's all this?' she asked brightly, hoping she wasn't blushing as she sat down beside them.

'Oh, hi, Alicia,' said Juliet, who was in her early thirties and wore floaty chiffon tops and pert-bum jeans. She had perfect eyebrows and a nose-stud, and a certain air of coolness that Alicia had always envied. 'I was just trying to persuade Wendy to come along to my belly-dancing class with me. It's a total scream. Go on, Wend, you'll love it.'

Wendy wrinkled her nose. She was younger than Juliet

and on the plump side, with a cloud of dark wavy hair, enormous boobs and a penchant for high heels. Today she was wearing bright-red strappy sandals with a two-inch heel, the sort of thing Alicia wouldn't have been able to walk in, let alone stride around a classroom with any confidence. 'Maybe,' she said hesitantly. 'I'm not sure it's my cup of tea, though.'

'Go on, you'll have fun. It's a beginners' class, so anything goes. And you feel great afterwards – really buzzy.'

Alicia couldn't remember the last time she'd felt 'really buzzy'. She couldn't even remember the last time she'd had fun. Before she could stop herself, she heard her own voice saying, 'I'll go with you. I'll give it a whirl.'

Juliet did a double-take as if the reply was unexpected. 'Seriously?' she asked. She didn't *quite* say 'YOU?' in a tone of disbelief, but she might as well have done. 'Okay. Excellent. Now you *definitely* have to come, Wend, if Alicia's brave enough.'

Alicia felt almost tremulous at what she'd just put herself forward for. Her – belly dancing? What on earth would Hugh say when she told him? The thought of his stunned face made her want to giggle. 'Yes, come on, Wendy, you know you want to,' she said, light-headed at her own daring. 'Life's too short not to give things a try, right?'

Juliet and Wendy were goggling at her breezy optimism.

It was a staffroom first. 'Um . . . okay, then,' Wendy said after a moment. 'Why not. We could make a night of it, couldn't we?'

'Brilliant,' Alicia said. 'You're on.'

Getting a nice haircut was one thing, but belly dancing . . . As the days passed that week Alicia began to wish she hadn't been so quick to put herself forward for it. What had possessed her? She hadn't done any dancing since she was a student, when she'd shuffled about self-consciously at the uni bop every week. Maybe the occasional embarrassed jig at friends' weddings, after a glass too many of bubbly, but that was her limit. Alicia had always been a fan of limits – and for good reason, she thought now.

Just as she was on the verge of backing out and composing an apologetic, untruthful text to Juliet about an unexpected family emergency, Hugh came back on Thursday with another carload of washing from Lilian, and something seemed to snap inside Alicia as he heaved it into the utility room. More drudgery. More washing. Was this really all she was good for?

Come on, Alicia, a voice said in her head. It sounded how she'd always imagined Christine's voice to sound – encouraging and kind. *There's more to you than housework and moaning. Don't back out now.*

'I'm afraid I won't be able to do that tonight,' she found herself telling Hugh as she went to get changed. 'I'm going out with some friends. Belly dancing, actually.'

So there she was that first evening, her face a study of trepidation, her body a mass of nerves, as she drove to meet Juliet and Wendy at the dance studio in Lyme for the class. *I can't believe I'm actually doing this*, she thought dazedly. Nor, it seemed, could Hugh.

'Have a nice time,' he said as she left. He still had that same confused, wary expression, as if he half-expected her to elbow him and laugh that of course she wasn't *really* going belly dancing, she was taking up flower arranging at the WI club. Silly husband! Had he seriously believed her?

'Thanks,' she said instead and shut the front door, feeling a prickle of excitement despite her nerves. She never usually went out in the evening. Occasionally there was something on at the school, a PTA meeting or a fund-raising event that she and Hugh tried to go along to whenever possible, babysitters permitting. But going out like this, just her on her own, before the children were even in bed – that was a novelty. It felt like a small but significant uprising.

'Alicia! You made it!' said Juliet when she walked in. Juliet managed to look chic in a pair of yoga pants and a clingy turquoise shirt, whereas Alicia instantly felt like a PE reject in her jogging bottoms and a black vest top. You were meant to wear something fitted on top, apparently, so that you and the teacher were able to see your muscles working as you danced, but Alicia wasn't sure she actually wanted her gut bobbling around on display to a room full of strangers. Not everyone was so modest, though. Some women in the studio were wearing floaty harem pants and cropped tops, which showed off sickeningly toned sets of abs. One or two of them even had golden coin belts around their trim waists, in proper Egyptian style.

Oh, help. Why had she ever thought she could do this? 'Where's Wendy?' she asked, looking around for moral support. There was no way solidly built Wendy would be in anything sheer or clinging either, she reassured herself.

'Bailed out,' Juliet said, with a hint of scorn. 'Said she's coming down with a cold. Coming down with skivilitis, more like.' She waved at someone across the room. 'Look, there's Martine. I'll introduce you, she's fab.'

Alicia just had time to say hi to Juliet's friend Martine when a blonde woman in a purple cropped top and matching yoga pants strode to the front of the studio and spoke into a clip-on microphone. 'Evening, all,' she said, beaming around at them as the chatter died down. 'I'm Debbie. Everyone ready for the warm-up? Then let's begin!'

To Alicia's surprise, the class wasn't as difficult as she'd been dreading. The warm-up seemed to be largely cardio-style exercises with big hip-circles and bottom-swings, then came a series of more focused exercises, such as squats and crunches. 'Squats and pliés will strengthen our legs for the shimmies and hip-accents,' explained Debbie. 'Whereas these abdominal exercises will give us beautiful belly-movements.'

Alicia was starting to care less and less about having beautiful belly-movements after countless agonizing stomach-crunches and it was a relief to move on to the dance steps themselves. Debbie showed them hip-bumps, ribcage-circles and snake-arms and, apart from poking her neighbour in the face during the arm-ripples and having to keep a hold of her ancient joggers every time she swung her hips, for fear of revealing her bum-crack to the woman behind, it wasn't long before Alicia realized that she was actually quite enjoying herself.

'Practise the routine over the week, and we'll keep adding to it throughout the term,' Debbie said at the end. 'That's it for tonight's class, thank you all very much. See you next time!'

Whew. Alicia was exhausted. She was absolutely hanging. She couldn't remember ever feeling so done in, apart from after childbirth perhaps. Despite the deep throbbing weariness of her limbs, and the embarrassment she'd felt when she discovered just how hopeless the elastic in her joggers was, she had what could only be endorphins a-gogo sprinting elatedly around her tired, hot body. She had done it: she'd leapt and stretched, she'd shimmied and swayed. What was more, it had even been a laugh, bum-flashing moments aside. She hadn't felt so alive and tingly for ages. Months. Years, even.

'That was FUN,' she said to Juliet as they went to put their shoes on. 'Thank you so much for letting me tag along.'

'Pleasure!' Juliet said. 'Really glad you could come. Are you going to join us for a drink? You'd be very welcome.'

Did she want a drink? Ohh . . . She *did* want a drink, she could absolutely murder a large, cold, ice-clinking gin and tonic, but on second thoughts she was sweaty and red-faced and probably a bit smelly too. 'Better not,' she said. 'Hugh's expecting me. Another time, though.'

'Brilliant. Well, see you tomorrow then.'

'See you. Bye, Martine! Nice to meet you.'

She was so glad she'd tried it. So glad she'd dared. She walked out of the studio humming the Egyptian music with a spring in her step. Christine would have been so proud of her. And just wait until she told Sandra!

Chapter Ten

'Hi, Lou – it's me, Izzy.'

'Hiya, love! God, I thought you'd dropped off the edge of the Earth. How are you?'

Hmmm, good question. *Increasingly paranoid*, she felt like replying. *Like I'm going mad.* As winter turned to spring, a whole new crop of worries seemed to be sprouting, namely the texts buzzing in from Gary, from a different number each time. She blocked them one by one, but that didn't stop him.

Dirty slag.

I want my girls.

I'm gonna find u, Iz.

It was doing her head in. It was really starting to scare her. Her fingers shook whenever she opened a new message, as if the phone might blow up in her hands. *Go away, Gary,* she thought desperately. *Leave us alone.*

'Things are a bit difficult' was all she said to Louise. She sighed, missing her friend suddenly, wishing she could walk into Louise's warm kitchen and have a cup of tea with her.

Louise had one of those bright, open faces you could tell anything to; she had always been on Izzy's side. She was the one who'd encouraged her to leave Gary in the first place, who had tutted and sighed with every new bruise and black eye. *You can't let him do this,* she'd said at the end. *You've got to have a bottom line — know when to get the hell out.*

'What do you mean, difficult? What's happened?'

Izzy shut her eyes and leaned back against the armchair. The girls were in bed, and she could hear the trees rattling in the wind outside. 'Gary's been in touch.'

'Shit. What did he . . . ? Hang on, I'm just going to take you in the other room. Wait there.'

Izzy tucked her feet up into the chair and put an arm around her knees. She missed having somebody hold her. Sometimes she even missed Gary, crazy as it might sound. She knew the girls did too; Hazel in particular was always asking after him. *No, we can't phone Daddy. Because we just can't. I don't know when we'll see him again. I'm sorry, but that's just how it is, I'm afraid. We live here now.*

Had she been fair, taking them away from him, ripping the family apart? God knows she'd hung on for as long as she could. But he had gone too far that last time. Staying put and hanging on wasn't safe any more.

'Hi, sorry — I'm here. Just wanted to go in the kitchen, because Ricky's watching TV and you know what he's like, getting in a hump with me for yacking over it.'

Izzy smiled weakly. 'Yeah,' she said. Louise and Ricky had the comfortable, easy sort of relationship where they only ever got annoyed with each other about things like what to watch on television, or who had scoffed the last biscuit in the packet. Lucky bastards.

'So tell me. What's happened? What did he say?'

'He keeps sending horrible texts,' Izzy said, lowering her voice, even though both the girls were definitely asleep. 'Threatening ones, saying he wants the children back and that he's going to find me. Horrible stuff.'

'Jesus. How did he get your number?'

'No idea. Only a couple of people know this new one. I don't suppose . . .' She licked her lips. 'Could he have got it from Ricky?'

'No way!' Louise sounded hurt. 'Of course not. Ricky doesn't even have your number, does he?'

'Sorry. I just . . .' Izzy felt bad for asking. 'Sorry, Lou. I'm freaking out. I'm scared. What if he finds out where we are?'

'Oh, love, don't worry. How could he?'

'I don't know,' Izzy admitted. She twitched the curtain back and gazed into the darkness beyond her window. He could be anywhere, she thought. He could be in the back garden watching me right now, plotting how he could break in and . . . and . . .

'There you go, then. Remember what a dumb-arse he is. He can barely count his own fingers, let alone find you. And he's lazy too, right? Even if he has a clue where you're living, can you imagine him getting off his fat bum and driving all the way down there? Not a chance.'

It was mad how, even now, after everything, Izzy could still feel protective of her ex. It wasn't Gary's fault his education had been so chaotic. He wasn't dumb, whatever anyone else said. She'd known him to be sharp, funny, switched-on. He'd held down his job with Little's Insurance for more than ten years now, hadn't he? Ten years – that was better than a lot of people. Louise didn't know him like Izzy did.

She let the curtain fall against the window again with a sigh. It was complicated, disliking and fearing a person you'd once loved. 'Lou, don't be offended, but I've just got to ask, so humour me, will you? Have you told *anyone* where I am, even Rick? Have you mentioned Lyme, or the south coast, or . . . ?'

'No! Of course not, what kind of mate do you think I am? A promise is a promise, and I never break promises. All right?'

Izzy cringed. Louise sounded really miffed now. 'All right,' she said meekly. 'Thanks. I'm sorry I had to ask. I'm just paranoid, sorry.'

'It's okay. Try to forget him. Block him on your phone, so that he can't contact you. Change your number! And keep your cool, love. He'll get bored soon.'

'Yeah. God, I wish you were here. I miss having a mate like you.'

'I wish I was there too. I've got Ricky's mucky football kit to wash here, and I'd much rather be with you.'

Izzy couldn't speak for a second, wishing her only problem was a pile of muddy football clothes. 'Give him my love, and lots to you too,' she said in the end. 'Bye now.'

'Bye, love. Take care and stop worrying, yeah? See you.'

Meanwhile Charlie was making life difficult as well. After the disastrous episode at his parents' house, he'd come crawling round to her flat, apologizing and grovelling, but she'd given him short shrift. She was through with men.

'I'm sorry, I didn't think,' he'd said, his voice crackling through the intercom. 'Really, Izzy – I'm sorry.'

'Go away,' she'd said, refusing to buzz him in.

The next day he came into the tea shop with a bunch of daffs. 'Don't take any notice of my family, they're all mad,' he told her.

'I'm busy,' she replied, ignoring the flowers and whirling into the kitchen where he couldn't get to her.

'Was that Charlie Jones I spotted?' asked Margaret, her

boss, making a tutting noise. 'He's a waste of space, that one. Don't get involved with him, whatever you do.'

'I'm not planning to,' Izzy replied, but Margaret was on a roll.

'He was meant to be decorating the building for us over Christmas last year, then made excuses at the last minute. Completely unreliable. I'm surprised he dared show his face in here.'

'He used to go out with my cousin's friend,' one of the other girls, Patrice, piped up, overhearing. 'He's full of shit – excuse my French.'

'Works at the garden centre now, I think, the one on the edge of town, doesn't he?' Nicci, the washer-upper added. 'God knows how long he'll last there.'

Izzy sighed. Did anyone have a good word to say for Charlie Jones? 'Thanks for the warning,' she muttered.

He had tenacity, though, you could say that much for him. Staying power. Bloody-mindedness, more like. He was waiting outside on the wall when she finished her shift that day, still clutching the daffs. They were drooping by now, but he wasn't. 'When can I take you somewhere nice, to make it up to you?' he said with his best smile.

It was the final straw. She already had one nutter stalking her by text; she didn't need another doing it in person, especially one with such a rubbish track record. 'Charlie, for fuck's sake, get it through your thick skull,' she said, snatching the flowers and throwing them to the pavement, 'I am not interested. It's not a game. It's not me playing hard to get. Just leave me alone, or I'll call the police. I mean it. Jog on!'

People had stopped and stared – you didn't usually get raised voices and flying daffodils in the middle of Broad Street – but she couldn't have cared less. She stalked away up the hill, furious, fists clenched, just daring him to run after her. He didn't, luckily for him.

When Saturday came around, she dreaded him turning up at her ballet class and making another scene, but to her relief Alicia dropped Matilda off and left without saying a word. Then, when she returned at the end of the lesson, she came over and quietly apologized for the awfulness of the Sunday before.

'I'm so embarrassed about the way Charlie's mum treated you,' she said, twisting her fingers around the handle of her smart leather bag. 'She was absolutely vile. I'm really sorry.'

Izzy shrugged, hardened against the situation now. It was no skin off her nose. 'It's not your fault,' she said, trying to brush the whole thing aside. Some mistakes were best left forgotten.

'I know it's small consolation, but she's got a lot on her plate right now,' Alicia went on. 'I'm not making excuses – she was rude to you, and shouldn't have been. But I promise she's not always like that. If Charlie invites you again, then—'

'Charlie won't be inviting me anywhere,' Izzy interjected. 'Or rather, if he does, I won't be taking him up on it.'

'Oh dear,' Alicia said, looking awkward. 'I'm sorry to hear that.'

'Well, don't be. I'm not.'

She was verging on rudeness, and it was only the whipped-dog look in Alicia's eyes that stopped her going even further. 'But thanks for being nice about it,' she managed to say. 'It's not your problem.' Alicia was her customer, after all – and a good one too, always paying Matilda's fees promptly. Izzy couldn't afford to start pushing people away.

To her relief, Alicia merely nodded and said, 'Okay,' before leaving with Matilda. Then Izzy was distracted by another parent wanting her attention and moved on. She felt guilty about her tone for the rest of the morning, though. Alicia seemed a nice person and had only been trying to build bridges, even if Izzy had gone about kicking them all down again. The problem was, it was hard to trust anyone when you felt as paranoid as she did right now.

Another week went by, and Charlie seemed to have taken the hint at least. No more calls, no more visits at work, no more apologies. Good. As far as Izzy was concerned, if she never saw that idiot again it would be too soon. From here on in, it was just going to be her and the girls, with no room for incomers.

If she thought she'd washed her hands of the Jones family, she was mistaken, though. Much to Izzy's surprise, Alicia approached her again at the end of the following week's lesson, looking rather pink. Oh God. Don't say Charlie had asked her to put a good word in for him now? Please, no!

'Hi,' Alicia said without preamble, as if in a hurry to get out her words. 'Listen, I wanted to ask you something. I've recently started a belly-dancing class on Thursday, and . . . well . . . I wondered if you wanted to come along sometime with me? It's right here in Lyme, in the community hall. No problem if you don't want to, though.'

It took Izzy a few seconds to process this. Alicia wanted *her* to go *belly dancing* with her one evening? Well, she hadn't been expecting that. Somehow she couldn't imagine this elegant, rather posh-sounding older woman in her nice navy coat shimmying to the Dance of the Seven Veils. Was it some kind of trick?

'This hasn't got anything to do with your brother-in-law, has it?' she replied cautiously.

'Charlie? God, no, don't worry about him. And honestly, just say no if you don't want to — it was only a thought.

And of course you might be really, really busy, and I know you've got the girls to look after too, obviously, but . . .'

'Okay.'

The word took both of them by surprise. Alicia coloured and licked her lips. 'You want to? Oh, good!' Clearly she hadn't been anticipating a positive outcome; she'd had defeat written all over her. Curious, thought Izzy. Why was she so nervy, so unsure of herself? 'I'm trying to challenge myself, you see,' she went on in a rush of new-found confidence. 'Trying to do new things.'

Izzy raised an eyebrow. 'What, and I'm a new thing, am I?'

She was joking, but Alicia looked mortified, turning even pinker. 'No! Not at all. Well, I am trying to – you know – broaden my circle, get to know some new people, but . . .' She laughed in relief when she realized that Izzy was grinning. 'You know what I mean. The belly dancing is the challenge. I'm going to be forty this year, you see.'

Izzy didn't see at all, if she was honest, but Alicia seemed harmless enough, if kind of flustered. Moreover it was the first time since Izzy had moved down here that another woman had extended the hand of friendship. Hopefully Mrs Murray would babysit for another evening. 'Right – you're on, then,' she said, conscious of her next lesson, which was about to begin. 'Here,' she said, scribbling down her number. 'Text me the details and we'll sort it out. See you then!'

The next week turned out to be much better than the last, thank goodness. Business was brisk at the tea shop and Izzy's dance lessons went well. Willow was elected to be her class's 'School Council' member, and Hazel came home with a 'Star of the Week' certificate, which seemed to be on a par with being awarded the Nobel Peace Prize, if her elation was anything to go by. Best of all, Gary had gone quiet on her. He hadn't sent a single text for almost a week. The relief was absolutely enormous; she felt lighter and more free with each passing day, less worried about spotting him on the beach or in the high street, less panicky whenever she heard a northern accent or glimpsed a tall, burly man with a crew cut. Lou must have been right – he'd got bored when she hadn't responded, had moved on to tormenting someone else.

Thank God for that.

On Thursday she met Alicia in Lyme for the belly-dancing lesson and ended up having the most fun she'd had for weeks. The actual dancing wasn't really her cup of tea – the music was a bit weird, and the steps were pretty repetitive, once you got the hang of them – but she loved the energy of the movements and the joyful feeling of shaking her tush with a room full of other women, all of whom seemed to be having a whale of a time as they swayed and swung.

Even more surprising was the way mousy Alicia let rip – really going for it with the hip-shaking and general jiggling. *Look at me! I am all woman! I am strong and gorgeous!* her body seemed to say, as she bounced about, boobs flying, thighs shaking, sweat pouring down her face. Her skin was flushed, her hair fell messily around her face and she wasn't remotely well coordinated, but there was no disguising her look of elation. Go, Alicia. Who would have thought?

'That was great,' Izzy said afterwards, once the class had clapped the dance teacher and started dispersing to gather coats and bags from the side of the hall.

'Isn't it wonderful? It always makes me feel so alive and happy,' Alicia replied breathlessly. She fanned her hot cheeks with a hand. 'As well as sweaty and unfit and completely ungainly, of course, but that's by the by.'

There she went – retreating back into mousiness, Izzy thought ruefully. Back into apologizing for herself and being the little woman. 'Who cares about being sweaty and unfit?' she replied. 'The main thing is enjoying it, and expressing yourself. That's what I love most about dancing.'

Alicia smiled and pulled on a shapeless black jacket. 'I hope it wasn't too much of a busman's holiday for you tonight,' she said. 'I hope you didn't mind me asking you along, it was just . . .'

'No way!' Izzy said. 'I'm glad you did. Thank you – I loved it. Can I come along next week too?'

Alicia beamed. 'You're on.' Then she paused. 'Um, I think a few people are going for a drink now – someone I know from work and her friend. Just in the local, nothing wild, but . . . well, would you like to join us?'

Izzy glanced at her watch. Almost nine o'clock. Not late by any means, but she didn't want to antagonize Mrs Murray, not when she needed to keep her onside. Besides, she couldn't afford to pay for drinks and any more baby-sitting, on top of what she'd already shelled out tonight. 'Sorry, no,' she replied regretfully. 'I told my neighbour I'd be back by nine, and I don't want to mess her about. Another time, though, definitely.'

'Okay,' Alicia replied. 'See you on Saturday then – for ballet, I mean.'

'See you.'

Izzy walked into the cold night feeling as if she'd made a new friend. An unusual sort of friend, yes – not someone she'd have picked out immediately as being friend material, but she couldn't help liking Alicia. Maybe something good had come out of the Jones family after all.

Chapter Eleven

Having David to stay was a godsend in Lilian's eyes. They said middle children were the awkward squad, but he'd always been the easiest of her boys: the sunniest, most good-natured and thoughtful. Hugh was solid and practical, Charlie made everyone laugh, but David was the one Lilian could really talk to – the one she felt was most emotionally engaged with the other members of the family.

It had broken her heart, seeing him so disillusioned of late, so tired of his life. His demeanour had reminded her of a man left in the airport, still staring at the baggage carousel going round and round after everyone else had grabbed their luggage and moved on. Thank goodness she had him under her roof again now. Home cooking and some hard work helping Eddie – that would see him straight.

Eddie, too, appreciated David being there. Charlie hadn't exactly been dependable when it came to building and decorating work in the past, however well-meaning he was, but they'd always struggled to take him to task on it.

Charlie was different from the other two, that was the thing. He'd been a sickly little boy, skinny and weedy, asthmatic from the age of six. Those night-time trips to Dorchester hospital, where he'd wheezed and struggled for breath and she'd actually thought she was going to lose him, had been the cause of her first grey hairs. She was not a religious woman, but she'd found herself praying by his bedside when he was hooked up to the ventilator, watching his oxygen levels until her vision blurred. *Please, God, let him be okay. Please, God, I'll do anything.*

Those days were long gone, of course, and nowadays he was a strong, healthy man, but when she looked into his eyes, she still sometimes glimpsed that frightened little boy, cheeks concave, skin turning blue as he gasped helplessly. You never got over something like that. It changed you.

It was simpler with David. Barring a few dodgy girl-friends, he'd never given them any trouble and was good company, easy to be with. Her favourite photo of him was one taken when he was about ten and they were holidaying in Ilfracombe. There was skinny, freckly David holding a mackerel he'd caught after a fishing trip, with the most enormous grin. Lilian knew that at least half the triumph came from the fact that Hugh hadn't caught a thing, and Charlie had been repeatedly sick over the side of the boat. Boys, eh?

Twenty-five years later, he'd slotted back into the house

as if he'd never been away, and she enjoyed having him there. He wasn't bossy, as Hugh could sometimes be, or as needy as Charlie; he merely got stuck into whatever needed doing: wallpaper-stripping, plastering, painting, fixing . . . He'd even helped out with the gardening and breakfasts on occasion, always whistling cheerfully as he did so. Already the house felt transformed.

You could see the difference in him too, within a week. His skin had changed from pasty grey to a healthier pink; the bags under his eyes had vanished, as if he was sleeping well. Hard work was good for a person, Lilian had always thought. And he was smiling again, enjoying the satisfaction of making a difference to the house. His home. If only he'd move back for good!

'I think the country air suits you, David,' she'd said innocently a few times. He'd put up some feeble argument about loving city life in Bristol, but she wasn't fooled. Dorset ran in his veins, she knew.

He wasn't daft, though, her son. Hugh and Charlie might not have noticed anything different about their father lately, but it took just three days for David to realize Eddie wasn't himself. 'Is Dad all right, Mum?' he asked that evening. They were in the kitchen together and he was drying the dishes as she washed them. 'Only he seems a bit . . . absent-minded.'

Her hands felt numb in the hot water and she floundered

for what to say. *A bit absent-minded* . . . Yes. He was that, all right. Just that morning he'd left the tap running in the bathroom sink with the plug in. It was only when water began dripping through the kitchen ceiling that she realized what had happened. It took six bath towels and a lot of mopping before the flood was dealt with.

Then there was the fact that words seemed to escape him. Of course, it happened to everyone sometimes – you'd grasp around for the phrase you wanted, only for it to slip away into the shadows of your mind, tantalizingly out of reach. Eddie seemed to have forgotten some really basic words, though, words so everyday that she wondered how his brain could have misplaced them.

'Have you seen my . . . my . . . you know,' he'd asked the day before, pointing at his wrist. 'My clock – my hand-clock.'

There was a lump in her throat. 'Your watch, love? It's on your bedside table,' she'd replied. She'd had to busy herself hoovering bedroom four for the Flint family, who were arriving that afternoon, to stop herself dwelling on it any further.

Now she took a long breath and looked at David. 'I'm not sure,' she replied candidly. 'He's been like that for a few weeks now. It's probably just stress, he's worked so hard lately. But we should keep an eye on him.'

'Yeah.' He was frowning; the exact same frown she'd

seen him wear as a boy when he was puzzling something out. 'It was just . . . We were stripping the wallpaper in bedroom two earlier and he put the steamer on without filling it with water first.' He cleared his throat. 'I know it's an easy mistake, but it could have been really dangerous – would have shorted-out the electrics, if I hadn't noticed. And when I reminded him, he seemed . . . well, quite confused about the whole thing.'

Lilian was silent for a moment, lips pressed together as she pictured the scene. Confused was a good way to describe her husband right now. A couple of times recently he'd woken in the night and had seemed completely disoriented, sitting bolt upright and staring at her wildly as if he didn't know her. 'It's great you're here, helping him, love,' she said finally, hoping to soften the tension on her son's face. 'I'm sure that's making things a lot easier for him.' *Not to mention saving him from being electrocuted or buggering up our power supply.*

'Yeah,' he said again. 'Well, I'll stay as long as you need me anyway. You're probably right – he just needs a break. You two should book a holiday after the summer, put your feet up for a change.'

She scrubbed at the casserole dish, a hollow laugh bubbling in her throat. A holiday indeed! Chance would be a fine thing. She couldn't even think about time off, when the Whartons were due on Thursday for a long weekend, along with Mr and Mrs Miller from Suffolk, and then a whole group of young women who were on some cycling tour or other the week after (she hoped they wouldn't be too much trouble; girls nowadays got so rowdy at the drop of a hat). And then once they'd gone and the dust had settled, their Easter regulars would start arriving: the Brook family from Hampshire and . . . goodness, now *she* was forgetting. Lots of people anyway. Lots of hoovering, lots of cooking, lots of washing. The thought of a holiday was almost enough to make her cry with longing.

'Seriously, Mum,' David was saying. 'While I'm staying, let me carry some of the load. Okay?'

'Thanks, son,' she replied. 'I'm glad to have you here.'

'In fact . . .' An idea seemed to have taken root in him. 'Listen, I've been thinking. I'd love to get Em down here for a few days soon, show her how great the house is looking. Persuade her to think seriously about the two of us taking the place on. Why don't you and Dad get away for a breather sometime next week? Just a couple of days. You could go and see Aunty Jean in Bournemouth maybe. Have a proper break.'

Lilian felt quite overcome. Nobody had ever suggested such a thing to her before. Could she really leave Mulberry House in the hands of her son? She and Eddie never took time off once the busy season started, not properly. Even when it was Eddie's brother's funeral, they'd made a day trip of it, all the way up to Nottingham and back, rather than spend a whole night away and put their guests out.

'You'll have to let go sometime,' David pointed out while she wrestled with the thought. 'This could be our trial run. Emma might fall in love with the place, like I have, and then . . .'

He left the sentence hanging tantalizingly unfinished. And then . . . they might move in for good and take up the reins. And then . . . she and Eddie could retire and live the quiet life.

'Go on, be a devil,' he coaxed. 'Have some fun together. You said yourself that Dad needs a break.'

That was what swung it. Eddie *did* need a change of scenery, a chance to put his feet up and relax. An image slid into her head of the two of them sagging into deckchairs on the front at Bournemouth, watching the tide roll in and out.

'All right,' she said. 'You're on.' She swallowed. 'And about your dad – perhaps it's best not to mention this to your brothers. For now anyway. We don't want anyone to worry, do we?'

Chapter Twelve

Dear Mrs Timms,

*I'm delighted to be emailing details of our proposal for your
fireplace order. As you will see, I am suggesting the Henley
Asquith limestone, with the cast-iron insert and granite hearth,
which has all the classic beauty I know you were keen to find.*

*Could you let me know your thoughts sometime this week,
please? If you are happy with the style, I can go ahead and order
that for you.*

Best wishes

Emma Jones

Emma pressed 'Send' with a flourish, and ticked 'Fire-
place/Timms' off her list. She liked her job, but sometimes
– just sometimes – she was reminded how ridiculous it
would seem to an extraterrestrial. Sourcing the perfect
cushion for a client . . . Deliberating for the best part of an
hour about the exact paint shade required for a child's
bedroom . . . Costing up an Italian light fitting that was

running into the high hundreds (when she knew damn well you could get something similar from BHS for fifty quid) . . . She'd done all of these things within the last week, and each one had made her die a little inside. Pandering to the whims of rich people with too much time on their hands was hardly akin to being a paramedic or a social worker or a teacher.

Her phone rang and, as if to amplify her convictions about her career's worthlessness, the caller was Jennifer Salisbury, one of her most demanding clients. Jennifer had more money than sense, and was constantly fretting about some trivial design detail or other. Emma wouldn't have minded if she kept the fretting to the quiet confines of her own head, but she insisted on involving other people — namely Emma — every single bloody time.

'Oh, hi, it's Jen,' she said. 'I'm having a total trauma about the rug. It's just not working for me, I'm afraid. Could you come and give me your opinion?'

Emma sighed inwardly. The rug in question was a typically colourful Paul Smith design, made of Tibetan wool, and absolutely gorgeous. The only 'problem' any sane person could possibly have with such a beauty was deciding which room was lucky enough to feature it. But after ten years in this business Emma knew that the customer was always right, even if it meant they were a complete pain in the neck.

'Of course,' she said. 'I've got another client to see in Clifton this afternoon, so why don't I drop in afterwards?'

'Oh, would you? You're such a sweetheart. What would I do without you?'

What indeed, thought Emma, hanging up. That was the question. Might Jennifer actually have to confront her loneliness, the pointlessness of her life, if Emma wasn't there to be badgered day and night with an opinion about this, and advice about that? Might she gaze around her enormous, spectacularly proportioned Victorian house, which she'd spent tens of thousands of pounds on styling and decorating in the four years Emma had known her, and think *what the hell have I been* doing *all this time? What's this all* for?

But then Emma knew the answer to that already. The endless lavish design plans and consultations, the purchases, colours and tweaks – they were merely an attempt to stave off Jennifer's encroaching boredom at being married to a millionaire who spent most of the week working in London. It gave her something to do, something to witter about to her posh friends over wine-bar lunches. They were all at it.

Still, each to their own. Who was Emma to judge anyway? She'd spent much of her free time chatting online to other pregnancy-obsessed women lately, when she wasn't popping disgusting fertility supplements into her gob. Her life wasn't exactly a triumph, either, right now. She'd even found herself reading up on all the barmy conception attempts that other women put themselves through – post-coital headstands, acupuncture, hypnoconception CDs (whatever the hell they were), temperature charts . . . even secret one-night stands with men without protection. The last was probably a step too far, admittedly, but she could see how the desperation took hold of you. It was already sinking its claws into her so deep she knew there would be scarring.

She added 'Rug/Salisbury' to her list, then returned to the top of her 'to do's. *Lighting for Newsom Family Room.* Ah yes, the Newsoms, who were in the throes of the most wonderful barn conversion out near Queen Charlton. Now that she thought about it, there was another family, the Barratts, who were decorating their master bedroom over in Bath and wanted some lighting samples too. *Goody*, thought Emma, getting to her feet and putting her Mac on standby. *Time to go shopping.*

Her assistant, Flo, a dreamy, dark-haired girl who never seemed to be fully in tune with the world around her, looked up and blinked. 'Going out?'

'Lighting,' Emma replied briefly. 'And then a couple of appointments in Clifton.'

'What's that, hair appointment followed by a manicure?'

teased Greg, one of the other designers. 'Jonesy, Jonesy, Jonesy. When are you going to start doing some actual, you know, like, *work* around this place?'

There were six designers in the agency, and Greg was the joker of the pack. Tall, broad and ridiculously confident, he definitely fancied himself as Alpha Male, even competing with his own colleagues for business or prices.

'Manicure? Brazilian you mean,' Emma retaliated. 'Shall I book you in for your usual back, sack and crack while I'm there? Followed by your . . . what was it you like, again? "Happy Ending" massage?'

He laughed, then leaned forward, his eyes sparkling. 'Have you *really* got a Brazilian, Jones? I've never actually seen one before. Hester refuses to do any kind of waxing down there – it's all I can do to persuade her to give the hairy beast a trim now and then.'

'Oh, Greg, stop, we don't want to know! Too much information, dude!' screeched Lottie, wincing and clapping her hands over her ears. She was, as usual, sitting with an open wedding magazine in front of her, ignoring her phone and not doing any work. Dressed today in a clingy fuchsia jumper, with the kind of cleavage that meant men never looked her in the eye, Lottie disapproved of almost everything Greg did or said. 'The poor woman. Her ears must constantly be burning, having to put up with you and your big trap.'

'At least her minge isn't burning,' Flo put in mildly. 'Turns out I'm allergic to bikini waxes. Came up in a rash the first time I tried one. Never again.'

'And on that bombshell...' Emma said. 'I'll see you lot later.'

'Missing you already!' Greg yelled after her.

Her mobile rang as she left the building: David. 'Fancy bunking off?' he asked.

'Always,' she replied. 'What did you have in mind?'

'A few days in the countryside ... a lovely big old house to ourselves ... fresh air ... romping in the meadows ...'

'Really?' she asked, a smile stretching across her face. Then she clocked what he meant. Oh. Not a mini-break in the Cotswolds, then. More like Mulberry House with the in-laws and wet paint. 'Are you talking about your parents' place?' she asked, trying not to sound too dispirited.

'They're away,' he said. 'We'd have it to ourselves.'

'Oooh!' God, it was like being a teenager again, she thought, remembering the secret fumbling sessions she'd had with sixth-form boyfriends while her parents were out. 'Take your time!' she'd trill under her breath, dashing for the phone whenever they went to Neighbourhood Watch meetings or a Caravan Club get-together. She could never hear 'Love Is All Around' by Wet Wet Wet without a flashback to the longest three minutes of her life, losing her virginity under her Laura Ashley duvet to Marc Abrahams, while her parents were out eyeing up new bedding plants in the Walsall Road garden centre.

'What, all night? How come?' she asked now, quickly blotting out the image of Marc Abrahams huffing and puffing before collapsing stickily on her.

'I persuaded them to take some time off. So what do you think? Fancy playing Lady of the Manor?'

She gave a snort. Lady of the Manor indeed. He made it sound like he was inviting her to Downton Abbey – Fawlty Towers, more like. But he sounded happy; so much happier than he'd been all year, and he wanted to be with her again. Given that the alternative was sourcing French curtain trim for Clifton Yahs, frankly she didn't need to think twice. She coughed fakely into the phone. 'Now you mention it, I think I'm coming down with something,' she told him. 'Better take a few days off to recover.'

'A few days in bed, that's what I prescribe,' he said, and the words gave her a jolt of desire. Absence might well make the heart grow fonder, but it also seemed to be making the husband randier.

'You read my mind, Dr Jones,' she said huskily. 'See you later.'

Skiving work was surprisingly easy. After her client visit that afternoon, she phoned Tracey saying that she was going to finish early as she felt ropey, adding a few more pathetic coughs into the receiver for good measure. Then she drove home and packed a bag of silky undies, scented bath oils and a book she'd been meaning to read for ages.

Oh, this was going to be *fun*, she thought to herself, singing at the top of her voice as she drove south. This might be exactly what she and David needed to get their marriage on track, some time off for good behaviour. She wasn't ovulating for another ten days, so they could enjoy lots of no-pressure sex and smooching. You never know, she might even be able to drag him back to Bristol with her when she left.

It wasn't until she arrived at Mulberry House and saw an unfamiliar black Volkswagen and a silver Ka parked outside that she realized she and David wouldn't actually be alone.

No way, she thought, gripping the steering wheel with unnecessary tightness. No frigging way. She'd assumed that Lilian and Eddie were going out of town because they had no bookings this week – not so that she and David could step in and play 'mine host' in their absence. Over my dead body, she thought grimly.

David must have been watching for her arrival because he was there in the doorway before she'd even hauled her bag out of the boot. 'Hello,' he said, crunching over the gravel drive and kissing her.

She tried to let go of the tension in her shoulders as she

hugged him, but couldn't help commenting, 'So I see we've got guests' in a strangled-sounding voice.

'Yeah, the Whartons and the Millers,' he said, taking her weekend bag from her as if he was the resident butler. 'Thought we could give it a practice run – you know, managing the place.'

A practice run. Managing the place. Stop right there, she wanted to shout, one hand up like a police officer. But just as she was opening her mouth a portly gentleman appeared in the doorway.

'Mr Jones! About that travel iron . . . ?'

'I'll be right with you, Mr Miller,' David replied. 'This is my wife, Emma, by the way.'

'Hello,' Emma said weakly. This was starting to feel like a bad dream. She wished she hadn't laid on her fake illness quite so thoroughly to Tracey earlier; a miraculous recovery might well be in order at this rate.

'Hello there!' he cried jovially. He was in his fifties, she reckoned, with a bulging gut that must have taken many whisky evenings to cultivate and a horrible thick moustache. For an awful moment she imagined how it would tickle against one's bare thigh and felt nauseous. 'My wife wants to borrow an iron, you see – your husband wasn't sure where such a thing was kept!'

Don't look at me, love, she wanted to say. *I haven't the foggiest.*

This may come as a shock, but being female doesn't give me the superpower to sniff one out like a hound.

She put on a bland Stepford smile, just to freak out David. 'Let's go inside, shall we?' she said pleasantly. 'I can track a domestic appliance from twenty paces, you watch.'

Once the iron had been located and presented with a flourish to Fatty Miller, Emma poured herself a strong gin and eyeballed David. He hung his head guiltily, like a dog told off for pinching biscuits. 'Sorry, Em,' he said. 'I should have been straight with you. I just thought it might be . . . a laugh.'

'A laugh,' she repeated, necking such a massive mouthful of gin it made her eyes water.

'I still think we could make a go of this place,' he said earnestly. 'Honestly, I've loved being down here for the last few weeks. We could transform the house, the pair of us, make it really special.'

She cast an appraising eye around the old farmhouse kitchen they were standing in: a well-proportioned square room with big windows overlooking the garden. There was a large table with six chairs around it, a proper old-fashioned larder cupboard and a wooden dresser stacked with Lilian's beloved Chinese willow-pattern dinner service.

Emma, who could never switch off her designer mode,

Lucy Diamond

had always thought there was so much potential in this room, if only her in-laws had the inclination to change it. For starters, she'd paint the whole room Joa's White, with brilliant-white gloss around the skirting and the larder door. She'd get a joiner to replace the tired old units with some lovely old-fashioned wooden cupboards, rip off the peeling Formica worktop and lay a massive marble strip in its place; she'd grow herbs along the sunny windowsill, hang a bright Roman blind from the window and...

'We could,' she agreed thoughtfully, 'but—'

'This could be it, Em. Our way out of the city. A family home of our own – even better than the Bishopstone house.'

She bit her lip. She'd loved the Bishopstone house, the one they'd almost bought before David lost his job and everything started going wrong. It was meant to be their happy-ever-after home. The first time they'd stepped over the threshold she'd almost been able to hear the pitter-patter of tiny feet on the gorgeous Victorian tiling of the hall floor, the laughter and excitement of their children on Christmas mornings and at birthday parties. She'd imagined this whole life for them there: the dog they'd have, the dinner parties they'd throw, the tasteful Farrow & Ball walls, the bread-smelling kitchen...

He could tell she was weakening and pounced. 'Just give

it a try while you're here, yeah? Open your mind to how things could be, and—'

'Hello-o? Anyone home?' The door handle turned and Alicia appeared. 'Laundry delivery,' she announced, rolling her eyes. 'Oh, Emma! Hello, I didn't know you'd be here.' She hauled two heavy-looking bin liners in behind her. 'How are you?'

Emma got up to kiss her on the cheek. 'Fine,' she said. 'God, are you still doing all the laundry for this place?' She arched an eyebrow at David. 'Staff. That would be my first rule.'

He looked delighted that she was even entertaining the idea. 'Done,' he said at once.

Alicia looked puzzled. 'What's all this? Staff? And where's Lilian anyway?'

'Bournemouth,' David told her. 'Can I get you a drink? Emma and I are holding the fort while they're away.'

Alicia's eyebrows shot up. 'Oooh! Does this mean . . . ? Has he actually talked you round?' she asked.

'No,' Emma said, just as David said, 'Not yet.'

Alicia beamed. 'I thought you were dead set against it,' she said to Emma, 'but it would be great if you two moved down here. And you could make this place look amazing, I know it.' She checked her watch. 'Damn. I wish I could stay for a drink so you could fill me in, but I've got my dance class tonight. I'd better push off. Can't wait to tell Hugh!'

'There's nothing to tell!' Emma called after her, feeling ganged up on. She put her head in her hands as David went to see Alicia out, and glared at the laundry bags. Oh God. What was she getting herself into?

Chapter Thirteen

The evening progressed into drunkenness — well, on Emma's part at least. After Alicia had vanished, she and David ordered in a Chinese, then started on a bottle of Sauvignon Blanc. While they waited for the food to arrive he showed her around the place, wine glasses in hand. She had to admit, the house had come on in leaps and bounds. David and his dad had painted two of the bedrooms so that they gleamed fresh and light, some of the old carpets had been ripped up and the floors sanded and waxed, and there was even progress on one of the outbuildings — or the holiday chalet, as he optimistically called it. (You'd have to be some kind of freak to want to holiday in that draughty, cobwebby old wreck, Emma thought, but David assured her it was going to be brilliant once they'd finished.)

'Just imagine us living here,' he said as they walked back to the house. 'Kids playing on the lawn, the Christmases we could have together.'

She stopped walking in surprise. 'You still want that? Kids, I mean?'

He stopped too. 'Of course I do! Did you think—?'

'You seemed to have gone off the idea, that's all.' She put her arms around herself. It was almost dark now and the warmth had melted from the air.

'I've always wanted a family, Em. I thought you knew that?'

'I did, but . . .' *But you've been so distant*, she wanted to wail. *You shut me out for so long, I didn't know what you wanted.*

Suddenly the garden seemed too public a place to be having this conversation. She began walking again, feeling the need to top up her glass.

He kept pace with her. 'I know things have been difficult lately. I know I've been a miserable bastard. I felt as if I was in a sort of . . . tunnel. I couldn't see how I was going to get through it.'

They went through the back door, past the box of badminton rackets and the croquet set that Lilian kept for the more athletic guests. He paused beside a row of old coats and gardening shoes. 'Being here, it's made me realize what I *do* want. I want you, and a family . . . and I'd like it to happen here. I can see us here.'

Oh God. This was almost exactly what she'd been dying for him to say for weeks and weeks – all apart from the 'living here' part anyway. She took his hand and squeezed it. 'I'm glad you want me and a family,' she said simply. 'I'm really glad.'

The food arrived, more wine was drunk, and David's words seemed to settle deep into the marrow of Emma's bones as the evening went on. The main thing was: he wanted a future with her. It was only hearing him say this that made her realize just how unhappy she'd felt, how estranged they'd become until now. Would it be so awful moving to the countryside, if he wanted it so badly?

Evening became night, the sky deepening to an inky black, and Emma found herself looking for positives as they staggered up to bed. Of course there would be plenty of good things about living here. The dense quietness of the nights, for instance, the spaciousness of the house. The slower pace of life, the fresh sea air . . .

Could she actually *live* here, though, rather than visit? she agonized, getting ready for bed. Was she ready for a quiet, slow existence? She still loved all the things Bristol had to offer: wine bars, theatres, restaurants and shops, not to mention their friends. More to the point, for all David's talk of settling down with a family, neither of them had mentioned the fact that they didn't actually *have* a family yet. They didn't even know whether or not such a thing was possible. She couldn't just snap her fingers and pluck a couple of kids out of thin air, much as she'd like to.

As she pulled the curtains, her eyes lingered on the luminous crescent moon and a sprinkling of stars, like spilt silver glitter. If they *did* have children here, they would grow up falling asleep to the soft hootings of owls, she thought with a wrench of yearning; they'd wake to the high screech of gulls. They'd scramble up trees and splash through the woods in wellies and macs. It would be a different kind of childhood from the one she'd had in Coventry; a different sort of life from the one she'd envisaged in Bishopstone, but idyllic nonetheless. And a move here didn't have to be forever, she reminded herself. They could always try it for size, see what happened. Bristol would still be there if they wanted to go back.

She brushed her teeth, thinking hard and staring at herself in the mirror. She could feel herself slipping across to David's side of the debate and felt slightly sick at the thought. *I won't say anything yet*, she resolved. *Just in case I've changed my mind by the morning.*

Whatever the future held, it was certainly liberating being able to have sex in Mulberry House without Lilian and Eddie down the hallway. Once in bed, she pulled her T-shirt over her head and flung it to the floor, kissing David wantonly with a sudden rush of lust, pressing her hips hard against him. Lady of the Manor, he'd said. She could get used to that. 'Oh yes,' she moaned when he thrust into her. 'Oh yessss . . .'

'Excuse me — are you there?'

She became dimly aware of an officious voice somewhere below, as well as the bell ringing in reception downstairs. 'Mr Jones? Are you there?' Oh Christ. It was Fatty bloody Miller again.

'For fuck's sake,' David grumbled.

'Ignore him,' Emma urged, grabbing his bottom. 'Don't listen.'

The bell jangled insistently. 'MR JONES?' Mr Miller called in an even louder voice.

'I can't ignore him,' David groaned. 'He's going to wake the Whartons.' He rolled off her and pulled on his dressing gown. 'Hold that thought,' he muttered and left the room.

Emma heard the old stairs creak as he padded down them, followed by Mr Miller's voice again. 'Ah, there you are. We seem to have run out of loo roll. Would you mind . . . ?'

Having originally anticipated a lazy lie-in the next morning, Emma found herself in for a rude shock when the alarm shrilled at six-thirty. David rolled over and slammed his hand on it to stop it ringing, and they both lay there for a few moments feeling hungover and tired. She'd assumed the alarm was a mistake, but then before she knew it David was hauling himself out of bed.

'What are you doing?' she asked groggily.

'I need to make breakfast for the Millers. They wanted an early start,' he replied.

'Fuck the Millers – it's the middle of the night,' she groaned.

'Shhh! Don't say that, they're paying good money to stay here.'

Emma pulled the duvet over her head. 'Do you want me to help?' she asked in possibly the most grudging voice ever. Short of tattooing 'Do not answer yes' on her forehead, surely nobody with half a brain could fail to pick up on her reluctance.

'Please,' he said, stuffing his feet into slippers. The door shut behind him and Emma let out an exasperated sigh. At the end of the day, David could blah on about love and children until he was blue in the face. But there was no way on earth she'd ever willingly choose to get up early to cook other people's breakfasts, and that was that.

Mr Miller, unsurprisingly, was a hearty eater. He polished off eggs, bacon, sausages, fried bread, tomatoes, black pudding and baked beans. He was disappointed to hear that kippers were off the menu and asked for a second round of toast instead. (It was a lie about the kippers. Lilian kept the fridge well stocked at all times, but Emma thought that if she so much as sniffed a kipper at this hour of the morning she might very well throw up.) Mrs Miller, by contrast, merely nibbled on a slice of wholemeal toast and a scrape of Flora as she perched on her chair, tremulous and weedy in a drab brown dress and thick glasses.

The Whartons came down at eight-thirty. They were a young couple, in their twenties at a guess, lithe and sporty-looking in matching tracksuits, with large white teeth and glossy hair. They seemed much more demure than Emma had envisaged, after all the noisy shagging-rumpus she'd heard from their room in the middle of the night. They too had healthy appetites this morning, although Emma wished they could hold back from canoodling over the scrambled egg. Good God. To think Lilian started every working day like this, pandering to the freaks staying in her house. No wonder she was always so foul-tempered. No wonder she'd leapt at the chance to escape for a few days.

It was a gorgeous spring morning and Emma would have liked nothing more than to sit out in the sunshine with a newspaper after breakfast, or even slope off back to bed with another coffee and her as-yet-unopened book. But then Charlie arrived and he and David took a toolbox down to the 'holiday let', and somehow or other it was left to Emma to hoover the breakfast room and wash the saucepans. And then the phone was ringing with people wanting to book themselves in, and the Millers requested a map of the South West Coast Path, and the Whartons appeared to be having bondage sex or at the very least killing something noisily in their room – oh, and she still hadn't actually phoned in sick again at her real job yet.

Deep breaths, Emma. You can do this. You're a competent, practical woman, you can handle these problems. Just deal with them, then the rest of the day will be yours.

She booked in the new guests in her best phone voice. She printed out a map for the infuriating Millers, who were now clad in hideous Lycra walking gear, complete with Nordic sticks. She hoovered and scrubbed, knowing damn well that Lilian would check up on her work when she deigned to return. She answered another call from a prospective guest wanting to know which sort of pillows they had, because her husband could only sleep with a hypo-allergenic pillow ('The sort with anti-microbial polyester fibrefill,' the woman said, like she was a talking catalogue.) Emma said she'd have to get back to her.

At last the house seemed quiet, so she picked up the bucket of cleaning cloths and sprays and set off to give the bedrooms and bathrooms a once-over. She put her ear to the door of the Whartons' room. There was nothing to be heard, but she was still scared to investigate. She'd start with the Millers', now that they'd gone on their ramble, she decided. With a bit of luck they'd ramble right off a cliff and she'd never have to see that moustache again.

Humming under her breath, she let herself into their room, wrinkling her nose at the pong of masculine deodorant spray. Ugh. Her nostrils were burning. Then she pushed open the bathroom door – only to let out a scream of horror. There was Mr Miller, trousers around his ankles, sitting on the toilet with the *Daily Telegraph*, less than a metre away from her.

His eyes boggled in shock. 'I say!' he shouted.

'Oh God!' she cried, stepping back so quickly she almost fell over the Hoover.

'Get out!' he yelled, just as there came an unmistakable plopping sound.

She bolted from the room, feeling hysterical. Oh shit. So to speak.

'I don't understand how it could have happened,' David said afterwards, when she sneaked down to the holiday chalet to fess up. Charlie, of course, roared with laughter, but David looked ashen. 'Didn't you check the room was empty? Why did you just burst in like that?'

'I didn't burst in – I thought they'd gone out! I was sure I heard their car!' Emma's poor traumatized brain could still hardly process the image of Fatty Miller sitting there on the bog; she kept visualizing it again and again, much to her revulsion. 'Oh God, it was so awful. Your mum's going to kill me when she finds out. How can I ever look him in the eye again?'

Charlie was still laughing. 'You've got to admit it's quite

funny,' he sniggered. 'We could hear your scream all the way down the garden.'

'Funny? I'm scarred for life, mate,' she moaned. 'My retinas are permanently damaged from the sight. There are some things in life you just aren't meant to witness. Or hear.' She shuddered and pulled a face, trying to blot out the sound of that plop.

'We'd better buy them a nice bottle of wine as an apology,' David said. 'Maybe put some flowers in the room.'

'Nice bottle of Penis Grigio,' Charlie suggested, chuckling at his own wit. 'Or ... what's it called? Pooey Fumey?'

Emma giggled helplessly. 'Stop it. And it's Pouilly-Fumé, you div.' She groaned. 'What a nightmare.'

'Could have been worse,' David said, relenting at last. 'You could have walked in on the shaggers.'

'Please – don't,' Emma said, holding up a hand. 'I know it's going to happen. Only a matter of time. I should probably stock up on a whole case of apology bottles of wine while I'm there.' She eyed David on her way out. 'And it's your turn to do the cleaning tomorrow, by the way. I'll be helping Charlie down here and keeping away from the guests from now on.'

Both cars had vanished by the time Emma went back to the main house, thank goodness. She seized the chance to quickly clean the Whartons' bedroom – braced to discover a sex dungeon with dodgy leather harnesses attached to the bed frame and empty baby-oil bottles littering the floor – but thankfully there was only a discarded pair of pants to show for their shenanigans and she was able to hoover safely around those.

Still, it was a gigantic relief to flee the premises and drive into Lyme. Some romantic mini-break this was turning out to be.

She parked outside the library on Silver Street and wandered down to the florist and off-licence. There. One bunch of gladioli and a bottle of mid-price Shiraz – that ought to go some way to making amends. She added a second bottle of the Shiraz (personal; medicinal) and a box of Celebrations (personal; ironic) on impulse at the till. Then she hesitated, not exactly in a tearing hurry to return straight to the house and more chores. Sod it, this was a day off work, she reminded herself, striding into the nearest tea shop. She more than deserved a breather, after the horror of a morning she'd endured so far.

The tea rooms were chintzy and dated, with laminated menus and gingham-lined baskets of fudge at the till. The clientele consisted largely of white-haired pensioners accompanied by tartan shopping trolleys and small dogs.

'Hi, what can I get you?' asked the waitress, notepad in hand.

Emma glanced at the menu. 'Just a tea, please and—' She

broke off as she looked up at the woman. The long, dark hair and cat-like eyes were familiar for some reason. 'Have we met?'

The waitress had recognized her too. 'Er . . . yes,' she said. Her accent was northern. 'You're married to Charlie's brother, aren't you?'

'That's it! And you're his girlfriend. Izzy, was it? Nice to see you again.'

Her mouth twisted. 'Not his girlfriend, actually. Never was. And certainly not after that fiasco,' she said.

'Oh God, it was awful, wasn't it? I really felt for you,' Emma said, remembering just how excruciating Lilian's behaviour had been that day. She gestured impulsively at the empty seat opposite her. 'Do you want to join me?'

Izzy glanced at her watch. 'Go on, then,' she said. 'I'm due a break, and my boss is at the cash-and-carry. I'll just get your tea.'

Emma couldn't help thinking what a shame it was that Izzy and Charlie were no longer together as they sat and chatted over tea and chewy flapjacks. She was a cut above all his other ex-girlfriends – she had a brain for starters, and there was a sparkiness about her that Emma really liked.

'How come you're down here then?' she asked, adding sugar to her tea. 'Can't keep away from those lovely in-laws of yours?'

Emma explained the situation. 'David – that's my husband – he seems all fired up for us to move down and run the B&B, but I'm not so sure. I've never lived in the countryside before and...' She shrugged. 'After this morning I'm starting to think I'm not very good at looking after people, either. I'm totally channelling Basil Fawlty right now.'

Izzy laughed. 'It's all right here really,' she said. 'I'm a city girl too but I love Lyme now. Yeah, so there's no big Primark or T. K. Maxx, and the nightlife isn't exactly rocking, but it's friendly and feels safe. Loads going on, if you look for it. And there's the sea too!'

Emma nodded. 'I do love the sea,' she agreed, 'but after the morning I've just had, I think I'd need the Mediterranean on my doorstep, not the English Channel.' She told her about walking in on Mr Miller on the toilet, making a proper horror story of it, and as they sat and laughed about the utter dreadfulness, she started to feel a bit better. 'What happened with Charlie then – is it definitely all off with him?' she blurted out before she could stop herself.

Izzy stopped laughing and Emma felt she'd just crossed a line. Whoops.

'It's definitely off,' Izzy replied. 'And the more I hear about him, the more I think it was a lucky escape. Apparently he's unreliable, lazy, a waste of space...' She ticked them off on her fingers. 'Plus he showed me up in front of all of you lot. Plus his mum gave me the total heebie-jeebies!'

'You've got a point,' Emma agreed, then felt disloyal. 'But he's a nice guy, you know. There are worse ones out there.'

Izzy drained her tea. 'I'm kind of done with guys right now, to be honest,' she said. 'Listen, I'd better get on anyway. Nice to have a chat.'

'You too,' Emma said. She paid her bill and headed off. *Back to the workhouse with you, Mrs Jones.* With a bit of luck, the guests would stay away all day and she could sample some Afternoon Delights with her husband. She reckoned she'd bloody well earned it.

Unfortunately the house had descended into chaos when she returned. A family of five had arrived, claiming to have phoned a week earlier to book two interconnecting rooms, and not remotely happy to discover that neither David nor Charlie knew anything about this.

'We don't even *have* interconnecting rooms,' David said as Emma walked in. 'Are you sure it was this place – Mulberry House – that you booked with?'

'Quite sure,' the woman said, over the din of the two toddlers chasing around her legs. She was tall and anoraked, with a squirming baby on one hip and a blue potty dangling from her other hand. 'I spoke to a very nice man who assured me you had plenty of room for us, and that you offered a babysitting service too. I specifically requested it.'

David quailed and exchanged a look with his brother. 'Well, we do have two empty rooms next to each other,' he said tentatively.

'And the babysitter?' the husband put in. 'We're going to a wedding do tonight, you see. Very good friends, we can't miss it. No children allowed though, unfortunately.'

David ran a hand through his hair. 'I . . . er . . .' He shot an agonized look at Emma, who glared at him. *Don't you dare,* she thought. 'My dad's been getting a bit muddled up recently,' he said. 'I'm really sorry. We can certainly put you up, but . . .'

'Please tell me you have a babysitting service,' the woman said, as one toddler fell over and started crying. The other one, meanwhile, had vanished into the depths of the house. Their mother seemed to shrink inside her anorak as if shrivelling from sheer despair. 'Is there anybody local you could recommend? We'll pay extra. Please!'

David crumbled. 'Don't worry, we'll keep an eye on them,' he said, avoiding Emma's eye. He swallowed. 'Now, if I can ask you to sign in here . . .'

The next morning, Saturday, when Emma loaded her bags into the car, she felt as if an enormous gulf had opened between her and David; as if she'd lost him all over again.

'If we were here, it wouldn't be like this,' he had tried saying, when they finally got to bed at one-thirty, having spent hours soothing the crying baby to sleep and trying in vain to calm the crazed demon-toddlers with endless stories. The incident with the potty had been the final, disgusting straw. And wouldn't you know it, the parents had had no mobile signal, so there had been no way of calling them to beg for their immediate return.

It occurred to Emma that you could see this as a test of their capabilities as prospective parents. If so, she and David had failed spectacularly. By the time Mr and Mrs Anorak, or whatever their name was, had returned to their hell-children, Emma felt as if she'd aged ninety years in a single night. Of course, no sooner had they clambered into bed than the rampant Whartons had embarked upon yet another vigorous, wall-shaking shag-endurance-marathon.

'Em? Did you hear me?' David said, his voice barely distinguishable over the racket. 'If we ran this place, it wouldn't be like this, I know it wouldn't.'

She was almost too knackered to speak. 'I can't do it, David,' she replied after a few moments, trying to tune out the enthusiastic banging noises from the next room. 'Honestly, I gave it a shot, I was open-minded, but it would send me mad, working here.'

'But if we were to just *live* here, as a family, we wouldn't need to take in guests at all,' he said, running his hand down her thigh.

'And live on what – fresh air?' she snapped. 'We'd need

to earn something, wouldn't we? Where we would find jobs down here? I can't imagine there's a massive demand for designers or architects!'

They lay in silence for a few moments until Mr Wharton let out an enormous orgasmic roar a few metres away. At least someone was getting their rocks off, Emma thought glumly.

'I know you love this place,' she said when David didn't reply, 'but we've got to be realistic. We can't just buy it off your parents and move in. We're talking a major business deal here – one that I don't think I can sign up to. And in the meantime . . . we've got a life in Bristol. When are you going to come home?'

He hesitated. 'It's difficult,' he said. 'I kind of promised Mum I—'

She stiffened. 'What, so you've taken her side, have you? Chosen her over me?'

'No! Of course not. It's complicated, that's all.' A high-pitched squealing had started up – it was hard to tell if it was a just-woken child or Mrs Wharton approaching climax. Whichever, Emma did not want the sound in her ears.

David groaned. 'I can't think straight, with those two going at it,' he said, rolling over. 'Let's talk about it tomorrow.'

But they hadn't talked about it – too busy juggling all

the breakfasts and finding high-chairs and lying about kippers again. And now she was packed and ready to go, and they still hadn't found a way back to the conversation. He'd asked her to stay on until his parents returned that afternoon, but she cited a string of work commitments that she needed to catch up on. *I'm an interior designer — get me out of here!*

'So I'll see you soon then,' she said, kissing him politely. God, it felt terrible, as if they were strangers.

'Yep,' he said shortly. 'Have a good journey.'

She started the car and drove away. *Back to square one*, she thought dismally, as she turned out of the driveway and Mulberry House vanished from sight. *Back to frigging square one.*

Chapter Fourteen

Alicia had been really excited at the thought of Emma and David moving to Mulberry House, until Hugh went out for a drink with David and said that unfortunately he thought Emma had gone right off the idea — something to do with sex maniacs, a fat man on the toilet and a gang of marauding toddlers. Shame, thought Alicia. She'd have liked to see more of Emma, not to mention less of the multiplying laundry. Any day now her washing machine would go on strike and demand a pay rise for working overtime.

Lilian, though, seemed to think a deal was in the bag. Fresh from her mini-break, she was already amassing estate agents' particulars of chalet bungalows on the market. 'This one has a smashing sea view,' she sighed the next time Alicia went round, wafting the papers in the air. 'Whereas this one backs onto woodland. What do you think?'

'Lovely,' Alicia replied politely, deciding that she was probably better off not getting involved. The last thing she wanted was for the limelight to fall back upon her and

Hugh as potential buyers. They'd talked about it for at least two minutes before deciding that they'd prefer to stay put. Neither of them was the sort of person to get emotional about bricks and mortar anyway. If Lilian and Eddie wanted to sell up, then good luck to them, frankly.

She decided to email Emma about it.

Dear Emma,

Hope all's well. Sorry to hear you aren't keen to take on the B&B – must admit, I can't say I blame you. I hope I wasn't too much of an eager beaver when I was round the other night – just got a bit excited at the thought of you two moving down, but really didn't want to put you under pressure!

Hope work's going well and your clients are all behaving themselves. I'm—

She broke off, wondering if there was any point to this email after all. Would Emma even *want* to hear from her? She was probably too busy partying in Bristol. Alicia still cringed whenever she remembered the only time she and Hugh had gone to stay with David and Emma in their flat, when Lucas and Rafferty were tiny. Nobody had expressly said so, but Alicia knew that she and the children were definitely cramping everyone else's style, whether it was the aborted trip round a gallery exhibiting some artist she'd never heard of (baby Raffy had cried the entire way round), the cut-short restaurant lunch (Lucas didn't like any of the fancy food on the menu and had an enormous cutlery-hurling tantrum) or the fact that Alicia wasn't keen on letting some teenager she'd never met babysit her brood, so that they could go out that evening to see a play. 'But I've got us all tickets — it's an RSC production!' Emma said in dismay. 'But the boys are still tiny — they'll freak if I'm not here!' Alicia replied miserably. They had never been invited to stay again.

Then she remembered the way she and Emma had bonded at the anniversary lunch. For a moment she had felt as if they were both on the same side. Sod it, she'd make an effort and be friendly. Why not?

I'm rushing towards 40 and trying to do some exciting new things before I'm past it, she typed. *The haircut was one. I've started belly dancing with Izzy too — you know, Charlie's ex. (She's lovely.) Next up . . .*

She hesitated again and then her fingers seemed to start working before she knew what was happening.

Next up, I reckon a treat is in order. Is that outrageous, do you think?!
See you soon.
Love Alicia x

There. Nice, friendly, short and sweet. She pressed 'Send' before she could change her mind and was about to switch off the PC when she hesitated. The children were in bed and Hugh was out at the gym (again! she was starting to wonder if he was undergoing his own midlife crisis), so she poured herself a glass of wine and reopened her Action Plan spreadsheet. *A treat is in order*, she'd typed just two minutes ago. But what?

While she was sitting there, thinking, there came a soft pinging noise, which meant she had a new email. She opened her in-box, expecting it to be a new offer from Ocado or the Lakeland newsletter, only to see, to her surprise, that Emma had replied straight away:

Hello Alicia,

Lovely to hear from you! Yes — me + Mulberry House = disaster. It was AWFUL!!! No wonder Lilian is such an old bag (don't tell Hugh or David I said that). Really, I did try to love it for David's sake, but it was all just a total nightmare. I was so glad to get away.

David was all 'Let's live here and have a family', but we can't both afford to give up work. Maybe it would be different if we already had children and were ready to leave Bristol, but . . . Well, to be honest, I'm worried we can't actually have a baby, much as we want one. We've been trying for ages, but nothing's happening. Yet!

*Enough of my problems anyway. A treat! Yeah — do it! Make
it a big, proper, Hell-I'm-going-to-be-40 treat too, the kind you
wish someone else would buy for you. That's an order. (And
when is your actual birthday, by the way? Sorry — for some
reason it isn't on the calendar.)*

Take care anyway, love to Hugh and the kids.

Em x

Alicia smiled as she read the message a second time.
Permission granted to treat herself — just the kind of order
she had wanted. But oh, she'd had no idea that Emma and
David were trying to start a family. How did you go about
replying to something like that? She wrote:

Hi again,

*Well, at least you gave it a go — at the B&B, I mean. At the
end of the day, it's only a house — it wouldn't be the end of the
world if they had to sell it. We don't want to move in, either,
and I think everyone knows Charlie isn't really in a position to
take on that kind of mortgage. I think it'll do L & E good to
move out now anyway — it's got a bit much for them to cope
with.*

*Sorry to hear that the baby thing hasn't worked out yet.
Fingers crossed for good news soon. Ring me if you ever want to
chat about it.*

Off to research treats now . . . half a glass of wine down, and I'm feeling reckless!

xxx

PS My birthday is 10 April.

She pressed 'Send', then opened Google. Emma was right. If she was going to do something nice for herself, she should do it properly, make a bit of a song and dance about the whole thing. Now she just had to decide what to do.

The glossy magazines she occasionally flicked through in the staffroom were always urging women to indulge in pampering weekends and spa breaks. Alicia didn't really have much truck with that sort of thing – she hated the idea of taking her clothes off and letting some complete stranger rub scented oils into her skin, for instance. However, the thought of actually going and doing something special on her own, just for her, definitely appealed. Was it disloyal of her not to want to invite Hugh along too, though? Was it somehow un-wife-like to want to be alone, to enjoy her own company?

She wrestled with the idea for a moment, then remembered the stream of stag weekends that her husband had been on in the last fifteen years, the golf trips he and his friends sometimes organized, the conferences he went to, often in interesting cities or even abroad, and, to a lesser extent, his constant gym visits. Hugh got plenty of time to do his own thing. She couldn't imagine him ever losing sleep worrying that his behaviour was remotely 'un-husband-like'.

'Do it,' she muttered to herself, and began typing into the search engine.

An hour or so later Alicia felt flushed with her own daring. After much enjoyable deliberation, she'd whittled down the vast wash of options to a shortlist of four. They were:

1) A walking weekend in Dartmoor. She'd never properly gone there before – never camped, never truly braved the harshness of wild beauty on her own. Stopping off for a picnic en route to north Cornwall didn't count. She wanted to experience being truly alone somewhere remote and barren and potentially rather dangerous. Was that crazy of her?

2) A watercolours weekend in Somerset. It would mean staying in a beautiful old manor house with a group of other painters, exploring the grounds and taking the time to create something beautiful. It sounded tranquil and relaxing, with the simplicity of only having herself to think about.

3) A trip to London to a concert. She didn't know which concert yet, but she'd always wanted to go to the Albert Hall to hear an orchestra. Obviously she'd have to stay in a gorgeous hotel as well, for the full experience . . .

4) Finally, she'd like to go to Paris. Oh, Paris! She could admire the beautiful buildings, dawdle through the Louvre, climb the Eiffel Tower, enjoy the ambience of Notre-Dame. She would sit in a bar watching the world go by, with a strong French coffee and a buttery croissant. She could walk the Champs-Elysées, drink good red wine, wear silk knickers and—

She broke off in surprise at her own thoughts. Silk knickers! That was Sandra's bad influence. But all the same: when in France ...

She clicked on a link and started looking at hotels before she lost her nerve.

'Paris?' Hugh repeated, taken-aback. Then his face cleared. 'Oh – I see, as a romantic weekend away?' He smiled, dropping his gym bag to the floor (where it would later be picked up by her, no doubt). 'What a wonderful idea, Alicia. I'm sure Mum would look after the k—'

'No,' Alicia said, awkwardly. 'Not as a romantic weekend. I mean, at some point, yes, it would be wonderful to go there together, of course. Definitely. But this time I meant ... just me.'

'What, with a friend or something? Some of the book-group girls or—?'

'No, Hugh,' she said patiently. 'Just me. On my own.'

He stared at her. She might as well have spoken the

words in Cantonese, for all the comprehension he displayed. 'Just you?' he echoed.

'Just me. I feel I need to stretch my wings. Do something exciting. Have a little adventure. Just me, before I get too past it.'

His face changed again, as if he'd worked something out. Then he nodded. 'Ah. This is your panic about getting old, isn't it?'

'Well, kind of. But it's something I've always wanted to do. To be honest, there are other options, though. Hiking on Dartmoor. Seeing a concert at the Albert Hall. Oh yes, and there's this painting weekend I've seen in Somerset that I'd like to do too. Watercolours. I haven't made my mind up yet.'

'But . . .' He'd gone back to flummoxed, three steps behind her. 'Wait. I don't understand. Why do you suddenly want to go off and do all those things? And why don't you want me to come with you? I haven't been to Paris for years.'

'Yes, you have,' she replied. 'You went there for that conference eighteen months ago.'

'Yes, but . . .' He'd lost the ability to finish a coherent sentence again. 'But, Alicia . . . I just . . . WHY?'

She shrugged, a proper Gallic shrug. It was rather enjoyable, to be honest. 'Because I thought it might be fun, that's all.'

Fun! That word again. It seemed to be cropping up in her vocabulary with increasing regularity these days. Great fun. What fun. Just for fun. It was so light and easy on the tongue, so much more pleasing than 'routine' or 'housework', for example. It kept taking Hugh by surprise, though.

'Fun,' he repeated haltingly.

'Yes,' she said, smiling. Perhaps now wasn't the right time to tell him about the silk knickers she'd ordered online, in a fit of bravado, she decided. He'd probably collapse with a coronary from shock.

'Is everything all right?' he asked when they went to bed that evening.

'Why?'

'It's just . . . you seem different lately, that's all,' he said.

She let the words hang for a moment in the velvety darkness. 'I feel different,' she admitted. 'In a good way, though. I feel as if I've suddenly come to life, as if I've woken up from a long, boring sleep.'

They were lying as they usually did before drifting off, her head on his chest and his arm curled around her. She felt him freeze at the word 'boring' and realized she'd offended him.

'Not *boring*,' she amended hastily, 'but . . . unchanging. As if we've been caught in a tessellating pattern and have forgotten how to – you know – strike out and surprise ourselves.'

He was quiet, so she rushed on before he could speak again. 'Approaching forty feels rather momentous; I want to mark it somehow, have a last hurrah. Or maybe two hurrahs. I don't know, maybe we should have a massive round of hurrahs, share some hurrahs together. We could both carve out time to focus on ourselves again, Hugh, couldn't we? Because in a family like ours it's so easy to plod on and on, and for the years to float by, and you realize you're just running around after everyone else, but never really thinking about yourself any more. Do you know what I mean? And, actually, there are still things I want to do in life. I don't want everything to be the same for the next forty years as well. Don't you think?'

He didn't reply. Oh dear. Was he taking this personally? 'Don't get me wrong, it's not that I'm bored with *you* – that would never happen, Hugh. Never. I just mean . . .'

He snorted in derision and she fell silent, worried that she was perhaps protesting too much.

'Please don't sulk, darling,' she said, propping herself up on her elbow and trying to make out his expression in the darkness. His eyes were tightly closed as if he couldn't even bring himself to look at her.

Then he snorted again . . . but this time she realized it

wasn't a snort of sarcasm or disagreement. He was snoring. He'd actually gone and fallen asleep, right when she'd been pouring her heart out!

She sighed crossly. 'Well, I bloody well will go to Paris then, if you're that uninterested,' she muttered, rolling away from him. 'So there!'

The next evening Alicia took down the calendar that hung on the kitchen wall and flipped through to April, her birthday month. The only dates already pencilled in were those marking the Easter holidays, a dental appointment for Hugh and a reminder that the buildings insurance needed renewing. The empty, unmarked spaces didn't promise thrills so much as threaten a dull trudge of name-tagging new cricket kit for the boys, horrendous queues in Clarks to buy all the school shoes, sandals and trainers that the children would need, and boring evenings slaving over the iron as she tackled the Mulberry House laundry mountain. Same old, same old. She could almost write herself a script.

ALICIA'S BIRTHDAY she wrote on the 10th in big letters, with three jaunty exclamation marks. She wondered if Hugh had even thought about it yet, if he'd started planning special treats, maybe even a surprise party. Much as she hoped he had, with every cell in her body, she knew with immense certainty that he wouldn't have. For the last few Christmases and birthdays he'd actually said, 'Just buy yourself something you want and let me know how much I owe you.'

Not wanting to be seen as greedy or extravagant, she'd gone for sensible, practical choices each time: a jumper she'd liked in Marks and Spencer, a pair of walking boots, a new nightie. All things that she needed, nothing luxurious or special. What had she been thinking? Why had she sold herself short for so long, as if she didn't think she was worth more than a machine-washable jumper?

It was Hugh's fault, though. If he'd bothered to think for ten minutes, he could have chosen something perfectly nice himself. But no. He'd taken the lazy way out, got her to do the legwork. Well, if he *dared* try that for her fortieth, she would refuse to play ball. 'Surprise me,' she imagined herself saying archly to him. Her mind boggled, trying to compute what he might come up with. As long as it wasn't oven gloves or a cake tin, she wouldn't care.

She leaned over the calendar thoughtfully and then, seized by a sudden decision, wrote in big letters through the Friday, Saturday and Sunday before her birthday 'ALICIA AWAY'. It was the first weekend of the school holidays, her last weekend as a thirty-something. Damn it, she would have some fun, whatever Hugh said.

Seeing the words in black and white on the calendar made her feel better already. All she had to do now was book her Eurostar ticket and find somewhere to stay. She hurried off to the computer, a thrill rippling through her. The thrill of the unknown, a frisson of daring. She was sure that Christine was applauding her every step of the way. *Paris, here I come!*

Over the next week Alicia fine-tuned her plan. She spent an enjoyable few evenings drawing up a list of all the Parisian sights she wanted to visit, and researched some wonderful-sounding restaurants. Her silk knickers arrived – they were very *Ooh la la!*, to say the least – as did the train tickets she'd booked. Then, after much website clicking and consulting the French teachers at school about where to stay, she finally plumped for a small, cosy-looking hotel in Le Marais, a stone's throw from the Place des Vosges, the oldest and perhaps most beautiful square in the city, as her new guidebook informed her. It wasn't flashy or cool – Alicia didn't do flashy or cool – but it looked gorgeous, sounded friendly and was in a brilliant location. 'This is the one,' she said to herself, scrolling through oodles of fabulous pictures and glowing reviews.

Gripped by a surge of can-do energy, she picked up the phone and booked herself in, there and then. Not even the mortification of having the receptionist reply to her rusty GCSE-level French in faultless English could dampen her spirits. This was really happening. It was official. She was off on an adventure!

'I've done it, I've booked myself into a hotel,' she said to Hugh when he arrived home that evening. 'I've sorted out my train tickets too. I'm going to Paris, Hugh. I'm going!'

'Right,' he said, his voice barely more than a grunt as he read a message on his phone. It was blindingly obvious that he didn't share her delight, but she was so full of happiness and excitement that his disapproval didn't touch her.

Humming cheerfully, she set about making dinner. Just knowing that she had the trip waiting there for her on the next page of the calendar made everything more bearable. She couldn't wait to tell Sandra, either. Even her sister would be impressed by this!

Glancing over at Hugh again, she saw him slumped in a chair, staring at his phone, his face tense. 'Everything all right?' she asked.

He didn't reply immediately; he seemed stunned by whatever message he'd just read. Or was he really in a massive sulk?

'Hugh?' she prompted.

He dragged himself away from the screen at last. His mouth had gone strangely saggy. 'I . . . Yes,' he said eventually. 'Yes, of course. It's just a work thing.' He turned his phone off and stuffed it in his pocket, getting up abruptly.

Something was not quite right, but Alicia wasn't sure what. Maybe he had the hump that she was off to Paris and he hadn't been invited. Fair enough. She'd be a bit cheesed off too, if the boot was on the other foot. Perhaps there was a way she could cheer him up, she thought, remembering her pristine silk lingerie, still wrapped in pink tissue paper on top of the wardrobe.

Letting the wooden spoon rest against the pan of frying onions, she went over to him. 'I've got something that might perk you up,' she said, snuggling against him. She felt rather like a bad actress in a porn film, but tried not to let that put her off. 'Let's have an early night, and I'll show you.'

'Er . . . maybe,' he said distractedly. He was all but prising her arms off him, so keen did he seem to escape her embrace. 'I've got a ton of work to catch up on, though, and . . .' He wasn't meeting her in the eye. 'And I'm a bit tired,' he finished feebly.

Alicia stepped back, hot with the embarrassment of rejection. 'Fine,' she said, covering up her hurt by returning to the sizzling frying pan and resuming stirring.

Hugh left the kitchen without another word and she stared after him. Was he trying to guilt-trip her about Paris? Was this his way of telling her she shouldn't go?

The exhilaration she'd felt just ten minutes earlier drained away. Maybe she was doing the wrong thing, she wondered unhappily. Was she sacrificing her relationship with Hugh in the name of a selfish weekend jolly for herself?

The doubts lingered with her for the rest of the evening.

Even email replies from Sandra and Emma saying 'Woohoo! Love it!' and 'Magnifique!' respectively didn't quite restore her equilibrium. Hugh remained distracted and uncommunicative, and although she made a point of slipping on her beautiful new silk and lace underwear and waiting gift-wrapped in bed for him, she'd read almost fifty pages of her book by the time he made an appearance.

She pulled back the duvet so that he could see her, and lay there in her camisole and knickers, goosebumps creeping up her arms, jaw aching from her posed smile.

He merely glanced at her before pulling on his old SuperDad T-shirt, the one with the torn neck that had lost its shape and most of its colour after ten years' wear. 'Very nice,' he muttered, getting under the covers and lying on his back.

She bit her lip. Was she going to have to do all the running?

Rolling towards him, she spooned against his body. *Come on, Hugh. Take an interest. I'm trying to cheer you up here.*

He patted her arm cautiously. 'Night, then,' he said, and turned over.

She lay in the darkness, feeling rejected all over again. 'What's wrong?' she asked after a moment. 'Hugh?'

He didn't answer immediately. 'It's nothing,' he said eventually. 'Just work stuff.'

She sighed, her excitement draining away. She could

always tell when he was lying. And it wasn't like him to refuse her advances, either — usually he was only too willing to get her undies off. Not tonight, though. She hoped he was okay. She lay there for a while longer, eyes open, wondering if independence and adventures were really all they were cracked up to be.

Chapter Fifteen

Spring was coming; Izzy could smell it in the air. Warm breezes blew in from the west, daffodils pushed up boldly in front gardens, golden trumpets blaring a silent chorus, and leaves were shyly uncurling on the branches of the trees, pale green and new. When the sun shone and the sky was blue, the sea became magically enticing with its long froth-topped waves and sparkles of light on the sleek, rippling surface.

She wondered if the leaves were appearing on their old street in Manchester yet, whether the snowdrops had been out in Fog Lane Park. It was strange to think of it all going on without her this year.

Did I do the right thing? she kept agonizing. *Should I have moved the girls away, wrenched up their roots?*

On one level – the most important level – she was sure the answer was Yes. She only had to remember how she and Gary been fighting that last night, how he'd punched her so hard she'd literally seen stars, how he'd pushed her up against the wall, his hand around her throat . . . and she felt nothing but relief to have escaped. If she still had any lingering doubts, then remembering the terrified light in Willow's eyes as she'd appeared at the living-room door in her nightie, face puffy with sleep, hair tousled, only to witness the scene and hear her dad threatening to kill her mum . . . Well, that was the clincher. Willow had let out a frightened cry, she'd shrunk into the doorway and whimpered, 'Don't hurt Mummy!' – only for Gary to round on her, a madness in him, his fist clenched as if ready to strike his own daughter.

It made her shiver every time the image flashed into her mind. And that was when she'd known beyond doubt: staying put was no longer an option. She could not – would not – let Gary's violence seep through to the girls and damage them as well. When they'd gone to the shelter in Dorchester, the other women there had inspired her and given her renewed strength. They'd made her see that the bruises and black eyes, the fear and constant treading on eggshells were not things she had to put up with any longer.

'Telling you he loves you and he's sorry does not make it all right,' said Roz, one of the support workers. 'Ever.'

That was all very well, but Hazel only knew Gary as a good guy, her beloved daddy. She didn't understand why they'd left in the first place. 'When *are* we going to see him again?' she kept asking.

A few times Izzy had attempted to tell Hazel, as gently as possible, that sometimes Daddy hadn't been very nice to Mummy, but her daughter stubbornly refused to believe it. Lately, there had been lots of requests for Daddy to tell her a story, or Daddy to cuddle her. What was she supposed to say to that?

Alicia had proved a good person to talk to about all of this. They had met for belly dancing three times now, and went for a drink the last two. Without venturing into too much gory detail, Izzy found herself explaining why they'd had to leave Manchester, then voiced her worries that maybe she'd handled it wrongly.

Alicia could not have been clearer in her response. 'You're a mother. Of course you did the right thing. You couldn't have stayed there, knowing that he might turn his anger on them any day.'

'I don't think he would have done,' Izzy had replied. 'Not really. He absolutely adored them.'

'He adored you too, though, at first, didn't he?' Alicia parried. 'And look what happened to that.' There was a fierceness about her that Izzy hadn't seen before. 'You had to leave.'

'I know, but now they don't have a dad. And they loved him!'

'You can find ways of reopening contact without putting them in danger,' Alicia said. 'I see it all the time in the school where I teach. You could arrange for him to have supervised visits, so that he's not alone with the children. It doesn't have to be total severance, not if you don't want it.'

Izzy bit her lip. 'I wouldn't know where to start.'

'The shelter you went to must have outreach workers who could advise you,' Alicia replied, 'or even child psychologists who could help with what to say to the girls.'

'I'm scared he's going to come and find us,' Izzy blurted out, her voice trembling. It was the first time she'd let the words out of her head since she'd spoken to Louise about it. 'He's been sending me texts – threatening stuff. I feel so jumpy, like I'm expecting him to pop up at any minute.' She glanced at her watch. 'I'd better get back to the flat soon. Talking about it is making me feel twitchier than ever.'

Alicia looked concerned. 'That must be horrible,' she said. 'You know you can always call me if you're worried, don't you? And listen, why don't I send Hugh round to your place with his toolbox? He could check all your locks and windows are secure, just to put your mind at rest. Hopefully Gary won't turn up, but just in case he gets any silly ideas in his head...'

'Thanks,' Izzy said. It was such a relief, being able to speak like this. Alicia was so kind and practical, the perfect person to confide in. 'I'd appreciate that. Just in case.'

*

Alicia had texted to say that Hugh would come round at eleven o'clock the following Sunday morning, but when Izzy answered the knock on the door, it wasn't Hugh standing there in front of her with a toolbox, but Charlie.

Oh God. She couldn't speak for a moment. She felt bamboozled by his good looks, his insouciant smile – but she also felt a stab of betrayal that Alicia could have set her up like this. Was it all some horrible trick?

'Oh,' she managed to say coolly, while her brain raced for the best way to deal with this awkward situation. 'It's you.' She hadn't seen him since bawling him out on the high street and throwing flowers at his feet. It was discomfiting having him right there in solid flesh on her doorstep. Solid, handsome flesh, no less. Damn. What should she do?

'The door was open downstairs, so I just came up,' he said. 'I hope that's all right.'

Annoyance pricked her. There were six flats in the building, and someone – she suspected the twenty-something lad with the low-slung jeans and shifty eyes – kept forgetting to lock the front door. Even closing it would be a start.

'Oh,' she replied, not moving.

'Look – can we start again?' he asked humbly. 'Hugh said he was coming round, so I persuaded him to let me do it instead. My way of saying sorry. Because I *am* sorry that I upset you, dragging you to my mum's house for the

Anniversary Lunch of Doom. I wasn't thinking properly.' He shrugged. 'I was just so into you that I wanted everyone else to meet you, so I could . . . well, show you off, I guess.' He shuffled his feet, looking less certain by the second. 'I thought I'd come here so I could do you a favour, show you I'm not a total dickhead, but if you really want me to go, then . . .'

Before Izzy could say anything – she was melting in the face of such an abject apology, it had to be said – Hazel appeared behind her. 'Who's that at the d— Oh! Charlie!' she cried, her face breaking into one big smile. 'We haven't seen you in AGES, have we, Mum?' She spun round on her toes. 'Willow! Willow, Charlie's here!'

Izzy opened her mouth to speak, but wasn't sure what to say. Hazel had no such hesitation.

'Come in,' she urged, leaning forward and grabbing Charlie's hand. 'Would you like some Ribena? Come and see our house, Charlie!'

There was a lump in Izzy's throat all of a sudden. Look at Hazel, so happy to have a man around the place again. Just the other night she'd heard the girls reminiscing about fun times with Gary: games of cricket in the park, the Halloween last year when he'd dressed up as Snape to their Harry and Hermione, and last Christmas when they'd had the most brilliant snowball fight. Willow, admittedly, had been less effusive than Hazel, but even so, the longing in their voices was unmistakable.

Charlie was still looking at Izzy, waiting for her to respond. Oh, what the hell, she thought. He wasn't Gary. He was just a bloke with a toolbox, who'd come here to do a favour. So why not let him?

'Come in,' she said, rather grudgingly. 'Thanks,' she added, with even greater reluctance. 'Can I get you a tea or coffee? Or Ribena?'

Hazel still had his hand. 'Come into the kitchen, Charlie,' she said grandly. 'You can see my Star of the Week certificate, if you want. I got it for this really excellent story I wrote, about a dolphin called Bellamy.'

Izzy tried to compose herself as they walked the few steps to the kitchen, Hazel still chattering on. Get things in perspective, she told herself. Charlie had been a disappointment at the end of the day, he'd made her feel embarrassed and uncomfortable for a short while, but that was it. He hadn't hurt her or lied to her or deceived her in any way. The anger she'd felt at the time was more directed at herself than at him: anger that she'd let her guard slip, that she'd forgotten so quickly the damage done by Gary and had started fancying someone else, even if it was only a tiny bit.

She could be civil to the man, especially as he had given

up his Sunday morning to help her. *Deep breaths, be normal. No more fancying, no more entanglement.*

Filling the kettle, she tried not to listen to how nice he was being to her daughters, tried not to notice how they were both giggling and trying to impress him in return.

'Look, here's my certificate,' Hazel said, shoving it under his nose.

'I've got a best friend,' Willow put in. 'And my teacher's going to have a baby.'

'Whoa – Hazel, that's awesome,' Charlie said, showing the certificate proper respect, with a long, solemn look. '"An excellent story, with very good spelling – well done, Hazel,"' he read aloud. And then, 'Oh, Willow, that's ace news. What's your best friend called? Is she anywhere near as cool as you?'

Izzy's heart softened. She couldn't help it. She broke open a packet of chocolate digestives and put some on a plate. 'Here,' she said, offering one to Charlie. 'Can't have you starving on the job, can we?'

Charlie went around checking everything carefully. He added a couple of window locks, tightened the catch of the kitchen window and put a new chain on the front door. He was far more thorough and competent than Izzy had anticipated. 'There we go,' he said eventually, unplugging the drill and putting it back in the toolbox. He cocked his head to check on the girls, who were now both busy with arts and crafts projects at the table, having finally tired of following him around asking countless questions about what each particular tool was for. 'Alicia said you've had some problems with your ex,' he added in a low voice.

Izzy tensed. She didn't want him to know all her troubles. 'He's been in touch, yeah,' she replied. 'Nothing I can't handle, though.'

'Good,' he said. A few seconds ticked by before he added, 'But let me know if . . .'

'Yeah,' she said. 'I will. Thanks.' She cleared her throat. 'I was just about to make some food. You're welcome to stay if you're hungry.'

He smiled. 'That would be great,' he said. 'Thanks.'

Thankfully there was enough mince and spaghetti for Izzy to cook what she prided herself on as her speciality dish: spaghetti bolognese. It might seem ordinary to some, but the way she made it, adding extra garlic and black pepper and letting the sauce simmer and bubble for a long, tantalizing while, until it had cooked down to a thick, jammy consistency . . . *Mamma mia*, she'd never had anything but compliments afterwards.

Izzy had always been a good cook – you had to learn fast, when you grew up without a proper mum or dad to do it all for you. Also, when there wasn't much money in the pot, you needed to be creative as well as organized – think of new ways to cook with cheap cuts of meat, and have plenty of tricks up your sleeve when it came to adding flavour and punch. She'd been meaning to phone the landlord of the flats and beg a strip of garden in which to plant herbs and salad leaves, maybe even soft fruit and tomatoes too, to enjoy over the summer. You didn't need much space if you used it cleverly.

'So,' she said as they ate. 'You're working at the garden centre, are you?'

'Now and then,' he replied. 'Not the most exciting job in the world, lugging around bags of John Innes for old ladies and watering the delphiniums, but, you know – it pays. I've been helping my dad and brother at my parents' house as well.'

'Doing what?'

'Painting and decorating, doing up the old outbuildings,' he replied. 'They—'

'Have you got any children, Charlie?' Hazel interrupted through a mouthful of spaghetti.

He shook his head. 'Sadly not,' he replied. 'Never been lucky enough yet. Never met the right woman, either.'

'My friend Madeleine from school told me where babies come from, you know,' Hazel announced. 'What happens is, the man puts—'

'That's enough, Hazel,' Izzy said in the nick of time. 'Eat

your food now.' She glanced over at Charlie, but he had his head down to twirl up some spaghetti. Never met the right woman before, eh? Or was it that he had always bailed out before things got serious? The girls at work would know all about it, she was sure.

'That was amazing,' Charlie said, a little later, when he'd scraped his plate clean. His eyes were glazed over with bliss as he leaned back and rested a hand on his belly. 'Wow. I am as stuffed as a turkey on Christmas Day.'

'It's Daddy's favourite as well, isn't it, Willow?' Hazel put in. 'He LOVES it.'

Willow nodded. 'It's *my* favourite too,' she said, and there was a flash of something — sadness? loyalty? — on her face that made Izzy's insides twist.

Charlie seemed to take the mention of Gary as his cue to go. 'I'd better leave you ladies to it,' he said, jumping up. 'Thanks again,' he said. 'Absolutely delicious. And thanks, girls, for showing me your beautiful pictures.'

Izzy stood up too, feeling as if a spell had been broken. 'Thank *you*,' she said, trying not to sound disappointed. 'Very much.' She followed him through to the front door. 'Well, see you around then.'

'Maybe we could...' He hesitated, then seemed to think better of the idea. Instead he nodded briskly. 'Take care now. I'll see you around.'

And that was that, off he went, and the door was shut.

Izzy leaned against the wooden jamb for a few moments afterwards, wondering what he'd been about to suggest and why he'd changed his mind.

The flat seemed empty without him, quieter too. She wrinkled her nose as she stacked the plates in the sink and squeezed in washing-up liquid under the hot water. *Don't go there, Izzy. You don't need anyone, remember? You and the girls, you're a team. No room for anyone else.*

That said, the girls were drooping around too, as if they missed having Charlie there. 'Come on,' Izzy said in the end, when the kitchen was clean. 'Let's go down to the beach for the afternoon. We'll take the buckets and fishing nets.'

'Just us?' Willow wanted to know.

'Just us,' Izzy confirmed. 'Hazel! Get your wellies! Let's go!'

Willow nodded. 'Good,' she said approvingly. 'I like it best of all when it's just us.'

Izzy hugged her. 'Me too, chick,' she said, holding her close. 'Me too.'

After a lovely beachy afternoon and jam sandwiches for tea, Izzy ran the bath, swishing bubble bath around in the running water. She was glad, on reflection, that Charlie had taken the initiative and come round. She was far too proud ever to have contacted him, having written him off as a mistake. Maybe she'd been wrong though. He was actually—

Willow burst in at that moment. 'Dad's on the phone,' she said.

Izzy nearly fell in the bath. *'What?'*

'Your phone was ringing and Hazel answered,' she said. 'She's talking to him now.'

Izzy ran out of the bathroom in a blind panic, her heart galloping. Sure enough, there was Hazel curled up in the armchair looking absolutely delighted as she chatted away. 'Lyme Regis,' she was saying. 'It's by the sea, Daddy, haven't you ever heard of it? There are loads of fossils and – hey!'

She cried out as Izzy snatched the phone out of her hand and jabbed at the 'End Call' button. 'But that was DADDY!' she wailed, tears swelling in her eyes. 'We were *talking!*'

The phone started ringing again in Izzy's hand and Hazel made a swipe for it. 'No,' Izzy said, her voice cracking.

'But . . .'

'No,' she roared, and threw the phone against the wall. It dropped to the floor and she stamped on it again and again, the plastic crunching underfoot until it fell silent.

Hazel was tearful and bewildered. 'But it was *Daddy*,' she sobbed. 'I was only telling him . . .'

'What did you tell him?' Izzy asked. 'Did you tell him our address?'

Hazel buried her face in her hands. 'I just wanted to *talk* to him,' she wailed. 'I miss him!'

Izzy felt as if there was an enormous knot in her throat. 'What did you tell him, Hazel?' she repeated frantically. 'What did you *say*?'

Chapter Sixteen

David had been away for four weeks now and it was getting Emma down, sloping back alone to their titchy flat every night and holing up with the TV or the Oh Baby! mums for company. The two of them had barely spoken since the Poogate debacle, and she was starting to wonder if he was ever coming home. Still, she was reliably informed by her temperature chart that ovulation was starting *now*, so planned to head down to Dorset that very evening. She would get herself up the duff if it killed her.

Before then, she had an afternoon's work to endure, although she was out on client visits at least. Her first appointment was on Norland Road, up towards the Downs. This was a new client for Emma, but as she drove along the street something familiar about its handsome Edwardian houses set a bell ringing insistently in her mind. She'd been here before ... but when?

She parked, trying to work out why the scene resonated so strongly in her memory. She'd definitely walked along this road; she'd been upset, she remembered. Looking for one house in particular . . .

Cutting the engine, she leaned back in her seat, still puzzling it over. She couldn't think of a single client she'd worked for on this street – and why would she be upset anyway? It didn't make sense. Yet the more she pondered, the more she could remember the tears on her cheeks, and that it was gloomy, early evening. She had sat on a wall just near here, outside one of these houses, and wept.

Then she remembered, like a slap bringing her round. Oh God. Of course. *Nicholas* had lived here, with his wife and three blond children, and his art studio in the back garden. Nicholas bloody Larsson. That was why she'd been crying.

A shiver trickled down her spine as the memory sprung fully formed into her head. He'd been her former lecturer, back when she was a gauche young student at the university. He was thirty-five to her nineteen years; old enough to know better. Dirty old bastard.

She unclipped her seatbelt and got out of the car, a strange, uncomfortable pain lodging in her chest. Oh, he'd broken her heart all right, Nicholas Larsson. How she'd worshipped the man – and how he'd brought her to her knees! For almost a whole year they'd had an illicit affair, most of which had happened in the confines of his office in Woodland Road. History of art had never been so fascinating; she'd hung on his every word during lectures and tutorials, believing herself to be a woman now, convinced that their love affair could transcend all the traditional boundaries that society had put between them.

Then . . . Well, then, everything had gone wrong. Trouble in paradise. She'd got pregnant just as the second year had ended and – surprise, surprise – he hadn't wanted to know any more. She'd never been able to forget the appalled look on his face as she'd broken the news, the way he'd actually flinched. 'Oh God,' he'd said, with none of the joy or excitement she'd hoped he might feel. 'Shit. You'll have to . . . Shit. Let me find you the number of a clinic.'

It had been that brutal, that cold. He'd washed his hands of her there and then, choosing his wife and children, even warning Emma to stay away. That was loyalty for you. That was love. The fall back down to earth had been nothing short of agonizing. Hence her tear-streaked visits to Norland Road, desperate to claw back the ecstasy and passion they'd shared not so very long ago.

And what did he do, that noble love of hers? He gave her a cheque for two hundred pounds, of course, and told her to get rid of the baby.

Stupidly, miserably, she'd done exactly that. She had never been able to get pregnant since.

In her darkest hours she wondered if it was a punishment – her inability to conceive David's baby. What if she'd only had one viable egg and she'd chosen to destroy it? What if that had been her single chance at a baby and she'd blown it, carelessly, caught up in the whirl of devotion she'd felt for that tosser Nicholas?

It had been another reason she felt angry with her body: the fact that it had blithely produced this poor foetus back when she was a penniless teenager and didn't want it; yet now, when she had everything in place and longed desperately to be a mother, her own flesh steadfastly refused to yield to her wishes. Not for the first time she wondered what would have happened if she'd kept Nicholas Larsson's baby. Okay, so she'd probably have had to drop out of college, and she might not have ended up with David or her current career . . . but she'd have had a child, wouldn't she? A teenage son or daughter now. She'd have coped somehow; she always did. What if she'd made the wrong decision back then?

Trying to collect herself, she grabbed her bag and locked the car. There was no point thinking about what might have been, she reminded herself. What was done couldn't be undone. All the same, she found herself gazing up and down the road, trying to pinpoint exactly which house Nicholas Larsson had lived in . . . and wondering if he might still be there.

'So, I'll get back to you with some ideas for carpeting and paint colours in this room, a floor-plan for the . . . er . . .'

'The drawing room,' Mrs Bentley supplied, one eyebrow raised.

'Yes, of course, the drawing room,' Emma said gratefully, 'and I'll ask one of our in-house architects to take a look at the building work for your new wet-room, in order to provide you with a full cost breakdown. Is there anything else?'

'Well, no, apart from . . .' Mrs Bentley gave a small, embarrassed laugh. 'That's my pen.'

'Your pen! I'm so sorry,' Emma said, handing it back to her. She was all over the place; this woman must think she was a complete bimbo.

'I wouldn't ask, only it's silver and was a present from my husband.'

'No, no, of course, absolutely, I wouldn't dream of walking out with your pen.' *Pull yourself together, Emma.* She smiled what she hoped was a winning smile. 'So I'll be in touch!'

She followed her client down the hallway, feeling an idiot. Thinking about Nicholas Larsson had knocked her for six; she'd spent the whole meeting trying to staunch the flow of memories and failing abysmally. She wondered if his house was a twin of this one, and found herself trying to visualise his decor and style. Was he still married?

'Thanks very much,' she said on the doorstep, patting her bag surreptitiously to check that she had her keys and phone. The fluster she was in, it wouldn't surprise her if she'd left her shoes behind, let alone anything else.

Memories swirled around her like dark clouds as she walked along the street. She shouldn't think about Nicholas any more. She mustn't. What was the point?

Because he was the only man to ever make you pregnant, a snide voice piped up in her head. *That's the point.*

She closed that thought quickly, as if slamming a door shut. *Not going there*, she told herself firmly. *Don't even think about it.*

She got back into her car and then, feeling like a mug, drove slowly all the way down the road, eyeballing each and every house. Then she stopped and parked again, staring closely at one with a copper-beech tree in front of it and a dusty Volvo on the drive. This was it – the Larssons' house. Yes, she was certain of it.

For reasons she wasn't altogether sure about, she found herself jotting down the number, her fingers shaking. And then, at last, she pulled away and went to solve the terrible problem that had arisen with Jennifer Salisbury's curtain tie-backs. The trivial nature of the task was oddly comforting.

'Anyone home? Hello-o?'

It was early evening and Emma had just stepped into Mulberry House, bags in hand. She could smell fresh paint and glanced around appreciatively. Wow. Busy, busy. In the two weeks since she'd been here the shabby old reception area had been cleaned up and decorated, and now appeared infinitely less like a cave of gloom.

David appeared in the doorway. 'Hey!' he said warmly. That smile of his was enough to dissipate some of the tension she'd felt on the journey. It had been a strange day.

'Hiya,' she said, hugging him tightly and breathing in his lovely familiar smell, in the hope it would see off the memories of Nicholas still lingering around her subconscious. 'How's it going? Looks great in here.'

He kissed the top of her head. 'It's going really well. We've got so much done! The chalet is actually going to be habitable soon.' He let go of her and kissed her properly, tenderly. 'It's good to see you again. I'm sorry about last time.'

'Me too,' she said. Her knees turned liquid as he kissed her again, long and slow. This was what she'd been missing.

'Oh! Emma, it's you. I didn't hear the bell,' came a familiar voice. Was it Emma's imagination, or were Lilian's lips actually puckering in disapproval at the sight of her precious son with his arms around another woman?

I'm his wife, Emma found herself thinking, hackles rising. Then she took a deep breath. 'I didn't ring, the door was open, so I . . .' Her spirits were sinking with every word. 'So I just came in,' she finished.

'Oh,' Lilian said, evidently unimpressed by this display of bad manners. Anyone would think Emma was a member of the family or something. 'Got to get on anyway,' she added, before busying off again towards the kitchen.

Rude, rude, rude. Not even a *hello,* or a *come in,* or *would you like a drink,* or *how was your journey?* Not even a *Thanks for sparing your husband for the last four weeks, I'm sorry if this has inconvenienced you at all.* That would be the day.

She tried to return to the happy place she and David had been in just moments before the interruption: the kissing, the holding, the smile in his eyes . . . but it was too late, her mood had curdled.

'Let's take this upstairs,' David said, heaving up her weekend bag. 'We're in number six this weekend – the other rooms are either being decorated or booked out.'

Oh, great. Bedroom number six was right next to Lilian and Eddie's bedroom. If oodles of baby-making sex was to be on the agenda this weekend, they'd have to be extremely discreet. *Where there's a will, there's a way,* Emma thought grimly, following her husband up the stairs. And visions of Lilian, or indeed Nicholas Larsson, would not distract her for a single second.

She quickened her pace as she remembered that there was, at least, an en suite in the bedroom. 'I wouldn't mind a shower,' she said, in what she hoped was a seductive purr. 'I feel kind of . . . dirty after the drive.'

She had an eyebrow arched suggestively, but David was

fiddling with the key in the door and, for a moment, she wasn't sure he'd heard. But then he grinned. 'Dirty, eh?' he said, pushing the door half-open, so that she had to press against him to enter the room. 'Come to think of it, I'm feeling dirty too. Mind if I join you?'

Mind? She'd practically stripped naked by the time it took him to shut the door. 'Be my guest,' she murmured, setting the water running.

Sex in the shower had never been Emma's favourite place but, hell, a quick one to serve as a starter suited her just fine. Besides, after missing last month's ovulation opportunity, she needed to make up for lost time. She planned to ravish her husband every single chance she got. The only small snag was that, immediately after he'd come inside her, the tiles cold against her back, water pouring over her gasping face, she just wanted to be on the bed, bottom up, thighs taking the strain as gravity helped guide the plucky sperm on their way to victory. She did not want to be standing upright in a shower, letting all the little fellas drain down her inner thighs.

'That was great,' she said, extricating herself carefully from his grasp. *Hang in there, little swimmers, hold tight!* Then she threw a towel on the bed and dived onto it, stark naked and sopping wet, lifting her bum up in the air, as she'd been advised by all the fertility websites. Would a conception-assisting headstand be too much? she wondered. Hell, why not – anything was worth a try, she thought, launching herself into an ungainly upside-down position.

'What the . . . what's going on? Don't you want to wash your hair or . . . ?' David was leaning out of the cubicle, looking confused. Then he clocked her contortions and his face sagged slightly. 'Oh, right,' he said, without a great deal of enthusiasm.

'Sorry,' she said with a smile, hoping he'd see the funny side, but he vanished back into the cubicle, and then all she could hear was the sound of running water for a while. She rested her feet against the wall, suddenly feeling cold and exposed and extremely self-conscious. It would be different once she was pregnant, she reminded herself, the blood draining to her head. It would all be worth it.

This weekend they were sharing Mulberry House with a whole new bunch from the odd squad. There was a young couple down for a sailing weekend, who had the poshest accents Emma had ever heard. There were two elderly sisters, Joan and Nora (or Moan and Borer, as David rather meanly christened them), who seemed to lurk around every corner of the garden, waiting for an opportunity to show off their horticultural knowledge. Then there was a family of four – two adults who were down for the True Light Christian Conference in Weymouth, and their decidedly

ungodly teenage sons, who had already faced the wrath of
Lilian for smoking out of the bedroom window.

After a smoochy early-morning bunk-up (with another
sneaky headstand afterwards while David was in the bathroom), breakfast on Saturday morning reminded Emma of
a social experiment that had gone badly wrong. Moan and
Borer had plonked themselves down at a table with the
Hoorays and were earnestly quizzing them about the bedding plants they were planning for the forthcoming summer.
'Terribly chalky soil in your neck of the woods,' Moan (or
was it Borer?) kept saying authoritatively. 'You'll never grow
a decent rose in chalky soil, you know. Don't even think
about geraniums!'

'Scabby potatoes too,' Borer (or perhaps Moan) added,
like the Gardener of Doom.

'They don't want potatoes in their *flowerbeds*, dear,' Moan
chided.

'I was just *saying*, dear!' said Borer.

'We were thinking a Zen garden, to be honest,' Mrs Hooray
said. 'Lovely white gravel, a fountain, a meditation zone . . .'

'Oh Lord,' said Moan. 'Are you thinking what I'm
thinking, dear?'

'Yes,' said Borer. 'One giant litter tray for all the local
moggies. Bad idea, darling. Bad idea.'

Meanwhile, over on the other table, the Christians were
saying grace – well, the adults were anyway. Their teenage

offspring, dressed from head to toe in black, were rolling their eyes and muttering, 'For fuck's sake,' to each other.

Emma couldn't help a smile as she walked through to the kitchen. The more awful the guests, the better as far as she was concerned – just extra ammunition in her attempt to bring David back home again.

Unfortunately, despite this latest collection of nutters, David didn't seem in any hurry to leave Mulberry House, as she soon found out. Emma had brought along details of various houses for sale in Bristol that she was keen to view, as well as two job ads she'd clipped out of the newspaper, but he barely gave them a second glance.

'Things are going really well here,' he said, as they headed into Lyme for the afternoon. 'All the returning guests love the new decor, and we've already had some people rebook for next year. We reckon the holiday chalet will be ready to let soon too – Charlie and I are about to start decorating inside now.'

'You're taking bookings for *next year*?' Emma said. 'Isn't that a bit . . . ?' She frowned out of the car window. 'What if your parents decide to sell up? I mean, they definitely want to move out, right?'

He glanced at her sideways. 'It's an ongoing business, though,' he replied. 'And if they do end up selling, then any new buyers will be pleased to have bookings in the diary.'

'I suppose.' She paused. 'Anyway, listen, if neither of those job ads I brought grab you, I was wondering: have you considered setting up as a freelance architect? I had to call one in the other day, and it made me think – well, *you* could do that, couldn't you? You must have loads of contacts, and—'

He parked down by the Cobb and cut the engine. 'Em . . . Just let me do this for now, yeah? I've got my hands full with the B&B.'

She gritted her teeth. 'Yes, but for how much longer? It's getting ridiculous. I feel as if we've split up, like I'm not married any more. You haven't been home for weeks!'

He was looking out at the sea, his eyes far-away. 'I know, but . . .' He shrugged. 'It's complicated. They need me right now. I can't leave just yet.'

'They need you? *I* need you, David! I'm your bloody wife, remember!'

He sighed. 'I know. I'm sorry. It's not exactly ideal.'

'You're telling me!'

'But that's just how it is at the moment. Okay?'

It was not okay. It was many miles from okay, and if Emma hadn't been counting on at least three more shags before the end of the weekend, then she might have pursued the argument and said so. Instead she nodded. 'Okay,' she said, putting a hand on his. 'I just miss you, that's all.'

He turned his hand over and squeezed her fingers. 'Me too,' he said. 'Enormously. Like you wouldn't believe.'

They got out of the car and she breathed in lungfuls of briny air. With a bit of luck she'd be pregnant by Sunday and then — *then* — she'd have the best reason of all for forcing him home.

To: *aliciajones104@teachermail.co.uk*
From: *emmaj@HughesMcPheeInteriors.co.uk*
Re: *Babies*

Hiya,

    Hope you don't mind me emailing. I was just wondering: when you got pregnant with your three, did you feel different very quickly? I've got another week before my period's due, but I've just got the strangest feeling that something's going on. I keep needing the loo, and I haven't been able to stomach breakfast for the last few days. I don't want to get my hopes up too high, but . . . !

    Love Em x

To: *emmaj@HughesMcPheeInteriors.co.uk*
From: *aliciajones104@teachermail.co.uk*
Re: *Babies*

OOOH! How exciting. Yes, I did feel different very quickly each time. I swear I even felt the implantation of Raffy and

*Matilda, both about a week after conception. Can't explain it —
just a strange sort of twingey ache. And yes, I think you do 'just
know' sometimes. Keep me posted anyway. Crossing my fingers
for you.*

    Lots of love
    Alicia

PS Just a week until Paris now. Whoopee!!

Chapter Seventeen

A few days after Hazel spoke to Gary on the phone, Izzy and the girls came home from school to discover that they'd had a visitor. An egg had been thrown at one of the windows and a handful of dead flowers dangled from the letter box. Izzy went cold all over. She actually thought she might faint right there on the doorstep. Violence and peace offerings within seconds of each other – it was Gary all over. Had to be.

Her heart thumping, she rushed the girls through the front door of the building and locked it. Then she hurried them up the stairs and into the flat, sliding the new bolts across and locking the mortice once she was over the threshold. She checked the window locks, then pulled all the curtains across, her breath coming in short, harsh gasps as if she'd been running. Shit. SHIT. She should have known it was too good to last. She'd been expecting something like this ever since the call. It looked like he'd tracked them down at last.

She held on to the kitchen table, trying to breathe deeply.

There were brick walls around them now; he couldn't get in. *Do you understand, Gary? You're not coming in, however much you huff and puff.*

She wished more than ever that she hadn't smashed her phone like that the other night. Right now she could do with it, to text Lou or even Alicia.

'It's too hot indoors,' Willow moaned, coming into the room. 'Can't we go to the beach?'

'Can we play in the garden?' Hazel asked, appearing too.

'Not now,' Izzy said, trying to keep her voice even and normal-sounding. 'Let's . . . do some baking,' she added desperately. 'We could make Easter cookies for your teachers as an end-of-term present.'

Hazel wrinkled her nose. 'Can't we make them for *us*?'

Grateful for the chance to laugh, even if it felt as if there was a desperate hysteria rising behind the sound, Izzy hugged her tight. 'That's an even better idea. Let's make cookies for us.'

And so, with a whirl of hand-washing and ingredient-finding and flour-sieving, she found a kind of temporary comfort, blocking out as best she could the worries beating about her brain. All the same, the peace was uneasy. A storm was on its way, and she knew it was closing in. Any moment now, it would hit her fragile ship and they'd be in all kinds of trouble.

*

The cookies — vaguely rabbit- and egg-shaped — had only just gone into the oven when there was a knock at the door. 'Anyone in there?'

It was him. He was right outside the flat, having got into the building somehow — no doubt that idiot Jonah, of the low-slung jeans, had left the front door hanging open again, even though she'd made a point of securing it earlier. Izzy felt her insides contract and put a finger to her lips. 'Don't say anything,' she warned in a raggedy whisper. If they just kept quiet and brazened it out, he might think there was nobody home and give up.

'That sounded like Daddy,' Hazel commented, eyes wide. 'Was it actually . . . What?'

'Shhh,' urged Izzy, panic spiralling inside her. *Go away, Gary. Leave us alone.*

The knocking came again, louder this time. 'Girls, are you there? It's me, Daddy!'

'Daddy!' squealed Hazel joyously. 'I knew it was you!' And before Izzy could stop her, she'd leapt away towards the front door.

'Don't let him in!' Izzy screamed, running after her. 'Hazel — stop!' She caught hold of the little girl just as she was reaching for the latch. Willow, who'd followed, hung back, more cautious.

Izzy swallowed. 'Gary — what are you doing here?' she called through the door. Her vision swam dizzily with the stress, and she could feel a full-blown panic attack just waiting to descend.

'What am I doing? I've come to see my girls – what do you think?' he replied. 'Are you going to let me in, or what?'

'No,' Izzy replied, clenching her fists. 'No, I'm not. This is not a good time. You can't just turn up like this.'

He ignored her. 'I saw you walking up the road,' he said, his voice thick. 'Proper little beach girls, aren't you? Hazel, you've got so many freckles now! And Willow, you must have grown a whole inch since I saw you.'

Willow was still hanging back, wary, but Hazel was like a puppy, bouncing with excitement. 'Oh, Daddy, have you come to live with us?' she cried happily. 'We can show you our school and all our fossils and . . .'

'No,' Izzy put in quickly, conscious of everything that was at stake. 'Girls, go and wait in the kitchen, I'll be two minutes. I need a word with your dad.' She refused to refer to him as 'Daddy'. That sounded too nice, too cosy.

Neither girl moved, both seemingly transfixed by the idea of their father standing on the other side of the door. 'I was thinking, maybe we could go out for a pizza tonight . . .' he said coaxingly, and Hazel spun round to Izzy, thrilled.

'Can we?' she begged.

'No,' Izzy replied. 'Go on – into the kitchen, both of you and shut the door. Now, please.'

Willow turned and left without another word, but Hazel wasn't so sure. Bottom lip trembling and eyes suddenly tearful, she stamped her foot. 'I want pizza with Daddy,' she said mutinously until, catching sight of Izzy's face, she eventually dropped her gaze and slunk away.

Izzy waited until she heard the kitchen door click before speaking. She was trembling so hard she had to fold her arms around herself, as if she might break apart otherwise. Oh God, she'd imagined this moment so many times. She had to get it right. 'Gary ... what do you want?'

'I told you – to see the girls. They're my children too, don't forget. I have rights!'

She shook her head. 'This is not the way to go about it,' she said slowly. 'Sending me messages, turning up out of the blue ...'

'What was I meant to do: wait for an invitation? You left! You walked out! Did you think I'd just let you go?'

She shut her eyes, not able to speak. He was so close she could hear him breathing through the door.

Then his tone softened. 'Look, I know things went wrong between us. I'm sorry,' he said. 'I wasn't myself, I wasn't thinking straight. All I know is, when you left . . . I was gutted. Devastated. It hit me, what a mess I'd made of everything.' She could imagine his eyes soulful and imploring, just like Hazel's had been moments earlier. Just like every other time he'd apologized.

'Go on, darlin',' he urged. 'Let us in. Let's just talk about it. Me and you together again, yeah?'

She hesitated. For a second, she was tempted. Of course he missed the girls – he was their father. Deep down she felt a pull inside too; there was still a part of her that wanted everything to work out between them. She missed the Gary who'd once been her true love, her best friend.

The realist in her held firm, though. That Gary was long gone. And if she let him in now, it could prove really difficult to get him out again. She shook her head. 'Another time,' she said.

It was like pulling the pin on a hand grenade. 'You bitch!' he shouted, thumping the door. 'Who the hell do you think you are? Let me in this minute, or I'll break your fucking door down.'

The last of her courage was shrinking away. She stood there, feeling small and frightened, knowing that he meant every word. 'Go away,' she said, trying to swallow her fear, 'or I'll call the police. I mean it, Gary.' A sob caught in her throat. 'Go away.'

'Excuse *me*, but what's all the noise for?' came a voice just then, and Izzy wanted to die. Mrs Murray had come out of her flat for a nosey. Brilliant. One letter of complaint to their landlord about noisy neighbours coming right up, not to mention future babysitting favours hanging perilously in the balance.

'Who the fuck are you?' Gary replied, and Izzy cringed.

'Leave her alone,' she called. 'Mrs Murray, don't worry, I'll sort this out.'

Her neighbour was already replying to Gary in the frostiest of tones. 'Barbara Murray, not that it's any of your business,' she countered, before adding, 'Izzy, dear, are you all right? Is this man bothering you?'

'What's happening, Mummy?' whispered Willow just then, and Izzy jerked in alarm to see her there beside her. 'Why's Daddy so angry?'

Izzy shooed Willow back, then put the chain on the door and opened it a crack. 'I'm really sorry you've been disturbed, Mrs M. Gary's just leaving now.'

Gary made a lunge at the door, but she slammed it shut again before he could get his foot inside. He battered on it instead. 'Don't think you can get one over on me, Iz. I'm not done with you yet.'

Izzy stood against the door, not knowing what to do while he hammered at it a while longer, all pretence at niceness and pizzas forgotten as he bellowed a torrent of insults.

'You should be ashamed of yourself,' Mrs Murray shouted. 'I'm calling the police this minute!' Her own door slammed moments later.

'Mind your own business,' Gary yelled in response, kicking at Izzy's door again. It shuddered in its frame and she felt paralysed with fright. Any moment now he was going to bust in there, in a roaring temper . . . and then what? What should she do?

Hazel had reappeared too, and both girls stood holding hands silently in the hall. Tears rolled down Hazel's face and Willow put an arm around her, although she looked pale and terrified herself. Izzy felt as if her heart was breaking. This had gone far enough. 'I'm calling the police, Gary,' she told him. 'Don't worry,' she mouthed helplessly to the girls as she went to the phone. Her fingers shook as she dialled, but he'd left her with no choice.

'Police, please,' she said, and gave her details. 'My ex is trying to break into my flat and I've got two young children here.'

'We've already had reports of a problem at that address, Miss – a car should be with you in less than a minute,' the operator assured her.

'Thank you,' Izzy gulped. She held the girls close. They were both trembling. 'I've got you,' she whispered. 'Everything's going to be all right.'

With one last deafening kick at the door, Gary suddenly stopped. A siren was wailing outside; he had heard the arrival of the police too. His footsteps clattered down the communal stairs and the front door slammed behind him. He was gone.

Hazel and Willow sagged in Izzy's arms and all three of

them wept. 'It's all right, it's all right, I'm sorry he scared you,' Izzy soothed, choking on her own words. Then the smoke alarm began to screech. The cookies were burning.

She barely slept that night, braced for Gary to come back and smash his way in. The police hadn't been much help; just listened to the story and told her to phone again if he came back. It didn't reassure her for a minute.

The next day she was in two minds about them going out to school and work, but couldn't bear the alternative of cowering in the flat all day. When they finally ventured out of the building, looking nervously in every direction, she noticed that the pots of daffodils and tulips outside the main door – the ones Mrs Murray had taken great pride in planting – had been kicked over and broken. Someone had trampled all over the bright new flowers, completely destroying them.

Izzy gazed miserably up at Mrs Murray's window. She wanted to run back upstairs and warn the old lady, apologize and promise to buy replacements, but there just wasn't time before the school run, and then she would have to go straight on to work. The thought of her neighbour's face when she saw the damage made her feel absolutely terrible. Gary wouldn't be happy until he'd trashed everything for her here in Lyme, that was obvious.

Thankfully there were no incidents on the way to school,

despite Izzy's fears, and she felt her heart slow a fraction once she'd seen the girls into the building. There at least they would be protected. She went to the reception desk just to be on the safe side, and waited until the knot of mums handing in late dinner-money payments and returning slips about next term's cycling proficiency course had melted away.

'Can I help you?' asked Mrs Hastings, the terrifying, gimlet-eyed woman who ran the school's administration like a colonel on a battlefield.

'Yes, it's um . . .' Izzy glanced around warily. 'I just want to let the school know that my daughters, Willow and Hazel Allerton, are only to be picked up by me, and me alone. Their father may try to . . .' She felt sick; she couldn't even say the words. 'He might turn up,' she managed eventually. She swallowed hard. 'He's not . . . very nice.'

'I see,' Mrs Hastings replied, jotting down the girls' names. 'Thank you for making me aware of this.'

'Hopefully he won't come to the school,' Izzy went on. 'But just to warn you: he might take a punt and try it on. And if he does . . .' She swallowed again, remembering the ruined tulips wrenched from the earth, boot-marks branding their colourful petals. 'If he does, I'm sorry for whatever happens.' She clutched her hands together miserably, hating that she'd been forced into this conversation. It would be all round the staffroom, no doubt, that the Allerton girls had a violent thug of a father. Soon everyone would know the shame she felt.

Mrs Hastings nodded. 'It's happened before, it'll happen again,' she said. 'But while they're in our care, they'll be safe. You have my word on it.'

Tired and vulnerable after her long sleepless night, Izzy had to turn abruptly before she did anything awful like cry. 'Thanks,' she said on her way out.

No more tears, she vowed. She had the law on her side, she had Mrs Hastings on her side. She hoped it would be enough.

At eleven o'clock that morning the call came. Mrs Hastings. 'I'm sorry to ring you at work, Mrs Allerton, but I wanted to let you know that the person we were talking about earlier has just left the premises,' she said crisply.

Izzy felt her legs buckle. She wasn't supposed to take calls during work time, but with her mobile now broken, she had given the school the tea shop's number, just in case.

'Excuse *me*,' snapped Margaret, her boss, coming through with a tray of cream cakes.

Izzy barely heard the reproach. 'What happened?' she asked.

'Well, it was as you anticipated, to be honest,' Mrs Hastings said. 'He was aggressive, wanted to take the girls out of school, became very abusive . . . I threatened to telephone the police, but that didn't make any difference. In the end, Mr Collingwood and Mr Liddell had to escort him from the building.'

Oh God. The head teacher and the elderly caretaker, no less. Izzy's face flamed. Why was Gary so hell-bent on wrecking everything?

'I'm so s—' she began shakily, but then, slamming through her consciousness, came a shout from the café. 'Where is she? I know she works here. Where's Izzy?'

'Oh God,' she whispered into the phone. 'He's here. I've got to go.'

Blindly she stumbled into the seating area. The floor seemed to pitch dizzily before her. There was Gary, towering above a table of scared-looking old ladies, virtually spitting with rage. It was happening.

'Do you mind, sir, you're upsetting our customers,' fumed Margaret, holding an empty tray in front of her like a shield. 'Kindly lower your voice at once.'

'I'm sorry, Margaret,' Izzy said, stricken. It was like being in the most terrible dream; everything had an unreal, filmic quality to it. 'I'm sorry, everyone,' she heard herself say, high-pitched and frightened. 'We'll go outside and leave you in peace.'

Margaret was muttering indignantly and there was a stream of hushed, nervy voices in her wake, but Izzy couldn't register the content. All she could see was Gary in front of her, a raging force of nature. The rest of the café seemed to fall away as she walked mechanically towards him and they went outside.

Her throat felt as if it was constricting as they stood there face-to-face at last. 'Look,' she said bravely. For some reason the old wisdom about not showing a wild dog that you were afraid came into her head, and she pulled her shoulders higher. 'This is out of order. You can't just turn up here and start creating – this is where I *work*, Gary. You've made a show of me in front of everyone now. What do you think my boss is going to say?'

His eyes were deranged, and he didn't seem able to hear her. 'You're coming with me,' he said. 'Get in the car, now.'

'No,' she said. 'I'm on a shift until two – I can't just walk out and—'

He grabbed her wrist so tightly she thought he was going to shatter her bones. 'I *said* you're coming with me,' he repeated as she let out a cry of pain. 'Now get in the car, before you make me angry.'

People were staring at him – red-faced and shouting, pulling on Izzy's arm. He glared back belligerently and not a single person held his gaze.

Izzy was overwhelmed by panic. What should she do? Gary had never been so publicly aggressive to her before; in the past it had always happened behind closed doors. But now he didn't seem to care who saw them. His possessive rage seemed to have smashed down all social boundaries; there was a madness about him. And now he'd caught up with her, he'd hunted her down. *Help me*, she thought, gazing around desperately for a potential rescuer. *Somebody help me.*

'Now,' he repeated, with devastating softness, pulling her towards his car and opening the passenger door. She could see it all unfolding like a horror film, flashing before her eyes – Gary forcing her to get the girls from the school, the long drive back up north like captured prisoners, all manner of violent punishments that might ensue . . .

'No,' she replied, struggling to free herself. She couldn't bear that terrible future, which lay ahead like a threat. She didn't want to go back. 'No, Gary. This is not how—'

He wrenched her arm behind her and she screamed as pain roared along it. 'Get in that car *now*,' he hissed, shoving her inside. 'We're going home.'

'Margaret, call the police!' she shouted, seeing her boss hovering uncertainly outside the café, the empty tray still in her hands. 'Please! Help me!'

She fought him as hard as she could, but he was too strong, too determined. Before she knew what was happening, he had bundled her into the passenger seat and slammed the door. She fumbled to let herself out, hands shaking on the lock, her heart almost pounding through her ribcage, but Gary was already in the driver's seat, revving the engine so hard it shrieked and speeding up the road.

'Gary, please,' she sobbed.

'Shut up!' he yelled, swinging his left arm out to hit her. He caught her full on the nose with a horrible crunching sound of cartilage, and she cried out with pain and the shock of blood on her face, warm and wet.

The road swam in front of her eyes; she hardly dared watch. His driving had always been macho and selfish, never letting anyone pull out in front of him, but today he seemed more reckless than ever. He rammed his foot on the accelerator, and Izzy bounced against the door as they swerved around corners at top speed.

They were heading for the school, she realized within moments, and she shut her eyes, summoning every bit of courage that she could find inside her. *Please let me wake up now. Please let this be over.*

Then, as he screeched maniacally into a dangerous right turn, she screamed and shielded her head. A police car was coming towards them; the road was too narrow. 'Gary, STOP!'

Gary didn't hesitate for a second. He drove straight into the other car, ramming the bonnet. There was the most deafening thud, a terrible metallic grinding and then everything went black.

It's over, was Izzy's last bewildered thought. *It's over.*

Chapter Eighteen

Alicia was surely in a dream. A wonderful, exciting dream where she had actually packed a bag in order to head off to Paris that very evening, all on her own, with a whole weekend of indulgence ahead. There was no way she was going to pinch herself; this was one dream she was in absolutely no hurry to wake up from. All week she'd felt fizzy and fluttery, and now it was Friday lunchtime and there were only two classes left before an amazing freedom opened up before her. Hooray!

Every time she thought of her smart weekend bag (new!), filled with a carefully planned collection of outfits covering all eventualities and weather situations (a rather daring scarlet evening dress, for example, nestled alongside her pac-a-mac), a frisson – an actual frisson – of excitement shot through her. Now *this* was living!

She was due to arrive in Paris that night at nine o'clock. Less than ten hours and she'd be there – she'd really be there, on French soil, *in true life*, as the children said. Her plan was to grab a taxi from the Gare du Nord to the hotel, change for dinner and then waft out in a cloud of perfume to see where she fancied eating. Perhaps somewhere serving good old-fashioned *steak frites* for the first night, the steak thick and bloody, the food washed down with a large glass of red wine. And then . . . well, who knew?

She might venture to a bar and watch the world go by, sipping champagne and inventing stories about the passers-by to amuse herself. Perhaps she'd fall into conversation with some Parisians, who'd been wondering just who *was* that mysterious woman in the scarlet dress with the big smile? *Come with us*, she imagined the Parisians saying in beautifully accented English. *We will show you Paris by night. Allons-y!*

Dreamily, she pictured herself whizzing around the darkened city on the back of a moped, like something from a film. Somehow she was much younger and more carefree in this fantasy, was laughing gaily and wasn't wearing a safety helmet – none of which was likely to happen, but never mind. Daydreams were private.

Of course, there was also the possibility that she'd decide to return to the hotel after dinner and run herself a bubble bath instead, but even that would be a treat. Lying back in the fluffy white bubbles, sipping wine, with all of Paris on the doorstep outside . . . bliss. It would certainly be a humongous step up from trying to bath at home, when she was always accompanied by the nagging guilt that she should be marking or ironing, and constantly being interrupted by one or more children banging on the door saying they needed her for something or other.

The point was, when in Paris, it was up to her to call the shots — her weekend, to spend however she chose. She couldn't remember the last time she'd felt that way.

'Alicia?' Beth Middleton, the school secretary, popped her head around the staffroom door, jerking her out of her reverie. 'There's a call for you. She said it was urgent.'

Alicia blinked her daydreams away and followed Beth to the small crowded office space, where a receiver lay on the desk, amidst a kitten mug, fluffy framed photos of various pop stars and a bag of Haribo Tangfastics. 'Hello?' she said into the phone. 'Alicia Jones here.'

She heard a sob. 'Oh, thank God. It's me, I'm in hospital, one of the nurses helped me track you down.'

One of the nurses? Hospital? Alicia lowered herself into Beth's chair, feeling confused. 'Who is this?'

'It's me, it's Izzy.' Another sob, and then the sound of a nose being blown. 'Oh, Alicia, I've been in an accident and I really need a favour. Can you — would you—'

'Goodness, Izzy, whatever's happened?' Alicia asked, shocked and alarmed as her friend broke down in a storm of weeping.

'It was a car crash. Gary came back. He—' Again the words were engulfed in a sob. 'Listen, I need someone to pick up the girls for me. I've got no one else. Please can they stay at yours tonight?'

Alicia was trying to take all of this in, her head reeling. An accident . . . hospital . . . little girls with nowhere else to go . . . Could they stay with her tonight?

She hesitated, dismay sweeping through her. But tonight was supposed to be Paris: red wine and a scarlet dress, a moped, good wine, the city in all its night-time beauty.

Her lip quivered as the dream slipped past like a train that wouldn't stop, a mirage that was never actually real. 'Of course,' she said at last, stumbling over the words. 'Of course I'll pick up the girls, and it's fine for them to stay, for as long as you need, we've got plenty of room.' She swallowed, the enormity of what she'd just said sinking in by degrees. Goodbye, Paris. *Au revoir.* 'But what happened to you?' she managed to say, dragging herself back to Beth's office. 'Are you badly hurt? Should I bring them to visit you later on?'

Goodbye, Paris, she thought again dully, as Izzy began pouring out the whole dreadful story, still racked with sobs. *You would have been wonderful, I know. But it looks like I won't be seeing you tonight now after all.*

The girls were quiet and wary when she collected them, Willow in particular. She looked sidelong at Alicia, sizing

her up with serious grey eyes, and barely spoke the whole
way home. 'Mummy's not very well,' Alicia prattled cheerily,
strapping them into the car. 'So you're having a sleepover
with Matilda tonight – won't that be fun?'

'Where *is* Mummy?' Hazel wanted to know.

Alicia hesitated. 'She's . . . having a rest,' she said carefully. 'She said she'd phone you a bit later for a chat, okay?'

'What about Daddy?' Hazel asked. 'He came to see us
yesterday. He said we could have pizza.'

Alicia saw in the rear-view mirror that Willow had
elbowed her sharply. 'Shut up,' she hissed.

'I . . . don't know where Daddy is,' Alicia said, trying her
best to concentrate on the traffic. She shuddered, remembering the scant details Izzy had given her. The fear, the crash
. . . the aftermath. Because Daddy, the bad penny, was dead,
killed on impact apparently. Not that she was going to say
as much to the girls on the Axminster Road.

Back at the house, she busied herself getting out camp
beds and spare pillows. She decided to splash out on a
takeaway for dinner, because she simply could not face
cooking after everything else. *Kiss goodbye to that* steak frites,
she thought ruefully, hunting through the menus. Matilda
and the boys had been brought home by a neighbour, and
she relaxed her usual rules about them watching the television and let them have brownies and squash in the living

room, trying not to think about how many chocolatey crumbs would end up embedded in the sofa. Never mind. Such things didn't seem so important now.

Hugh came home early, looking alarmed to find the house full of children. In all the chaos she'd completely forgotten to tell him she wasn't even going away any more.

'What time are you off then?' he asked, striding into the kitchen and loosening his tie.

She didn't reply immediately, feeling small and stupid and sad. 'I'm not,' she said. 'I've had to cancel.'

If there was one thing worse than the crushing disappointment she felt at not going to Paris, it was the expression on Hugh's face as she said those words. He actually dared to smirk. Just a tiny smirk, only the very corners of his mouth, but she knew it was there. She could tell what he was thinking: that she'd bottled out at the last minute, that she couldn't do it alone.

'Izzy – my friend – has been injured in a car crash,' she said, coldly furious. 'Those are her girls playing on the Wii with Matilda. I said I'd look after them. Their father just died, not that they know any of this yet.'

That wiped the smirk off his face. 'God,' he said, stricken. 'Bloody hell.' There was silence for a moment, then he cleared his throat. 'Well, I'm sorry that you didn't get to go,' he added more apologetically.

'Yeah,' she muttered. There didn't seem much else left to

say. She waited for him to tell her: No, she should still go, he could cope perfectly well with two extra children in the house, she mustn't miss her trip.

He didn't. 'Oh well,' he said. 'What's for dinner then?'

'You choose,' she snapped, slapping the menus on the worktop. 'I'm going to unpack.'

She ran upstairs, tears spilling down her face. What a fool she'd been ever to think she could get away and have an adventure. Like life was ever that simple!

That evening Izzy phoned to say goodnight to the girls, keeping her voice cheerful and bright and, as far as Alicia could tell, not letting on about any of the trauma she'd gone through. 'Are you up to a visitor later?' Alicia asked, after Hazel and Willow went off to get ready for bed, both looking perkier.

'Please,' Izzy said. She sounded wrung-out, as if she'd used up her last shred of energy faking normalcy to her daughters.

'I'll find out when visiting hours are and come over when I can,' Alicia promised. 'Have a think if there's anything you want me to bring, and text me a list. Hang in there.'

No list arrived, but Alicia hunted out a few things that she knew she'd have wanted in Izzy's place: a clean nightie, a spare toothbrush and toothpaste, a magazine, some fluffy bedsocks and the get-well cards that the girls had made.

Rifling through her drawers, she found two brand-new, unworn pairs of knickers and stuffed them in the bag too. They were probably miles too big for Izzy's tiny bum, but it was better than nothing. She also put in some shower gel and shampoo, a couple of apples and a slab of chocolate cake.

Seeing Izzy in the hospital – tough, capable Izzy, who'd always seemed so in control – upset Alicia more than she could say. She looked like a frightened little girl in the bed, pale and wan, her foot bandaged and up in some sort of sling. Tears sprung to Izzy's eyes when she saw Alicia.

'Thank you for coming,' she said, her lip trembling. 'And thank you so much for having the girls. I don't know what I'd have done without you.'

Alicia sat down and took her hands. 'Oh, love,' she said. 'How are you doing? I've brought you some things.'

Izzy's eyes became wetter still as she saw the assortment of goodies Alicia had packed, and she sniffled when she read the felt-tipped cards from Hazel and Willow. 'Thank you,' she said again, blowing her nose. 'Are you sure they're okay? Did they say anything about Gary?'

Alicia chose her words carefully. 'Hazel mentioned that he'd been to see you. I didn't tell her anything. Willow seemed a bit anxious, until she spoke to you on the phone.'

A tear rolled down Izzy's cheek. 'How will I tell them?' she said, choked. 'What will I say?'

Alicia hugged her, feeling desperately sorry for her. 'It'll be all right,' she soothed, stroking Izzy's dark hair, and wishing she could come up with something less bland to say. 'It'll be all right. I promise.'

'It's all my fault,' Izzy sobbed. 'I should never have come here. I—'

'No,' Alicia said firmly, still holding her. 'It's not. None of this is in any way your fault. Ssshhhh. It's okay.'

They stayed like that for some moments until Izzy had cried herself out. She blew her nose again, hands shaking, and attempted a watery smile. 'Bet you're wishing you'd never met me now.'

'I'm not wishing any such thing,' Alicia told her. 'You're my friend. Now. Tell me what the doctors have said. How long do they think you'll be here?'

The doctors felt Izzy had got away lightly, apparently. 'You've been very lucky, Mrs Allerton,' one of them had said, with no trace of irony, according to Izzy. She had a compound fracture of the bones in her lower leg, the tibia and fibula, probably where she'd been 'sympathetically braking', the doctor explained, leaving her leg locked and bearing all her weight. She would need surgery in the morning and pins inserted to keep the broken bones in place, as well as a plaster cast for at least six weeks. On top of that, she had mild concussion, whiplash, a cut on the head and the most horrendous bruising, lividly marking where her seatbelt had been. Not to mention the psychological trauma of having her ex-husband die in the driver's seat next to her, the unenviable prospect of having to tell all of this to her little girls, the guilt that the police officer driving the car was also injured and in hospital, and the prospect of no longer being able to work as a dance teacher for a while. When you looked at the sum of the injuries, it didn't strike Alicia that her friend had been 'lucky' at all.

'I should have stopped him,' Izzy said, pleating the bedcover between her fingers in agitation. 'I should have calmed him down. If I'd sorted things out better in Manchester rather than running away, he'd never have been so angry with me. He'd still be alive today.'

Alicia squeezed her hand. 'And you'd still be black and blue, and living in fear,' she pointed out gently. 'He was the one who made bad choices, not you.'

A nurse popped her head around the curtain and walked in with a clipboard. 'Just need to do your observations,' she said. 'How are we doing for pain?'

'It's . . .' Izzy looked as if she was about to tough things out, but then dropped her head. 'It's pretty bad actually,' she admitted.

The nurse bustled around her. Any misgivings Alicia might have felt about cancelling Paris and being Izzy's 'phone-a-friend' had long since evaporated, leaving only a dreadful feeling of selfish shame for even *thinking* of complaining.

Once the nurse had left, she took Izzy's hand. 'So, I guess you'll be out of action for a little while, if you're going to be in plaster,' she began. 'And I doubt you'll be able to manage the steps up and down to your flat — second-floor, did you say? No chance. So let's work out a plan . . .'

Izzy nodded. 'There's one thing I really need you to do,' she began.

The following morning was Saturday, the start of the Easter holidays. Fortuitously Izzy had no dance classes on anyway, and the boys' cricket club was taking a fortnight's break, so Hugh nobly took all five children to the beach, while Alicia sped round to Izzy's flat armed with a set of keys and some empty bags. According to the hospital, Izzy had had a reasonable night's sleep and was due to have surgery later that morning. They anticipated that she could leave hospital the following day, providing she was fully recovered from the anaesthetic, although she was going to need some looking after for a while.

Alicia stopped at the florist's on the way and bought, as per Izzy's instructions, several pots of spring flowers and a large bunch of freesias. Then she drove the short distance to the flat and parked the car. Izzy's flat was in a modern block, boring and boxy to the eye. The whole of the front garden had been given over to car parking, with just a scraggly little hedge offering any sort of greenery or screening from the main road.

As she approached the front door, she could see that one of the glass panels there had been shattered and someone had clumsily patched it up with cardboard and masking tape on the inside. The front area had been swept clean, with just one tiny blue fragment visible from the smashed flowerpots that Izzy had described.

Alicia carefully set down the pots she'd brought by the entrance and brushed the soil from her hands. The flowers bobbed their heads in the breeze, the flashes of yellow, red and blue breaking up the monotony of the brick and concrete around them. It was a start.

Then she unlocked the front door and went up two flights of stairs, shaking her head at the thought of her friend being able to manage them herself any time soon.

After dropping the freesias in to Mrs Murray and explaining what had happened, Alicia opened the door to Izzy's flat . . . and let out a gasp. The inside of the flat was, in complete contrast to the outside, colourful and vibrant. The hall had been painted a cheerful pink, and a large red heart had been added around the small mirror that hung on the wall. MUMMY LOVES WILLOW AND HAZEL was spelled out above the coat rack, and a series of bright flowers painted in a wild assortment of colours and styles blossomed along the skirting boards. Inside, the living space was similarly dazzling. Children's artwork lined the walls, shell-mobiles dangled from the ceiling, the sofa had a stuffed monkey and a beaming blue bear in its corners and a collection of library books adorned a small bookcase.

Alicia felt a lump in her throat. The furniture might be shabby and old, the building might not be the prettiest, but with every slap of paint, with every Blu-tacked picture, Izzy had turned this into a home — a happy, fun place for her and the girls. A place of refuge, their little pocket of safety. Until yesterday anyway, when Gary had done his best to wreck everything.

Poor Izzy. The desperation had been quite naked in her eyes, the panic in her voice unmistakable. The girls had no grandparents, no aunties and uncles whatsoever. All the family they had in the world was her. 'And what use am I, like this?' she'd fretted. 'How can I possibly look after them? They're going to end up in care, just like me. I know it!'

Alicia had had to use her strictest, most no-nonsense teacher's voice. 'That is absolutely not going to happen,' she had said, looking Izzy straight in the eye. 'They can stay with me for as long as you need. Nobody will put them in care, or anywhere else. You've got me now, and I'll help you.'

The fierceness of her own voice had startled even her, but now she was glad she'd laid it on the line so clearly.

They just had to think of a way to make it work so that everyone was happy.

Unzipping her holdall, she went into the girls' bedroom and started to pack some clothes and toys, thinking hard.

Chapter Nineteen

'Have you ever,' Emma began thoughtfully, 'done something really, really awful that you knew you'd probably regret . . . but you just couldn't help yourself?'

She was speaking to Flo, her assistant, but her voice must have carried across the office because an awful lot of ears seemed to prick up at the question.

'I took this job, didn't I?' Flo said grumpily. She had an enormous pile of invoices on her desk and looked sorely tempted to stuff the lot in the bin. 'I'm totally regretting that today.'

'Why do you ask, Jones? Are you plotting mischief?' Greg put in, an eyebrow raised as he leaned over the desks.

'I wasn't talking to you, Big-Ears,' Emma replied, but it was too late, the others had taken up the question as if some kind of personal challenge.

'A friend and I once did a runner from the Hotel du Vin restaurant,' Lottie confessed coyly. She was on a protein diet and had been nibbling slices of ham from a packet since she'd arrived that morning. 'I was so pissed – I'd been on cocktails all night – and it seemed a good laugh at the time. Right until we got hauled back by the manager anyway. Walk of shame or what.'

'Oops,' said Emma. 'Does the future husband know about your dreadful life of crime, Lottie?'

'No, and you mustn't tell him!' she giggled, a manicured hand flying to her mouth. 'Really, you mustn't. He thinks I'm a nice girl.'

'Poor sod,' mumbled someone, possibly Greg.

'Once, when I was a teenager and had been grounded, I sneaked out with a mate and went to a gig in town,' Rhodri said. 'Climbed out my window, into a tree . . . proper SAS stuff. Had to sleep in the shed that night and had the most wicked hangover the next day. Didn't regret a thing.'

'I once smuggled some drugs into Malaysia for a mate,' Greg said airily. *Of course, he had to go one further than anyone else,* thought Emma, rolling her eyes. 'Stuffed a bag of smack up my arse and tried to blag it.'

'No *way*,' Flo breathed, open-mouthed.

'You didn't,' cried Lottie, appalled.

He snorted, bemused. 'Of course I didn't, you muppets,' he roared. 'What kind of a man do you think I am?' He waited a good two seconds for effect, then added, 'I stuffed it up Hester's arse, of course, got her to do it instead. Like I'd take that kind of a risk myself!'

The others laughed, but Lottie still looked disapproving. 'The worst thing is, Greg, I can actually believe you'd do something like that,' she said primly, her mouth pursing into a tut.

He pulled a face at her. 'Nah. I'm too busy stuffing her other orifices with—'

'ENOUGH!' Emma yelled hurriedly. 'Honestly, Greg, why does every single conversation have to end up with poor Hester getting dragged into things? Can you not leave her and her orifices out of it?'

Greg sniggered.

'Sounds like a Woody Allen film,' commented Rhodri. *'Hester and Her Orifices . . .'*

'Oh, not you as well,' Emma sighed. She rubbed her eyes wearily as she shut down the browser page she'd been looking at: Bristol Uni's Art History Faculty, where a photo of Nicholas Larsson gazing cool-eyed out of the screen had given her pause for thought for the last few minutes. She was clearly going insane. *Insane.* Why else would she be reading up on *him*, after all these years? Why on earth had she dredged up so many old memories, as if returning to a neglected, locked room and stirring up the dust?

'I once cheated on someone I really loved,' Flo put in suddenly. Her eyes were on Emma and the mood changed. 'Biggest mistake of my life. One I'm still regretting.'

Emma shivered and a favourite phrase of her grandma's

slipped into her head. *Like someone walking over my grave.* She wished Flo would stop gazing at her so intently. It was almost as if she knew what Emma was plotting.

She got up abruptly, claiming to be heading out for a lunch meeting. I'll just grab a sandwich and wander over to Queen Square to clear my head, she told herself. Even as she was thinking the words, she knew they were a lie.

As soon as her miserable period had started yesterday, regular as clockwork, and she'd found herself arguing on the phone to David, the obsessive need to do something – anything – had seized hold of her and wasn't about to let go.

Nicholas Larsson was about to take a trip down memory lane, she'd decided. And what better time to start his journey than now?

The university buildings looked remarkably unchanged from when she'd been a student there, she thought, driving through the campus a short while later. She half-expected to see Sally or Kez waving at her from outside the Union bar, lecture notes tucked under their arms, their clothes a mismatch of charity-shop finds with the uniform clumpy Doc Martens on their feet. Happy days.

She shut her eyes for a moment after she'd parked and rubbed her temples gingerly. This might, of course, be an enormous mistake. Catastrophic. She could be on the verge of something very, very wrong and very, very bad. But desperate times called for desperate measures, wasn't that right? And, put simply, she'd never felt more desperate. She wanted a baby so badly, the longing had taken over her whole life. Sometimes the end justified the means. David never had to know.

She checked her lipstick in the rear-view mirror and faked a smile. Her eyes were as hard as diamonds. For a split-second she wondered what the hell she was getting herself into, and whether she should just start the engine and drive away again, fast.

This is madness, Em. What good can come of it? Go back into town and get your wretched sandwich before you do anything you regret.

She tamped the thoughts down and got out of the car. *Remember me, Nicholas? You soon will.*

The art history building felt distinctly empty when she stepped inside. No footsteps, no voices, no ringing telephones. Then it clicked. Of course. Easter was approaching, term must be out; the students had evidently all buggered off back to their parents' houses with bin bags of smelly washing in tow. She hesitated, feeling self-conscious with no crowds of students to hide amidst. Would the staff be away too, putting their feet up in their own homes or sunning themselves on distant beaches?

Well, there was only one way to find out.

Her heart stepped up its pace as she went over to the

main reception desk. A printed note on the counter informed Emma that the office was closed for the next two weeks, and that all enquiries should be taken to the main reception. *I don't think so.*

She glanced around, trying to gather her thoughts. The whole notion of turning up here had been so impulsive that she'd barely had time to plot a convincing cover story. In the car, she'd decided she would gush out some nonsense about being on campus to meet an old friend, but the closer she came to Larsson's office, the thinner and more easily picked apart the lie began to feel. *Yes, I was just randomly walking past your office door – what a coincidence! How ARE you these days? It must be years...*

Hmmm. He'd have to be stupid to fall for that one. And she'd have to be stupid to think it might suffice.

Her eye fell on the staff pigeonholes behind the desk, an old-fashioned wooden construction, rectangle built upon rectangle, the exact same place she'd handed in essays herself once upon a time, as well as secret love notes, tucked deep into the shadowy corners, saying, *I dreamed about you last night* and *When can we see each other again?*

The thought of her round, curling handwriting, the adornments of biroed hearts, gave her a pang inside. She'd been such an innocent, after all. Practically still a child.

She skimmed the names – PROFESSOR K. MALLORY,

DR V. KHAN, M. CURTIS – and then there was his, printed black on white, DR N. LARSSON, and her legs suddenly felt boneless. He'd been here all these years, right where she'd left him.

Leaning slightly over the reception desk, she eyed the trays of paperwork, the files, the Rolodex – all abandoned for two weeks, according to the printed notice. What information might she find stored there? she wondered, adrenalin rising in her like sap. What might she be able to unearth about dear old Nicholas?

The sudden sound of footsteps behind her made her jump and she whirled around, feeling shifty, only to see . . .

Whoa. His presence hit her like a physical blow as he approached along the corridor, as dapper and smart as he'd ever been. His hair was now shot through with seams of silver-grey, and his frame was somehow smaller than she remembered, but his eyes were still so piercing they made her shiver. *Dr Larsson, I presume.*

'Can I help you?' His voice was just how she remembered: brisk and dry, with only the faintest trace of the Norwegian fjords beneath, hinting at snow and ice and wolves. That voice had once whispered the dirtiest of things into her ear, had been low and witty and suggestive. She felt a stirring in her knickers at hearing it again. But he hadn't recognized her.

She gulped, as if she'd been caught stealing. 'I . . . I was looking for . . . for Dr Khan,' she lied with atrocious fluency. 'I . . . Hey. Wait. Have we met before?'

God, this was awful. She was fake and wooden and completely unconvincing. This was not at all the scene she'd envisaged.

He paused and frowned, and she was just about to gabble an apology and sprint away, when his face cleared.

'Good Lord,' he said. 'It's you. It's you, isn't it, ah . . .' He struggled to remember her name, gaping helplessly.

'Emma,' she said. 'Oh, my goodness. Nicholas. I mean . . . Mr Larsson.'

'Dr Larsson now,' he said, the pride unmistakable. His eyes were steady on hers, blue slivers of ice. Amused blue slivers, she noted, as if he too was now recalling their rumpled encounters upstairs in his office with a certain fondness. 'Well, well, well. And you're here to see Dr Khan, are you?'

'Uh . . . Yes. He wanted to talk to me about . . . some business,' she blustered haltingly.

The ice chips narrowed, his mouth twisted. 'Ah. Unfortunately she's abroad for a week, I believe. It's the Easter vacation here now.'

She. V. Khan was a she. Own-goal to Emma. 'We haven't actually met, just been in contact via email,' she lied, feeling a blush creep through her skin. 'Not to worry, though, it can wait. I'll . . .' She shrugged, not wanting the conversation to end so soon. She hadn't managed to steer things round to reminiscing and good times yet.

'Listen,' he interrupted, not seeming to hear her ramblings. He touched her arm and her breath caught in her throat. 'Why don't we get a coffee?'

History seemed to be peeling back as, minutes later, Emma trotted across campus beside him. *Well, well, well. Haven't we been here before?*

A chill went through her, even though it was a bright, clear spring day. Flowers were blooming, the trees were in leaf. It was the season of fertility, after all.

'How funny to be here with you again, after so long,' she found herself saying demurely as she slipped off her jacket in the coffee bar. She knew all about men like Larsson. He had never been able to say no.

Chapter Twenty

Izzy was in the darkest place she'd ever been. Despite the numbing bliss of the morphine and whatever other drugs they were sticking in her, despite the kind attentiveness of the nursing staff and the novelty of being looked after by somebody (a whole team of somebodys), she ached all over, inside and out. Gary was dead. She would never see him again. He had scared her and hurt her, but there was a part of her, just the tiniest shard, that still loved him for the Gary he'd once been, the one person who'd really understood her, the father of her children. She couldn't believe he was gone, just like that, in a single, final heartbeat.

'Can you give us a contact number for his family, love?' the police officer asked when he came in to question her.

She had to shake her head. 'He doesn't have any family,' she replied dully. 'Only me and the girls.' A funeral would need to be organized, she realized, friends told, official paperwork dealt with, only she didn't have the energy to think about any of that right now.

Telling the girls was the worst ordeal of her life. Their little faces as they appeared in the ward — cowed and anxious, holding tightly to Alicia's hands . . . that alone was enough to rip her heart in two. They deserved better than this. Better parents, a better life full stop. She'd messed everything up, just like she always knew she would.

'Hey!' she said softly as Willow burst free from Alicia and ran over to her, burying her dark head in Izzy's chest. 'Hello, gorgeous,' she said. 'Oh, I missed you. Are you okay?'

'Mummy, what happened?' Willow asked. 'When will you be better?'

Hazel was there too in the next second, looking uncharacteristically worried. 'Mummy, are you very, very poorly?' she asked, shifting from foot to foot, eyes huge and round.

Alicia pulled the curtains around Izzy's bed for some privacy, then mouthed that she'd leave them to it and made a discreet exit.

Izzy patted the side of the bed and they both scrambled up to sit beside her. 'Well, I had an operation on my leg this morning, but it's going to take a while to heal up. Maybe a few months.'

'You're going to be in hospital for a few months?' Willow wailed instantly.

'No! Hopefully I'll be out tomorrow but they want to keep me in today because I bumped my head in the accident.

They need to make sure nothing's wrong. Check I've still got a brain in there, you know. Then I'll be out, only I'll have to walk with crutches, while my leg's mending.'

'And will we go home then?' Hazel asked.

Izzy took a deep breath. 'Not straight away, no,' she admitted. 'Not back to our flat. I don't think I'd be able to go up and down the stairs very fast with crutches, do you?' She was doing her best to sound upbeat, as if this was merely the latest episode in a marvellous adventure they were all having, but both girls looked anxious. 'We'll find somewhere different,' she went on quickly. 'Alicia's said we can stay with them first of all, then we'll go somewhere else, just us three.'

She felt tired having to think about such practicalities. The nurses had been unanimous in saying she needed looking after for a while, that she couldn't be expected to manage single-handedly straight away. Going home was not an option. However wonderful Alicia was being, for the first time in ages Izzy had found herself wishing that she had a mum to lean on.

'Does that sound okay?' she asked when neither girl reacted. 'Has it been all right staying there with Matilda?'

Willow nodded. 'Alicia's really nice.'

'The house is *massive*,' Hazel whispered, then perked up a fraction. 'And they've got a Wii. I'm really good at *Mario Kart* now, you know.'

'Good,' said Izzy, stroking her hair fondly. 'That's great news.'

'Matilda was pleased too,' Willow said. 'She didn't want her mummy to go to Paris anyway, she told me.'

Izzy did a double-take, the words spiking into her like darts. 'She didn't – oh *no*. Was Alicia meant to go to Paris? This weekend?'

'Yes,' Hazel replied, shrugging. 'But she said we were more important.'

'Oh God,' Izzy croaked. Not only had she called in the most enormous favour from this woman she barely knew, but in doing so she'd wrecked her special birthday treat. Izzy had never seen Alicia so bright-eyed and excited as when she'd told her about the trip, the other week in the pub. How could she have forgotten?

Hazel leaned against Izzy's legs, her long hair fanning across the sheet. 'Has Daddy been to see you again?' she asked.

Izzy stiffened. Here we go. 'Er . . .' she began. She was still spacey from the anaesthetic and hadn't slept at all well the night before. Could she seriously do this conversation now? She paused, her mind churning through the pros and cons. It was tempting, frankly, to take the coward's way out and palm Hazel off with a simple 'no', or even lie, make up some story about how he'd gone away and wouldn't be coming back . . . It wasn't all that far from the truth, really, was it?

But no. She couldn't lie to them.

'Actually, there's something I need to tell you about Daddy,' she said. She took Willow's hand and held it tightly. 'When I was in the car crash, it was Daddy who was driving. And I'm really sorry to say that . . . he was badly hurt too.'

'Is he in the hospital as well?' Willow asked, sitting very still.

'No, love.' She swallowed. 'I'm afraid to say that Daddy . . . Daddy died in the car crash. He's . . .' Oh God. How should she do this in a way that wouldn't completely crush their little worlds? 'He's . . . up in heaven with the angels now.'

There was a moment of shocked silence before Hazel erupted into an absolute frenzy of weeping, clutching at Izzy's legs. 'I want Daddy back!' she screamed. 'I want him BACK!'

Tears spilled down Willow's face. She had gone completely white. 'Is it true, Mummy? He's really dead?'

Izzy nodded, trying to enfold them both to her. 'I'm so sorry, chicken. I know how much you loved him. It's really, really sad.'

'I never got to say goodbye,' Hazel railed, rearing up, eyes glittering. 'And you never even let him into our house, Mummy. Why didn't you let him in?'

The guilt was unbearable. 'I was cross with him,' Izzy managed to say. 'I thought he might hurt us.'

'Daddy would never hurt *me*,' Hazel cried hotly, wrenching herself out of Izzy's arms. 'He wanted to take us for *pizza!*'

'Darling—' Izzy tried to reach for her, but she pulled away.

'You're wrong. Daddy's not dead. You're WRONG!'

'Hazel . . .' But she'd already scrambled off the bed, fighting through the curtains with a choking cry, before vanishing from sight.

'I'll go after her,' Willow said, and disappeared.

Izzy could hardly breathe with anguish, just gripped the bed sheet helplessly, wishing she could run after Hazel too, catch her in a huge hug, hold her and hold her, assure her that everything would be okay, that Mummy was here and would never leave . . .

But instead, she was stuck in this stupid bed, with her stupid leg, and couldn't do anything other than wait. She wanted to scream with frustration. She wished she'd lied now, wished she hadn't bludgeoned them with the terrible truth. As if they didn't have enough to cope with right now, what with her being trapped in hospital and them uprooted from home. What had she been thinking?

The longest minute in the history of all time ticked

slowly around and neither girl returned. Izzy was becoming deranged with agitation. Where were they? Her mind raced with frightening images: Hazel bursting through the hospital and outside, into the road. Hazel falling over, hurting herself, becoming lost. Willow searching for her, tears pouring down her little face ...

'Nurse?' she called out wildly, her heart thundering. 'Is anybody there?'

Nobody came. It was no good, she couldn't wait a second longer. She had to go looking for them, broken leg or not.

Gritting her teeth and ignoring all the doctor's instructions about keeping immobile, she gingerly tried to lever her foot off the bed . . . then yelped with the sudden roaring agony of her injury.

'What are you *doing*?' exclaimed a nurse, rushing in and just preventing Izzy from toppling onto the floor.

'I'm sorry, I . . .' gabbled Izzy, then heard the sound of voices: Alicia and the girls, thank *God*. She leaned back against the pillows, limp with relief, no longer caring about the throbbing, angry pains shooting through her leg. 'Oh, *girls*,' she cried, as they returned through the curtains, Hazel red-faced and wild-eyed, Willow looking wobbly with shock. 'Are you okay? I'm sorry I had to tell you, I wish it wasn't true.'

'I think that's perhaps enough excitement for today,' the nurse said briskly, folding her arms across her chest as she glanced from Izzy's tear-streaked face to her daughters. 'For everyone.'

'They'll be fine with me,' Alicia assured Izzy. 'Girls, let's go back and have some tea, shall we? We'll come and see Mummy again tomorrow.'

Izzy reached out for a cuddle, but only Willow came and let herself be hugged. She wept into Izzy's shoulder and her body shook with emotion. 'It'll be all right,' Izzy murmured, stroking her hair. 'You won't feel like this forever.'

'I don't want him to be dead,' Willow sobbed.

'I know, love. I don't either. We'll do something extra-special to remember him when I'm out of here,' she said desperately. 'Something lovely, like – we'll plant a tree, or we'll make a beautiful memory book or . . .'

Willow nodded. 'But, Mum, part of me is really sad, but part of me is—' She broke off into fresh sobs, not able to finish her sentence.

Izzy held her close, completely understanding her confusion. 'Me too,' she said, choking on the words. 'Me too. But we'll just remember the good bits, yeah? We'll remember all the happy times.'

Hazel would not be hugged. She held herself defiantly, not even looking at Izzy. It was obvious who she blamed for Gary's death.

Alicia leaned over and gave Izzy a kiss. 'Try not to worry,' she said. 'I'll look after her.'

'Thanks,' Izzy replied dully, but oh, how it hurt to see her girls walk away, so distressed, with her unable to follow. It went against every maternal instinct, staying put when all she wanted was to comfort them, to make everything better.

It was only after they'd gone that she remembered what Willow had said about Alicia's aborted trip to Paris. She hadn't even apologized for ruining her plans.

I'll make it up to her, she vowed fiercely. *I don't know how, but I'll make it up to her*, and *the girls. I'll put everything straight once I'm out of here.*

Izzy fell into an uneasy doze, drifting from one troubled dream to another. The nurses were monitoring her hourly, shining lights into her eyes and checking her temperature and blood pressure in case of any complications arising from the bump on her head. She woke with a jerk to find Charlie Jones sitting next to her bed, and blinked groggily, wondering if this was still part of the dream. Then he spoke.

'Hello,' he said. 'How are you?'

She struggled to a sitting position. 'Well, I've been better.'

'What a fucking nightmare,' he said, his eyes soft. 'I can't imagine—' He broke off, shaking his head.

I can't imagine what it's like being such a screw-up. Tears welled in her eyes for what felt like the hundredth time and she dashed them away defensively. 'It's okay,' she said.

This was patently untrue, but he was kind enough not to argue. 'So, do I get to write rude messages on your plaster then?' he asked, indicating her enormous white cast. He winked. 'I could really embarrass you, couldn't I? Shock the doctors and nurses with some choice language, get them all talking about you behind your back. *Have you SEEN what's written on her cast? Seemed such a nice girl, as well.*'

She raised an eyebrow. 'I'd better just point out that I could probably kick *really* hard, now I've got this thing on,' she replied. 'And a dancer's kick . . .' She took a sharp intake of breath and shook her head. 'Believe me, you don't want to experience one of *those*.'

He grinned, the dimple flashing in his cheek. 'Ah, then I'll just have to find a spot where you won't actually be able to *read* what I put, where only the doctors will be able to see it.' He fished in a battered rucksack and withdrew a pen, then pretended to write with it in mid-air. 'Izzy smells . . .'

She laughed, a proper gurgling laugh. It was the first real laugh she'd had in days. 'Don't you dare,' she warned, grabbing one of the satsumas that Alicia had brought in for her. 'I have missiles and I'm not afraid to use them.'

He held up his hands in surrender. 'Whoa!' he yelped, feigning alarm. 'Now you're frightening me.' He leaned back in the plastic chair and put his arms behind his head, as if sunning himself on a beach. 'So,' he said. 'Do you come here often?'

'Oh, shut up, Charlie.'

'Because, I've got to say, you are looking *hot* in that nightie.'

'Really.' She struggled to suppress a smile. Alicia's nightie was not exactly her style, it had to be said. It was on the voluminous side, and rather tired, with loose threads hanging from the sleeves and bobbly fabric where it had been washed so many times. Still, it was way better than the hospital gown they'd first put her in at least.

'You know it, girlfriend. Winceyette is so this season. And—'

'Winceyette? Where did you get that from?'

'Alicia, at a guess.'

She pulled a face. 'I'll winceyette you in a minute,' she warned. 'And don't you dare be mean about Alicia.'

'Wouldn't dream of it.'

'Or her nightwear.'

'Wouldn't dream of that, either. Seriously. It'd be a scary dream. More like a nightmare.'

'Shut up, Charlie.'

'Although she does make a bloody good pie, Alicia, I'll give her that,' he said, as if pie-making was the most important criterion when judging a person's worth. 'Her pastry's better than her choice of nightwear, that's for sure.'

'Whatever.'

'Don't worry, I haven't forgotten that spaghetti bolognese you made me the other week. No need for jealousy, all right?'

Izzy shut her eyes briefly. Charlie was exhausting. 'Well, she's a total goddess as far as I'm concerned,' she replied after a moment. 'Honestly, I don't know what I'd have done without her the last few days. I've got no one else.'

'You've got me,' he offered.

'Thanks,' she replied after a moment, trying not to sound too doubtful.

He laughed. '*Really*. I know you might think I'm a flake or, I don't know, a loser.'

'I don't,' she said, even though this wasn't strictly accurate.

'And you've probably heard all sorts of stories about me being a failure or an idiot, or someone who's never been able to commit to anyone else.'

'Yeah, loads. It's all anyone can talk about.'

'Well, I'm afraid it's all true,' he said, wrinkling his nose. 'I've been a bit of a twat, if I'm honest, lost the plot a few times, been skint, been in trouble, been called all the names under the sun by various women.'

'You're really selling yourself to me.'

'But I'm not a bad person,' he went on earnestly. 'I'm a good friend. I'm loyal, and if I say I'm going to help, I won't let you down.'

'Really.' She couldn't even be bothered to make it a question.

'Seriously. I want us to be friends. I like you, and I like your kids. And if you want anything, I swear I'll help out if I can.'

'Thank you.'

'That wasn't a sleazy come-on, by the way,' he put in quickly. 'I'm not trying to hit on you, while you're trapped in a hospital bed. Although it is tempting, I must say.'

'Thank God for that,' she said. 'Or I'd have to press my emergency button and get you manhandled out of here.' She smiled. 'Cheers, though. I could do with someone to carry my shopping for me now.'

'Anything.'

'And do the hoovering and make dinner, and iron the school uniform and help with the homework and...'

'Yep, got it, on the case.'

She laughed. 'Charlie, I'm joking,' she said. 'But thanks anyway.'

He leaned forward, his eyes bright. 'Ah, but I'm not joking, so there you go. Think of me as your new man-slave, at your beck and call.'

'What about your job?' she reminded him. 'For all you know, I might turn out to be an extremely demanding boss. What makes you think you'll be able to help all those old ladies with their compost bags *and* be a man-slave?'

'They're cool at the garden centre,' he told her. 'I'm mates with the manager, so he's been all right about me switching shifts around to help my dad out recently.' He got to his feet suddenly. 'Anyway, I'll leave you to it. You look like you could do with some more beauty sleep, if I'm honest.'

'Thanks a bunch. Visitors are meant to make patients feel better, not worse, remember.'

'You know me. Can't resist breaking the rules,' he said. 'See you, then, Hop-Along.'

'Bye, Charlie.'

She leaned back on her pillows as he loped away. Despite what she'd told him, he *had* made her feel better. Obviously she still didn't trust him as far as she could throw him – leopards never became tigers – but she couldn't help liking him. Just a little bit.

Chapter Twenty-One

Alicia was starting to wonder if she'd bitten off more than she could chew. It had been second nature for her to take in Hazel and Willow in Izzy's hour of need — any mother would have done the same — but really, she was completely out of her depth when it came to dealing with distraught, bereaved children, and felt as if she was floundering around like a toddler without armbands. Comfort zone? Where was that?

Poor Hazel had wept steadily for over two hours now, right from when they'd left the hospital in the early afternoon. Nothing could comfort her, not cuddles or chocolate brownies or unlimited goes on *Mario Kart*. Alicia was struggling to know what to try next. Was the child hysterical? Her own three had never been given to such fits of torment or passion; they were all stoic plod-alongs like her and Hugh. The wailing and sobbing bounced off the walls, a recurring accusation of Alicia's uselessness.

Willow, meanwhile, was white-faced and seemed to have

withdrawn completely from the world, replying only in monosyllables whenever anyone tried to engage her in conversation. She was perched on the sofa, knees up, arms wrapped around her legs, as if attempting to make herself as small as possible.

Hugh had vanished off to the gym, of course, the minute she walked into the house, weeping children in tow. 'No, wait,' she protested, but he'd gone, his sports bag flashing past before she could stop him. Surprise, surprise. He was even worse at dealing with people's emotions than she was. The merest whiff of tears and he was haring for the hills, or the bench press in his case. He seemed to be spending more time at the gym than at home, recently.

Meanwhile, the misery had seeped through to Matilda, who drooped mournfully about the house, her valiant attempts at friendship and suggestions to play all having been rejected. The boys had got the best idea; they'd escaped outside and were currently skateboarding up and down the street, a pastime that invariably set Alicia's nerves on edge. Today, for once, it was the lesser of two evils.

To top it all off, Lilian had just telephoned, asking querulously if Alicia would mind popping out to the supermarket for her – only she had one of her heads coming on, and would like to go back to bed.

Wouldn't we all, Lilian, Alicia thought savagely, jotting down the list of shopping – at least thirty things, several with detailed instructions attached ('Don't get it from the chiller, make sure you ask the butcher at the deli to cut you some fresh,' for example, when it came to the stewing steak. 'And watch he doesn't put his finger on the scales while he's weighing it.')

'It's lucky you're around to have the children after all,' Lilian said in a long-suffering voice. 'I don't think I'd have been up to it today. You know how I get with my bad heads.'

Before Alicia could query this – what did she mean, having the children today? That had never been the plan! – the line was cut off with a click. 'Thank you very much, Alicia,' she muttered waspishly to herself. 'Very kind of you to give up your Saturday afternoon on my behalf. It's not like you've got anything else to do. How ever would I manage without you?'

She would have to do it later, when Hugh got home, she decided, glancing over at a tear-streaked Willow, still immobile on the sofa, and at Hazel, who was weeping into a cushion at the other end, shoulders shaking. A trip to buy Lilian's stuff wasn't exactly top of anyone's cheer-up list. Besides, she couldn't wedge all five children in the car even if she wanted to, she realized, unless she asked a neighbour to have the boys maybe, or . . .

Oh, sod it. Lilian would have to wait. Hugh should be back soon, and she'd pop out then.

'Anyone want a glass of juice?' she tried brightly. 'Squash?' No answer came. Matilda, she noticed through the window, had given up on the Allerton girls and was now outside with her brothers. 'Well, let me know if you change your minds.'

Sighing, she retreated to the kitchen just as her phone pinged with a new text. Sandra. *So how's Gay Paree? Done anything naughty yet?!*

She made a low growling noise in frustration and despair. How's Paris? How the hell would she know? She wasn't bloody there, was she?

Oh, if only she *was* there and none of this was happening!

She didn't bother replying. How Sandra would gloat! She wouldn't be able to resist sticking the knife in, either, when Alicia told her of the recent dramas that had burst, unasked-for, into her life. *Hold on a minute, sis*, she imagined Sandra drawling, barely able to contain her triumph. *Correct me if I'm wrong, but I thought you wanted life to be more interesting and challenging. Don't tell me you're wishing you could go back to your boring old routine now. Make your mind up!*

Putting the kettle on, she seethed at the thought. *Be careful what you wish for*, her mum had always (pessimistically) warned. And hadn't she been moping about only a month or so ago, pining for something to happen? Well, now it had happened, and guess what? It turned out she wasn't up to the challenge, not remotely.

And meanwhile, she raged, catching sight of Lilian's shopping order, she was more of a mug than ever, when it came to falling over herself to help other people. What a bloody doormat. Nobody else she knew let things pile on top of them like this; nobody else was so flaming acquiescent and willing when it came to helping others. Was it some pathetic need she had to be useful, a pitiful attempt to make herself liked by others?

Well, no more. She'd reached her limit. Any minute now she would explode or have a nervous breakdown, and then they'd all be sorry. Except they probably wouldn't even notice until they needed more shopping or laundry or dinner . . .

'Alicia?' It was Willow, nervously tapping her arm.

Alicia took a deep breath. *Do not explode, Alicia.* 'Yes, honey?'

'Maybe we could bake a cake. For Mummy, I mean.'

Baking! The perfect solution. Her black mood evaporated immediately, as if Willow had undone an enchantment. Shame on you for complaining so selfishly, she reprimanded herself. When the poor girls have gone through so much. When they've lost their father!

She knelt down and put her arms around Willow. 'What a kind idea,' she said. 'A cake would really cheer her up, I'm sure. Hazel, would you like to help?' she called. 'I bet you two are brilliant at baking. Now, what flavour would she like best, do you think?'

Hugh didn't return until hours later, looking odd. 'Where the hell have you been?' Alicia hissed coldly, hurrying to greet him in the hall. 'What have you been *doing*?'

'Sorry,' he said. 'I lost track of time.'

'You lost track of time,' she repeated, hands curling into fists by her sides. In other words, he'd seen a mate at the sports bar and had stopped for a pint. Oh, and the football would have been on, she could picture it now. The thought of him taking it easy, while she'd had the most emotionally exhausting day for months, tipped her over the edge. 'For heaven's sake, Hugh, did it not occur to you that I might need a hand?' she snapped. 'I . . . Hold it!' she commanded shrilly, as he started taking his shoes off. 'You can leave those *on*. You're going straight off out again — your mum wants some shopping picking up.'

'But . . .'

'Don't argue. I'd have done it myself, if you'd bothered to get back sooner, but it's too late now. Here.' She thrust the list into his hand before he could say another word and stalked off, shaking with anger. Honestly! Talk about thoughtless. She couldn't remember the last time she'd felt so furious with him. Was this his way of punishing her, of making her feel even worse about Paris? *You've made your bed, Alicia, now lie in it.* Was that was he was trying to say?

Fuming, she went to start dinner. Having baked the most fabulous chocolate cake with whipped cream and fresh straw-berries earlier (which had done wonders for the girls' spirits – full marks to Willow for the idea), the kitchen was now a complete bombsite, with chocolatey mixing bowls, wooden spoons and the whisk needing attention. The children, thank-fully, were all playing a rowdy game of football in the garden, though, and Alicia turned a blind eye to her trampled flowers and mud-churned lawn for the sake of peace and harmony. Now for the washing up and then dinner. Oh, the end of this day could not come soon enough! Once the children were in bed, she was definitely going straight back to her list of treats to plan something new for herself.

Just as she was rolling out pastry for tuna puffs, there was a knock at the front door. Charlie.

'Hello,' she said in surprise, wiping her floury hands on her apron. 'Come in. Hugh's out shopping for your mum, but he should be back before long. Are you all right?'

'Fine, thanks,' he said. 'I've just been in to visit Izzy, actually. Listen, is this a bad time? Only I've been thinking . . .'

'You haven't!' She pantomimed shock and ushered him in.

'Ha-ha,' he said politely, following her down the hall,

almost tripping over Hugh's gym bag in his haste. 'Anyway, the thing is, I've had an idea. About Izzy. Have you got a minute?'

Alicia had patiently sat and listened to many of Charlie's ideas before. There had been his brainwave to rig up an ice-cream van and tour the Dorset coastline during the summer some years ago, making a fortune in Mr Whippys. (Or not, as it had turned out.) Then he'd come up with a plan to start his own mechanic business, if he could just use their garage as a base. (No.) His painting and decorating business had hit a brick wall pretty fast, leaving him with a terrible reputation and mounting debts, whereas his idea to rent out the recently closed cinema for private screenings had suffered a similar premature death. (A mercy killing, Alicia thought in secret.)

Still, he kept trying, you had to give him that. He always bounced back, beaming and full of a brand-new idea that would solve everything. And, to be fair, once in a while one of his mad schemes did work. He and a friend had imported a load of trinkets from India following a trip there, and had made a small fortune on them some years earlier. He'd actually got a flat and a nice holiday out of that masterplan, although this meant he'd blown all his profits and couldn't afford to reinvest. That was Charlie all over.

She made them both coffee – the tuna puffs could wait,

and actually she could do with the caffeine — then, after a quick glance outside to make sure the children were still okay (Hazel seemed to be bossing everyone around, despite being the youngest; Alicia took that as a Good Sign that she was feeling better), sat down at the table. 'How was Izzy?' she asked, not in any great hurry to hear the latest incredible Charlie Jones brainwave.

He sipped his coffee. 'She was doing okay, actually,' he replied. 'Toughing it out, you know how she is.' He put his mug down and drummed his fingers on the table. 'I want to help her, Lissa. I want to be able to do something for her.'

Ah. Of course. She should have guessed: his chance to play the knight in shining armour and rescue the damsel in distress. Well, Izzy might well be in distress right now, but Alicia wasn't so convinced Charlie was the perfect rescuer. Knight in patched-up, second-hand armour he'd wangled from a mate in a used car was more his style.

'Right . . .' she replied doubtfully, not even sure if Izzy would *want* to be rescued by Charlie.

'And I was thinking — well, why don't we see if she wants to move into the holiday chalet at Mum's for a while, just until she's better? It makes perfect sense.'

Alicia stared. She hadn't been expecting such a normal, practical suggestion to come from her brother-in-law's lips. 'I've said they can stay here,' she replied. 'She'll need some help doing day-to-day stuff, you see, getting the girls to school and—'

'I can do that.' He was beaming. 'I can drive them. Think about it. I know you've got a lovely house here, but, you know, three extra people, for however long . . . it's a big ask. If they're in the chalet, then she's still got some independence, plus we – me, David, Mum and Dad – are all on hand to help out.'

'I don't think she and your mum really hit it off,' Alicia pointed out. *Understatement of the flipping year,* she thought.

'Well, I reckon it could work,' Charlie said, shrugging off this minor obstacle. 'We could even make out she'd be doing us a favour, having someone in the chalet to road-test it, like. There's everything there that she needs, it's all been freshly decorated. Maybe I'll just ask Dad for now, see what he thinks. Bypass Mum, for the time being.'

Alicia snorted. It was very difficult, she had learned, to keep the smallest crumb of knowledge from Lilian. The woman could sniff out a bypass attempt like a Jack Russell after a rodent. 'Good luck with that,' she said mildly.

He nodded. 'Cheers,' he said. He got up, draining his coffee. 'Anyway, I just thought I'd run it past you, sound you out. Hugh won't mind, will he? No skin off his nose. Now to get Dad onside.'

Oh, right. So he'd assumed she was 'onside', had he? She

could picture it now, him marching in to Izzy and saying, 'Alicia and I think . . .' and then Izzy might wonder if Alicia was getting cold feet about having her to stay.

'Hang on, Charlie,' she said quickly. 'I'm not sure that—'

'Relax. I'm on the case,' he said airily. He grinned that confident Charlie grin, one that had sent countless women (Alicia excluded) soft in the head before now. 'I'll just say hello to the kids, then I'll be on my way.'

Charlie was 'on the case', eh? Alicia sighed. She should give him the benefit of the doubt, she supposed but . . . Well, they'd been here before. Several times. At least he hadn't asked to borrow a vast sum of money this time, though.

Out in the garden Uncle Charlie was greeted like a home-coming hero. He hugged all the girls, ruffled the boys' hair and tried to get them both in a headlock simultaneously, then scored a goal that smashed the last red petals from her tulips. Then came an energetic victory lap around the garden, punching the air and cheering. The children fell in behind him forming a mad conga, whooping and dancing as they went, even Willow and Hazel.

Alicia couldn't help but smile at such exuberance. He was a good guy, Charlie, she reminded herself. He always meant well. It was just that his latest brainwave involved the lives of three very fragile people, who needed security and stability like they'd never needed it before. Hand on heart, she really wasn't convinced he'd be up to the job.

But anyway she'd been forewarned, so that was something. She could oversee the whole thing with a beady eye, make sure that Izzy knew she had a choice, and pitch in if need be. It would be okay.

On with the cooking then. And she should probably pick up Hugh's gym bag before it caused anyone an injury. The last thing they needed was another person in hospital right now.

Snatching it up, she unzipped it, meaning to stuff the contents straight into the washing machine. Then she paused as her fingers touched a bone-dry towel. Strange. Had he not showered?

She pulled the bag open suspiciously. Hugh was a sweaty kind of person; he'd soak through a T-shirt and shorts pretty quickly during a session on the rowing machine or treadmill. Not today, it seemed. His kit was daisy-fresh, still neatly folded. She stared at it for a few moments, not comprehending. How . . . ?

He hadn't used it, she realized, with a thud of shock. And so, unless he'd completed his routine stark-naked, she could only conclude that he hadn't actually been to the gym at all. In which case, where had he been?

*

Alicia fully intended to get to the bottom of the matter that evening. 'Where exactly *were* you today?' she would bark, lips pursed. Maybe she'd even put her hands on her hips in a show of attitude. 'Because you sure as hell didn't go to the gym.'

That sounded good. Tough and to the point, no punches pulled. He would be caught off-guard; he would probably blink and stutter in surprise, but he'd have to be honest in reply. And he'd say . . .

That was the bit where her nerve failed: trying to imagine what he could possibly say that would make his lies acceptable. She didn't think Hugh was the lying sort. He *wasn't* the lying sort! That was what she loved about him: the fact that he was so good, so solid, so decent. He didn't deceive people or sneak around, pretending to be somewhere he wasn't. Did he?

Somehow she managed to navigate through the evening meal on automatic pilot. The girls were less tearful, thank heavens, and now just looked shattered, in need of a hot bath and an early night. Hugh seemed to be tiptoeing around her, but she remained tight-lipped, unable to look him in the eye. Oh, Hugh! How could he have let her down? Not only that, but he'd made it so obvious, leaving his unused gym stuff there, knowing she wouldn't be able to stop herself from putting it in the wash. Did he *want* her to find out?

The thought shook her. Maybe he was building up to telling her something awful. Maybe he was seeing someone else. What if he had been playing away all this time, cheating on her, weaselling out behind her back to meet some temptress under the pretence of being at the gym, week after week after week? He had been there a lot recently, even by his standards. Something else struck her. Was that why he'd sneakily roped in Lilian to look after the children while she was meant to be in Paris? Was he planning a little trip of his own, with this woman? Talk about a tangled web!

She felt like crying as the questions kept unfolding in her head. It was only the process of running a bath for the children, pouring in the bubbles and fetching clean towels that stopped her from collapsing in a puddle of dread. Hugh ... and somebody else? Hugh ... having an affair?

She tried to get a grip of herself as she bathed the children and helped them get ready for bed. Silly woman! One unworn gym kit and she was leaping to all sorts of ridiculous conclusions. There was probably a perfectly good explanation for it. Perfectly good. Maybe Hugh would even offer it up himself that evening. *You'll never guess what ...*

It was sure to be nothing. There was little point in her even mentioning it really, was there? She didn't want to cause a fuss.

Wuss, taunted the voice in her head. *Hiding your head in the sand? Scared of what you might find out?* The voice sounded more like Sandra every day, thought Alicia, trying to block it out. Where was Christine when she needed her?

'Alicia?'

There was Willow again, looking younger somehow in her pyjamas, with clean, shining hair. It was uncanny how she seemed to know when Alicia needed a distraction. 'Yes, darling?'

'Can we go to see Mum again tomorrow?'

'Of course you can, my lovely. And hopefully tomorrow we'll bring her back with us, won't that be good?'

'Maybe we could make her a welcome poster,' Willow said. 'And some balloons. She likes balloons.'

Alicia cuddled her. Willow was adorable. 'What a good idea,' she said. 'And what a lucky mummy she is, having you to think of all these special things for her.'

Hazel was already in bed, her thumb in her mouth. 'Do you think it's nice in heaven?' she asked when Alicia leaned over to kiss her goodnight.

Ah. Good question. As a scientist, Alicia didn't have an awful amount of truck with the notions of heaven and hell, or religion full stop actually, but she knew exactly what was required of her here. 'Oh, I imagine it's wonderful up there,' she said, stroking Hazel's hair tenderly. 'And I bet Daddy will be looking down on you and blowing kisses, and thinking what a lovely, brave superstar you are.'

'And Willow too,' Hazel said, sounding sleepy.

'Definitely Willow too,' Alicia agreed, tucking the covers in around her. 'Night-night, sweetheart. Sleep well.'

Willow hugged Alicia tightly before climbing into bed. 'Thank you for being so nice to me and Hazel,' she murmured. 'I really like being here.'

It was enough to slay even the flintiest person. 'You're welcome,' Alicia replied chokily. 'You wait until I tell your mum how good you've been. She'll be so, so proud of you. Even more proud than she already is.' She bent down to tuck Willow in. 'You sleep well, okay? Tomorrow will be a better day.'

Tomorrow *would* be a better day, she repeated to herself as she went back downstairs. Today had been pretty tough, all things considered, with worse possibly yet to come. Could she really bring herself to grill Hugh on what he'd been up to?

She hesitated on the bottom step, her hand on the newel post. He was in the kitchen, opening the fridge. Seconds later she heard the pop of a wine cork.

Should she do this? Did she really want to find out the truth?

Steeling herself, she marched in. She had to know what was going on. If she didn't ask, she'd be wondering and wondering and the doubt would eat away at her.

Hugh waved a wine glass at her as she entered the room.

'Glass of Château le Bordillot?' he asked amiably. '2006 — it's a good vintage apparently.'

She ignored him. *Tough and to the point.* 'Hugh,' she said abruptly. 'Be honest. What were you really doing all day today?'

Chapter Twenty-Two

It was the same Saturday and Emma braked as she nosed her car into the Mulberry House driveway. She was frowning, still puzzling over the strange thing she'd seen on her way down. She'd stopped for petrol near Ilminster, but, as she slowed to park at one set of pumps, she'd been certain that David's brother Hugh was getting into his car beside the pumps opposite. She waved and smiled – coincidence or what! – but he hadn't seen her. Too busy talking to the young woman in his passenger seat.

Emma had stared in shock, her eyes actually boggling in their sockets like a cartoon character. Wait a minute . . . Had she made a mistake? She yanked on the handbrake and turned off the engine, but before she could go over and say anything, Hugh – if it *was* him – had driven away.

She'd sat there for a good twenty seconds with her mouth open. Hugh . . . and a pretty auburn-haired woman? No. No way. She must have been mistaken. But if it wasn't him, it was the spitting image of him.

Shaking her head, she got out of the car. She was definitely mistaken. It was almost laughable, the thought of good old Hugh cheating on good old Alicia. It was probably someone he worked with, that was all. (Did he work on Saturdays?) Or maybe he was kindly giving a girl from their street a lift somewhere. But Hugh, doing the dirty? Never. That was her, leaping to warped conclusions, her with cheating on the brain because . . .

Because what, Emma?

She wrinkled her nose as she slotted the petrol nozzle into the tank. To be fair, she wasn't exactly *cheating* on David as such. Not technically speaking. Not if you forensically analysed the evidence so far. That wasn't to say that cheating on David hadn't crossed her mind during the last week. It had.

She and Nicholas had met again since their first 'chance' encounter on campus. He'd taken her for lunch on Thursday, to Bordeaux Quay, one of Bristol's classiest restaurants. Her stomach felt light and fluttery as she walked up to the entrance, her heart actually flipped when she saw him seated at a table, smartly dressed in dark jeans and a soft grey cashmere jumper. The older man. History repeating itself. This time she was going to make sure events panned out her way, though.

They sat there together, terribly polite, talking about this and that, safe subjects, all of them. They clinked wine glasses and admired the food, the sun twinkling off the harbour outside. It almost felt like it was the first time they'd met, had it not been for all the deep, murky history washing unmentioned between them. By the time they finished eating she could feel the tension throbbing like an electrical charge. Was he still attracted to her? He didn't have the same thrall for her any more – she wouldn't have looked twice at him in the street. But if he could give her what she wanted, then who cared? Ironically, it might even save her marriage from imploding.

'It's so good to see you again,' he said once she'd dragged out a coffee for as long as she could get away with. 'I can't remember why we ever lost touch.'

Her face flushed. Did he really not know? Was she merely one of a string of affairs, which had melded into an amorphous blob of memory over the years?

She probably should have held her tongue, but after a midday glass of wine she'd never been able to rein herself in. 'I got pregnant. That's why we lost touch,' she blurted out, more accusingly than she'd meant to.

A lesser man might have flinched, but Nicholas had always been one to keep his composure. 'Ah yes,' he said after a moment. 'That's right. Now I remember.'

Silence fell while they both remembered. She remembered sitting on his wall weeping, being shooed away in no uncertain terms in case his wife saw her. She remembered the sterile clinic, the weeks of crying and heartache afterwards, the emptiness inside her.

Suddenly she wanted to get out of the restaurant, to run as far from him as she could possibly go. Reopening the wound was more painful than she had expected. The scarring was deep and still tender. And her being here at all was a completely mad idea.

The chair squawked as she pushed it away. 'I'd better get back to work,' she mumbled. She had a three o'clock meeting with a client about a bathroom refit; she mustn't rock up there red-faced and dishevelled, stinking of wine, lust and bad memories.

He put a hand on hers. 'Wait. I'm sorry,' he said. 'I didn't mean to embarrass you.' He cleared his throat. 'And I'm sorry for how things ended between us. I behaved very badly. I was unkind. Yes,' he said firmly, holding up a finger as she opened her mouth to protest. 'We both know I was.'

And there it was, an apology of sorts: words she'd wanted to hear, fifteen years too late.

She tried to brush it off, not wanting him to know how much pain he'd caused. 'Don't worry about it,' she said. 'Water under the bridge.'

'Do you have children now?' he asked and she winced. Tactful, Nicholas.

'No,' she said.

'But you are married, yes? I noticed your ring.'

'Yes.' She felt wrong-footed, suddenly, no longer in charge of the situation, and half-rose in her seat. 'Listen, I really do have to go. Let me leave some money.' She pulled out her purse and began fishing for a twenty-pound note, but he waved a hand.

'No need,' he said. 'This one's on me.'

Now she'd definitely lost the lead. 'Honestly, no, let's go halves,' she said.

He'd already placed his credit card on the table. 'My treat,' he said. 'Next time, maybe you could take me somewhere.'

She managed a smile, although she felt as if she'd just slipped out of the shallows and into uncharted, turbulent waters. He was playing her just like he always had. How had she let it happen? 'That would be nice,' she said and brushed an imaginary crumb from her skirt. 'Well. Thank you.'

He smiled back. *Come into my parlour, said the spider to the fly.* 'I'll ring you.'

She stumbled away from the restaurant feeling like an idiot — a teenage fool lusting after the sexy lecturer all over again. Oh God! So much for her calling the shots. So much for going in, taking what she wanted and exiting again. Already the situation had become complicated. Was he hitting on her? Could she seriously go through with what she'd been planning?

The lunch date wasn't her only transgression. To her shame, the very next night she had . . .

She blinked. The fuel tank was full, the nozzle had cut off, and was silent and still in her hand. How long had she been standing there in a daydream? Quickly she fastened the cap on her tank and shut the little hatch. The less she thought about last night, the better.

She paid for the petrol, her head still full of Nicholas's enigmatic smile, his low chuckle, the frisson she'd felt whenever his skin touched hers. She had to tread carefully, she told herself. Very, very carefully.

It was a relief to come down to Dorset, to escape the temptations of the city for a weekend, she thought, sliding back into the car and starting the engine. And she was definitely losing her marbles if she thought she'd seen Hugh Jones with some young fox on a Saturday afternoon.

She drove away, resolving to put Nicholas Larsson firmly out of her mind from now on. The man was nothing but trouble.

Mulberry House felt rather subdued when Emma arrived forty minutes later. According to Eddie, Lilian was in bed with 'one of her heads', Charlie had gone to visit a friend in hospital, and David was hard at work in the holiday chalet, down the garden.

'I'll make him a cup of tea,' Emma said, still feeling

guilty about her shenanigans over the last forty-eight hours. 'Would you like one?'

'Bless you, love, I could kill for one,' Eddie said. He'd come in from mowing the lawn and smelled of grass clippings and sweat.

More caffeine. She'd been mainlining the stuff all day, trying to shake off her horrendous hangover. She had needed a Diet Coke, two cups of tea and the mother of all bacon sandwiches before she could even stagger into the shower that morning.

Her hands shook as she set out the mugs. What was happening to her? She seemed to be falling apart, as if her carefully constructed self had cracked and the secret mess inside her head was leaking out everywhere.

She couldn't even properly remember what had happened last night. It had begun innocently enough, as a post-work drinking session that she had actually bothered to go to for once. She'd been drinking too fast, too much, but she was having fun for what felt like the first time in weeks and didn't care. Drinks and chat in the pub turned into a pounding club night, and Emma had gone with the flow. Why not? she'd thought impulsively. There was nobody to hurry home to, was there? Nobody to text explaining her whereabouts. She remembered bright-pink cocktails, fruity with a kick. She remembered laughing like a drain at her colleagues' banter and thinking what a laugh it was, going out with them. She also remembered dirty dancing with Greg, provocative and too close, his hand on her back, his hips grinding into hers.

Oh God.

And then . . . What happened next was a blank, however hard she tried to piece together the details. How had she even got home? She had absolutely no recollection of leaving the club or making her way back. Her next definite memory was of the flat spinning around her at about three in the morning, then of being repeatedly sick, pinkly sick, in the loo for some time afterwards. They didn't advise that as best practice on the getting-pregnant websites.

She had woken up still dressed, her tights ripped, make-up smeared across her face and some deely boppers wedged on her head. Deely boppers? Where had *they* come from?

She shuddered now as she poured the tea. If Nicholas Larsson was trouble, Greg was worse. Much worse. Greg was loud, indiscreet, shameless. He wouldn't have thought twice about putting his hand up her top – or any other woman's, for that matter. She hoped she hadn't snogged him. Please let her not have snogged him. Surely she'd have remembered *that*? She gritted her teeth, feeling queasy and already dreading Monday morning's recriminations at the office.

My marriage is on the rocks, she thought grimly, stirring in the milk. *I'm behaving badly. David hasn't even bothered to say hello. What's to become of us? And is there any way back?*

'Ta, love,' said Eddie and she jumped, having forgotten he was still in the room with her. She hoped he couldn't smell alcohol seeping from her pores. He went back outside with the mug, whistling, and she watched him go, wistfulness and angst clashing inside her. He was a proper husband, if ever there was one: dutiful and steadfast, spending his free time making his home better for him and his wife. That was how a marriage should be. Not the two of them spending weeks apart, barely speaking and misbehaving.

She saw Eddie walk down the garden and then David appeared, coming towards the house.

At that moment her phone buzzed with a text. Greg. *MADAM!* it read. *Never knew you had it in you! ;)* G x.

Oh shit. Madam? Winking emoticons? This didn't look good. This didn't look good at all. The back door was opening and so, with a deep breath, a big fat fake smile and creeping nausea, she stuffed her phone into her pocket and waited to greet her husband.

They drove out to Charmouth and walked onto the beach together. The sea breeze tugged at her hangover, pulling it away, and she gulped in the salty air, feeling slightly more alive.

'You'll never guess who I saw on the way down here,' she said as they tramped along. 'Hugh — and some woman. Don't tell me he's got a bit on the side?'

'Nah,' said David. Did she imagine it or was there the slightest hesitation before he answered? Did he *know* something? 'Not Hugh. You must have been mistaken.'

'I'm sure it was him,' she persisted, wondering uneasily if Alicia knew about her husband's mysterious rendezvous. Should she mention it, or would that throw a spanner in the works?

David said nothing. The Joneses closing ranks once again. There had been a time when she and her husband had told each other everything, trusting one another not to break a confidence, even that of a brother or close friend. Now look at them, clutching their secrets protectively close.

She shook herself. She must be imagining it. Probably just hangover-induced paranoia, she thought, deciding against pressing him any further.

Her mobile buzzed again and she opened the text without thinking. *Thinking about you. N x.*

She rammed her phone back into her pocket, and a hot flush reared up through her skin. She was sure her heartbeat was audible through her clothes.

David glanced over. 'Everything all right?'

'Fine,' she said, wincing at her own lie.

They walked in silence for a while, then sat down on

some dry rocks, watching the waves roll in and out, glittering in the weak April sun.

'I'm not pregnant,' she blurted out miserably before she could stop herself. The words seemed louder than the sea for a moment; the world shrank to the two of them, together but alone on the rock.

He said nothing for a moment, then reached out and took her hand. 'Sorry,' he said.

There seemed to be nothing more to say as they sat together, joined by their fingers, yet miles apart. A mob of seagulls jeered overhead and she felt utterly desolate. *What now?* she wondered. *Where can we go from here?*

Chapter Twenty-Three

Typical. The one afternoon Lilian actually admitted defeat and took to her bed, the whole house of cards collapsed around her. Her head had been throbbing constantly since she'd got up that morning, the pain pinching her temples so hard and tight she could hardly see. Somehow she'd managed to call Alicia and beg her to buy in the groceries they needed (vaguely registering that Alicia seemed uncharacteristically irritable at the request), then closed the bedroom curtains and collapsed back into bed, plunging into a troubled sleep.

Some hours later she woke to the sound of shouting downstairs. Eddie's voice, rising to a wail. 'Where are you?' he called. 'Where is everyone?'

Instantly she sprang from the bed, adrenalin shocking her fully awake. Downstairs her husband was wild-eyed and holding out a bleeding hand, which dripped onto the kitchen floor. 'Oh my goodness,' she cried, rushing over to examine it. 'What did you do? How did this happen?'

'I was putting away the . . .' He paused, his eyes clouding over. 'The . . .'

'You were putting away the . . . ?' she prompted, trying to keep her patience, although panic was spiralling inside her. 'Come on, let's rinse this while you think.'

She led him to the sink and turned on the cold tap, letting the water wash the cut. It didn't look too deep, thankfully; she didn't think it needed stitches. Blood swirled into the stream of water, the vivid scarlet becoming pale pink and then clear as it disappeared down the plughole.

'The grass-cutter,' he said eventually. 'I was putting it away.'

'The lawnmower?' she suggested, her mind sifting through all the sharp implements in the shed – once useful, now each a threat. 'Oh, Eddie. I thought you were going to wait for David to help?'

'Emma came,' he remembered, as she turned the tap off and gingerly patted his hand dry with a folded square of kitchen roll.

'Emma – oh goodness, I'd forgotten she was coming today.' Another thing to flap about. Lilian wasn't sure she was up to more visitors right now, particularly Emma, who always seemed to be turning up her nose. Her headache slammed back with a vengeance as she tried to remember what she'd planned to cook that night. And what had happened to her groceries anyway?

There, see? she reprimanded herself as she carefully bandaged her husband's hand. This is what happens when you go to bed in the middle of the day, Lilian Jones. Don't do it again, even if you're on your deathbed. She dreaded to think what other accidents might have befallen her husband, blundering around in the garden shed on his own. Next time, she'd pay more attention. Next time, she'd blooming well do it herself.

The boys arrived shortly afterwards, one after another, like homing pigeons returning to roost. Hugh first, with the boot full of groceries. (Clearly it was beneath Alicia to fetch and carry for her now. Fancy sending her husband out to do the shopping – and on the weekend, too!) 'Thanks, love,' Lilian said as he brought in the last few bags. 'Very kind of you. Can I make you a nice cold drink while you're here? Something to eat?'

He seemed awkward, she noticed. 'Better not,' he said. 'Alicia's waiting for me with the kids.'

Probably with some other jobs for the poor man to do, she thought sourly, waving him off. Honestly! Emma and Alicia didn't know they were born sometimes. Didn't appreciate just how lucky they were to have fine men like her sons looking after them.

Talk of the devil . . . here came David and Emma next,

parking in the drive, both looking rather distant. Their body language was unfriendly as they got out of the car. No doubt Emma had been nagging him to go back to Bristol again. Couldn't she see that David was needed here, in his family home?

'Come in,' she said. 'Had a nice afternoon?' It was on the tip of her tongue to tell David what had happened to Eddie while they'd been out, but she decided not to at the last second. The lad had worked his socks off, after all; it wasn't his fault Eddie had got himself tangled up in the shed. (She still hadn't quite established how the accident had actually happened, she remembered, making a note to go down there later on and put all the sharpest things out of reach.)

'Yes, thanks,' David said. 'We went to Charmouth.' He stooped to kiss her cheek. 'Are you feeling better?'

She pushed her lips up in a little smile. 'Much better,' she said, even though it was far from the truth. 'Hello, Emma,' she added. 'How are you?'

Emma's eyes looked bloodshot. Had she been crying? 'Fine,' she said, in a not-very-fine way.

Oh dear. Trouble afoot. 'I'd better get on with dinner,' she said, making a quick exit to the kitchen.

Later on, as she was dishing up the evening meal — a rather dreary affair of lamb chops and mash, she just didn't have the energy to conjure up anything more spectacular —

Charlie appeared, breathless and agitated, as he dropped into a seat at the table. 'Mum, Dad, have you got a minute? I need to ask you something. A favour.'

Lilian did her best not to sigh but it was hard to prevent the resigned feeling of déjà vu. Here we go again, she thought. 'Can it wait, dear? Only we're just about to eat. Have you had anything, by the way? Would you like a chop? They're not the best, unfortunately – I did give specific instructions to Alicia about what I wanted at the meat counter, but...'

He waved the chop aside (she couldn't blame him, it was a little on the scraggy side) and leaned forward, elbows on the table, obviously dying to impart news of whatever he'd cooked up now.

'Remember Izzy?' he began without preamble. 'She came here once – your anniversary lunch. Two little girls. Remember?'

Lilian's head thumped. She remembered all right. It had been the last thing she'd wanted that day when, fraught with everything else she was trying to cope with, Charlie had appeared with three surprise guests. Rude, it was. Plain rude. 'Yes,' she said guardedly. What had this woman gone and conned him into?

'Well, she's in hospital. She's the one I went to see earlier, and the other day.'

'In hospital?' Emma exclaimed. 'Is she all right?'

Eddie put his fork down. 'Trees,' he said suddenly. 'Her little girls. They're named after trees, aren't they?'

'Yes, Dad, that's right. Hazel and Willow,' Charlie replied. 'She's been in a car crash,' he said to Emma. 'Broken her leg. Anyway, they've got nowhere else to go right now because – well, it's a long story, but she's going to be on crutches for a while and—'

'Beautiful tree, a willow,' Eddie said conversationally, sawing at his chop as if Charlie wasn't speaking.

'What? Yes, Dad. Yes, it is. Anyway. So they don't have anywhere to stay, so . . .'

Lilian felt very, very weary. Wearier, perhaps, than she'd ever felt in her life. 'No, Charlie,' she said quietly, guessing where this was going. 'Whatever you're about to ask, the answer is no. We've got too much on.'

He gaped at her. 'But – wait, I haven't . . .'

'Of course, a hazel tree is very nice too,' Eddie went on. He was staring into space, lost in thought.

Lilian reached out and patted his arm. 'All right, love,' she said gently.

Charlie eyed his father. 'Dad, are you even listening to me?' He sounded annoyed. 'What did you do to your hand anyway?' he added after a moment.

'Leave your dad alone,' Lilian said. David and Emma were both looking at Eddie in concern now too, she noticed, and a hot defensive wave of feeling swelled in her. 'He's fine.' The words came out with more vehemence than she intended.

Luckily Eddie seemed to come back to earth just then, the fog clearing suddenly, and he chuckled. 'Of course I'm fine,' he said, sounding himself again. He did this quite often; seesawing between normality and this other confused state, often with unnerving speed. 'Just a scratch. You know what your mum's like for fussing over me.' He gave her an indulgent wink, as if they were in on a secret together.

She smiled back, despite the slow churn of despair that hadn't let up for weeks now. He was worth fussing over, her Eddie, after all.

'So anyway,' Charlie went on doggedly, 'I was wondering...'

David put up a hand. 'Charlie, mate,' he said. 'Maybe not now, yeah?'

Charlie's eyes glittered: a danger sign that he was feeling combative. He'd always been one for explosive tantrums as a boy, could never bear not getting his own way. 'Look,' he said, straightening up in his chair, 'I wouldn't ask unless it was a desperate situation. Mum, Dad – don't you see? She's got nowhere to live. Her ex-husband – her *violent* ex-husband – has just died in a car crash. The poor girls are traumatized, she's injured, she physically can't get up to her flat without a lot of pain and difficulty. All I'm suggesting is...'

'Bloody hell!' Emma cried. 'How awful!'

'We don't have room,' Lilian replied flatly. Good grief. It was like an episode of *Coronation Street*, listening to this tale of woe. Violence and death, trauma, injuries . . . she didn't want that lot under her roof, if that was what Charlie was angling for. She had enough to worry about, with Eddie's unpredictability. They were not a charity. 'We're booked up right over the Easter break. And the week after.'

He was smiling, one step ahead. 'Ah, but I'm not asking for a room here. I was thinking – if we got the holiday chalet finished, they could stay there. Self-contained, isn't it? And I'll be on hand to help them. I can do everything for her.' Nobody spoke. 'I *want* to do everything for her.'

Good Lord, there was such stubbornness running right through the boy. Determined, that's what Charlie was. Well, at first anyway. He tended to peter out halfway through these grand plans of his, leaving a mess for somebody else to clear up. Not this time. though, son. She was going to have to put her foot down. 'I don't think—' she began.

'Please,' he said. '*Please*, Mum. Just until she's back on her feet. You won't even know she's there. I really like her. I just want to help her. I'd put them up at my place, but there's not enough room. Please?'

Eddie cleared his throat. 'Sounds like she's had a rough time,' he said gruffly. 'What do you think, Lilian?'

'They've been staying with Alicia until now – the girls, I

mean,' Charlie rattled on, sensing he might have an ally at last. 'Good as gold, they are. No trouble.'

Lilian could feel the walls closing in on her. The argument was starting to wear her down. And while on another day she might have been able to dig her heels in fully and resist Charlie's barrage of pleas, today was not that day. Today she was tired and anxious and vulnerable. Today she just wanted to eat her dinner in peace and not be pressurized any more. 'Oh, all right,' she said ungraciously in the end. 'I suppose so.'

Charlie leapt up and kissed her. 'Thanks, Mum,' he said. 'Thanks, Dad. Listen . . . David, I don't suppose you'd be able to give me a hand getting the place finished tonight? With a bit of luck she'll be out of hospital tomorrow and I want it to be really nice for her.'

David rolled his eyes comically. 'Go on, then,' he said. 'Who am I to stand in the way of love's young dream? You don't mind, do you, Em?'

Mind? She looked like she might very well spit at the question. 'Of course not,' she muttered, not meeting his gaze. Her mouth twitched as if she was trying to control her feelings and then she drank the last of her wine in a single gulp. 'Why ever would I mind?'

After dinner Charlie and David vanished outside with paint pots, hammers, drills, the mop bucket and Eddie's toolbox.

Emma went out to help for a while, but came sulkily back, claiming that they'd told her they didn't need her.

'Man's work, eh?' Eddie said jovially, putting on the television in time for *Casualty*.

Lilian was sure she heard a growl under Emma's breath as she helped herself to another drink and sat at the far end of the sofa, feet tucked under her like a cat, but she made no comment.

The programme began and Lilian tried to concentrate. She and Eddie never missed an episode, but tonight she was finding it difficult to follow the plot. Her thoughts kept skewing back to the conversation over dinner, and the way Charlie had steamrollered blithely over her in order to get what he wanted. Typical. He didn't even seem to have noticed that his father wasn't himself. Didn't care how tired or overworked they were – that clearly didn't matter. And now this Izzy woman had turned his head, and the whole family was expected to fall in with his wishes!

'Honestly,' she muttered crossly. Emma shot her a look before pouring herself another large glass of wine, but Eddie was glued to the television and oblivious. Lilian wished Emma would go somewhere else so that she could have a good moan to her husband about Charlie's thoughtlessness. She just wanted someone to tell her, 'It'll be all right', and for her to believe it. Was that too much to ask?

The programme finished – goodness, she'd barely noticed

what was happening tonight – and Eddie flicked off the television with the remote. Then he leaned back on the sofa and put his hands behind his head. 'Be nice to have a couple of kiddies about the place,' he said, to nobody in particular.

Lilian thought he was referring to the guests they had booked in for Monday, until she realized he meant Izzy's girls. 'Hmmm,' she muttered darkly.

'And that Izzy our Charlie's so keen on, she seemed a friendly sort of lass, didn't she?' he commented.

Lilian gritted her teeth. 'Goodness knows how she's managed to wheedle Charlie into *this*,' she huffed, getting out her knitting. 'Sounds like trouble to me.'

Emma – who appeared to have polished off most of the bottle of wine – made a scoffing sort of noise. 'Nobody's good enough for Charlie, are they?' she said cattily.

Lilian narrowed her eyes. 'And what do you mean by that?' she asked. Try it on with me, love, and you'll get it right back, she thought. Just you dare!

'I *mean*,' Emma slurred, 'nobody's good enough for your precious sons, are they? Kate bloody Middleton wouldn't have been good enough!'

Eddie, to her annoyance, merely raised an eyebrow, but Lilian gripped her knitting needles so hard her knuckles blanched. 'I beg your pardon?' she said in her iciest tones.

'You've never been nice to me,' Emma stated, 'you treat Alicia like some kind of skivvy, and now you're writing off

Izzy before you've even bothered getting to know her.' She leaned forward, pointing a finger, like a spiteful, drunk harpy. 'What's your problem, eh? Why can't you give us a break?'

The nerve of the girl, it almost took Lilian's breath away. 'How *dare* you!' she managed to say. 'I've never heard so much rubbish in my life.'

'Now then,' Eddie said mildly. 'Let's not argue. More wine, anyone?'

'All I ever wanted,' Emma went on, 'was to love your son. All I have tried to do is make him happy, to be his best friend, his wife. Is that such a terrible crime?'

Lilian opened her mouth to answer, but didn't get a chance. Emma ploughed straight on. 'How do you think it makes me feel, coming here, when you're always so unfriendly to me, so rude? Every single bloody time there's some dig, some nasty little remark. Thank God you've stopped asking when we're going to have a baby. Because — hello! Newsflash! — we've been trying and trying for a baby for nearly a year. And guess what? We're finding it really hard, actually. If you're interested. If you care!'

Lilian felt winded. 'I—' she began, but Emma was still in full flow.

'I would love to be a mother. I am desperate to be a mother. I am trying my bloody hardest to get pregnant so that I can be a mother. And I've also been trying to help

David get his life back together again. Okay? So don't you dare look down your nose at me any more. Because all I've done is love your son the best I can.' She was breathing hard. 'Your boys might think you are the most perfect mum ever, but I'll tell you something, you're a bloody rotten mother-in-law. The worst!'

'Now come on, that's a bit harsh,' Eddie said, just as David came striding into the room.

'What the hell's going on?' he asked, looking from Emma to Lilian. 'What's all the shouting about?'

'Your *wife* is just telling me what a dreadful mother-in-law I am,' Lilian said sharply, trying not to show the wound Emma had caused. Her hands shook so violently that the knitting needles clicked against each other like chattering teeth; she was reeling from Emma's rant. Each word had been spat out with sheer hatred.

'*What?*' David looked incredulous. He turned to Emma. 'What have you said? What's happened?'

Emma's face crumpled and she got up, swaying. 'That's right, take her side as always,' she shouted. 'I knew you would!'

'I'm not taking anyone's side,' he replied. 'Not until I know what's been said.'

'Forget it,' Emma spat. 'Just forget it!' And she pushed past him and out of the room, the door banging behind her.

Still stunned, Lilian clutched at her necklace, gripping it

so hard that the string broke and a hundred small blue beads bounced down to the carpet, rolling everywhere. 'Oh no,' she cried, the words becoming a sob. She had never felt so attacked, so demonized. And in her own home too!

'Oh, Mum,' David said, coming over and putting an arm around her. 'I'm sorry for her behaviour. She's . . . I'm sure she didn't mean it.'

She didn't reply. What was the point? Because Emma *had* meant it, every stinging word of vitriol, that much was obvious. The way the diatribe had poured out of her with such ferocity, she had clearly been storing those words up, unsaid, for a long time.

Lilian rubbed her eyes. A rotten mother-in-law, Emma had called her. The worst. She wasn't that bad, was she? *Was* she?

Chapter Twenty-Four

Emma flung herself onto the bed and wept angry tears into the pillow, images of burning bridges flaming in her mind. She'd really gone and done it now; blown the situation sky-high with a heady combination of wine and pent-up frustration.

Wrapping her arms around herself, she cried and cried; emotions breaking over her like waves on a sea wall. *Stupid, stupid woman*, she raged. David would never forgive her for this. Never in a million years!

Eventually, when she was all cried out, she lay numbly on the lumpy eiderdown, gazing up at the shadowy ceiling. An owl hooted softly outside and the wind moaned around the chimneys. In the next room she could hear the couple who were staying — the burble of their television, the low murmur of their voices, occasional muffled laughter — and the sounds seemed to mock her. It seemed an age since she and David had done anything as ordinary and domestic as watch television in quiet togetherness. He hadn't even bothered to come and see if she was all right. No doubt he was too busy comforting his mum, mopping up those crocodile tears. She'd walked right into Lilian's hands this time.

Oh, Emma, she groaned to herself, pulling on her night things and washing her face in the tiny en suite. *You and your big mouth.* All those angry words that had boiled up out of her.

But really . . . who could blame her for cracking? Friends of hers had long said how amazed they were that she'd lasted this long without retaliating to Lilian's jibes. Sally had actually called her a saint at their wedding, when Lilian had a face on her more appropriate to attending her son's funeral than marriage to his beloved. Frankly, she *had* been a saint the whole time they'd been together, ignoring the snide remarks, slapping on that brave face for the umpteenth time when asked yet again when she was going to give David a baby.

Still . . . She found herself squirming uneasily as her own words came back to mock her. She might have talked the talk about loving David as best she could just now, but really . . . had she? Did she? When she thought of her recent behaviour with Greg and Nicholas, she couldn't justify the statement with any sincerity.

She spat out her toothpaste, rinsed the brush and met her gaze in the bathroom mirror. There were secrets locked away in her eyes; she looked shifty, not to be trusted.

Maybe she wasn't such a saint after all.

*

The next morning Emma woke early to find David's sleeping body next to her, his back decidedly turned against hers, even in sleep. She shut her eyes again, feeling hungover and tired, before deciding that she simply couldn't face the repercussions today. Instead she'd take the coward's way out, skulk downstairs without another word, jump in the car and just go.

Cooling-off time, that was what they needed. Space to think about what, exactly, they both wanted – and whether or not it was each other any more.

Bloody hell. How had things become so precarious that she was now sliding gingerly out of bed, washing and dressing in silence and scooping up all her belongings? It was hardly the sign of a happy marriage. She imagined the couple next door spooned dreamily against one another's warm, slumbering bodies and tears sprang to her eyes.

She cast a last glance over her sleeping husband, slightly sickened at what she was about to do. *Lame, Em. Not very wifely.*

Well, duh, she thought defensively. He hadn't exactly been very husbandly lately, had he? Moving out, refusing to make plans for the future with her . . . The pair of them might as well be strangers.

She pulled the door gently to and crept downstairs. The house was still – it was only just past six o'clock. She knew that Lilian didn't open the breakfast room for guests until seven-thirty on a Sunday, so she had plenty of time to make her escape. In fact, she'd have time for the quickest of coffees, she decided, setting her bag quietly down in the hall. A shot of caffeine might go some way towards stripping away one layer of her hangover, too.

But as she padded into the kitchen she froze in horror at the unwelcome sight of Lilian already at the table with a bowl of porridge. Damn. Emma's armour and pride crumbled instantly, leaving her vulnerable, caught off-guard in enemy territory. Worse, she'd been spotted, so she couldn't just turn and flee, however desperately she wanted to.

Lilian's face was impassive. 'Good morning,' she said.

Emma hovered in the doorway. No, she simply could not go in and make coffee now. She couldn't take another step towards her nemesis; she felt physically repelled, as if they were clashing magnetic forces. 'Morning,' she muttered. 'I'm just heading off actually, so——'

'Wait,' Lilian said quickly. 'Emma . . . please. I'm glad I caught you. I wanted to . . .' She cleared her throat, almost swallowing the next word. 'Apologize.'

Emma blinked. Hold on a minute. Was she still dreaming?

'Sit down,' Lilian said, motioning towards the table. Her hands flew back to her lap and she twisted her fingers, uncharacteristically nervous. 'There's coffee in the pot, if you want some.'

'Listen, about last night . . .' Emma began hesitantly, not moving.

Lilian waved a hand. 'You were right.'

Emma stared, not convinced she'd heard her mother-in-law correctly. She wasn't sure the phrase 'You were right' had ever come out of those thin lips before, especially not addressed to her.

'Please,' Lilian said. 'Sit down.'

Still wary – was this a trick? – Emma lowered herself cautiously into a seat. Now what?

'You were right,' Lilian said again, pouring her a mug of coffee. 'I haven't been the most welcoming mother-in-law in the world.' She gave a short, brittle-sounding laugh. 'I know I've been overprotective of the boys. David especially. But you see . . .' Her mouth twisted. 'That's my job. It's always been my job. And it's hard to let go.'

Emma said nothing. *It's not your job to be a bitch, though*, she thought.

'I've been unfair to you,' her mother-in-law went on, her gaze unflinching. 'Things have been tricky here. Eddie's not himself. You've seen how he is. I'm worried he's got . . .' It was obvious she could hardly bring herself to say the words. 'Alzheimer's, or some kind of dementia.' She bowed her head. 'I'm terrified, Emma.'

For the first time ever, Emma felt a stab of sympathy for her. It was true, Eddie had been acting oddly the last few times she'd been down. 'Must be worrying,' she said tentatively.

Lilian's eyes were wet. 'I just don't know what to do,' she said quietly. 'And I've let myself lean on David and keep him here longer than I should have done.' She reached into her pocket for a tissue and blew her nose. 'I knew it was wrong, but it helped, having someone else here with me. I felt so alone before. And he's a good lad. I put him in a difficult position and he's just been trying to support me, that's all.'

'It's fine,' Emma said, because suddenly it was. There she'd been all this time, thinking David had stayed away because he didn't want her or a baby, when this whole other drama had been unfolding in the background. 'Really, Lilian. I didn't realize what was going on; he hadn't told me.'

The central heating suddenly came to life; a flame leapt in the boiler behind them and it rumbled gently in the background. 'But, Emma, I've got to say, while David's been staying here I've seen how much he's missed you, and how much he loves you. It's taken me a long time, but I do believe that you are good for each other.' She gave a small smile. 'I should have recognized it much earlier of course, but I'm a stubborn old woman. And I'm sorry.'

Emma swallowed. Of all the times her mother-in-law could have made this peace-offering, of all the times she could have said these words, she'd picked the very moment when Emma herself was having massive doubts about her future with David. 'Thank you,' she murmured. But the omission throbbed inside her, and she couldn't be dishonest.

'Although actually,' she blurted out, 'I'm not so sure that's true these days – that we're good for each other, I mean. I don't know if we still are.' Her gaze drifted to a framed photo on the wall of David as a boy, holding a fish and beaming gappily. He looked so happy, she thought with a pang. 'Since he's been here, I feel like I've lost him. I don't know what he wants any more – and if he even wants me.'

Ugh, Emma Jones, what are you doing? She felt sick for showing her hand with such frankness, to her old enemy of all people. 'I should probably just go,' she added, rising to her feet.

Lilian put a hand on hers. 'Don't go,' she said.

Emma looked helplessly at the gnarled fingers on hers, the dull silver gleam of Lilian's wedding band, and sank back onto the seat. 'Things have become so strange between us,' she admitted after a moment. 'I felt jealous, as if he'd chosen you over me. And lonely, too. I just want him home. I've been so desperate to get pregnant, Lilian.' She rubbed her eyes, feeling self-conscious. 'I must sound like I'm mad.'

Lilian patted her arm. 'Not to me, you don't,' she said. 'I remember that desperation myself. After David was born, there were complications. I was ill for a while and they said

I might not be able to have any more children. It was the worst kind of pain, like a terrible hunger gnawing away at me inside.'

'Yes,' said Emma. 'That's how I feel.'

'I was so desperate for another baby that we looked into adoption,' Lilian went on. 'I just knew our family wasn't complete. Eddie wanted a girl, and we'd been approved by the adoption agency and were on their waiting list, when two weeks later I discovered I was carrying Charlie. Our little miracle.'

There was silence for a moment while Lilian topped up their coffee. 'Probably just as well we didn't have a daughter, I've often thought. I've not been very good at having daughters-in-law, let alone the real thing.'

'Oh, but . . .' Emma started, feeling obliged to argue the point. This was her cue to say, *Don't be silly, Lilian, you've been a wonderful mother-in-law!*, but they both knew it wouldn't be true.

'It's all right,' Lilian went on. 'You don't have to be polite. I really need to cut those apron strings once and for all, don't I?'

Emma smiled. 'I've got some scissors you can borrow,' she ventured.

Lilian smiled too. 'You know,' she said, 'I think David has been hiding down here because he's afraid to face up to the future and find a new job. He's always hated losing face, even as a boy. He couldn't bear it when Charlie learned to ride a bike before he did.' She sighed. 'I should have done what I did back then – told him to get back on the bike and keep trying. Instead, I put my head in the sand too. I've kept him here for selfish reasons.'

It was quite a speech. 'Oh, Lilian . . .' Emma began.

'I'm sorry,' Lilian said again. 'I'll send him back to Bristol, to you. I need to face facts just as much as he does, and you need him more than me.'

'Thank you,' Emma said faintly, not quite able to believe how this conversation had turned out.

'You'll sort things out, I know you will,' Lilian went on. 'And if a baby doesn't come naturally, well, it's not the end of the world, Emma. Adoption can be just as wonderful. You can have a family yet, you know.' She sipped her coffee. 'Don't give up, that's all I'm saying. Not without a damn good fight.'

There were tears in Emma's eyes all of a sudden. 'Don't worry,' she promised. 'I won't.'

Chapter Twenty-Five

You had to hand it to Charlie: once he got an idea into his head there was no stopping him. As soon as the doctors said Izzy was ready to leave hospital, he turned up in the ward, breezily announcing his plan, as if that was that – got it, okay?

Thankfully, Alicia had already forewarned Izzy, laying it on good and thick that she *did* have options, whatever Charlie might say, and she was absolutely welcome to stay with her and Hugh for as long as she wanted. It was a hard choice, though. Could she really trust Charlie not to let her down? Could he seriously guarantee that he'd be able to take the girls to school every morning, along with the great list of other things he'd assured her he'd do? That was the fulcrum on which her entire decision rested: the reliability of Charlie Jones. Izzy wasn't used to relying on anyone for anything, had deliberately trained herself not to be dependent. Unfortunately, she just wasn't confident that Charlie's glib words were enough.

Obviously, she wished they were. How easy life would be if, for example, she could lean on him for support without a second thought, allow him to help her with everything. But she was used to fighting her own battles, and self-preservation was too deeply ingrained in her, etched into her very bones. Everything she'd heard about Charlie in the past told her to just say *No, thank you, we can manage,* and walk briskly away. Well, hobble slowly away on her new crutches anyway.

He was a difficult person to say no to, though. 'Look, just give it a go,' he kept urging. 'If it turns out you're not keen, or you change your mind, we can sort out somewhere else. I'm not asking you to sign a six-month contract or anything. I won't dump you in the nearest gutter if it doesn't work out.'

It was the thought of having their own place, just her and the girls, that swung the decision in the end. Although staying at Alicia's would have been fine, she knew the three of them were fragile right now. They might not be up to boisterous family dinner times or cheery conversations 24/7. She, for one, was looking forward to being on her own again and just having an enormous, no-holds-barred cry — one that wouldn't depress the other patients in the ward or send a nurse rushing round to comfort her. She didn't want *anyone* to feel they had to try and comfort her, she just wanted to let the grief pour out and release some of the pressure. Whether they realized it or not, the girls needed the same.

'Okay,' she said in the end. 'If you're one hundred per cent sure it's all right with your mum.'

'Leave her to me,' Charlie assured her. 'Besides, she's a pussycat really. I swear.'

Hmmm. Izzy had been prepared to suspend a little disbelief in order to trust Charlie's word, but calling his mum a pussycat was stretching it.

Anyway. Resistance was futile. Once the doctors and the physio were happy that she could get about okay on crutches, and had booked her in for a follow-up appointment at the fracture clinic for ten days' time, Izzy was free to go and hobbled down the corridor with Charlie.

Sitting in his car, watching through the window as he drove back towards Lyme, she felt as if a new page in her life was turning, a new chapter starting. Part one – her childhood – was long over. And now part two – married life with Gary – was almost closed, bar the funeral. Part three was about to begin, but she had no idea what it would bring.

Part three actually felt pretty Grimsville at first, she decided, later that afternoon once she and the girls were reunited. They clung to her, Hazel weeping, Willow silent, and Izzy was engulfed by the awful fear that she wasn't strong enough, that she simply wouldn't be able to cope. *I can't do this, I can't do this*, she thought, frightened by her own doubts.

'They've been such stars,' Alicia said, holding a box of clean linen and food that she'd put together for Izzy. 'And they're welcome to stay again any time – as are you too, okay? Any time.'

Izzy wanted to weep herself at the kindness Alicia had shown. She was the nicest person Izzy had ever met; the best mother, the most thoughtful friend. 'I gather you had to delay Paris because of me,' she said, her voice wobbling. 'I am so sorry about that. I feel terrible, Alicia.'

'It's fine,' Alicia said bravely, although you could see the disappointment was still there in her eyes. 'I can go another time – don't worry about it.'

Izzy hugged her. 'I'll make it up to you,' she promised. 'I mean it – I owe you big time, and I'll make it up to you, just as soon as I'm back in action.'

'Don't be daft,' Alicia said. 'Honestly. It's fine.'

'Let us know if you need anything,' said Alicia's husband, Hugh, as they went out to Charlie's car.

'You can borrow my Gwyneth Rees books if you like,' Matilda offered Hazel and Willow. Then she looked up at Izzy, winding one leg self-consciously around the other like an anxious flamingo. 'Will you still be teaching me ballet?'

Izzy bit her lip. 'Not immediately, sweetie, no,' she replied. Sore point. She didn't know what she'd be able to do to earn a crust, now that she was crocked. She wouldn't be able to work in the tea shop any more, either – imagine, hopping around on crutches while she carried teas and coffees to the tables; she'd be the stuff of Health and Safety nightmares – but she had to support her little family somehow.

In her darkest moments she had wondered miserably whether the girls would be better off in care, now that she was jobless, broke and destitute. If they could be farmed out to a loving, rich foster family who'd give them ponies and a bedroom each, surely they'd be ten times better off . . .

She'd had to shake the image away, slap herself with a major reality check. Families like that were few and far between, the stuff of *Annie* and care-home mythology. She'd certainly never come across her own Daddy and Mummy Warbucks when she'd been stuck in the system.

Don't go there, Isabel, she ordered herself. *You're not done yet.*

Charlie drove them to the flat so that the girls could pick up anything they wanted from their bedrooms, but Izzy didn't feel she could manage all the steps safely, so she stayed in the car. It was strange being back, unnerving even. She couldn't help thinking about the last morning she'd left, glancing over her shoulders as she took the girls to school, terrified that Gary would come after them. It seemed so long ago, completely out of reach now. Everything had changed.

Once the girls were loaded up with every precious felt-tip and bangle that was required, and Charlie had carried down the small TV, everyone's pillows and a collection of pot plants that appeared to be in their death-throes, they set off once again to the house in Loveday. The whole day was starting to feel like a strange dream.

Mulberry House had a number of cars parked outside it when they arrived, and Charlie's brother David came out to help carry their belongings through to their temporary new residence. The chalet was down at the bottom of the garden, almost hidden from view behind a large spreading beech tree. 'Ta-da!' cried Charlie as he unlocked the door and showed them in. 'So what do you think?'

Hazel entered first, followed by Izzy, awkwardly on her crutches, with Willow hanging back. What did she think? Her first impressions were ones of pleasant surprise. She'd felt so flat recently that she had pessimistically envisaged their new home to be a shed in Charlie's parents' back garden, the way he'd described it.

Instead, what had once been some kind of outbuilding was now a sweet little two-bedroom chalet, complete with dinky loo and shower, with a small kitchen and living space at the front. It was all on one level (a godsend to a person getting used to crutches) and had been freshly decorated, plastered and tiled — you could still smell the paint.

The kitchen was small and plain, with four sets of white crockery and some cutlery on the spotless work surface. The living area was more homely, with a comfortable-looking red sofa (Hazel immediately threw herself onto it), a rug, a vase of flowers and a couple of well-thumbed novels on a window-ledge.

She realized she'd been holding her breath and let it all out in a rush. 'It's great,' she said, sagging on her crutches with relief. 'Oh, Charlie, it's perfect.'

'Brilliant,' Charlie said, sounding equally relieved. 'Budge over then and let me in with this telly. I'll set it up for you, shall I? Make myself useful.'

David followed with the box of essentials that Alicia had packed – tea, coffee, bread, butter, ham, cheese and a home-made fruit cake – and set it on the side in the kitchen. 'Thank you,' Izzy said faintly.

Once everything had been carried through, Charlie said he'd leave them in peace. 'I'll only be in the main house,' he said. 'Just find me if you want anything. I'll get us some fish and chips or a takeaway tonight so you don't need to cook, but if you write me a proper shopping list of what you need, I'll do you a supermarket trip tomorrow, okay?'

'Thank you,' she said again. 'Charlie – thank you. I can't believe you're doing all of this for us.'

He grinned, flushing with pleasure. 'I'm your friend, aren't I?' he said, shrugging off her thanks. 'Anyone would have done the same.' He stuck up a hand in goodbye to the girls and sauntered off up the garden, whistling.

Izzy sank carefully into the sofa, watching as he vanished

behind the beech tree, which was covered in new leaves. She could hear birds singing, there were irises and anemones in the flowerbeds closer to the house, and the air felt clean and good. A rope swing dangled from a branch of the beech tree, and there was glorious countryside all around. They would be safe here. They could start again.

Hazel snuggled up to her on the sofa, her thumb in her mouth. 'I like it here, Mummy,' she said, and those five small words were enough to dissolve some of the tension still in Izzy's battered body.

'I like it too, chick,' she said. 'But not as much as I like being with you two again. Me and my girls back together – it's the best feeling in the world.'

Willow came and cuddled into her other side, and Izzy sat with her arms around them both, counting her blessings. She was alive, her daughters were safe and they were reunited, thanks to the help of some kind new friends. It was a start. A really good start.

Not two minutes later, though, she heard a rustling sound and saw a figure approaching, at which point the tentative shoots of hope she'd felt promptly retracted and disappeared. Her heart sank as she recognized Charlie's mum marching towards them, pinny flapping and a determined look in her eye. Oh God. She should have known the brief moment of peace was too good to last.

Let me guess, she thought nervously. Charlie's only just

remembered to tell his parents that we're staying here. Now Mummy Dear's on the warpath, come to chuck us straight out again, while Charlie's been grounded for a week and has been sent to his bedroom with a smacked bottom. Great. Here comes the thunderstorm.

The door was still open, but Lilian paused on the threshold. 'Knock-knock,' she said.

'Come in,' Izzy said, struggling to heave herself up from the sofa with her crutches.

'No need to get up on my account,' Lilian said. She was holding a bottle of milk. 'Just thought you might need this.' She went into the kitchen, and Izzy heard her open the fridge door. Then she reappeared and hesitated for a moment before saying, 'Charlie told me what had happened, and you're very welcome here.'

Whoa. What the . . . ? Was there something wrong with her hearing? 'Th-thank you,' Izzy stuttered in surprise. 'Thanks so much, that's very kind.'

'No problem,' said Lilian briskly, and marched away again.

Izzy watched her go. 'Well, I never,' she murmured. So the old bag was human after all. Who knew?

The next few days were spent trying to finalize the funeral arrangements. It was an odd situation, sorting out a funeral for a man she'd been scared of, a man she'd stopped loving, but there was nobody else to do it. She couldn't just let the council dispose of him.

So she booked a service at the crematorium, broke the news to Lou and Ricky and asked them to pass on the date to their other friends, and phoned Gary's boss to let him know too. Gary had always hated his job and bitched about his colleagues, so Izzy was surprised when Gary's boss, Diane, broke into shocked sobs down the line. 'That's just tragic,' she said. 'He was so young. And he was on track for his sales targets for the quarter, too. I'm so sorry for your loss, love.'

Sorry. Everyone kept saying how sorry they were, as if they felt they had to apologize personally. Don't be sorry, she wanted to reply. Because I'm not. Not really anyway. It sounded awful, but in some ways Gary being dead was a relief. Did that make her a terrible person?

In the meantime, at least, the chalet at Mulberry House was proving to be something of a sanctuary, a place where Izzy could lie low and recharge her energy. Willow was still subdued, and Hazel kept drawing endless pictures of Gary with angel wings and a halo (hmmm), but despite the recent traumatic events, they were coping remarkably well on the whole. It was the Easter holidays, the sun was shining and they enjoyed having a big garden to play in, whether it was hide-and-seek, doing their best to scramble up the trees or spending hours one afternoon making a 'fairy house' in an unused corner – with fallen petals for rugs, a long white feather as a bed, moss for cushions, twigs shoved into the ground to make hat-stands, and a large round stone as a table.

Charlie was working most of the time, but his dad Eddie brought out a comfortable sun lounger for Izzy to relax on while the girls played, and David, who was helping him finish off one of the bedrooms in the main house, appeared at intervals with cups of tea, glasses of squash and plates of chocolate brownies or shiny red apples for them. Even Lilian put her head in the chalet door again and said in that same brisk tone that when Izzy wanted any washing doing, she just had to add it to the basket in the laundry room.

It was as if she'd walked into this ready-made family – the three-generational family she'd never had – and they'd folded her into their mix, accepting her without question. This was what a proper family felt like, she kept thinking dazedly. People helping each other, looking out for one another. Caring. She still half-expected to get her marching orders at any moment, to find that the doors had been closed to her and she was dumped back in the wilderness, but so far it hadn't happened.

On the Tuesday Lilian put her head round the chalet door again. 'Knock-knock,' she said.

Izzy was washing up in the tiny kitchen while the girls played tag outside. 'Come in,' she said, hoping that Lilian wasn't about to complain that they were too noisy and disturbing the guests. 'Um . . . can I make you a tea or coffee?' It felt rather as if the Queen herself had deigned to visit.

'No, thanks,' Lilian said. 'I was just wondering: would you and the girls like to join us for dinner this evening? Save you having to cook every night.'

Izzy stared in surprise before remembering her manners. 'Um . . . yes. Thank you, that would be lovely,' she said. 'Are you sure? I don't want to put you out.'

'Not at all,' Lilian replied. 'Is six-thirty all right?'

'Yes, that's fine. That's brilliant. Thank you.'

And then Lilian was gone, just as quickly as she'd arrived. Well, well, well. Invited in this time, then. That was a first.

By six-twenty-eight she and the girls were walking up towards the house. Willow and Hazel had never looked cleaner or smarter. Their hair shone dark and glossy, they were wearing their nicest dresses with clean white socks and school shoes, and all the mud and grass had been scrubbed from their fingernails and limbs in the titchy shower.

As they approached the house, Izzy could see through the window that the dining-room table had been set with gleaming wine glasses, and that Eddie was bringing in a stack of warm plates, smiling at some quip or other David had just made. Then her heart gave an unexpected thump as the younger man turned and she realized that it wasn't David after all. It was Charlie.

He spotted them approaching and his face broke into a smile. She'd hardly seen him over the last few days; he'd given them space just to unwind. She'd missed him, she realized, smiling back fondly. Life had felt duller, less interesting without his presence.

'Hello, Charlie!' Hazel shouted through the window, noticing him too and bouncing about Tiggerishly.

Willow held up her hand in a shy little wave. 'Oh, good,' she said. 'I like Charlie.'

Izzy squeezed her shoulder. 'Me too,' she said.

The house was beautiful from the front, but more haphazard from the back, with new bits built on here and there, the roof a patchwork of mismatched slates and some of the paint peeling around the higher windows. It had been well loved, though, she thought, as they went in through the back door and into a porch. You could tell this had been a happy family home for many years, before becoming a B&B, just from the fact that there were still some small wellies lined up under the shelf, and a row of pegs that once must have been the dumping ground for little coats and woolly hats. There was even an ancient cricket bat and ball. She must ask if the girls could have a go with it – well away from any windows, of course . . .

Charlie came into the hall to find them. 'Hello,' he said. 'Goodness, look at you two. What smart young ladies you are today!' His eyes crinkled as they met Izzy's. 'Your mum doesn't scrub up too badly, either,' he teased.

'Hi,' Izzy said, suddenly feeling as shy as Willow. Her mind flashed back to the awful scene that had ensued last time they'd been in this house, how she'd fled a mere ten minutes after arriving, vowing never to have anything to do with the rotten Jones family again.

'Come on through,' he said, holding out an arm and ushering them into the dining room. She could smell herbs and garlicky chicken, and felt weak with hunger. Proper food, cooked by somebody else. What a treat. 'Sit down,' he added. 'I'll just go and see if Mum wants a hand.'

The room was empty, apart from Izzy and the girls, and she hesitated for a moment, wondering if the family had particular places at the table and whether sitting in any old seat was going to be a terrible faux pas. Hazel was shifting from foot to foot. 'I need a wee,' she whispered urgently.

'Okay, let's find a loo,' she replied. 'Willow, do you want to stay here, or . . . ?'

'Come with you,' Willow said immediately.

'Okay,' Izzy said, hoping the nearest loo wasn't upstairs. She was still pretty slow on her crutches and hadn't dared tackle proper stairs yet. 'Come on, let's investigate.'

Back out they went and into the long hallway, moving

forward towards the front door now, past a reception desk with an old-fashioned brass hand-bell on its top. There was a large staircase on their right, and to her relief Izzy spotted a door built into the side of it. Cupboard or loo? She opened the door hesitantly . . . to see a small, spotless bathroom. 'There you are, Haze,' she said. 'We'll wait out here for you, okay?'

The front door was slightly ajar and the last rays of golden evening sun were shining through the gap, sending long, bright fingers of light onto the tiled floor. She arranged her crutches carefully so that she could lean against the wall, and dimly became aware of voices from outside. Male voices.

'So how was it on Saturday anyway? I didn't want to ring in case . . . well, you know. Anyone overheard.'

'It was . . . God, it was pretty amazing actually. We really clicked. I feel so much better for seeing her.'

It sounded like David and Hugh talking, but she didn't know their voices well enough to be certain. Then Hazel flushed the loo, so Izzy missed the next bit of conversation. Once the water finished rushing in the cistern, the second speaker said, 'I just don't know how I'm going to break it to Alicia, though. I mean – how can I tell her?'

Izzy's ears pricked up and she felt cold. Break what to Alicia? she wondered uneasily. What had happened?

There was a pause and then the first man said, 'I think

you're going to have to, mate. Emma saw you with her on Saturday, you know – at the petrol station, she said. I fobbed her off, don't worry, but chances are someone else will see you two together and...'

'Finished!' sang Hazel, unlocking the door and emerging. The voices fell silent immediately.

'Did you wash your hands?' Izzy asked distractedly, still tuned into the conversation she'd overheard. What was it that Hugh couldn't tell Alicia? Something about him being with another woman, by the sound of it. She grimaced. Please, no, she thought. Not Hugh. Husbands and other women never made for a good starting point.

'Yeeees,' Hazel said, just as David pushed the front door wider and stepped over the threshold, a couple of folders under one arm. He turned and waved at his brother.

'See you then,' he called.

He smiled briefly at Izzy as he went past and dumped the folders on the reception desk. She found herself blushing for having eavesdropped. 'Come on, girls,' she said quickly. 'Let's go back to the dining room. Smells like dinner's about ready.'

She led them back, wondering and worrying. She hadn't known Alicia long, but anyone could tell she was the married-for-life type, someone whose family meant everything to her. If Hugh had been doing the dirty on her . . .

Ugh. Izzy couldn't bear to imagine how her friend might react. Her whole world would cave in.

Her dilemma now was, having overheard the snippet of conversation, should she report back faithfully to Alicia, or was it kinder to keep it to herself?

It was hard to decide anything with the funeral looming at the end of the week, though. Lou and Ricky were travelling down, plus another couple they'd been friends with, Jane and Liam. When the day came, Charlie drove them to the crematorium in Chard. 'Do you want me to come in too?' he asked when they pulled into the car park. 'Bit of moral support?'

'No,' she said. 'But thanks. I might need some support later on, though. The kind that comes in a glass.'

The service before Gary's had attracted a large crowd of black-clad mourners, many openly weeping and clutching at each other for comfort. A whole florist's worth of bouquets were laid out in the display area, along with poignant notes: *A wonderful mother and friend. Goodbye, Grandma xxx. For Vera, sadly missed.*

In contrast, Gary's send-off was a much smaller affair; his life less celebrated. Fewer people and just one bunch of flowers: *From everyone at Little's Insurance, with best wishes.* Despite her complicated feelings for him, it gave Izzy a pain inside.

She'd loved him once, after all, before everything went wrong. The dispassionate way in which the rest of the world was letting his life slip by seemed an injustice.

The room where the service took place was echoey and spacious, and Izzy felt self-conscious, with only seven of them there, all on the first row of seats. Tears pricked her eyes, wondering what Hazel and Willow were making of this. It seemed wrong, somehow. Not enough.

Afterwards she and Lou embraced. 'So I take it you'll be up soon to clear out the flat?' Lou said. 'Would be lovely to see you properly.'

Izzy bit her lip. She hadn't actually thought about the practicalities of Gary's possessions, and what was left of her belongings in the Manchester flat. It would all need boxing up, and then she'd have to sell it, she supposed. She certainly didn't want to go back and live there any time soon. 'I guess so,' she replied heavily. It was not a job she was looking forward to, that was for sure.

'I'll help you,' Charlie said when she mentioned it on the way back to Mulberry House. She'd bowed out of putting on a wake – she didn't have the money for any kind of catering, for one thing. The others were going to find a pub nearby and drink to his memory, but she hadn't wanted to.

'Are you sure? What about work?' she replied. 'Isn't your boss getting fed up with all this time off you keep taking?'

'He's a mate,' he said. 'He understands. Besides, I don't want to work there forever anyway. I'm trying to convince my parents that I'm "mature and sensible enough" — he took his hands off the steering wheel to make quotation marks — 'to run the B&B when they retire.'

'Oh! Is that what you want to do?'

He nodded. 'I know it's sentimental, but I love that house. I don't want it to be sold to a load of strangers. But Mum and Dad think I'm too disorganized to take it over. They don't think I've got the staying power.' He grinned. 'Can't think why, when my career history has been so glittering so far!'

Izzy smiled faintly, just as Hazel, who'd valiantly kept it together all day, suddenly burst into noisy sobs in the back seat. 'I miss Daddy,' she cried. 'I still miss him. Am I going to feel sad forever and ever, Mummy?'

Izzy reached back and took her hand, her heart aching. 'No,' she promised. 'Not forever, my love. You'll always be a little bit sad, but soon you'll be able to feel happy about other things again. I promise.'

She stared unseeingly out of the window as Hazel hiccupped, tears still flowing. *Please God*, she thought fiercely. *Let that be true. We all need to feel some happiness again soon.*

Chapter Twenty-Six

Alicia had one single day left as a thirty-something. Less than twenty-four hours before the clock ticked that decade out with a terrifying finality. It was a weird feeling, as if she was standing at the docks, waiting for a ship to slowly pull away without her, never to return. *Goodbye, youth,* she kept thinking mournfully. *I never really made as much of you as I could have. And just as I've realized this, you're leaving me forever. I've only got the Dull Ship Forty on the horizon now, and the prospect of wrinkles, heavy-duty moisturizer and support stockings in its wake.*

'Don't be so melodramatic,' Sandra had snapped on the phone the night before. Her voice was odd, muffled as if she had a cold. 'For heaven's sake, Al. You should try counting your blessings for a change.'

Alicia was taken aback by the advice. Counting blessings? Not so long ago her sister had been prescribing counting orgasms and sexual adventures. 'I suppose,' she replied.

'You're so lucky,' Sandra said, a distinct sniffle in her

voice now. 'You're so bloody lucky, and you don't even frigging realize it!'

Oh. Okay. So perhaps it wasn't just a cold. 'Is everything all right?' Alicia asked cautiously. Sandra was the kind of person who bit your hand off if you dared make her feel vulnerable.

Now came a definite sob. Bloody hell. Sandra never cried. She'd sooner punch a wall, or an unlucky bystander, rather than let actual tears rain from her eyes. 'What is it?' Alicia asked in alarm.

'Ohhh . . . Just men,' came the reply. 'Fucking bastard shitty MEN!'

Alicia flinched, hearing the soft thump of fist meeting pillow. At least she hoped it was a pillow and not some poor unsuspecting bloke that her sister had trussed up on her sofa. 'What happened?'

'Matt decided he wanted to stay with boring fucking Penny, his boring fucking wife, that's what. The lying shitball. The tossing great tosser!'

Another broken sob. Alicia couldn't bear it. Despite a sneaking sympathy for boring fucking Penny, she felt a ferocious surge of rage for tossing tosser Matt. 'Bastard,' she said sympathetically. 'After stringing you on for so long!'

'Don't rub it in,' Sandra snarled. 'Two sodding years of promises, and it turns out they were all a crock of horse-shit. I hate him!'

Another muffled thump. 'Do you want me to come over?' Alicia asked.

Sandra gave an almighty sniff, the sort for which Alicia would have sharply scolded her own children had it come from their nostrils. 'Seriously?' she said, her voice softer. 'You'd do that?'

Alicia made some rapid calculations. It was a three-hour drive to Sandra's house in Cheltenham. It was eight in the evening now, she could be there by eleven. She'd have to arrange for Hugh to drop the children with friends the next morning, of course, so that he could go to work, but she could whizz back down the following day in time for lunchtime, say, to pick them all up . . .

It would all be a gigantic palaver, quite frankly, but then this was her sister. Alone. *Crying.* Punching random objects, by the sound of things. If ever there was an emergency, this was it. 'Of course,' she said. 'No problem.'

Sandra started weeping even more copiously. 'You're so nice,' she sobbed. 'I don't deserve you. You're so kind.'

'Nonsense,' Alicia said bracingly. 'You'd do the same for me, wouldn't you?'

There was a slight hesitation. They both knew Sandra wouldn't, any more than Alicia would ask it of her.

Sandra gave a snorting sort of laugh. Not a horrible one for a change, more the snotty, choking laugh that you sometimes manage even when crying. 'I wish I was like you,' she wailed.

Alicia thought there must be a fault on the line. 'What? You wish you were like *me*? Ha!' She shook her head. 'I wish I was more like *you*. More confident, more adventurous . . .'

Sandra sniffed again and Alicia only just managed not to suggest that she find a handkerchief. 'Well, don't,' she said. 'You really shouldn't wish that right now. You wouldn't wish this on your worst fucking enemy.' Her voice cracked. 'I'm a total mess, Alicia. Think yourself lucky that you're not me.'

'We're just different, that's all,' Alicia said gently. 'Now then. What can I bring for you? Wine? Chocolate? Some posh bubble bath?'

There came the sound of Sandra blowing her nose — thank goodness — and then she spoke. 'Listen. You don't need to come, Al. Seriously. It's a long way, and you've got stuff going on at home.'

'It's fine,' Alicia replied. 'Honestly. If you want me there, I'll—'

'No,' said Sandra. 'I'm not saying I don't want you here, but it's too much. Just talking to you like this is enough.'

'Are you sure? I don't mind—'

'I know you don't. And that's the most amazing, lovely

thing about you. You're so, so kind. And I love that you were willing to trek up the M5 in my hour of need – I absolutely love that. It makes me feel really . . . loved.'

Goodness. This was the most intense conversation Alicia had ever had with her sister. More intense, even, than the one when Sandra had stolen Alicia's first teenage boyfriend and Alicia had threatened to kill her, with her bare hands if necessary.

'You *are* loved,' she said quietly. 'Even if Matt, the wanker, is dumb enough not to stick around, there are other people who will.'

'Thank you,' Sandra said. Then she chuckled. 'I'm loving hearing you slag him off, by the way. Swearing and everything. You really hate him!'

Alicia smiled. 'Too right I do. The shitty wanky bastard motherfucker!'

'MUMMY!' came a shocked voice just then, and Alicia whirled around to see Rafferty standing there in his pyjamas, staring at her, his eyes as round as ten-pence pieces.

Sandra, who had obviously heard this, burst into fits of laughter, and then, before Alicia could stop herself, she was laughing too. Great gales of laughter from deep in her belly. 'Oops,' she giggled, as Raff vanished. 'Lucas, guess *what*?' she heard him call in glee.

'I'd better go,' Sandra gurgled. 'Leave you to explain that one. Good luck.'

'Are you going to be okay? Ring me back later if you want to chat.'

'I'll be fine,' Sandra said. 'You know me. I'll be over it tomorrow.'

'You will,' Alicia agreed. 'Take care of yourself, then.'

'Yeah, And thanks, Al. For being there. I appreciate it.'

So, as Sandra had suggested, she was counting her blessings. Grateful for the children. Grateful for Hugh. Bless him, he'd fabricated this whole story about going to the gym, just so that he could go shopping for birthday presents for her. Originally he'd arranged for Lilian to look after the children while she was in Paris, so that he could go shopping alone, he explained. The pleasure of discovering that he'd been so thoughtful swelled inside her. What on earth had he bought for her? she wondered excitedly. It definitely wasn't a Marks and Spencer jumper this year, if he was going to such trouble.

'You could have just *said* you were going shopping,' she'd laughed, delighted. To think she'd had her doubts about him! To think she'd gone in all guns blazing, ready to accuse him of playing away, of all things. 'Why didn't you just *say*?'

'I wanted it to be a surprise,' he'd said. 'Because you really are the most wonderful wife, Alicia. I honestly don't know what I've done to deserve you.'

His words touched her, reached right to her heart. 'He

looked as if he was about to cry,' she told Izzy when she went to visit her later that week. 'Seriously! Hugh doesn't normally do emotional, but he was all choked up, his voice sort of thick and gruff. *And* he brought me flowers the next day – for absolutely no reason!'

Izzy opened her mouth, then closed it again, as if changing her mind about what to say. She seemed a bit quiet but then she had just been to her ex-husband's funeral the day before. 'So . . . things are good between you, yeah?' she asked, turning a dandelion stalk between her fingers. It was a warm afternoon and they were sitting out on the lawn at Mulberry House, intermittently cheering and clapping as one of the children scored a rounder or made a good catch.

Alicia looked at her in surprise. 'Between me and Hugh? Yes, very good, thanks.' She leaned in conspiratorially. 'How about you and Charlie? It sounds as if you've really turned his head.'

Izzy wrinkled her nose. 'Do you reckon? He's hardly been anywhere near me since we moved in. I mean, he's been perfectly nice and polite, making sure we've got everything we need, and I'm massively grateful to him, but that's it.'

'Oh.' Alicia felt rude for having asked. 'Sorry. I just assumed . . .'

'Well, so did I, to be honest. I thought it would be game on. But I don't think he's interested.'

Alicia laughed. 'He's interested, don't worry,' she said. 'Charlie doesn't do anything for anyone unless—' She could have bitten her own tongue off; just stopped herself from saying 'Unless there's something in it for him', which made the arrangement seem tawdry, almost prostitute-like. 'Unless he really likes someone,' she said quickly instead.

'Hmmm,' said Izzy, and Alicia thought that perhaps she should leave the conversation there.

The night before Alicia's birthday Hugh and the children went up to wrap presents in the master bedroom – 'You must *not* come in, Mummy,' Matilda ordered, eyes gleaming at this role reversal – and she was left sitting idly on the sofa for once, flicking through the newspaper, feet propped up on the coffee table. She felt deliciously spoiled, imagining the children writing loving messages in their cards and carefully wrapping their gifts. Yes, all right, so the chances were they were actually fighting over the Sellotape and dashing off a brief 'Love X' in the cards before scurrying back to their far more interesting DS games, but you never knew. Miracles did happen, even in Dorset.

Then the phone rang. Sighing at the interruption – typical! – Alicia heaved herself off the sofa and went to pick it up. 'Hello?' she said.

There was an intake of breath down the line, a hesitation . . . and then the connection promptly went dead. 'Goodbye to you, too,' Alicia muttered, replacing the receiver on its base and thinking no more of it.

Ten minutes later the same thing happened. Down went the newspaper, and up she rose. 'Hello?' she said, this time with an edge to her voice.

Again, there was no answer, just the burr of the dial tone as the other person hung up. She frowned, wondering if it was a prank, teenagers messing about. But no – they were ex-directory, had been ever since she started teaching. Perhaps, then, it was one of the children's friends calling, struck dumb with shyness when an adult answered. Perhaps it was one of those spam calls that dialled ten numbers at once, and someone else had picked up first. Perhaps it was somebody who didn't want to speak to her, who'd been hoping a different person would answer...

No, she thought, returning briskly to the article she'd been reading about bloodshed in Syria. No more perhapses. It was probably nothing. A fault on the line.

All the same, when the phone rang again and Hugh happened to be back in the room, she gestured towards it. 'Would you get that, love? Whoever it is keeps hanging up on me.'

Hugh picked up the receiver. 'Hello?' he said. 'Yes?'

Alicia, watching intently, noticed his face change. He flicked a glance over to her, then turned his back, hunching over the receiver.

A feeling of dread gripped Alicia as he left the room. 'I see,' she heard him say in a polite, clipped voice. 'Just a minute.' And then he was gone, door shut, and she heard no more.

Doubts swirled blackly through her mind. Who was it who wanted to speak to her husband, but not to her? After a few minutes he re-entered the room, running a hand through his hair with what appeared to be faux casualness, and she all but pounced on him.

'Who was that?'

He didn't answer immediately, but went over and replaced the handset on its base. 'It was nothing,' he said eventually. 'Just Izzy, wondering what you wanted for your birthday.'

She narrowed her eyes while she processed this information. Well, then, she told herself. That must be it. He wouldn't lie about something that would be so damn easy for her to check, would he?

'So that was her earlier, was it, hanging up on me twice when I answered?' she persisted.

He was flicking through the TV guide, not looking at her. 'Must have been,' he said, shrugging. His defensive body language was enough to start warning bells ringing loud and shrill in Alicia's head.

Something was going on here. She didn't have a clue what it was, but something was definitely going on. Surely

Izzy wouldn't have hung up, even if she did want to talk in secret to Hugh. If it had been her, planning a mystery present for a friend, she'd at least have said hello to the friend and then asked if she could speak to the husband, rather than rudely hanging up without a word. You would, wouldn't you?

She stared at Hugh for a few moments, wondering how hard to push him. 'So did—' she began, but he was already speaking.

'Excellent,' he said, snatching up the remote. '*Panorama*'s just about to start.' And then he was turning on the TV, the title music was blaring and the moment had gone.

Gone but not forgotten. The phone call worried away at Alicia for the rest of the evening. She wondered about ringing Izzy back on some pretext or other, just to check Hugh's story was right. But that would be as good as saying that she didn't trust her husband, and of *course* she trusted him. Hugh was nothing if not trustworthy — always had been, always would be. It was one of the things she loved best about him.

Despite being a rational person, a lot of irrational thoughts kept bubbling up in her head, refusing to be popped. She remembered the deceit about his gym visit the weekend before. The frequency of his gym visits in the last month or so. The phone calls he would leave the room to take. Then she thought of Sandra, bitching about 'boring fucking Penny', and cringed. What if there was another woman madly in love with Hugh somewhere, moaning about 'boring fucking Alicia', just praying that their marriage would fall apart so that she could sweep in victorious to claim him?

No. Of course there wasn't another woman. She was just being silly. Tomorrow was her birthday, and any secrets would be revealed. Or so she hoped.

The next morning she woke to the sound of three children and a man singing tunelessly at the bottom of the bed. 'Happy birthday to you, happy birthday to you, happy birthday dear Mummy . . .' ('Aliciaaaaa,' sang Hugh), 'Happy birthday to you!'

'Breakfast in bed!' she said, struggling to sit upright as Hugh laid the tray carefully across her lap. 'Darlings, what a lovely surprise. Thank you!'

'I picked the flowers,' Matilda said, hopping from foot to foot. 'Do you like them?'

'Oh, forget-me-nots, yes, I love them,' Alicia said, pulling her in for a kiss. She was glad that someone had pulled some of them up, to be honest; they always went rampant across the flowerbeds at this time of year, a pale-blue army advancing in all directions.

'Here's your card, Mum,' Lucas said, leaping onto the bed and thrusting a yellow envelope under her nose. Goodness, he was getting so big these days, his limbs seeming to lengthen every day.

'Thank you, love,' she said, ruffling his shaggy blond hair. (It was so unfair that her boys had such lovely thick mops of hair, whereas Matilda's was fine and thin and could only make weedy little plaits.)

'You'll never guess what I've got you,' Rafferty said, pushing the present at her and almost knocking the flowers into the plate of scrambled eggs.

'I'd better open it and see, hadn't I?' she replied, beaming. 'I'm sure it's something lovely.' She was *forty*, she remembered with a jolt as she took a sip of coffee. This was it – new decade, ta-da!

She waited to pass out with the sheer horror of being so ancient, glanced at her hands to check if some enormous liver spots had sprung up there, patted her face in case it had shrivelled like a walnut overnight. No difference. She didn't even *feel* different, much to her surprise. In fact, she'd even say that she felt remarkably sanguine about being forty, after all that angst and dread.

So far, so jolly. She had the children beaming at her; flowers, breakfast, presents. Hugh . . . well, she'd think about Hugh later. *So up yours, forty*, she thought, with a burst of energy, ripping open the first card. She wouldn't let it stop her doing anything.

*

There was no school that day – still another blissful week of the Easter holidays to go – and Hugh had taken the day off work, so the present-unwrapping was a leisurely, unhurried affair. The children gave her chocolates, a book and a pretty vase between them. Sandra had sent a voucher for a massage and a bottle of perfume. Her parents, who lived on the Costa Brava, had posted a fuchsia-pink sundress (the sort of thing she'd never wear in a million years) and a matching feathery corsage. (Had they turned to mind-bending drugs in their old age? she wondered, as Lucas tried on the corsage, batting his eyelashes and simpering, and the children all fell about laughing.) A pair of dangly silver earrings and floral card had come from Lilian and Eddie, also signed by David and Charlie. Very nice, even if she didn't have pierced ears. Emma sent champagne and a card that sang 'Happy Birthday' when you opened it. There was a card from Izzy too, decorated with felt-tipped hearts and flowers, presumably by the girls. Inside was a message: *Sorry, I haven't been able to get you a proper present, but I'm making you a cake! Will send Charlie round with it on the big day. Have a brilliant one, you deserve it. Love Isabel.*

Alicia smiled, trying to blank out the fact that she was now sure Hugh had lied to her about the mystery phone call. *Don't go there*, she instructed herself. *Stay in happy birthday mode for a bit longer.* Now there was just one present left, and it was the biggest of them all, wrapped up in pink polka-dotted paper with an enormous white bow on the top.

'Happy birthday, love,' said Hugh, bringing it over to the bed. He looked tired, she noticed. Guilty conscience?

'Thank you,' she replied, becoming quite excited as she felt how heavy it was. 'Goodness, whatever is it? It's huge!'

'It's a——' Matilda started, but her brothers leapt on her at once.

'Shut up, idiot!'

'Don't tell her!'

'You'll just have to open it,' Hugh said. He was smiling, but it was stretched thin, as if he couldn't keep it on his face for much longer.

Alicia looked away. *Stop it*, she told herself. *Stop doubting him.* Her suspicions were polluting her birthday mood, tainting the happy feelings. But she was convinced he must have lied the night before. Why? What was going on?

She ripped off the wrapping paper . . . to see a large boxed KitchenAid mixer. 'Oh . . .' she said, lost for words. 'How lovely.'

'It's just like Nigella's,' Hugh said encouragingly. 'I remember you admiring it on one of her shows.'

'Yes,' she agreed, although she could remember no such thing. She couldn't help it – she was disappointed. Was this the big surprise? A bloody food mixer? So that she could spend even more time in the kitchen preparing meals for the ravenous hordes? *Wow, Hugh. You shouldn't have. Seriously – you shouldn't have, mate.*

348

She tried not to think what Sandra would say to such a present and found herself wishing, disloyally, that Hugh had tried a bit harder, that he'd actually chosen something that *wasn't* useful and practical, that didn't make her feel like a middle-aged housewife. 'Thank you,' she said again, trying not to think about glossy handbags or sparkling jewellery. 'Aren't I lucky?'

She *was* lucky, she told herself, as she went to run a scented bath. Remember Sandra, remember how upset she'd been, think about her turbulent life and remember that you're the lucky one who's got everything she could possibly want.

Other women would have been pleased with their KitchenAid. She *was* pleased with it. But she couldn't prevent a sinking feeling of dismay that that was all she was to Hugh these days: the little woman in the kitchen, who could be fobbed off with a shiny new contraption. It didn't seem enough any more.

She found herself thinking about Christine, as she always did on her birthday. *Happy birthday, Chris. Wish you were here. Would you have wanted a KitchenAid?*

Later that day the sun obliged by venturing out from behind the clouds, and they had a lovely walk around a nearby National Trust property with a picnic and the football. When they came home they found that Charlie had delivered Izzy's birthday cake – a fluffy Victoria sponge with edible silver glitter all over the top – and the second rendition of 'Happy Birthday' probably broke speed records as everyone was so desperate to tuck into a slice.

That evening, Hugh had – shock! – actually arranged a babysitter off his own bat, and – gasp! – booked a restaurant for dinner, and – no way! – ordered a cab to whisk them away at eight o'clock. This was more like it, Alicia thought approvingly as she clip-clopped out to the car in her nicest going-out dress (the scarlet one Sandra had all but forced her to buy from Gloucester Quays during a rare 'girls' day out'; the one she should have worn in Paris). Turning forty was all about being more sod-it, she decided, adding more make-up than she usually wore, then slipping on her one and only pair of high heels (terrifying). Yes, sod it, she'd wear scarlet; so what if it drew attention to her belly and bum. Yes, sod it, she'd splash on her new perfume, even though normally she'd eke it out over a whole year, one careful squirt at a time. She'd wear her heels too, even though she was likely to break her ankle or skin her knees, stumbling over in them. And yes, sod it, she'd damn well confront Hugh about what the hell was happening – birthday or no birthday, restaurant or no restaurant. Forty-year-old Alicia Jones wasn't about to take this lying down any more.

✻

The restaurant Hugh had picked was a good choice, if entirely predictable. She'd celebrated so many birthdays and anniversaries in Axminster's Grove Bistro that she could reel off the menu in her sleep. It was a small family-run place, with dusty candles rammed into Mateus rosé bottles on the tabletops, a laminated menu littered with spelling mistakes (the 'samlon fishcakes with tarter sauce' being Alicia's particular favourite) and the kind of yellow-varnished wood-panelled bar that wouldn't have been out of place in a skiing lodge. They were also playing Norah Jones. They *always* played Norah Jones.

Still. Who was she to turn her nose up? The food was perfectly decent, and the staff were friendly. And yes, all right, so perhaps steak-and-kidney pudding wasn't *everyone*'s idea of a romantic dinner – Hugh could never resist the slightest hint of suet on a menu – but it could have been worse; she might have had to make dinner herself (with the wretched KitchenAid!). At least Hugh had made an effort, getting them there at all, even if, for his fortieth, she'd pushed the boat out and taken them to a new French restaurant on the seafront in Lyme. (Okay, so it had given him food poisoning and he'd puked his guts up all night, but it had been memorable.)

The waiter handed them menus, but she didn't even bother reading hers. She knew already she'd have the 'smocked mackerrel' for starters and the 'chicken beast with white wine sauce'.

'Everything all right?' Hugh asked, leaning in towards her. They were sitting at 'their' table in the window, the one he always requested. She'd never bothered saying that actually she'd prefer to sit further into the restaurant, especially as she always seemed to end up nearest the front door and suffer its constant draught. She opened her mouth to say as much, then decided to choose her battles. Tonight was all about uncovering the secrets she knew he was keeping from her. Next time they came here – if there *was* a next time, she thought queasily – that would be the occasion to state her seating preferences.

'Fine,' she said, trying to get comfortable on the chair. She was sure they were the same chairs that had been here ever since they'd first come to this restaurant, twenty or so years ago. The velvet had inevitably faded and the padding wasn't what it was, after the imprint of so many thousands of bottoms. She sighed. 'Actually, Hugh—'

'Would you like to order something to drink?' The waiter was back in a cloud of Lynx and frying onions, pen and notepad at the ready.

'Ah yes, I think we'll have—' Hugh began.

Alicia couldn't help interrupting. It was her birthday, after all, and she'd just realized how much it irritated her, Hugh always taking control of the ordering. 'I'd like some fizz, I think,' she said, smiling at the waiter and then at Hugh. 'Not every day you turn forty after all, is it?'

'Absolutely,' Hugh said. 'I was just about to suggest—'

'Let's see . . . the Prosecco, please,' she said before he could suggest a single damn thing, almost breathless at her own daring. She never usually spoke over him like that. For all the years that she'd been his girlfriend and then wife, she'd been deferential when it came to matters like choosing wine or deciding where to sit in restaurants. Tonight she felt as fizzy as the Prosecco, no longer so acquiescent. *You go, girl*, she heard Sandra call in her head and imagined her shaking cheerleader pom-poms at her big sister's sudden spunkiness.

'Perfect,' Hugh agreed. 'Yes, we'll have the Prosecco, and a jug of tap water too, please. Thank you.'

'Very good, sir,' the waiter said, jotting it down. It was as if Alicia hadn't spoken.

'Thank you,' she made a point of saying. Hugh was looking at her oddly, as if he didn't recognize her. Fair enough. She wasn't sure if she recognized herself, sitting here in her flamboyant dress, taking the lead and talking over him, plumping for bubbly as if she was used to the high life. It was fun, though, being this confident new Alicia. Exciting.

The Prosecco arrived and the waiter poured them each a glass, then hovered expectantly. Usually Alicia waited for

Hugh to taste the wine and pronounce on it, but tonight she put hers to her lips and took a mouthful first. It was creamy and fizzing, sweet and celebratory. 'Delicious,' she told the waiter. 'Thank you very much.'

'So here's to you,' Hugh said, raising his glass, once they'd ordered their food and the waiter had left again. 'Forty years old. Happy birthday, darling.'

'Thank you,' she said, hoping he wasn't trying to put her back in her box with a reminder of her age. 'Forty years young, you mean,' she added with a laugh.

'Of course.'

'It's funny,' she went on with another large mouthful of her drink. (God, it was lovely. Worth breaking into a brand-new decade for the bubbly alone, in fact.) 'I do feel different – but in a good way.'

'I can tell,' he said.

'I feel . . . more assertive. More ballsy.'

He paled. She never usually said things like 'ballsy'. In fact, she never made any references, even oblique ones, to male genitalia, unless she was teaching an anatomy module in class. 'That's good,' he said, not sounding wholly convinced.

'It is,' she agreed. The alcohol buzzed through her, lending her courage. 'For instance, I'm just going to come out and ask you straight, because I deserve to know the truth. Are you cheating on me, Hugh?'

He choked on his wine and his eyes bulged. 'Alicia!' he

cried, then lowered his voice to an agitated hiss. 'What sort of question is *that*? In *public*?'

Oh, help. This wasn't looking good. This wasn't the instant denial she'd been hoping for. 'It's a simple question,' she said, drumming her fingers on the table. 'Yes or no. Have you been seeing another woman?'

His mouth fell open as if he wanted to speak, but then it snapped shut, seconds later. 'I . . . I . . .' he stammered.

'Tell me,' she ordered. 'Or, I swear to God, I will make a scene in here.'

'I . . . It's not what you think,' he said, stricken. His face had turned an interesting mix of blotchy red and white, whereas his eyes were large and frightened.

She leaned forward, tension crackling between them. 'Yes or no, Hugh. Yes or bloody no?'

'So, that's one smoked mackerel and one crispy duck salad,' the waiter said just then, having appeared unnoticed at the table. He set the plates down with a flourish. 'Enjoy!'

They ignored both him and the food. 'Well?' Alicia prompted icily. 'You were saying?'

Hugh's face had crumpled. She couldn't remember ever seeing him look so unhappy, not even when Badger, their Labrador, had been fatally hit by a short-sighted pensioner in a Fiat Panda back in January. 'I don't know if this is the best place to talk about it,' he said so quietly she had to lean forward to hear.

'Oh, I think it is,' Alicia said. She picked up her fork and stabbed the smoked mackerel, suddenly tired of the whole day. 'Just tell me. Spit it out. I'm all ears, Hugh.'

'I'm not having an affair,' he said in a small voice. 'And I'm not cheating on you.'

Good. Well, that cleared that up at least. *Phew*, she thought, with a dizzying wave of relief. *I should have known. I should have trusted him.*

Wait, though. He hadn't finished yet.

'But . . . I . . . I have been keeping something from you,' he said, his voice cracking.

She said nothing, merely posted a forkful of mackerel and granary toast into her mouth and chewed without tasting a thing. Her head swam with possible revelations, none of which she wanted to hear. *He's dying. He's lost his job. He's gay.*

He took a deep breath. His hands shook on his cutlery. 'I have another daughter,' he said.

Chapter Twenty-Seven

On Monday morning Emma entered the office warily, dreading having to meet Greg's eye after Friday night and his subsequent text. She still had only the haziest memories of what had happened and none of them were good. Never had a week-long sicky in the comfort of her own duvet been so damn tempting.

Greg was already at his desk, messing about on Facebook, by the look of things. 'Ah,' he said as she walked past. 'The woman herself.'

Oh God. She could hardly bear that teasing glint in his eye, the way his lips were already puckering with a smirk.

'Morning,' she said. Most of their colleagues hadn't yet arrived, she noticed. It was probably best to get this conversation over with as soon as possible. 'Can we have a word, please? In private.'

'I knew it,' he said, getting to his feet with a slow, almost unbearable insouciance. 'Jones wants my body and she wants it now. In the stationery cupboard then?'

She tried to smile and not appear too humourless or frigid. It wasn't easy. 'How about Tracey's office,' she countered, knowing that their boss wasn't due in for another half-hour.

'I'm all yours,' he replied, flashing her a grin as he held the door open for her. His teeth were white and sharp; she felt as if she was going for dinner with the Big Bad Wolf.

Once the door was closed, a strained silence descended.

'Listen,' she said, 'about Friday night.'

'I'm sorry,' he said with what might actually be sincerity. His laddishness had vanished, like a mask being removed. 'I was bang out of order.'

She hesitated. 'I think I was too,' she replied, 'but the problem is . . .' Oh hell – out with it. 'The problem is . . . I can't remember much of what happened. The last thing I remember is mucking about on the dance floor with you, getting into a bit of a . . . clinch . . . and then, being back home.' She swallowed. 'Nothing in between.'

He perched on Tracey's chair and swivelled to and fro. 'Was I really *that* bad that you've completely wiped me from your memory?'

A shudder went through her, and the egg she'd had for breakfast seemed to curdle in her stomach with bile. Shit. This sounded worse than she'd feared. A lot worse. What had she actually *done* with him?

He leaned forward. 'Don't worry, I *did* wear a condom,' he said in a low voice. 'I'm not that much of a prat. And if you're worried about STDs, then...'

She made a choking sound and shut her eyes, the words hitting her like fists. So she'd actually shagged him. She'd shagged Greg and she couldn't even remember!

'Then don't. I'm quite clean. Apart from the crabs, which are bloody persistent...' he went on. Then he laughed. 'For Christ's sake, I'm *joking*, Jones. I know it's Monday morning, but you look catatonic. Liven up!'

She opened her eyes again. 'You're joking?' she repeated cautiously.

'Of course I am. I got rid of the crabs ages ago,' he said.

'Greg...'

'Sorry. Couldn't resist. No — we didn't have sex. Okay? Feel better, now that you know you are unsullied by the Gregster?'

She bit her lip. 'Yes,' she replied, hanging her head. 'Better' was an understatement if ever she'd heard one. She hesitated. 'Sorry. I feel a complete fool for even asking this — and if it goes any further I swear on my life I will actually kill you — but Greg... what *did* happen? It's a total blank.' He paused for a split-second and she knew he was on the verge of inventing something absolutely heinous. 'Truthfully,' she put in.

He wrinkled his nose. 'Truthfully? I was pissed and got a bit lairy, that's all. I tried it on, okay? And I'm sorry. It won't happen again.'

She waited for the punchline, or the laugh as he added, *Not really – you were gagging for it.* Neither came.

'Okay,' she said, still not completely sure if she was off the hook.

'I mean, I know I'm God's gift to all things female – well, the human race, let's face it – but yeah, okay, I shouldn't have flirted. Damn that tequila!'

She smiled, relief sloshing through her. 'So . . . what: I just peeled off your clammy, molesting hands and sent you packing?'

'Well, you did punch me quite hard on the jaw . . . Joking. Nah, you said something like *No way, you were married; and what about Hester?* That sort of thing.' He pulled a face. 'Make me feel a total wanker, why don't you? Majorly guilt-trip a dude when he's trolleyed . . . ouch.'

Her heart felt light with happiness. 'Sorry for making you feel a wanker,' she said. 'Although, you know, the truth hurts . . .'

'I think you even wagged a finger at me,' he said, demonstrating. ' "I'm married, you know," ' he added in a prim voice, obviously meant to be her. ' "Even though my husband is being a total twat right now, I'm still married." '

A laugh spilled out of her. 'That's what I said?'

'That's what you said. Married bliss, eh? The pisshead and the twat.'

She laughed again. 'I should get that printed up as one of those strips to go across our car windscreen,' she said.

'I was thinking his and hers T-shirts,' he said. 'The perfect anniversary gift.' He got up and stuck out his hand. 'So are we cool, then? We're mates?'

'We're mates,' she said, stepping towards the door. 'Thanks for' – she was about to say 'filling me in', but it seemed inappropriate given the circumstances – 'enlightening me. All's well that ends well, yeah?' *And let's never get into this situation again*, she added in her head. *Ever.*

'Yeah,' he said, sheepish now. 'Um . . . I'd appreciate it if you could not mention this to Hester, by the way. Not that I ever thought you *would*, but . . . you know. She'd turn my ball-bag into a purse, if she ever found out I'd been unfaithful.'

Emma mimed zipping her lips. 'It's forgotten,' she said.

'Cheers,' Greg said, and loped out of the office.

She followed him thoughtfully. Part of her wanted to tell him off on behalf of Hester, make him feel bad for messing about behind his girlfriend's back. But in truth she was so overwhelmed by relief that she didn't have it in her. Even when pissed and offered temptation, she had said no to Greg. And she knew damn well that at the back of her drunken mind a klaxon would have sounded at the time, heralding a potential sperm donor in the vicinity. (She wasn't proud of this, not at all.) But even then she'd said no. 'No way, I'm married.' Thank *goodness*.

So that was one fly in the ointment dealt with at least. The situation with David wouldn't be quite as easy to resolve, though. Lilian had promised to send him back home, but he hadn't appeared so far. He hadn't even phoned. Maybe he didn't want to come back? Maybe he had chosen Dorset after all. She kept picking up her phone and selecting his number, then her finger would hover over the 'Call' button without quite managing to press it each time. What if the marriage was over?

Still, she had a distraction at least – the lunch date she'd arranged with Nicholas on Wednesday. Good work, Emma: swing from one uncertain relationship to another, why don't you? As Tuesday night and Wednesday morning ticked by she found herself becoming increasingly tense, but tried to ignore her multiplying doubts. Needs must, she kept reminding herself. This was closure in its purest form.

They had arranged to meet at the bar in Butlers, a smart, upmarket hotel in Clifton. She'd met clients there before, as there was a large sunny lounge room full of squishy armchairs, perfect for coffees and chat, with a bar set further back, and a restaurant even deeper into the building with views over Clifton Suspension Bridge. There were also, of course, rooms upstairs. Emma felt slightly sick, wondering if Nicholas had optimistically booked a bedroom for them as well as a table in the restaurant. A mistress for lunch, and his wife for dinner. He'd probably already done a nubile, adoring student before breakfast. Once a cheat, always a cheat – but hers for the taking, if that was what she wanted.

She took a deep breath as she stepped through the front door of the hotel. Not for the first time she wondered if she was losing the plot, coming to meet Nicholas at all. If she was any sort of proper wife, she'd walk straight out of there and get on the phone to her husband. Instead she smiled at the receptionist and kept going.

The lounge was full, as usual, with a mixture of business types poring over paperwork, elegant women surrounded by shopping bags gossiping over a pot of coffee, and a collection of yummy mummies with babies and toddlers in tow.

'Emma! Is that you?' came a voice, and she spun round. 'I *thought* it was,' said Sally, beaming. She got up from where she'd been sitting in the corner with the mummies, podgy curly-haired Violet in her arms.

'Sally!' It had been so long since she'd seen her friend, it didn't feel quite real at first. She'd been in her own private world all day, focused solely on meeting Nicholas. Now the two worlds had collided, and the effect was disorienting.

The two women hugged, and Emma stroked Violet's soft cheek, feeling the familiar twist of yearning. This was what it was all about, at the end of the day – a babe-in-arms. Her arms. 'Hello, beautiful,' she cooed. 'Look at you, haven't you grown!'

'She's just started walking,' Sally said proudly. 'Actually took her first steps at her party – she's always loved an audience, haven't you, sweetie?'

'Wow,' Emma said, feeling bad at the mention of Violet's party and the unspoken accompanying fact that she'd bailed out of attending. *If only you'd been there, you could have witnessed the event for yourself . . .* 'Very impressive, putting on a show for your guests,' she added. 'I can't *think* who she takes after.'

They both smiled and any background awkwardness melted away. Paul, Sally's husband, was the loudest, most gregarious man she'd ever met, a total show-off and party animal. He thought 'shy' was something you put coconuts on.

'So how are things?' Emma went on. 'We should catch up sometime.'

'We so should,' Sally said. 'It's been months. Hey, why don't you join us – we're having coffee.'

Emma shook her head. She could see over Sally's shoulder that one of the babies had just been sick over its mother's creased T-shirt. 'I can't,' she said. 'I'm meeting someone here for lunch.'

'Oh, right. Another time, then.'

'Another time,' she agreed. 'Anyway. I'd better—'

'Hey, I was just thinking about you actually. Total co-incidence. You'll never guess who walked in, not five minutes ago.'

I bet I can, Emma thought, her heart bucking. 'Who?'

'That disgusting old lecturer you used to have the hots for – well, I say *you* had the hots for him; we all did secretly, I think.' She laughed self-consciously and shifted Violet on her hip. 'Remember? Nicholas Something-or-other. Hasn't aged brilliantly, I must say – like Bill Nighy's older, wrinklier brother – but I would have recognized him anywhere.'

'Nicholas Larsson. Yeah.'

There was a pause and then Sally's face changed. 'That's who you're meeting?'

Emma nodded. 'Yeah.'

Violet started squirming and Sally put her down on the carpeted floor, almost unseeing. 'Emma . . . What's happening?' she asked. 'Tell me you're not . . . involved. With *him.* Are you?'

Emma bit her lip. 'I . . .'

'Because I remember how he chewed you up and spat you out last time,' Sally said, her voice becoming shrill. One of the shopping ladies glanced up in interest. 'I remember how devastated you were, how shitty he was. Please don't—'

'It's okay,' Emma said. She remembered with a stunning

bolt of clarity how she'd wept in Sally's arms back then, how her friends had plied her with gin and Double Deckers, how they'd been united in their chorus of 'What a bastard!' fervour. It had been so long since she'd had a cosy girlfriends' night, she realized in the next moment. They'd all moved on, got married, settled down. How had she let this friendship with Sally slip so badly since then?

'Really,' she added, because Sally was still looking at her doubtfully. 'I know what I'm doing.'

'Do you?'

Emma hesitated. Did she? A long moment passed and then slowly, numbly, she shook her head. 'I'm not sure,' she said hoarsely. She struggled to get back to the cocoon she'd been in earlier, the world where this meeting had seemed to make sense, but reality was hitting her like wave after wave of cold water. What *was* she doing, coming here to meet Nicholas on the sly?

'Why don't you sit down for a minute?' Sally asked, looking concerned. 'Why don't we talk this through together?'

Emma felt rooted to the ground. If she sat down and talked this through with Sally, she knew what Sally would say. And Sally would be right.

'I wish you'd phoned,' Sally went on, one hand on her arm. 'You could have told me you were having a difficult time.'

'Yeah.' Emma shrugged, not knowing what else to say. Why *hadn't* she phoned? Because she'd cut herself off from the real world, swotting up on baby websites like a loser, obsessing about the one doomed time she'd ever been pregnant – that was why. And also, in fairness, because Sally only ever seemed to be able to talk about sleepless nights and teething these days, which only made her feel more unhappy. Even now the conversation had broken off because Violet was suddenly crawling very quickly towards the shopping ladies' pile of bags, and Sally had to make a fast lunge to grab her, apologizing over the sound of her daughter's indignant squawks.

'Whoops,' she said, returning to Emma. 'Listen – what are you doing tonight? It's been months since we had a proper chat without Madam here interrupting. Shall I come over?'

'Oh *yes*,' Emma said, struck by how badly she wanted the company. 'Would you? I'd really love that.' She couldn't remember the last time Sally had suggested meeting in the evening; she'd pleaded tiredness practically since giving birth, suggesting they meet during the day instead, which meant Violet being in tow. Much as she wanted to make life easier for her friend, it had secretly irked Emma, having the baby intrude on their friendship by constantly tagging along. She'd been jealous.

'Great,' Sally said. 'Well,' she went on, suddenly hugging

her again, 'whatever happens with him, I hope it all works out. Just ... be careful.'

Emma caught a sweet waft of Sally's shampoo as she hugged her back, mingled with the faint tang of ammonia emanating from Violet. 'I will,' she replied. 'See you later.'

She took two steps into the bar, saw Nicholas sitting waiting at a table with a newspaper and a glass of red wine and walked straight out again, trembling all over. She called Flo and lied that she was going to meet a new client and would be back in tomorrow, then went home and locked the door, her heart rushing. It felt like a near-miss, as if she'd screeched to a halt at the very edge of a precipice. After a few minutes she texted him a polite, formal message, saying she thought it best if they didn't meet again, and turned her phone off. *Goodbye, Nicholas. I changed my mind. I saw sense at the last minute, just before I made the most terrible mistake.*

He'd survive, of course. Knowing him, he'd already be chatting up the waitress.

She sank into a chair, feeling wrung out by the drama, but elated that she'd done the right thing. Having a baby with another man – with him! – would not have been the solution; it couldn't possibly have ended happily.

Thank goodness for Sally. Her friend had no idea what she'd just done back there, how her perspective and her unknowing comments had saved Emma from that devil on her shoulder. She owed Sally big time.

Gazing around, she realized just what a state the flat was in. Recently it hadn't seemed worth the effort keeping on top of the place – not when there was only her living there. As a result, the washing-up had mutated into leaning towers of saucepans and crockery, there was dust on the mantel-piece and fluff balls on the carpet, hair in the shower cubicle and toothpaste splatters adorning the basin. The bin needed emptying, the recycling box needed sorting and putting out, there was a pile of paperwork she had neglected ...

There was something quite cathartic about mopping and hoovering and scrubbing, though, she decided, an hour or so later when she'd tackled the worst of it. Not only did the place look a lot better, but she felt better as well, more in control. She went out to the supermarket and stocked up on healthy food, a bunch of pink gerberas and some wine for later. It was time to stop existing on ready meals and chocolate biscuits. It was time to get her life back on track.

That evening Sally arrived, drinks were poured and they tucked into posh crisps and nice cheese. 'This is sweet,' Sally commented, gazing around at the flat. 'What's the plan with this place, then – how long are you staying here?'

Boom. Straight in with the big question. 'Well, it's a six-month contract, but . . .' Emma sighed. 'It kind of depends on David, really.'

'What do you mean?' Neither Sally nor Emma had ever been the sort of wife who left massive decisions like where they might live to the sole direction of their husbands.

'Things haven't been too brilliant, to be honest,' Emma replied. 'David's been in Dorset for weeks, helping his parents. They're moving out of their house, and he's hankering for us to buy it off them.'

Sally gaped. 'Seriously? He wants to move to the sticks? God. And what about you?'

'I don't,' Emma said flatly. 'I want to stay in Bristol.'

'Oh no.' Sally reached across the sofa and took her hand. 'So . . . what's the latest? Where are you up to? I mean, there's room for negotiation, right?'

Emma shrugged. 'We're kind of stuck,' she admitted. 'Both digging our heels in. We haven't actually spoken all week.'

The words sounded awful said out loud, much more alarming than they'd been inside her head. 'Shit,' said Sally. 'What are you saying? Surely you're not looking at . . . Splitsville?'

Emma winced. Splitsville was the very last place she wanted to be, but she was no longer sure where they were heading. 'I don't know,' she said. 'We had this massive showdown at the weekend. And I do mean massive. I had a go at his mum – a proper drunken rant – and David took her side. And since then . . . nothing.'

'Ouch,' Sally said, then her lips twitched. 'Bet it felt good, though, didn't it – socking it to that miserable old bag. She so had it coming to her.'

'I did kind of let rip,' Emma confessed. 'Although, miracle of the year, we actually sorted it out the next day – me and the old bag, I mean. She even apologized, can you believe? Ironic, isn't it, when David and I aren't speaking.'

'Oh, hon. It's tough, isn't it. Paul and I haven't been getting on well, either. It's like – real life can be such a bloody drudge, can't it? We're constantly knackered. We never have sex. We're skint because I can't find a part-time job, so Paul's working extra hours to cover the bills.' She bit her lip. 'Don't get me wrong, I love Violet. I love her to bits. But it's not the happy-family thing I thought it would be. I miss my old life too.'

'Getting old sucks,' Emma agreed. 'It was so much simpler being young, free and single, wasn't it? Now look at us – all grown up, whinging about our rubbish husbands.' She tried to laugh, but it didn't sound very genuine. 'And here's me, so desperate for a baby that I was seriously considering . . .' She broke off at once. *Watch what you're saying, Emma.* But then this was Sally. If she couldn't tell her, who could she tell?

'What?' Sally prompted.

Emma twisted her wedding ring round on her finger. 'I've been so desperate,' she repeated. 'It's so awful, every sodding month: not pregnant, not pregnant, not pregnant. And then I build myself back up over the next fortnight – right, this will be the one, don't worry, plenty of time, it can still happen. Then I'm ovulating and absolutely frantic with this kind of madness that I must, must, must conceive. Poor David. Must be terrifying for him. Honestly, I turn into this raging wild beast of a sex maniac.'

Sally elbowed her. 'Poor David, my arse. I bet he loves that.' Then she squeezed Emma's hand. 'Oh, love,' she said in a softer voice. 'I had no idea. Why didn't you say anything?'

'I just felt so miserable,' Emma admitted. 'And obsessed. I felt as if talking about it might jinx my chances. And it's boring, too – nobody wants to hear endless moans about stupid useless ovaries.'

'You can always talk to me,' Sally said stoutly. 'Any time.'

Emma said nothing for a moment. She didn't want to remind her friend how often their phone calls had been called to an abrupt halt in the last year, if Violet was crying or hungry. 'Thank you,' she said eventually. 'I don't know what's going to happen now anyway. Because if David doesn't want to know, then . . .' She stopped and screwed up her face. 'Well, I had been thinking, maybe Nicholas . . .'

Sally had been taking a mouthful of wine, but swung her head round at the critical moment and nearly spat it out. 'Whoa. Rewind. Are you saying you'd have a baby with *him*? With *Nicholas*?'

It sounded so unspeakably dreadful coming from Sally's mouth that Emma cringed. 'I *was* thinking that,' she replied in a low voice, feeling ashamed. 'I was convinced it was the right answer. I know, I know, you don't need to tell me how insane that is. I wised up anyway, just talking to you earlier. I'm not going to see him again – game over. But now I'm back to square one.'

'Bloody hell.' Sally looked stunned. 'God, Emma. I'm even more glad I saw you, then. I can't believe you've been going through this on your own.'

The kindness of her words punctured the tough shell that Emma had been wearing for months and months. Tears gathered in her eyes. 'I'm glad I saw you too,' she replied, a lump in her throat.

'Oh, Em. Don't cry, babe. I'm sorry I haven't been around for you lately, I know I've been a crap friend. But all that's going to change, okay? And I'm here now. So tell me all about it, yeah? Then we'll make a plan together.'

It really was the best kind of therapy, spilling out her secrets to Sally, being listened to and taken seriously. She'd missed having a confidante, with David being away. Missed being able to go home from work and unload her mind, talk through worries and problems, make sense of the day. Without that outlet for her thoughts, her brain had become clogged, too full to think straight. Talking to Sally felt as if she was taking steps back towards a normal life again.

'First things first,' Sally said, holding an authoritative finger in the air. 'Stop being so proud, and phone David. Yes, I know that technically he should be the one ringing you, but we're not fifteen any more. Do the mature thing and just talk to him.'

Emma nodded. 'Yep,' she said.

'Two. You need to get some basics sorted out between you – this has gone on long enough, you being in your mad limbo. Like where exactly does he want to live, for one. And what are his plans, job-wise. He's got to start thinking about these things; they're both too big and important to keep burying his head in the sand.'

'Agreed.'

'Three. You need to think about what *you* want too. Do you want to stay with him – and if so, at what cost? Be prepared for what he might say. If he's desperate to move to the sticks, then would you give it a go and join him there, or would that be a deal-breaker? Think about your options.'

'Yep,' Emma said again. God, it was so much easier, having someone else tell you what to do.

'Most important thing: do not contact Nicholas. He's not worth it, however badly you want to get up the duff.'

'I know.'

'Really. Look me in the eye and promise me you won't touch him with a bargepole, unless it's to brain him with it.'

'I promise.'

'Now, give me a hug and let's have some more wine.'

'Done.'

Emma felt happier than she had for weeks as they put their arms around each other. Oh, why had she cut off her nose to spite her face, isolating herself from her friend? If only they could have had this talk a month ago, she never would have pursued Nicholas and she almost certainly wouldn't have snogged Greg. 'You should be a marriage counsellor,' she laughed as they pulled apart. Then she froze. 'Oh my God,' she hissed. 'Do you hear that?'

There was the definite sound of footsteps climbing the stairs to the flat. 'Is it David?' Sally whispered, her eyes wide.

'Must be,' said Emma. Oh, help. She wished she hadn't drunk so much so quickly now. They both stiffened as a key was put in the lock and turned.

Then the door opened and David walked in. 'Hiya,' he said. 'Oh, Sal – hello. How are you?'

'Great, thanks,' Sally replied, leaping to her feet. 'Just about to leave actually.'

Emma got up too, dazed by the unexpected appearance of her husband. 'Hi,' she said. Her mouth felt dry all of a sudden and her heart thudded.

'No need to leave on my account, Sal,' David began, but she brushed his comment aside.

'Ah, cheers, but I promised Paul I wouldn't be late.' She held up her hands as if to say, *What can you do?* 'I'll just dial a cab, then I'll leave you to it.'

Emma felt as if they were actors in a play as she went to embrace David. 'You okay?' she asked quietly.

'Yeah,' he said into her hair. 'It's good to be back.' He held her tight for a long moment and she felt herself moulding to his shape. God, she had missed him. Just being held by him felt like such a treat.

'Lovely to see you both,' Sally said in the background. 'I'm going to wait outside for the taxi, so...'

Emma disentangled herself from David and flung her arms around her friend. 'Thank you,' she said. 'For everything. Let's do this again soon. I've missed you.'

'Me too,' Sally said. 'I'll ring you. Bye, David.'

Emma shut the front door and they heard her clattering down the steps. Then came the bang of the outer door as she left the building. 'So,' Emma began, her breath catching at the enormity of the unsaid. 'I guess we should talk.'

Chapter Twenty-Eight

Izzy was starting to wonder if she'd done the right thing, phoning Hugh to have a little word — especially as she hadn't heard a thing from Alicia since then, despite the birthday cake and card, despite the Happy Birthday text. But really, what kind of friend would she have been if she'd turned a blind eye to Hugh's dodgy secrets? A rubbish one, that's what. 'I'll make it up to you,' she had vowed to Alicia, back in the hospital, and she'd been looking for ways to repay her ever since. When she'd heard Hugh and David talking about this other woman Hugh had met up with, the opportunity to help her friend seemed to have presented itself to Izzy on a silver platter.

All the same, she dreaded to think what a hornets' nest she might have stirred up.

She'd laid it on the line to him when she'd called — once she'd finally got Hugh on the phone, that was. It had been a nightmare, hunching over the Mulberry House reception phone when nobody was around, in order to call Alicia's landline. And of course Alicia had picked up the call — twice — and Izzy had panicked and hung up, not wanting to be detected. If only she'd had Hugh's mobile number, she could have avoided all the subterfuge, but she didn't want to prompt questions from Charlie by asking for it.

Third time lucky anyway. He'd answered and she'd put it to him straight: tell Alicia what's going on, or I will. Simple as that.

He hadn't liked that very much, of course. His voice had changed from assured to shaky in a single heartbeat. 'Is this a threat?' he asked. 'What ... what do you know?'

What did she know? Not a lot. Enough, though. 'I'm saying this as Alicia's friend,' she replied. 'I'm not interested in the gory details, I just don't want her to be hurt.'

'Neither do I,' he said sadly. She could practically hear him wringing his hands. *Shouldn't have cheated on her then, should you?* she thought, hardening herself to his anguish. Alicia deserved better. 'Well, that's that then,' he ended. 'Goodbye.'

Since then Izzy had kept an ear out for news down the family grapevine, but nothing had been reported. Not a word. She really hoped she hadn't completely ballsed this up. It had seemed the right thing to do, forcing Hugh to come clean — a show of solidarity with Alicia — but she couldn't help wondering if she might actually have made things worse, not better. Should she have kept her mouth shut after all?

'Were they there?' she asked Charlie, when he came back from delivering the cake. 'Is everything okay?'

'They must be out somewhere,' he replied. 'I've got a spare key, so I left the cake on the kitchen table. Had to put it back together again after I dropped it on the front path, but . . .'

She laughed despite her anxiety. 'You're such a bad liar.'

He grinned. 'Do you think I'd have dared show my face if I really had dropped it?' he asked. 'No, it's fine. Survived the journey. Tasted lovely, too . . . You did say I could help myself to a slice, didn't you?'

She threw a carrot at him. They were in Lilian's kitchen, and Izzy had offered to make everyone lunch. 'If I find out one crumb was missing . . .'

'I love it when you're angry,' he teased, taking a bite out of the carrot. 'Go on, start telling me off. Give me a proper bollocking.'

She laughed again. 'Don't tempt me, Charlie Jones. There are more carrots where that one came from, and I can think of plenty of uses for them, that's all I'm saying.'

'Kinky talk – even better,' he said, dodging as she tried to cuff him. 'This is like one of those hotlines, isn't it, where I pay a premium-call rate and you start promising me carrots up the arse. Dirty girl. I love it.'

'Ah, there you are, David,' Eddie said, coming into the room just then.

Charlie turned round. 'It's me, Dad. David's gone back to Bristol, remember?'

Eddie scratched his head. 'Of course he has,' he said after a moment. 'I knew that. Have you seen my glasses anywhere?'

'No, Dad,' Charlie said.

'I haven't, either,' Izzy said. 'Can I make you a brew while you're here, Eddie?'

He beamed at her. 'Now you're talking,' he said. 'You're my kind of girl, you know. She's my kind of girl, you know, Charlie.'

'Oh, she's mine too,' Charlie said, grinning. 'Make us one too while you're at it, babe.'

Izzy rolled her eyes, but couldn't help a flush of pleasure. *My kind of girl, eh?* Did he really mean that, or was he just messing about? She still couldn't tell if he felt anything more for her than 'just good friends'. 'You take over with these carrots then,' she told him. 'Are you okay there, Eddie?' she added, getting down some mugs. 'Do you want to have a seat? This won't take a minute.'

She'd been in the house less than a week and already adored big, gentle Eddie, as did the girls. He was so sweet and kind, softly spoken and mild-mannered, yet she'd seen the devoted way he looked at Lilian and his sons, and got a sense of the deep protective love he felt for them, like a daddy bear. Sure, he was in his sixties, with a paunch and greying hair, but she could just imagine him in his prime, squaring up to anyone who dared hurt a member of his family. She'd always wanted a dad.

There was this unspoken subject everyone was skirting round, though. Eddie was a frail old man, she thought, watching him lower himself carefully into a chair at the table, and age was creeping up on him, tapping on his rounded shoulder. He had started forgetting things – names, words, where he was going, what he was doing – and seemed to be in a fog for much of the time. So why was nobody acknowledging that there was a problem?

The kettle began hissing and Eddie turned his benevolent, guileless eyes around the room. 'I don't suppose you've seen my glasses anywhere, have you?' he asked.

Izzy was getting more agile on her crutches every day, and, as the girls were happy to play in the garden for hours on end, she took it upon herself to start helping out around the main house. At first Lilian had shooed her away, refusing her offers of assistance. 'You're meant to be resting,' she said in that brisk, clipped way of hers, but Izzy had insisted.

'It's the least I can do,' she argued. 'Besides, I'm not very good at resting.'

This seemed to strike a chord. A lifelong grafter herself, Lilian could relate to such an admission. 'Nor me,' she admitted after a moment, then gave a nod of approval.

'Well . . . if you're sure, then I suppose I could use a hand here and there. Thank you.'

And so Izzy got stuck in. Although stairs were still difficult, she was able to hoover (slowly) the downstairs rooms, help out in the kitchen (such a lovely big kitchen!) and take bookings for new guests online or over the phone. She rather enjoyed being involved with the personal side of the business too, greeting the guests and answering their queries if Lilian was too busy. (Lilian was *always* too busy, poor woman, what with it being Easter and Eddie not being himself. She also had to do all the driving now, as the family had banned Eddie from the car, following an incident in the lane with a Renault Mégane.)

It wasn't just the domestics that Izzy lent a hand with. Having seen Lilian struggle back with two enormous loads of groceries within the week, Izzy showed her how to order food online and have it delivered instead. It was clear that Lilian was extremely excited by this idea. 'So I won't have to go out and pick up the shopping myself?' she asked several times before the first delivery. 'Somebody will drive it all here for me?'

'Yes, and they'll bring the bags through to the kitchen if you want them to, as well,' Izzy assured her. 'All you have to do is put everything away. Simple as that.'

It was quite something, seeing Lilian's expression when the delivery van arrived that first time, and the strapping young driver carried through all her bags of groceries. The novelty of such a thing made her face light up, like the sun coming out. 'Thank you. This is wonderful!' she said, rummaging through her purse for a tip.

'You don't have to do that,' the driver laughed as she tried to press a pound coin into his hand. 'Really, Mrs Jones – it's just my job.'

'Well, you must take a piece of cake then,' she replied, wrapping up a slab of the lemon-drizzle cake she'd baked the day before. 'No arguments!'

Since then, Lilian had made a shopping list every few days, and Izzy ordered it online for her. Within a matter of weeks she knew the names of all the drivers, whether or not they were married and how many children they had. She always had a treat ready for them, too. 'If only you'd been doing this when my boys were little,' she was fond of telling them. 'The hours it would have saved me! Housewives these days don't know they're born, do they?'

In return for Izzy's work, Lilian's hard frostiness seemed to be thawing by the day. The Allertons now had an open invitation to every evening meal. Lilian didn't bat an eyelid when Willow accidentally cracked the bathroom window with a spectacular overhead kick of the football. And Izzy noticed that treats were appearing in the shopping lists, especially for the girls – ice lollies, which Lilian would produce with a flourish on sunny days, and packets of lime and strawberry jelly that she made with them in rare quiet moments.

They liked her too. Willow presented Lilian with a little clay cat she had made at school the previous term, which now stood proudly on the dresser next to the big red teapot. Hazel was prone to giving her impromptu handstand and forward-roll displays in the kitchen, after Lilian once let slip that she'd loved gymnastics as a child. Lilian had even taught them a few tunes on the old piano, and the girls could often be heard bashing out 'London's Burning' or 'Twinkle, Twinkle, Little Star' on there now.

It was funny how your first impression of someone could be so wrong. The battleaxe who'd all but shoved Izzy and her children off the premises that awful first afternoon seemed a completely different person now. Maybe Charlie had been right the whole time. Once you got to know her, his mum really was kind of okay.

Somehow or other the Easter holidays were almost over, and Izzy needed to start putting her life in order. She began by organizing someone to cover her ballet classes for the next six weeks, so as to keep them ticking along in her absence. The replacement she found, Ella, was newly qualified and full of enthusiasm. 'I'm free all summer if you need me,' she said, glancing down at Izzy's cast.

Izzy wasn't sure how to reply. She hoped to have made a full recovery by then, but it was difficult to predict. Charlie had taken her back to the fracture clinic for a follow-up X-ray and appointment, and the consultant had pronounced herself pleased with the healing process so far, but it was still early days. As for her other job, Margaret and the tea shop girls had sent flowers.

'There's a job here for you whenever you need it,' Margaret said when Izzy phoned to thank her. She sounded awkward. 'I'm just sorry I didn't do more to help you when – you know – he turned up,' she added in a rush. 'It all happened so fast.'

'Don't worry,' Izzy said. 'Please. I don't think anyone could have stopped him that day. I'm just grateful to be alive.'

She had to make her goodbyes and ring off quickly then, because her whole body had begun trembling from the flashback of that terrible day. *Don't cry, don't cry, it's okay.* The shock was still catching up with her, reluctant to be shaken off. Every now and then she was slammed with the enormity of what had happened, then traumatized by imagining the terrible outcomes she had been spared. She was lucky not to have suffered brain damage, spinal injuries, a broken neck. *I'm just grateful to be alive.*

She gripped the handles of her crutches, trying to breathe

normally as the panic attack rushed at her, like an enormous wave. *She was okay. She had survived. They were here, safe at Mulberry House, and they would get through this as a family.*

'Is everything all right?' Lilian asked, coming down the stairs just then with a bundle of washing. Izzy was sitting at the reception desk in the hallway, still immobile following the phone call.

She took a deep breath and pushed herself slowly to her feet. 'I'm fine,' she said. 'Just . . . having a moment.'

Lilian eyed her, with the measuring gaze of a woman who had seen it all before. 'I think you're overdoing it a bit,' she pronounced eventually. 'Go on, I can manage here today. You take it easy for a while, okay? Go and sit in the garden. I'll bring you a cup of tea once I've got this lot in the machine.'

Izzy said nothing. She wasn't good at taking it easy – but then she wasn't much good for anything, in the state she was in right now.

'No arguments,' Lilian told her. 'You look very pale. Go and get some sunshine and fresh air. It's lovely out.'

Izzy knew when she was beaten. 'Thanks,' she said. 'I will, if you don't mind. I've got some forms and stuff to go through about closing Gary's bank account anyway, I can get on with those.'

'The forms can wait; I'll help you with them later. You just sit in the sun and rest.'

Sometimes it was nice to be told what to do, Izzy thought gratefully, swinging herself through the house on her crutches and outside to the patio. She never would have done this, left to her own devices; she would have busied herself with another chore, pushed herself along. Having someone order you to stop and take it easy was a total novelty – but one she rather liked.

A few minutes later Lilian bustled out with a tray of tea things and a magazine one of the guests had left behind. The girls were busy further down the garden making a den, birds swooped across the blue sky, and the sun felt warm on her skin. Izzy sat quietly for a moment, sipping her tea and letting her tired bones sink into the old wicker garden seat. This must be what it was like to have a mother, she realized after a while, being fussed over, and looked after. It felt good, really good.

The next day a letter arrived that changed everything. If Izzy had been feeling remotely together, she might have foreseen it, but she hadn't. Hadn't imagined in a million years that, as Gary's wife (albeit estranged), she'd be in line for a massive life-insurance payment. He'd worked for an insurance company since leaving school, and one of the perks had been the most comprehensive personal-insurance package available. The money hadn't actually arrived yet – more forms to fill in and sign first, of course – but oh, my goodness. She was going to be rich. She, Isabel Allerton, wouldn't have to worry about scraping together pennies for bills for a long while. She wouldn't have to take back her dance classes if she didn't feel like it, or work for the next few years, for that matter. For the first time ever she would be financially solvent, and needed never to rely on anyone else again.

And, of course, she realized dazedly, the flat in Manchester had her name on the mortgage too. Once she cleared it out and found someone who wanted to buy it, she'd be richer still. Admittedly, it wasn't a palace – it was in a fairly rundown area of the city and wasn't what you'd call pretty – but they'd bought it years ago for a bargain price and she knew the value had risen. Her head spun at the notion of all this money coming her way. In life, Gary might have cowed her and hurt her, but in death he had set her free. He'd given the girls the best kind of security too. She was already looking into investment funds for the pair of them, so that, come eighteen, they'd have a good start as young women. Unlike her, they'd have real choices in their hands. They could go to university if they wanted, they could travel the world. And in the meantime the three of them could have some corking holidays too – ones that needed passports and everything. Bring it on!

Before she could start flicking through holiday websites, though, there were still the practicalities of selling the flat to get through; a job she both dreaded and wanted to get over with. So when Charlie told her that he had the last three days of the week off work, and asked if they should set off on a road trip to Manchester, there was only one possible answer. Needs must, as her granny would have said. 'Let's do it,' she replied.

He borrowed a six-seater van from a mate (Charlie had all sorts of useful mates, it was becoming clear) and off they went at the crack of dawn the following morning. It was a four-and-a-half-hour journey according to the satnav, but it turned out to be more like six hours on the road, after they'd stopped several times for food, coffee and loos. Still, the girls absolutely loved the novelty of being in a van, and Charlie proved to have a knack of tuning the radio to find the best driving songs. Plus, he was good company. Great company. She'd never spent so much time with someone who was just so easy to *be* with, who made her laugh so much. His stream of funny stories took the edge off her nerves all the way up the motorway. It was only as the signs for Manchester finally appeared that she began to feel a strange, anxious ache inside.

The girls picked up on it too. Once they were off the motorway Willow began complaining of a headache, shielding her eyes as if subconsciously she didn't want to see, whereas Hazel was glued to the window, with a nervous, almost hysterical energy radiating from her as she recognized landmarks. 'Hey!' she cried suddenly. 'That's our Asda. Mum, look. Asda!'

'Duh,' Willow said, somewhat unkindly. 'It's only a shop.'

'I know, but – Mum. Did you see it? We're nearly home!'

Izzy winced at the word 'home'. The poor girls had had so many homes in the last year: the flat in Manchester, the one in Lyme, Alicia's house and now the holiday chalet in Loveday. 'We're nearly back,' she agreed. 'And remember what I told you. The flat might not be how you remember it. You know how messy Daddy was. He might even have changed things around!'

Her words were lightly spoken, but she felt worried beneath them. Maybe it had been a mistake bringing the girls along. What if they arrived at the flat and he'd completely trashed it? All their memories would forever be tarnished. He'd been in such a dark place by the end of his life that she could imagine this manifesting itself in horrible graffiti on the walls, smashed furniture, the stench of rotting food . . .

'I can't *wait* to see our bedroom again,' Hazel said, bouncing on the seat, not seeming to have taken Izzy's warning on board. 'Are we going to start school here again too?'

'No, love,' Izzy said, as Willow made another rude noise of derision. 'No, we're just here for one last visit, to clean up and choose the nicest things Daddy left behind to take back to Dorset with us. We'll be here one or two nights tops, then we'll say goodbye to Manchester again, okay?' She eyed Willow, who had her arms folded across her chest. 'And there's no need to be unkind,' she added. 'It was a perfectly good question.'

'A perfectly *stupid* question,' Willow muttered, kicking her leg petulantly.

'Scooby-Dooby-Doo,' Hazel sang, oblivious to her sister's mood. 'Shaggy did a poo. He threw it out the win-dow . . .'

'Left down here,' Izzy told Charlie, her heart quickening as they passed the little row of shops where she'd bought milk and bread every day. 'Then it's the next right.'

'Scooby-Dooby-Dee, Scrappy did a wee. He—'

'Hazel,' Izzy said, feeling unusually irritable. 'Hush, love.' She hugged herself, gazing at the streets as if she'd never seen them before. They were so familiar, yet dream-like too. The houses appeared hunched and packed together, with some windows boarded up and a burnt-out car at one end of the street. The tiny front yards sprouted junk – bits of car, rubble sacks, overflowing bins. There were no trees, barely anything green at all. Even the sky felt small after the wide-open horizon at Lyme. 'This one,' she said quietly, pointing. 'Just here, on the right, Charlie. Number sixty-two.'

They were all silent as he parked and cut the engine. 'Well, here we are,' he said.

'Here we are,' she echoed.

'We're *home!*' Hazel sang, unclipping her seatbelt with a flourish.

Izzy's hands trembled as she opened the front door. She'd never imagined them coming back here, least of all under such extraordinary and traumatic circumstances.

She held her breath when the door swung open and she stepped cautiously inside. The flat felt still and deadened, as if it had been left on pause. There was a stale sort of smell in the air, the kind that made her want to push open all the windows and bring a fresh, cold draught rushing through the place.

'Come in,' she said apprehensively. It was daft. Even though she knew Gary was dead – she'd signed enough forms and letters confirming this, after all; she'd seen his lifeless body at the undertaker's, for heaven's sake! – there was still a part of her braced for conflict as she walked down the hall. Habit, she supposed. Gary had held her up against this wall by her neck one time, she remembered, his thumbs hard against her windpipe as she'd gasped for air. She couldn't even remember why – towards the end he'd picked a fight for any trivial reason.

'Are you okay?' Charlie asked from behind her. He had a tower of empty boxes in his arms; they'd come prepared with suitcases to pack and bin bags to fill too. An estate agent was due round the following day; there was a lot to do.

'Yeah, sure. Just . . . ghosts of the past, you know,' she said. She shook herself, then walked down to the kitchen. She could hear Hazel exclaiming over everything in the hall.

'Look, there's my old coat still hanging up! It's *tiny* now. Oh, and look – my Peppa Pig umbrella!'

'Peppa Pig is for babies,' Willow muttered witheringly.

Izzy filled the kettle – its handle sticky where it hadn't been wiped down for months – and stood looking around the room. It was only a tiny galley kitchen, certainly not one where you could sit and linger over a coffee, like in Mulberry House. The window looked out at a wooden fence, which divided them from the next house in the terrace, although she'd tried to improve the view by planting up a windowbox fixed to the ledge outside. Needless to say, the flowers had all died since she'd left. In fact, there was a prominent cat-turd in the box now; just what you wanted to look at when you were washing up.

While the kettle boiled she prowled around the rest of the flat, still on high alert, as if expecting something horrible to jump out from a cupboard, or for Gary himself to emerge. *Thought you'd got shot of me, did you? Gotcha!*

To her relief, it appeared much the same as when she and the girls had done their flit. It wasn't particularly clean, but she was surprised by how tidy it was, almost as if he'd known he wasn't going to come back. *No*, she thought quickly, not wanting to develop that thought any further. Then, when she went into the girls' old room and saw that the bunkbed had been stripped, save for an envelope on each mattress – one for Willow, one for Hazel – Izzy's knees suddenly felt very weak.

'Are those for us, Mum?' asked Willow, who'd sneaked in behind her.

Izzy handed Willow's over dumbly, wondering what on earth was inside. Then Hazel, sensing intrigue, appeared, demanding hers, and the small room was full of the noise of envelopes being ripped open.

Willow was first into hers and pulled out a letter. Izzy read it over her shoulder and tears welled in her eyes.

Dear Willow,
  I am so proud of you, babe. You are clever and kind and funny. And beautiful too.
  Lots of love from your Daddy xxx

Willow made a choking noise and promptly burst into tears, collapsing onto the lower bunk.

'Dear Hazel,' Hazel read aloud. 'Never forget that your daddy loved you. You are bright and . . . what's that word?'

'Thoughtful,' Izzy said.

'Thoughtful and make everyone laugh. Love you darling, Daddy xxx.'

'But I don't understand,' sobbed Willow. 'It's like he *knew* he was going to die, Mum. How did he know?'

Izzy sat on the lower bunk and put her arms around them, a knot clenching in her stomach. *Oh, Gary. You stupid bastard*, she thought angrily. 'I'm not sure, love,' she managed to say. 'I really don't know.' Had this seriously been his plan B – to kill himself, if he wasn't able to snatch the girls away? Was he really that desperate?

She opened her mouth to say something comforting, but nothing came. Who knew what had gone through his head, he had been so deranged that awful last day. A madness had overtaken him, its power working him like a puppet.

'I am thoughtful, aren't I?' Hazel mused, less affected than her sister. 'And I *do* make people laugh too.'

'You do,' Izzy said, stroking her hair. God, but she hated thinking of Gary sitting in the flat, maybe right on the bed here, as he wrote these letters to them, just in case he never got to say the words himself. He, of all people, knew at first hand the crushing pain of losing your parents when you were young. He, of all people, should have tried harder to keep himself together, for their sake. For everyone's sake. And what if she had died in the car with him? He'd have forced his own daughters into the very kind of foster homes he'd hated himself. *Good move, Gary*, she raged. *Genius!*

Charlie appeared just then, thankfully. 'Two girls are at the door. Tanya and Phoebe? They were asking if you wanted to p—' He broke off at Willow's tear-stricken face. 'Oh. Everything all right?'

'PHOEBE!' Hazel shouted, her letter forgotten. 'Can I, Mum? Can I go over?'

Izzy smiled weakly, grateful for the distraction. Tanya and Phoebe were the girls next door; their mum Ange was a friend of hers. You couldn't get anything past Ange, she was a perpetual lace-curtain twitcher. 'Of course you can. Tell Ange I'll pop in to say hello later. Willow, do you want to go and play with Tanya?'

Willow wiped her tears away and nodded. 'Yes,' she said.

Hazel had already skipped merrily out of the room, but Willow was more hesitant to leave. Izzy put her arms around her and held her tight. 'It's going to be okay,' she said. 'It's all going to be okay.'

Charlie was still in the doorway and ruffled Willow's hair as she went by. 'You all right?' he asked Izzy again once the front door had shut.

She nodded and pushed herself up. 'Yep,' she replied. 'Come on, let's make a start.'

*

They began in the kitchen, Izzy directing and Charlie following orders. There wasn't an awful lot of stuff that had sentimental value to her; she'd already taken the essentials when they'd escaped to Dorset. There were a couple of things she decided to keep — a bright-red vase Gary had given her one Valentine's Day, and the faithful wall clock which she'd had forever — but otherwise she culled brutally, piling up the crockery and pans. She'd give them to the nearest women's refuge, she decided.

The living room was harder to sort — there were boxes of photos, books, music and all sorts of artwork done by the girls over the years. She packed the photos and artwork to take, but did her best to be practical about the rest, sifting out only her favourite books and CDs, and bagging up the rest for the charity shop. She felt bad, ditching Gary's music — all his moody Joy Division albums, for instance. She'd loved them herself at first, but nowadays they just made her think about him, sunk into a chair, scowling, and taking no pleasure from the music or life in general.

'Call yourself a Mancunian?' Charlie said, aghast. 'And you're chucking out Joy Division? Isn't there a law against that?'

She wrinkled her nose. 'I know but . . . bad memories. I don't want to hear them again.'

As for the furniture, the curtains, the rug — they were

pretty faded and shabby, when looked at with an impartial eye. She didn't want or need them, they belonged to the past. Once the money came through, she decided, and she was back on her feet, she would buy a new home for them and kit it out just the way they wanted.

The trip next door hadn't been a total success for the girls – 'Phoebe said I talk funny now,' Hazel reported, confused. 'She said I sound foreign.' 'Tanya kept going on about new people at school that I didn't know,' Willow complained – but Izzy loved catching up with Ange, who willingly took two of the rugs and an armchair off her.

'Hey, and who's that fit bloke I spotted lugging boxes into the van, eh? That your new fella?' Ange wanted to know.

Izzy pulled a face. 'Not really,' she said. 'It's complicated.'

Ange rolled her eyes. 'Complicated? Doesn't look it from here. He's gorgeous. You're single – I won't say widowed, that makes you sound about ninety – so what's stopping you? He's not married or gay or freaky, is he?'

'No,' Izzy laughed. 'No and no. I just think it's too soon to be diving into a relationship with someone else.'

Ange raised an eyebrow. 'Don't give me that. You'd had enough of Gary for months before you left. Just because he's died now, it doesn't turn him into a saint overnight, does it? Don't feel you have to weep over him forever, not when he was such a bastard to you.'

Izzy was silent. She knew there was some truth in what Ange was saying, but it seemed so harsh.

'Sorry,' Ange said in the next moment. 'You're right, shouldn't speak ill of the dead. But he was, though, wasn't he?' She gave Izzy a sudden fierce hug. 'It's lovely to see you again. Sure I can't tempt you to stay, now you're back? Our Phoebe hasn't stopped talking about it.'

Izzy sighed. Ange had been a good friend – so had many people here. Manchester would always be her true home, the city that had shaped her and taught her some important life lessons. But she had a new life now, down in the soft greens and blues of Dorset. 'We'll come back and see you again,' she promised. 'Maybe in the summer. Or you could come down for a holiday with us!'

'You're on,' said Ange, then winked. 'And don't forget the invite to the wedding, now, will you?'

That night, when the girls were asleep, Charlie produced a bottle of red wine and poured them both a glass. 'Well done,' he said, handing Izzy hers. 'Today must have been tough, but I reckon we've made a good start.'

'We have,' she agreed. The sofa smelled of Gary when she leaned her head back. Gary who'd written notes to his daughters to read after his death; Gary who'd been driven to self-destruction, who'd nearly killed her too, not to mention two police officers. Ange was right – he definitely hadn't been a saint.

'I'm so glad you're here,' she blurted out to Charlie. 'I couldn't have done this on my own. Thank you.'

'No worries,' he said, reaching over and putting a hand on hers. 'No worries at all.'

She liked feeling his fingers on hers, the warmth of his skin. He was a good, good man, whatever his family thought, whatever Margaret in the tea shop might say. She couldn't think of another man who would have looked after her and helped her as he had done.

They sat there a while longer in a tired, companionable silence. The worst was over, she told herself. She'd returned to face down her demons, ventured back to the place where she'd been miserable for so long, and she had coped with it; she was undefeated. The only way now was up.

They watched a film together and drank wine. She could hear Mr Waters, the man who lived in the flat above, wandering about, his telly too loud as always. And there were Ange and Pete, laughing about something or other through the party wall, and Ange's phone was ringing, and she was yelling at her kids to stop mucking about and go to sleep. Teenagers passed by, shouting over one another, dogs barked, a police siren wailed in the distance . . . All sounds she'd heard a million times before, sitting on this very sofa. There was a difference now, though. Now she felt safe, able to relax, no longer having that ball of dread in her stomach as she waited for Gary to crash in from the pub, stinking of ale and in a blazing temper. Home, sweet home, she thought with a smile.

When the film was over, and the bottle was empty, and the lights across the street were going out, Charlie yawned and stretched. 'I'll kip on the sofa here, if you've got a sleeping bag, or something,' he said.

She hesitated. Her mind had been so full of all the things she needed to do that sleeping arrangements hadn't occurred to her. 'You can share the double with me,' she replied after a moment. 'If you want.'

They looked at one another, his eyes slightly narrowed as if he was attempting to read her expression. 'I don't mind going on the sofa,' he offered again.

'I'd like the company,' she said. 'I'm not trying to make a pass at you, don't worry, I just don't want to be on my own.'

He reached over and squeezed her hand. 'Fine by me,' he said. 'Although if you change your mind about making a pass ... that's fine, too.'

She laughed self-consciously. 'Right. Good. Well, let's get ready for bed then.'

It was strange, getting undressed and brushing teeth

together. She put a clean sheet and pillowcases on the bed, as the others had smelled of Gary, and she knew the scent would creep her out if she had to breathe it in all night. But soon the whole distraction of stripping the bed and remaking it was over. Now came the weird bit of actually being in it with Charlie.

They lay side by side in the darkness, both on their backs. The new sheet was cold against her skin and she shivered. Would she even be able to sleep in this bed, after all the bad things that had happened in it? Maybe she should be the one on the sofa. Charlie must be knackered from the long drive earlier – he needed the bed more than she did.

Just as she was thinking this, Charlie stretched an arm out. 'Come here,' he said, and she wriggled into his side. With his arm around her and her head on his chest, she could hear his heart beating, and smell the last traces of his aftershave. He was wearing a T-shirt and boxers and the hairs on his legs felt prickly as she moved closer into him.

She shut her eyes. It felt good lying next to him. 'Charlie Jones, what on earth did I do to deserve you?' she murmured.

He stroked her hair. 'You are the most beautiful and lovely woman I have ever met,' he told her. 'I should be saying the same.'

It felt as if her whole body was blushing. 'Oh, Charlie...'

'I mean it. You're so strong and together, the way you've dealt with everything, the way you look after the girls. I really admire you.'

'Stop it, you're embarrassing me,' she said, not wanting him to stop at all.

'I hate thinking of you being miserable here. I know you were.' He twined his fingers through her hair, his body solid and warm against hers. 'I wish I could go to bed every night with you in my arms like this. I'd be the luckiest man alive — and I'd never ever do anything to hurt you.'

She didn't speak for a moment. It suddenly felt wrong, disloyal to be having this conversation in this bed. 'Don't,' she whispered.

'I'm just saying,' he replied, kissing the top of her head. 'I just want you to know.'

'I know,' she replied. 'Thank you.' And then a swell of emotion — of happiness, relief and, yes, perhaps even love — overtook her and she found herself twisting her head so that they were lying face-to-face. 'I think I'm falling in love with you,' she said softly. Before she could stop herself, she was kissing him.

Chapter Twenty-Nine

It was the fact that Hugh had lied to her that hurt Alicia most. She had always thought she and her husband were each other's first loves, cherishing how special that made their relationship. And yet it wasn't even true. Another woman had gone before her, this other 'first love' of Hugh's. Just like that, the rock-solid core of their relationship cracked, and their precious wedding night became a travesty. The joke was on her.

'Her name was Sophie Bloom,' he confessed dully. 'We weren't together very long, only a few months. I didn't think it was worth mentioning.'

Alicia smarted. Didn't think it was worth mentioning, indeed. They were back home now, with vinegary parcels of fish and chips still wrapped on the kitchen table. It turned out she wasn't able to continue the conversation in the Grove Bistro after all, had quite lost her appetite for fizz and fancy food.

'She went to France for a year as part of her degree and

we broke up,' he said. 'I didn't know it, but she was pregnant when she left. Pregnant with Cathy. And she never came back to Oxford – she dropped out of university and went to live near her parents.'

'Cathy? That's your daughter's name?' The word 'daughter' set her teeth on edge. It sounded so wrong, using the word for someone other than Matilda. Catherine Bloom. Sophie Bloom. She prickled with irrational dislike for them both. She hated them for messing everything up like this!

'That's her name,' Hugh replied. 'And that's who I went to meet the other week, when I said I was at the gym. I'm sorry.'

'So you weren't at the gym, and you weren't buying my birthday present, either. You were with *Cathy*.'

Hugh swallowed audibly. 'Yes.'

'I should have guessed,' she said with a snort of derision, unable to keep the spite from her voice. 'I should have known that sodding food mixer wasn't the result of hours deliberating over the perfect gift.'

He coloured. 'I'm sorry,' he said again.

'And that was her, too, on the phone the other night, hanging up? The one you pretended was Izzy?' Pathetic, she thought. Absolutely pathetic.

'No,' he said. 'That really was Izzy. She overheard me talking to David about Cathy.' He looked as if he was ill –

his face greenish-pale with a sheen of sweat. 'She told me I had to tell you, or else.'

Alicia put her head in her hands. Oh, great. So everyone knew about this wretched Cathy except her, did they? She felt so angry and muddled and hurt that she didn't trust herself to speak for a moment.

'I'm sorry,' Hugh said like a broken record. 'I'm really, really sorry.'

'Right,' she replied, her voice sounding as brittle as she felt. *You're sorry. And that's supposed to make everything all right, is it?* This was the worst birthday ever, she thought, scrubbing at her eyes. Hadn't she known all along that forty was going to be shit? She'd certainly been proved right about that. Hadn't taken long, had it, for the shittiness to begin.

'I'm going to bed,' she said, no longer wanting to talk about this. 'And you can sleep on the sofa tonight. I feel so – so fed up, I don't even want to see you right now.'

'Alicia, wait,' he bleated, but she swept out of the room, ignoring the cooling fish and chips. Let him have them. She hoped he bloody well choked.

Hugh had already left for work by the time Alicia surfaced the next morning. She stumbled downstairs, feeling the most dreadful lurch inside whenever she thought of last night's awful conversation. Hugh had shaken their marriage to its very core with his deceit. How could she ever trust him again?

There was a note waiting for her on the breakfast table. *I'm sorry. Let's talk tonight. I want to work this out. X*

Yeah, and so he should be sorry, she thought crossly, crumpling the note into a tight ball and hurling it into the bin. She was sorry too – sorry she'd ever believed him. And to think how smug she'd always been about their marriage: how lucky she'd felt to have snagged 'a good one'. Turned out he was as much of a liar as Sandra's string of exes. Worse, in fact, because he'd let the lie fester for over twenty years. What a fool she felt, now that she knew the truth.

Oh, Christine, she thought helplessly. *What do I do now?*

You carry on, came the reply. *You keep going.*

She made herself a coffee and sat at the table for a while, still wrapped in her dressing gown. Carry on and keep going, she thought sourly, curling her lip. Great. Women like her always carried on and kept going, even when they felt like screaming at the top of their voice and flinging things at their husband. Stiff upper lip, chin up, keep calm and carry on. Well, what if she didn't want to keep calm?

She pulled a face. *I might have to disagree with you on this one, Christine*, she thought. *Besides, no offence, but what would you know anyway?*

*

The sun was shining, so once everyone had breakfasted Alicia slapped together some ham sandwiches, wrapped up the rest of the birthday cake and took the children off to Lyme for the day – anything to get away from the house. At the beach they discovered that the tide was on its way out, so they spent ages hunting for treasures in the rock pools with fishing nets, while dogs and welly-clad toddlers paddled splashily in the shallows around them. Afterwards the four of them picnicked on the pebbles, entertained by a couple of seagulls squabbling over the remains of an abandoned blueberry muffin nearby, then the boys pestered her to take them to the fossil shop in Broad Street to spend their pocket money on yellowing sharks' teeth and bits of old rock.

Alicia found herself eyeing passing young women, wondering if one of them was Cathy. Sod the stiff upper lip, sod trying to pretend that the conversation with Hugh had never happened. It had. She had to deal with it somehow – they all did.

Was that her, in the pink cropped jeans and gold wedges, arm-in-arm with a bunch of girlfriends, their hair uniformly long, streaked and straightened? Or was that her, in the emo make-up with a nose-stud and crimped black hair, looking too hot in black jeans and a studded leather jacket? Maybe that was her, smooching with a young man on the Cobb, oblivious to the world around them?

Oh God. It felt as if she was stumbling around a

minefield, waiting for the detonation. And there were the children, completely oblivious. What would they make of the news that they had a brand-new stepsister? Her mind raced with questions, trying to make sense of it all. Would it put Lucas's nose out of joint that he was no longer Hugh's eldest? Would Matilda be miffed that she wasn't the only girl any more? They would be a patchwork family now, with a half-sister stitched into the mix, changing their whole look and shape. And she would be a stepmother, she realized to her horror, a dozen gruesome fairytales springing to mind. It felt all wrong, as if she was wearing somebody else's clothes that didn't suit her.

She put a hand to her head, suddenly dizzy. The world seemed to be spinning too quickly, she felt confused and disoriented. She wished she could go back to the blissful ignorance of being thirty-nine, when everything had been in its proper place.

That evening Hugh seemed like a stranger when he came home. Dinner was a strained affair, with them both making polite chit-chat, yet essentially saying nothing. All Alicia could think about was how much she was dreading the 'talk' he had requested.

Hugh obviously felt the same. The very second after the children had gone to bed he turned to her, a weak smile on his face. 'Gin and tonic? Wine?'

'Not for me,' she said, wanting to keep a clear head.

'Probably wise,' he said, after one last look at the gin bottle. There was a pause. 'So,' he said, sitting down at the kitchen table and clearing his throat.

'So,' she echoed, sitting opposite him. They'd sat in these seats for so many important conversations before. The difference was, in the past, such conversations had always been good ones, ones that promised positive change. Where shall we go on holiday this year? Do we have enough money for a conservatory? What should we buy the children for Christmas?

'First of all,' he said, 'I feel terrible about this. I should have told you about Sophie right from the start, back in Oxford. I wish I had.'

'Why didn't you?' she asked. 'Not telling me is as bad as lying, Hugh.'

'I know,' he said miserably, hanging his head. 'She . . . she broke my heart, you see.'

It was like being punched, hearing him talk about her with such emotion. Hugh usually displayed as much emotion as a house brick. 'You loved her?'

He nodded, not looking at her. 'Yes.'

Ouch. She wished she'd taken up his offer of gin now; she could do with a large shot of something strong to soften the edges of this hard truth. 'More than me?'

'No!' Now he raised his gaze. 'No, of course not. I can't

even compare the two experiences. With Sophie, it was . . .'
He shrugged. 'Adoration. Teenage fantasy. You know, I'd
left home, I felt like a man for the first time ever, I was—'

She didn't want to hear any more. 'Shagging around?' she
finished waspishly.

'No!' he protested again. 'It was only Sophie – and then
you. That's it, my sum total of romantic experience.' He
seemed to shrink into himself. 'I was naive, Alicia. I didn't
have the first clue about love. I confused it with sex, for
heaven's sake, thought that because this girl – Sophie – let
me . . . you know, *do* things, that we must have this amazing
relationship. Realistically, we didn't at all. I can't even
remember what she looked like.'

'I still don't understand,' Alicia said through gritted teeth,
'why you didn't tell me about her, though. What was the
big secret?'

'The big secret, I suppose, was that I felt an idiot for
having believed I was in love at all. She finished with me
that summer, the end of my first year. Said she was going
to France and we should probably cool it, go our separate
ways. I was crushed.'

Alicia nodded, digesting the information. 'And then you
met me when I started at Oxford the following autumn.'

'And I realized what true love really was,' he said.
'Meeting you made me see that Sophie had been a mere
infatuation. It never would have lasted. Whereas you – I

knew straight away that you were the real thing, Alicia. I knew that what we had was special. Still is.'

Despite all her inner turmoil Alicia found herself unexpectedly moved. The house brick was really wearing his heart on his sleeve tonight. 'So when did you find out about Cathy?' she asked, trying to keep her composure.

'A few weeks ago – I got an email out of the blue one evening. You might remember: I was here in the kitchen at the time and nearly collapsed with shock.' He rubbed his eyes. 'I literally had no idea Cathy existed, hadn't given Sophie a thought since we were at university. But she knew about me.'

There was a pause, longer this time. 'What's she like?' Alicia asked, not entirely sure she wanted to hear the answer.

'She's lovely,' he replied, almost apologetically. 'She's two years into an art degree in Brighton, sweet and bubbly, a bit quirky, quite tall, long red hair and dimples . . . You'll like her.'

Alicia said nothing for a moment, imagining this red-haired intruder first as Annie, then as Jessica Rabbit. Neither was particularly good stepdaughter material.

'Does she want to meet the children?' she asked.

'Yes,' he replied. 'That's okay, isn't it?'

'I suppose so.' She didn't feel as if she had much choice. There was a pause where she examined her fingernails and Hugh stared at the table. 'Alicia . . . be honest,' he said after a moment. 'You didn't want a food mixer for your birthday, did you?'

She jerked in surprise at the abrupt change of subject. 'No,' she admitted before she could say something more tactful.

He sighed. 'I'm sorry,' he said. 'I feel as if I've got everything wrong lately. I wanted to give you something really special for your fortieth, but I just . . .' He spread his hands helplessly. 'I've got no imagination. I'm rubbish.'

He did look genuinely pained. 'Look, it's fine,' she said, after a moment. 'Really. I'm sure it'll be very useful. But . . .' Go on, she urged herself. Out with it. Tell him how you feel. 'Well, it's just that sometimes I'm worried that's all I am to you. A boring wife who cooks and cleans and lives a sensible, safe life. And, okay, so I know I haven't done very much to dispel this theory over the years. I *have* been boring and sensible and safe. But lately, I've wanted more. I've wanted some excitement, for you to see me as a . . . woman again. Feminine. Attractive. Not just a wife in a pinny with her hands in the washing-up every day.'

It felt quite a speech, all in all. These words had burned inside her for weeks and her heart raced as she finally released them out loud. There. Cards on the table.

To her relief, he was nodding. 'You're right,' he said.

'Not about me thinking you're a boring wife. I've never thought that. You are perfect to me. Perfect.'

His earnestness was verging on the unbearable; his sincerity without question. She opened her mouth to thank him, but he hadn't finished. 'When you asked last night if I'd been cheating on you, if there was another woman, I nearly fell off my chair,' he said. 'Why on earth would I ever want another woman when I have you? I mean it, Alicia. I've never meant anything more in my life. You are all I want – all I have ever wanted.'

She pressed her lips together, trying to keep her cool, but it was no good. A tear broke free from one eye and plopped onto the table. 'Thank you,' she whispered.

'And I'm sorry I haven't shown you that more often. I will, I promise, from now on. I'll make you feel the most loved and adored woman that ever walked this earth. The KitchenAid can go straight back to the shop,' he went on gruffly, getting up from the table as if preparing to despatch it there and then, 'and I shall spend all the money on jewellery instead. Jewellery and flowers and perfume and . . . lovely things. Whatever you want.'

'Oh, Hugh.' She got to her feet too and stood holding the back of her chair. 'You don't have to do that.'

'I know I don't,' he replied. 'But I want to.' He held his arms open for her and she walked into them. They stood there together in the kitchen, just holding each other.

'Thank you,' he said after a while. 'For being so understanding about all of this. But, most of all, for being my wife. I'd be nothing without you, Alicia.'

For a moment she felt stiff in his embrace, not quite able to let go of the image of Hugh pining over his lost love Sophie, weeping in his teenage bedroom in Mulberry House all those years ago. And he hadn't told her. He hadn't said.

But the truth was out now at least. They could pick themselves up and move on together again, couldn't they?

She leaned against him and let him hold her closer, then tightened her arms around his back. It was worth a try, she decided. Surely it was worth a try.

Chapter Thirty

Emma had shied away from difficult conversations with David for so long that the night he came home after his self-imposed exile, she almost bottled it again. But Sally's words chimed insistently in her head and she knew she must be brave. *Do it, Em. Just ask him.*

'David,' she began, with another mouthful of wine for Dutch courage. 'Tell me honestly, because I need to know. Do you still want us to buy Mulberry House and live there?'

If he was surprised at such a direct question, he showed no hesitation in giving her a direct reply. 'No,' he said. 'I don't.'

And there it was: a major worry answered and eradicated, just like that, after weeks of doubt and dread. Emma swayed in relief; it was as if someone had removed her bones and she was nothing more than jelly. '*Really?* Oh, thank God,' she sighed. 'Because I don't want to, either.'

He raised an eyebrow. 'I kind of got that impression.'

'So what changed your mind?' She couldn't stop smiling.

Maybe it wasn't polite to be so openly happy, but it was impossible to put a lid on it. He didn't want them to move to Dorset. He didn't want them to run his parents' decrepit B&B. It felt like Christmas.

'I tried to want it,' he said. 'I *wanted* to want it, because I knew that's what Mum and Dad were hoping. But the longer I stayed there, the more the guests started getting on my wick.' He pulled a face. 'They were always bloody complaining! They were meant to be on holiday, having *fun*, but my God, the moans and whinges were just endless: about the weather, or their view, or the room being cold. Some woman actually bitched that the birds were singing too loudly. I mean . . .'

Emma laughed. 'I'm not even going to mention Poogate.'

He laughed too. 'I don't know how my parents have the patience, I really don't.' He shook his head. 'And it wasn't just that. It was being stuck in the middle of bloody nowhere as well. I love the countryside and the beach, but I started to get stir-crazy. I missed going to the pub, the cinema, restaurants, being able to buy a decent coffee . . .'

Emma gave a theatrical cough. 'Anything else?'

'You, Em,' he said. 'More than anything. I wish I hadn't stayed away so long. I'm sorry. I just felt such a failure: not having a job or income, not being able to provide for us.' He swallowed and looked away. 'Not being able to make you pregnant.'

Her eyes filled suddenly. 'You idiot,' she said gently. 'You're not a failure.'

'That's not how it felt.' He fidgeted. 'Mum sat me down and gave it to me straight anyway. I think she's been watching too many soaps, because she actually told me I had to "man up" and start facing real life again.'

'Really?' She smirked, imagining the scene. To think that Lilian had taken her side for once!

'Yep. So here I am. Manning up. Facing real life. Telling you I'm sorry for not being around. But I'm back now, and I'm going to sort everything out, I swear.'

His words sent an enormous weight rolling from her shoulders, she felt light-headed with its release. 'I'm glad you're back,' she said. 'I missed you so much. It's been rubbish without you. I even started going a bit mad, I think.'

'Talking to yourself in public again?'

She forced a smile. 'Something like that.' That was one can of worms she would definitely leave closed, she decided, pouring more wine for them both. 'So, what's going to happen with the house then, now that we're out of the picture?' She couldn't help herself; she actually wriggled with joy saying the words. They were out of the running. They wouldn't be taking over the B&B. David had finally made his choice and he'd come home, to her. YESSSSSS.

'I don't know,' he admitted. 'Mum and Dad definitely

can't carry on there, though. I don't even know if they'll last the summer. Dad's . . . I think he's losing his marbles, Em. It's horrible. He's forgetful and confused, and it's all just too much for him.' He ran a hand through his hair, and she noticed how tired he looked. 'That's another reason I stayed so long, because Mum was struggling. But she's booked a doctor's appointment for him now, to see what they think, so . . .'

Emma winced. David wasn't the only one facing up to things then. Going to the doctor was official confirmation that something was wrong, and might be the first step in a whole flood of hospital appointments, tests and check-ups. You wouldn't wish it on anyone. 'Poor Eddie,' she said when he didn't finish the sentence. 'And poor Lilian.'

'Yeah,' he said heavily. 'But anyway. Let's not talk about them. Let's talk about us, and make some plans together. Me and you, what do you say?'

'I'd like that,' she said, as optimism and joy inflated inside her like balloons. She put her arms around him. 'Oh, David, I'd really, *really* like that.'

It was strange, having her husband moving back in. Good-strange. They had only been apart a matter of weeks, but Emma had become quite set in her ways without him around the place. David being home made her realize how lonely she'd been, with her single mug and plate in the morning; how she'd left the radio on almost constantly just so that she could hear someone else's voice; how she knew the weekly TV guide off by heart by the time it was Tuesday. Now that he was back, the small rooms filled instantly with his sounds again – the ringtone of his phone, his laugh, the low burble of sporting commentary from Radio 5. She slept so much more soundly with him in bed beside her too, somehow better able to block out the noises from the street below with the comfort of his warm body there.

It had crossed her mind that, for all his promises and optimistic words, he might well fall back into the slough of depression he'd been in, gradually becoming beaten down with negativity if a job didn't fall into his lap straight away, but on the first morning he got out of bed as soon as her alarm shrilled and went into the kitchen, where she heard him filling the kettle.

'You don't have to get up,' she said, when he presented her with a cup of tea and two slices of toast, with the perfect amount of butter and Marmite. 'Stay in bed, I would.'

'It's cool,' he said. 'I'm used to getting up and helping Mum with the breakfasts, remember. Looking after you is a breeze in comparison.'

He was trying, she realized happily as she came home in the evening to find him making risotto for them and saw that he'd circled job ads in the local paper and even arranged a couple of interviews with recruitment agencies. He wanted to make this work – to make *them* work as a team once more. It hit her then just how badly she wanted the same, not to mention how close she'd come to blowing everything, messing about with Nicholas and Greg.

Having David there in the evenings meant she had less time to spend obsessing on the pregnancy forum too. For the last month she'd felt close to the other women all tapping away online in their lonely bubbles of desperation, as if they were in it together. She knew their ovulation cycles almost as well as her own, had been typing them supportive messages and words of encouragement every night. Funnily enough, as soon as she switched off, she discovered that she didn't miss them one bit – if anything, she felt lighter, not having to worry about them. The website had been a good source of information, and a useful emotional crutch at first, but she could see now that it had long since stopped helping her. If anything, it had only made her feel more obsessed.

In its place she made more of an effort to reconnect with Sally and other friends, and began organizing nights out. She even agreed to go to baby Poppy's naming ceremony in May. Baby or no baby, she and David still had a lot to be thankful for, after all.

Two weeks after his return to Bristol, David greeted her

one evening with a bottle of champagne. 'It's not even cava, it's the proper stuff,' he said, popping it open with a flourish. 'Cheers!'

She squealed as the champagne foamed over the fat green lip of the bottle. 'What are we celebrating? What's happened?'

His eyes sparkled. 'I've got a job,' he said. Four words, and he could not have said them with any more happiness or pride. 'For an architect's firm in Bath. Great company – the MD is Robert Fletcher, remember me telling you about him? Amazing bloke.' He pulled a crumpled pile of paper from his laptop bag before she could say anything, and grinned. 'Picked these up on the way home, too,' he said tossing them onto the table. 'Houses for sale. Thought we could look at a few this weekend.'

Emma couldn't speak for a moment, she felt so delighted for him – for both of them. Finally, *finally*, the wheel had turned and they were moving once more, out from the dark place they'd been in and forward towards a bright new future together. 'I'll drink to that,' she said, kissing him full on the lips. 'Oh, David, well done. I'm so proud of you. Congratulations!'

The next few weeks passed very happily. David started work, throwing himself enthusiastically into his first new project – a modern extension to a Victorian villa, which seemed to consist of inordinately large pieces of toughened glass, so as to give incredible views down one of Bath's hillsides. The job was a twelve-mile commute away, but he was able to do it by bike, along the cycle path, which he absolutely loved. Within the week he was bragging about how he'd already shaved two minutes off his journey time. 'I feel a spreadsheet coming on,' Emma groaned, rolling her eyes.

Being employed again seemed to flick a switch in David's internal circuitry. The light in his eyes became brighter, he moved with more energy and purpose. He was David again, in short. Gone were the despair and moping – now he was back playing cricket with his mates every Thursday night, he was swimming his splashy butterfly at the Dean Lane baths, he was running around the park and getting sweaty in Lycra. (Mmm-mmm.)

Emma loved seeing this change in him. He hummed without realizing it. He laughed easily. He even sang in the shower some mornings. She looked forward to seeing him after work every evening and hearing what he'd been doing that day. If they met for dinner or a drink in town – which was quite often – she found herself feeling fluttery as she put on perfume and lipstick, just like in the early days when they'd started dating. It was as if she was falling in love with him all over again.

Even house-hunting was romantic. 'What a chore,' Alicia

had said sympathetically when Emma told her over the phone that they were about to start looking, but it didn't feel remotely chore-like to Emma. Walking hand-in-hand up the front path of what might be their new home actually felt really exciting, full of hope. Even going through specifications seemed to bring them closer together. 'We can't have this one, the garden's pathetic,' he would say. 'How are we meant to teach the kids football on one titchy patio?'

Such a line might sound throwaway and unimportant to another person, but to Emma it felt seismic, just as ruling out houses with fewer than three bedrooms did. Their checklist simply underlined what they both wanted to find, in a house and in life too.

Emma knew that house-hunting might well take them a long time. As an architect and an interior designer, they were tough customers and knew exactly what they wanted — she was fully prepared for it to be a long haul. 'There's no point settling for anything we don't love,' they had both agreed.

'It's got to be our happy-ever-after home,' she had added.

It came as a surprise, then, that the third house they looked around, a Victorian semi in Southville, spoke to both of them with the most persuasive of voices. It had a beautiful stained-glass inner-porch door, which Emma swooned over. It had the original Victorian doorbell that David loved ('It's an actual bell, rigged up on a cable, look!'

he beamed, pointing it out) and the ceilings were high, with all the original coving and plasterwork still in place. Emma knew quite well that she shouldn't be swayed by something as temporary as a shade of paint, but when she went into the back living room and saw the deep Brunswick green on the wall, she was smitten.

'This is it,' she whispered, as they walked into the kitchen. It was dated, with tired old units, a peeling lino floor and what might even be damp in the corner. *Whatever*, she thought. There were large windows overlooking the garden, a separate utility room, and she knew a reclamation yard where she could get her hands on a good butler's sink. With a spraygun of Flash and elbow grease, sandpaper, paint and a loving eye, she could turn this room into the very heart of their home.

'Check out the garden,' David murmured, gripping her hand, and she knew he was already planning where to put the football net. *If* I get pregnant, she reminded herself. *If* we have children to practise penalty shoot-outs with. But she was sure this house would be way more conducive to baby-making at the very least. They would be happy here.

With cash already in the pot from their previous sale, and no chain behind them, they were the best kind of buyers and were able to sneak in a low offer, which was duly accepted. They organized solicitors, contracts and a land search, and Emma began making moodboards for every room, gathering paint charts and fabric swatches like a woman possessed.

They moved in at the end of May, two days before her thirty-sixth birthday. They threw a double housewarming-birthday celebration, with friends bearing presents and Prosecco, and there was a huge cake filled with whipped cream and fruit that David had bought from Patisserie Valerie. They strung fairy lights around the grotty kitchen and everybody toasted their good fortune, and danced.

The occasion was tinged with a pang of anxiety, though. She was now thirty-six, and her conception chances were running out, trickling steadily away like sand through an egg-timer. Blowing out the candles on her cake only served to remind her that her fertile days were numbered – if she even had any left at all.

'Let's give ourselves one more year to get pregnant,' she suggested to David one evening soon afterwards, 'and then maybe we should look at other options. IVF, for instance, or adoption.'

He nodded. They were sitting out on their small patio on a rickety wooden bench, which had come with the house. Late golden sunshine fell warm on their faces, while a cool breeze ruffled through the too-long grass on the lawn. 'I've been thinking the same,' he said. 'And in the meantime we should make a point of doing all those things that our friends with kids envy us for. Dirty weekends away when we feel like it, lazy Sundays in bed . . .' He put a hand on her thigh. 'Screaming full-blown sex on the patio . . .'

She arched an eyebrow. 'David Jones, do *all* your ideas for things to do revolve around sex?'

He kissed her and slid his hand up her top. 'But of course,' he murmured throatily, while she gasped, and hoped very much that their nosey new neighbours weren't watching. 'Don't yours?'

Chapter Thirty-One

Down in Dorset, Izzy and Charlie were also embracing life – and each other – wholeheartedly. This was the relationship she had always wanted: someone who made her laugh, who was fun to be with, who was on her side. Best friend as well as lover, Charlie was the sunshine to Gary's darkness, the flipside of the coin. She'd always preferred the warmth of the sun to storm clouds.

Lilian surprised everyone – not least herself – by professing to being overjoyed about the blossoming relationship. She actually clapped her hands with joy when they broke the news to her. 'Oh! I was hoping this might happen,' she said, hugging Charlie, then Izzy, then Charlie again. 'You two are perfect for each other. Perfect!'

Izzy felt dazed by such enthusiasm. To think she'd once thought this woman a dragon – and look at her now, dabbing her eyes on the corner of her apron, having shed real wet tears of happiness that Izzy had got it together with her son. She hadn't seen that one coming, back at their first inauspicious meeting.

Later on, when Charlie was helping Eddie trim the front hedge, Lilian cornered Izzy for a woman-to-woman chat. 'I've never seen Charlie like this before,' she confided. 'I mean, I always knew that the girls he hooked up with in the past wouldn't last. They simply weren't good enough for him, and he didn't care two hoots. But the way he looks at you . . . well. He thinks you're a cut above, take it from me. And Eddie and I think so too.'

It was like receiving a blessing from the Pope. 'Thank you,' Izzy replied, trying to hide the stab of sympathy she felt for all the supposedly unsuitable girls who'd gone before. No wonder Charlie had never had long relationships in the past; she could well imagine Lilian terrifying each and every poor unknowing girlfriend with her gimlet eyes. 'I think he's pretty fantastic too. He's great.'

'Oh, he is. He's had his moments in the past, mind you, but I feel he's actually grown up a lot this year. And hasn't he turned out lovely?'

Izzy smiled, her nose wrinkling. She was so going to tease Charlie for being Mummy's Little Poppet. 'He has,' she agreed.

Term started and Willow and Hazel went back to school. Every morning Charlie appeared at twenty past eight to give them a lift in, and every afternoon he brought them home again. Within a few days the three of them had developed all sorts of in-jokes, and Charlie was party to umpteen items of gossip, about who was best friends with whom, and who had been sent to the head teacher for being naughty. Izzy might have felt left out, if she hadn't been so pleased at the new bonds the three of them were forming.

Hazel would often burst into giggles for unfathomable reasons when they were having their post-school biscuits and apples in the garden. 'Charlie was so funny in the car this morning,' she would splutter, suddenly remembering. 'Wasn't he, Willow? When he—'

'When he was doing all the voices!' Now Willow was cracking up too.

'What voices? What do you mean?' Izzy would ask, but both girls would be helpless, shaking with laughter. 'I guess you had to be there,' she would say, when no answer was forthcoming.

In the wake of Gary's death and the turbulent few weeks they'd had, Izzy had worried about Willow and Hazel coping at school, but being back in a busy routine seemed to distract them both, thankfully, and soon they were in the usual whirl of new playground crazes, school trips to look forward to, and spelling tests. If anything, they actually seemed happier and more settled than they had all year. Willow joined the drama club and was growing in confidence by the week, and

Hazel had discovered (to Izzy's horror) that there was a certain cachet to be had amongst her peers by dint of having 'a dead dad'. 'I've got an alive one as well now,' Izzy heard her say to a group of girls one Saturday afternoon at a birthday party. 'He's called Charlie and he's *really* cool.'

Izzy wasn't quite sure what to make of this. Pleased as she was that the girls had taken Charlie to their hearts so readily, she didn't know if they should yet be thinking of him as their new dad; it seemed clingy, even by Hazel's standards. But they liked him at least. That was the main thing.

Three weeks into the new term Hazel's long-suffering teacher, Mrs Anthony, called Izzy in for 'a little chat'. 'I know life has been difficult lately,' she began tactfully, 'but I'm slightly concerned that Hazel is being rather . . . er . . . well, ghoulish, frankly, about her late father. One parent has already come in saying that her child has had nightmares about, and I quote, "Hazel's daddy being a zombie".'

Izzy tried not to laugh, but it found its way out as a splutter. 'Sorry,' she said. 'I know it's not remotely funny.'

'I'm glad she's no longer quite so distraught about losing her father,' Mrs Anthony replied, her own mouth twitching with suppressed amusement. 'But perhaps you could have a word — ask her to tone it down a touch?'

'Leave her to me,' Izzy promised, then snorted again as she was leaving the classroom. A zombie, indeed. If Willow was showing a flair for amateur dramatics, then her younger sister seemed more inclined to no-holds-barred melo-dramatics. Still, she supposed she should be grateful that Hazel was talking about it at all. There was no chance of her ever bottling anything up.

Meanwhile, with the girls at school, Izzy had begun helping Lilian out more and more. The first morning that Charlie whisked them away, she sat twiddling her thumbs for all of ten seconds before deciding to hobble up to the house and see what needed doing.

She had never witnessed breakfast at the B&B before, and walked into the kitchen to find herself in a whirl of noise and action. Lilian was breathless and red-faced as she single-handedly flipped bacon, scrambled eggs, buttered toast and made pots of coffee, all apparently at the same time.

'What can I do?' Izzy asked.

Lilian looked faint with gratitude as she passed Izzy an apron. 'If you carry on here, I'll go out and clear the tables. Please.'

The next hour flew by in a hot blur of cooking, plating up food and making endless pots of tea and coffee, while Lilian took orders, wiped tables and delivered the breakfasts on enormous trays. By the end of it, Izzy never wanted to see a black pudding again. 'Whoa,' she gulped, when the last guests had finally left the dining room. 'Is it always like this?'

Lilian gave a small laugh. 'You want to see it when we're really busy.'

'And you've been doing all of this yourself? This whole time?'

'David helped me while he was staying, and Eddie used to chip in before that, but . . .' Lilian didn't need to finish the sentence. 'I have Becky and Lynne, girls from the village, in for busy weekends and the summer holidays, but otherwise I have to manage alone.'

'Wow.' Izzy felt exhausted already and it was barely nine-thirty. 'I've worked in pubs that were less busy than your breakfast room.'

Lilian smiled and set the dishwasher running. 'You get used to it,' she said as the machine rumbled sloshily into life. 'That's always the toughest bit of the day. The way I see it, hoovering and stripping beds feels like a holiday afterwards.'

'Right,' said Izzy politely, although she remained unconvinced. 'Well, look, you've got me now as well. I'm not going to be much help waitressing while I'm on crutches, but I don't mind taking over the cooking, if you've had enough of frying breakfasts.'

'Oh no, I couldn't possibly let you.'

'You could,' Izzy told her. 'Really, Lilian. You could.' Her eyes twinkled as she used one of Lilian's favourite phrases back at her. 'No arguments now.'

'But . . .'

'And no buts, either. I know you're a tough lady, but so am I. You've helped me out – and now I'm going to return the favour.'

From that day on, a new arrangement began at Mulberry House. Every morning at six-thirty Izzy and the girls would wake and get dressed, then come to the breakfast room for seven. It was quite unusual for any guests to emerge for food until at least seven-thirty, by which time Izzy had woken up properly over a coffee, the girls had eaten and she'd brushed their hair. Lilian appeared at eight, in time to supervise Willow and Hazel's tooth-brushing (she was proper strict too, much to Izzy's approval and the girls' dismay), by which time Izzy would be in full swing in the kitchen. Once she'd mastered the temperamental gas grill and got a routine going, she discovered she rather enjoyed being head chef. She did think Lilian was missing a trick with the menu, though.

'Listen,' she said one day, once the rush had subsided and the two of them were taking morning coffee together. This had become a new ritual too, a companionable un-winding session where they discussed the rest of the day's chores and divided them up. 'I was thinking – how would you feel if I changed things round a bit on the menu?'

Lilian frowned and dipped her Rich Tea into her mug. 'What do you mean, changed things round a bit?'

'Well . . .' Izzy knew she had to be tactful. Criticizing Lilian or her business was highly precarious. 'I think you do a great-value breakfast here – I mean, everyone enjoys a fry-up, don't they? But sometimes people want a lighter meal. A good old bacon-butty, for example, or pancakes for the children. My two would have pancakes every day if they could, and they're no bother to make. Banana pancakes are nice, or we could try blueberry ones, perhaps . . .'

Lilian said nothing, but her lips were tightening as if she was on the verge of disagreeing.

'Maybe eggs Benedict, too, I know how to cook that,' Izzy went on quickly. 'I once worked in a fancy café in Manchester, and that was dead popular. Or slow-cooked porridge with honey . . . We could have a pot of that bubbling away at the back of the stove, no problem. What do you think? We could give it a try.'

Izzy was feeling less and less optimistic by the second as Lilian remained silent. It was obvious she had served up the same old fry-ups day in, day out for the last twenty years. Was she affronted by Izzy wanting to muck around with her menu now?

Then Lilian nodded. 'Well,' she said slowly. 'If you think it's a good idea, I suppose we could try.' She looked far-away suddenly. 'I haven't had eggs Benedict since our honeymoon, you know.'

Izzy grinned. 'Then I'll make us all some for lunch,' she said. 'I can remind myself how to do it, before I'm let loose on the paying guests.'

They launched the new breakfast menu the next week, and Izzy's hunch quickly proved right. Her creamy smooth porridge was a big success (several people actually requested seconds) and the pancakes went down a storm too. Nobody seemed to miss the kippers and black pudding, especially not Izzy.

On a high from all the compliments she was receiving, she found her thoughts turning to the future, idly planning what she could introduce later in the summer. Strawberry pancakes would be nice – Eddie had some strawberry plants in his kitchen garden, she had noticed. Maybe she could try making her own fruity granola. She might even be able to persuade Lilian to invest in a waffle-maker . . .

Then it hit her. Summer? What was she thinking? She'd be long gone by then, of course. Once she was up and about as normal, she and the girls would be packing up and leaving here to go back to their flat in Lyme. Their contract on that place ran out in August, but if her money came through in time, she wanted to buy them a little house down near the sea front – a brand-new home for the three of them.

She paused, her hand on the black marble mantelpiece she'd been dusting. She would miss it here, though, she realized. Even after a month Mulberry House felt like home. She would miss the space here, the garden, the calm. She would even miss Lilian.

Poor Lilian. Izzy had a feeling that Charlie's mum would miss her, too, when she and the girls left. 'I don't know what I would do without you,' she had been saying with increasing frequency as Izzy worked tirelessly around the house alongside her. She looked so haggard and worried and tired lately, as Eddie slowly but steadily declined. They were like a pair of old clocks winding down together – her with exhaustion, him with mental illness. Lilian had finally taken him to the doctor's, where he'd undergone a whole battery of tests, with more to come at the hospital. The doctor later telephoned to say that Eddie was almost certainly suffering from the early onset of Alzheimer's.

The news, although not a shock, had come as a terrible blow to the whole family; Charlie had wept in dismay when he heard.

'I knew it,' he said wretchedly. 'I knew something was wrong. The worst thing is, there's nothing anyone can do about it. How is Mum going to manage?'

Izzy felt like crying herself. She hadn't known Eddie all that long, but he was such a lovely person, and it was heartbreaking seeing a man who'd clearly once been so capable and together gradually sinking into a state of bewilderment and frailty. They'd had to stop him answering the phone and the door now, after he had become a magnet for spam-callers and evangelical Christians alike.

Lilian was holding it together for the time being, but Izzy wasn't sure how much longer she could cope with so much on her plate. 'Go on, I'll do this,' she told the older woman whenever she could take a chore from her. 'You go and see what Eddie's up to in the garden, if you want. Sun's shining.'

Lilian had never seemed very good at accepting help before, but these days she was grateful for any extra assistance. In fact, one afternoon in late May she actually gave Izzy a sudden tight hug when she offered to finish cleaning the kitchen floor. 'Thank you,' she said. 'I hope you know how much I appreciate all you're doing for me. You're like the daughter I never had.'

The words took Izzy's breath away. Tough, no-nonsense Lilian was not the type for glad-handing or meaningless platitudes. She certainly wouldn't get sentimental for no good reason. 'Oh, Lilian,' Izzy said, the most enormous lump appearing in her throat. 'Nobody's ever said that to me before. I never really had a mum.'

Lilian patted Izzy on the back and they drew apart. Her eyes were moist. 'Well, you've got me now,' she said.

Eight weeks after the crash Izzy returned to the fracture clinic for the last time. Her cast was taken off and she was given a series of physio exercises to rebuild the strength of her leg. 'You should continue being cautious,' the consultant advised. 'It's best not to go straight back to jogging or anything that will put it under a strain for a while. Weight-bearing exercise such as swimming is excellent, though.'

'I take it dancing is still out?' Izzy asked, her heart sinking.

The consultant nodded. 'I'm afraid so. The bones have healed, but the leg isn't as strong as it was. It may be some time before you can dance again.'

The advice was about as welcome as a gigantic hairy spider in the bath. She had Ella, the new dance teacher, who was more than happy to continue taking lessons at least, but it was still a blow. Izzy was an active person by nature, and had found her limited mobility so frustrating. She'd been looking forward to running and jumping and dancing as normal.

'Try to be patient,' the consultant said, seeing her face. 'You'll get there.'

Better news came in June, when the estate agent telephoned to say that the sale of the flat in Manchester had just completed, and it was now the property of a very nice young family apparently. Days later the proceeds, coupled with Gary's hefty life-insurance payment, landed in Izzy's bank account with the most almighty thud. She felt cata-pulted into the air by it, sent soaring free, like a bird released from a cage. This was it – she was now a woman of means, able to do whatever she and the girls wanted, go wherever the wind took them.

But where would that be? When she searched inside her heart for the right way forward, she discovered she didn't actually want to go very far from the Joneses at all.

That evening, once Hazel and Willow were in bed, she and Charlie curled up on the creaky old love seat in the garden, swinging gently together. He was staying the occasional night with her in the chalet now, and she loved spending the whole evening and night together. Even some-thing as mundane as watching TV or having a beer was more fun with Charlie around. 'Listen,' she said, 'it's been amazing staying here, and I've loved getting to know your family. Thank you for everything. But now I'm off the crutches it's probably time that I left you lot in peace and went back to the flat with the girls, just until I can buy us somewhere nice for keeps anyway.'

Charlie looked dismayed. 'You want to go?'

'Well . . .' She bit her lip. 'It's not that I want to *go* exactly, it's just that I don't feel I can keep on freeloading here. I want to pay my way. This was only meant to be a temporary thing, right? I can manage again now. Maybe I could find a cottage in the village so that I can still help out here, but . . .'

His arm was around her and he stroked her shoulder. 'Izzy – you're not freeloading. And you've more than paid your way, with your amazing breakfasts and all the cleaning and guest bookings . . . and, well, just supporting my mum in a way that I'm not very good at. I know she feels the same. You can stay as long as you want.'

She swung her legs, enjoying how light her leg felt out of plaster now, as she hunted for the right words. 'Staying in the chalet has been lovely. But it's small. And it's not permanent. I just want to live someplace where I can put down roots again. Somewhere I can unpack everything. Our own space. Does that make sense? I'm not ungrateful, don't get me wrong, it's just . . .'

'I know,' he said. 'I get it. Stupid of me not to think about that.'

They were silent for a few minutes, each deep in thought. Then at last he spoke. 'I've had an idea,' he said slowly.

Chapter Thirty-Two

'What time will she be here, Mum?' asked Matilda, appearing in the kitchen doorway.

'Any minute now,' Alicia replied, wiping down the surfaces for the tenth time. Any minute now their family of five was officially going to become six. She wasn't sure why she was cleaning everything so obsessively – as far as she knew Cathy wasn't some hygiene inspector who'd be examining the kitchen for signs of slovenliness (hell, she was a student, she was probably pretty resistant to E. coli and domestic disorder), but first appearances did count, whatever people said. The last thing she wanted was for Cathy to report back to the saintly Sophie Bloom that her new stepmother (stepmother – her!) was a slattern.

Not that she would have any right to, of course – this was Hugh's house too, and technically he was every bit as responsible for the upkeep of the place as her, and she hated how it always seemed to be the woman who was judged on these things, but . . .

'I hope she likes me,' Matilda said, swinging on the doorjamb. 'Do you think she will?'

Alicia put down the cloth. 'Of course she will. Just think how lucky she is, to have a brand-new sister – you!'

'I told Mrs Brewster that I had a new sister and she said, 'Oh! Mummy's had a new baby?' and I had to tell her that actually . . .'

Alicia's smile became rather fixed as Matilda went into detail. Mrs Brewster was Matilda's teacher and the type who poked her nose into everything. She hadn't bargained for their dirty washing to be hung out quite so publicly yet, before she'd even had a chance to sort out her own feelings.

'Mrs Brewster said we're very modern,' Matilda finished. 'What does that mean?'

Alicia coloured. Modern indeed. How smug it sounded, as if the woman was mocking them. 'It means Mrs Brewster's an idiot,' she snapped, breaking her own golden rule about never criticizing the children's teachers in front of them. 'And she doesn't have a clue what she's talking about. Now then, why don't you go and look out the window, to watch for Daddy's car?'

Less than a minute later the shout went up. 'They're here! They're here!'

Alicia's stomach seemed to contract and she gripped the side of the (spotless) counter for a moment, before smoothing down her hair, brushing a crumb from her blouse and taking a deep breath. Oh, help. This was really happening.

She walked towards the front door, feeling as if she were in a dream. Her relationship with Hugh had been slightly discordant since the news about Cathy had come out. They hadn't argued again as such, but there had been this new mistrust between them, a certain coolness. Sure, he'd been as good as his word and taken the KitchenAid back to the shop just after her birthday. He'd even persuaded Izzy to go shopping with him and help choose an assortment of pretty things for Alicia. Yet they still stepped warily around each other, avoiding difficult conversations. Now his daughter was coming to meet the rest of the family, and it felt like crunch time.

However rational Alicia tried to be about the whole thing, she was aware of a deeply ingrained insecurity that kept making itself known. What if Hugh went back to his real first love? What if he decided he preferred the Blooms to her and the children?

It was astonishing just how jealous you could be of a person you'd never even met.

The front door was opening. 'Hello?' called Hugh, stepping into the hall.

Queasily Alicia forced herself to smile at the girl who walked in behind him. 'Hi,' she said with all the calm she could muster. 'You must be Cathy.'

Wow. Cathy looked so like Hugh, it was hard not to stare. Alicia had secretly wished for there to be no likeness whatsoever, and for Cathy really to be the daughter of some random Frenchman whom Sophie had sluttishly bonked while over there, but no. There was no getting away from it: Cathy was definitely Hugh's daughter. She had the same wide eyes and large forehead as her father, coupled with his tall frame. She was ganglier than Hugh, like a beautiful young deer, shy and unaware of her grace. Long red hair fell about her face, and she was wearing a short summer dress and silver gladiator sandals, with an armful of clinking bangles.

'Hi,' said Cathy, glancing from Alicia to Lucas, to Rafferty, to Matilda and then back to Hugh. She looked completely overwhelmed all of a sudden – terrified, even – and in that moment Alicia's maternal instinct rose to the fore. The girl was barely more than a child, at the end of the day.

'Come on in,' she said graciously. 'We've all been so looking forward to meeting you.' It wasn't strictly, forensically true, but as Hugh began making all the introductions, and the children fell over themselves to impress their new, glamorous big sister, Alicia realized, really for the first time, that this tall gorgeous creature was a human being, not just a 'thing' that had threatened her marriage. Judging by Cathy's defensive body language and the way she was clutching her bag to her side, she wasn't enormously comfortable with the situation, either.

'Come on, kids, let her into the house,' Alicia said, with a nervous laugh. 'We've got plenty of time to get to know each other, there's no rush. Cathy, would you like a drink? Something to eat?'

The six of them had lunch and then went out for a walk in a nearby country park. Half-child, half-adult, Cathy flitted between Hugh and Alicia and their children with ease, discussing Fine Art techniques one minute, then joining in wholeheartedly with a kick-about the next. She was polite, friendly and thoroughly nice. Moreover she was not remotely threatening. She was not, Alicia realized, about to barge into the Joneses' world and disrupt everything, throw their world into chaos. She hadn't come for financial reasons, or to emotionally blackmail Hugh; there was no hidden agenda whatsoever. She'd merely come to meet her half-family and, in doing so, added a refreshing spice to their mix, creating a new, and perhaps even better, flavour.

'She is so cool,' Matilda sighed later in the day, when Cathy had been dropped at the train station to go home. 'I love her hair.' She gave a little skip of pleasure. 'And I've *always* wanted a sister.'

'She's actually all right,' Lucas admitted. 'At least she's not as ugly as Dad.'

'She's awesome on the Wii, too,' Raffy said. 'Did you see, she broke my record for the 100 metres on *Mario & Sonic at the Olympics*?'

That night Alicia and Hugh held each other for a long time in bed.

'Thank you,' Hugh said into the darkness, his breath warm against her ear. 'Thank you for today.'

Alicia could hear his heartbeat, slow and steady. It made her feel safe. 'She's a lovely girl,' she said.

'I know,' he said. 'Thank you for being able to see that. You're a very generous woman.'

Alicia held him a little tighter. 'I'm a very lucky woman,' she replied.

'Good God,' Sandra said, spluttering on her cigarette when Alicia told her about the whole episode. She had come down for the weekend, and the two sisters were having coffee in the sunshine outside the Bay Hotel in Lyme, while Hugh supervised the children sea-kayaking.

'I know,' Alicia said. 'That was my reaction too.'

'Hugh – with a secret love child! I'm looking at the man with totally new eyes now, I'm telling you. I never thought he had it in him.'

'He didn't, either,' Alicia countered. 'It was a shock for him too. But I think it's going to be okay, you know. I think we're through the worst.'

'What about the ex, first-love-Sophie? Is she back on the scene too?'

Alicia shook her head. 'No,' she said. 'She lives in Norfolk. Has been married to someone else for fifteen years, apparently, so I think I'm safe there.'

Sandra elbowed her. 'Ah, well, you say that, but lots of women have a soft spot for their first loves, remember . . .'

'Don't start! I don't need anything else to worry about, thank you very much. I've had enough dramas this year to last me a lifetime.'

'Must be strange, though,' Sandra went on. 'Having an extra person in the family all of a sudden. I guess it would be like us, if we suddenly discovered that Christine had been alive all along, that Mum and Dad had just given her away when she was a baby because—'

A shudder went right through Alicia. 'Don't,' she interrupted. 'Really, don't. That's a horrible thing to say. They would never have done that.'

'I know, of course they wouldn't, but I'm just *saying*, imagine if they had.'

'Really – don't! It makes me feel weird.' She fiddled with her coffee cup, aware that Sandra probably thought she was overreacting wildly. 'I wish she hadn't died,' she said wistfully after a moment.

'I know. Sorry. Do you ever wonder what she would have been like?'

Alicia gave a hollow laugh. 'All the time,' she replied. 'And, most of the time, I measure up short against her. In my head she's like SuperTwin – you know, the perfect woman, brilliant at everything, leading the most exciting life ever lived.' Then her brow furrowed as something occurred to her. 'Although . . . that's weird. I haven't been thinking about her so much lately. For a while it was like she was in my head all the time. These days, hardly at all.'

'You know, I think maybe you've spent your whole life trying to overcompensate for Christine not being here,' Sandra said, out of the blue.

'How do you mean?' Alicia asked, startled.

'I mean . . . You've always tried that extra bit harder than normal people to please everyone, Al. You've almost been *too* nice, because you've been trying to make up for Christine not surviving. And maybe, at a deep subconscious level, there's some guilt, too, that you couldn't stop her dying, so you're running around trying to help everyone else instead. Does that sound crazy?' she added hastily as Alicia's face dropped. 'It seemed okay as a theory in my head, but now that I've actually said it out loud . . .'

'No, I get what you mean,' Alicia replied, and then didn't know what else to say. Whoa, Sandra the psychotherapist. It was rather scary, having someone analyse your behaviour with such unnerving perception.

'So if you've stopped dwelling on her, then maybe it's

because you're more relaxed – like you don't have to prove anything.' She raised an eyebrow. 'You can drop the nice act now, honey. We all like you anyway. Give us the real Al Jones for a change.'

Alicia laughed. 'It's not an act!' she protested. 'Some people *are* just nice, you know, Sandra. Although . . .' She hesitated.

Sandra looked delighted that there was an 'although'. 'Yes?' she prompted encouragingly. 'Go on – let rip with that mean streak. I know you must have one.'

'Well, it's not mean, exactly, but . . . oh, all right, I'll just say it.' She took a deep breath. 'Please, Sandra, stop calling me "Al". I've never liked it. It makes me feel like a man.'

Sandra's eyes widened and then she laughed and clapped Alicia on the back. 'You got it,' she said. 'Absolutely. Consider it done, *Alicia*. Now, can I get you another drink?'

If Alicia thought the family might be heading for calmer waters now, Charlie's phone call a few days later promptly shattered that illusion. 'I'm calling a crisis meeting,' he said dramatically. 'Mum and Dad's house, Saturday afternoon. Emma and David are coming too. Are you and Hugh free?'

'Crisis meeting?' Alicia immediately feared the worst. 'What's happened? Has Eddie––?'

'He's okay. Well, he's the same anyway –' He broke off. Charlie had taken the news about his dad hard, by all accounts. 'I've been thinking about the future, and I've got something to discuss with everyone, that's all. Not a crisis – not yet anyway. We can't keep burying our heads in the sand, though.'

Although impressed that feckless Charlie was taking the lead for once, Alicia couldn't help thinking that this sounded rather ominous. She hoped it wasn't going to be another of her brother-in-law's ludicrous money-making schemes, where he would attempt to tap everyone for an investment. Please, no.

Hugh didn't have much confidence in the forthcoming meeting either. 'If he says we need to put Dad in a home,' he started fiercely, 'I'll—'

'He hasn't said anything yet,' Alicia reminded him. 'Give him a chance.'

Privately, though, she had been wondering if Eddie's days in a normal home environment were numbered. The old Eddie who'd roll up his shirt sleeves and fix anything, who'd take on the boys at French cricket in the garden, the Eddie who made everyone laugh, who smoothed off Lilian's rough edges and kept them together as a family – he was a thing of the past, and nowadays there was just this anxious, befuddled old man in his place. Charlie was right: they had all been burying their heads in the sand. It was clear that Lilian and Eddie could not carry on as they were for much longer.

She braced herself all week for the meeting. Ever since

that anniversary lunch back in February, when Hugh's parents had announced their intentions to retire, the whole family seemed to have been nervously repositioning themselves in anticipation of the monumental change that was coming. She wasn't sure if she could handle any more changes, to be honest.

On Saturday afternoon the adult Joneses and Izzy gathered en masse around the dining table in Mulberry House, and it was almost as if the months had rolled back to that last fateful meeting. This time Charlie wasn't turning up late and in disgrace, though. This time he was a man with a plan, at the head of the table, no less.

'I've got a proposal to make,' he began without preamble. 'Or, rather, Izzy and I have.'

Eddie, who had been staring blankly into space, seemed to wake up at this. 'A marriage proposal?' he asked hopefully.

Charlie blushed. 'No,' he replied, glancing rather sheepishly at Izzy. 'Well, not today anyway. I know Izzy here is gagging to be Mrs Jones in the future, but . . .'

'Don't flatter yourself, love,' she put in, rolling her eyes. Anyone could tell she was happy, though. The pair of them had lit up from the inside since they'd finally got it together romantically. (Alicia was *thrilled* for them, it went without saying. She loved a romantic happy ending – all the best books and films had one.)

'No, it's about the business,' Charlie went on. 'Mum and Dad have done a brilliant job of running this place over the years, while still keeping Mulberry House our family home.'

'Hear hear,' David put in.

'And I know when I first offered to take over the business, back in the spring, none of you thought I was up to the job,' he said.

There was an embarrassed silence. 'Yes, we did,' Alicia said kindly after a moment, but it came too late to be convincing.

He laughed. 'It's all right, honestly. I *wasn't* up to the job, simple as that. I'd have been rubbish – hopelessly disorganized, however much I wanted to save the house. But . . .' He looked unsure of himself all of a sudden, as if the real Charlie was being revealed, the vulnerable youngest brother who'd always secretly felt a screw-up.

Izzy stepped in to rescue him. 'But now he's got me,' she said, glancing sideways at him. 'And I'm *really* organized. I've managed my own business before, and I like working here. And we think, between us, that we could make a go of running Mulberry House. If that's all right with everyone else, of course,' she added uncertainly when nobody spoke.

Alicia's mouth had fallen open. 'Gosh,' she blurted out. 'Wow!'

'Really?' said David. He looked delighted. 'Good on you!'

'How exciting!' Emma chimed in, her eyes crinkling at

the edges as she smiled. She was *very* smiley these days, Alicia thought, noticing how cosily 'together' she and David looked.

Lilian clutched a hand to her chest. 'Oh, that's *wonderful*,' she exclaimed. 'Truly wonderful! I've been hoping and hoping, you know. I didn't want to put any pressure on you, or say anything but . . .'

'Wait a minute. So, how's this going to work?' Hugh, of course. He always had to get the full facts before he was able to give any future project his approval. Some might say he'd just killed a lovely moment stone-dead, but Alicia knew it was only because he cared.

'Well, I've come into quite a large sum of money,' Izzy said.

'And I'm going to sell my flat,' Charlie added. 'We've got enough to buy Mum and Dad out, so that they can move somewhere smaller and retire.'

'Move out?' cried Eddie in alarm, as if this was the first he'd heard of the idea. 'But what about my garden?'

'Or,' Izzy put in quickly, as he began to look anxious, 'we can look at turning the holiday chalet – or one of the other outbuildings – into a more permanent place for you both to live. That way, Charlie and I are onsite if you two need anything.'

'Oh, Eddie,' Lilian said, taking his hand. 'Did you hear that? We could stay. We could stay here! You wouldn't have to leave the garden.' She put her face in her hands, clearly battling not to cry.

Alicia had tears in her own eyes, seeing her mother-in-law's undisguised relief. The Joneses had come good, she thought, as Charlie, David and Hugh began animatedly discussing how the new set-up could work. Those Jones boys – and Izzy – really had come good.

Later, when the meeting had descended into positive, hopeful chatter about the future, and Hugh had cracked open a bottle or two of wine, Alicia saw Izzy going to check on the girls and followed her out of the room, wanting a quiet word. It was all very well the Joneses having sorted out their problems, but with the best will in the world, this new plan was an enormous leap of faith for Izzy. Going into business with Charlie so soon after the tragedy of her ex-husband – did she really know what she was letting herself in for?

'Listen, tell me to mind my own business if you want, but . . .' She broke off, feeling guilty for being such a kill-joy when everyone else was so openly thrilled by today's developments.

Izzy just smiled. 'But am I rushing into things without thinking them through?' she finished. 'Following my heart instead of my head?'

Alicia bit her lip. They were standing in the hallway, the grandmother clock ticking discreetly behind them. 'Sorry,' she said. 'I don't want to pour cold water on anything; it all sounds wonderful — really, it does. I just can't help being boringly sensible. You know me.'

'Not boring at all,' Izzy replied. 'You're right. I know this must all seem a bit sudden. Normally I would never rush into something like this so quickly, but . . .' She shrugged. 'Sometimes you have to go with your instincts, right? And I don't think this is just a rebound response. I've got a really good feeling about it — like it's meant to be.' She laughed at herself. 'Hark at me, Mystic Izzy. But don't worry, we're getting a proper legal agreement drawn up, making everything official. If it turns out that my instincts are actually crap, and the whole thing is a disaster, I won't lose out financially.'

'Great,' Alicia said warmly. 'I've got a good feeling about you two as well. I always have had, to be honest.' She hesitated. 'And I know Charlie was only mucking about, but . . . well, it's nice to think there might another Mrs Jones in future. You, I mean — not some random other woman he's going to run off and marry.' She giggled and put her hand to her mouth. 'Sorry. This is all coming out wrong. Too much excitement.'

Izzy grinned. 'Isabel Jones sounds all right, doesn't it?' she replied, then added shyly, 'I always wanted to be part of a big family, you know.'

Alicia hugged her. 'Welcome to the family. It's good to have you.'

Much to everyone's relief, Lilian and Eddie chose to stay living on the premises, and the details of all the chalet bungalows that Lilian had accumulated went straight into the recycling pile. 'This will always be our home,' she said fondly to anyone who would listen. 'And you never know, Izzy and Charlie might want my advice on best business practices. I am an expert, after all.'

Once this had been decided, the whole family helped set the wheels in motion. David drew up plans to extend the holiday chalet so that it was more spacious and luxurious, and hired a team of builders. Emma advised on the interior design and helped Charlie decorate. Izzy borrowed a van and collected her last bits and pieces from the flat in Lyme, saying a fond goodbye to Mrs Murray while she was there. Then she and the girls moved into the big house with Charlie, and everyone began working in earnest on ways to improve the business.

Izzy discovered a local-ish company, Berry Botanicals, which made organic toiletries, and ordered a load of yummy smellies in for the bathrooms. Emma took her on a buying trip around an auction house, where she bought some beautiful pieces of furniture for the guest rooms, as well as boxfuls of quality new linen and crockery. Charlie installed a proper Wi-Fi system, Alicia ran up some new curtains on her sewing machine, and Hugh helped with a website overhaul. With just a few small touches, the house was becoming transformed from a tired bed and breakfast to an upmarket, elegant place to stay.

Not only that, but Izzy and Charlie quickly turned the private quarters of Mulberry House back into a proper family home once more. The kitchen became adorned with the children's artwork and school certificates, the dresser displayed colourful vases of flowers picked from the garden and Izzy's favourite cookery books. There were cuddly toys and Pixar DVDs up in the girls' bedrooms, and the garden rang with cheerful shouts and laughs. There was even talk of a new puppy.

'You've done an amazing job,' Emma told Izzy one Sunday in July. She and David had been invited over for lunch, along with Alicia and Hugh's mob, but it was such glorious weather that Charlie had stoked up the barbecue for al-fresco dining instead. Replete with steaks and salad, the three women were now lolling lazily in deckchairs on the patio, with tall glasses of Pimms, while the men organized a game of French cricket for them and the children. Even Lilian had been roped in to referee and was taking it all very seriously.

'Thanks,' Izzy said, twisting her hair up in a chignon.

'I'm loving it, to be honest. Everyone's been so nice to us – we've had so many people booking for next year already.'

'And he hits a six!' yelled Charlie excitedly, thwacking the ball into the orchard. The children all screamed and ran after it.

Alicia laughed. 'I was just about to say how sensible your Charlie is these days,' she said. 'But he's still about seven years old really, isn't he?'

'Young at heart,' Izzy agreed. 'The girls just love him. Do you know, Willow asked him if she could start calling him "Dad".'

'No! Really?'

'It was the sweetest thing,' Izzy said. 'Not Daddy, she decided, because that was Gary. But he could be her dad – because that's different, in her little world.'

'Bless her,' said Alicia. 'She's so gorgeous.'

'And what a compliment to Charlie,' said Emma. 'He makes a good dad.'

'HOWZAT!' Hugh screamed triumphantly just then, punching the air as he bowled Charlie out.

The three women laughed. 'Competitive, much?' Alicia spluttered, rolling her eyes.

'What are they like?' Emma said, as all three brothers began arguing. Lilian marched over, hands on her hips, and they watched in amusement. You could imagine the exact same scene taking place thirty years earlier.

'So, what's next for Mulberry House?' Alicia asked after a while.

'Well, we've been finding out about the glamping market,' Izzy replied. 'Boutique camping, for people who don't like roughing it. It's the hip thing, apparently. We've definitely got room for some big posh tents – yurts, I think they call them – in the orchard.'

'Ooh, that *is* a good idea,' Emma said. 'David and I are off to Cornwall next month with some friends, and we're all staying in yurts. We can be your researchers.'

'You and your trips,' Alicia teased. 'New York last month, Thailand in December . . . You two are becoming the best-travelled couple I've ever met.'

'I know,' Emma replied with a grin. 'The last few months have been really fun. David's used up half his annual leave already with all our adventures. And we've decided . . .' She lowered her voice, even though the rest of the Joneses were still arguing heatedly a safe distance away. 'We've decided we're going to try IVF next year, which is why we're doing all these things while we still can.' She drained her Pimms with a rattle of ice cubes. 'Any excuse, right?'

'Too right,' Izzy said. 'And good luck with the IVF. How exciting.'

'It all sounds a bit medical and undignified,' Emma said ruefully. 'I'm not looking forward to that side of things, but . . .' She shrugged. 'Fingers crossed anyway. We've had some tests, and the doctor said there's nothing actually physically wrong with us, so it's worth a go.'

'It's definitely worth a go,' Alicia echoed. 'Medical science is *amazing*. You've got every chance.'

'Thanks,' Emma said. 'We're both feeling hopeful. It's going to happen, I'm sure of it.'

Alicia was glad for her. Hopeful was good. But, whatever the outcome, Emma and David seemed so much happier these days, full stop: settled in their new home, with David working again. She and the family had gone over to stay with them for the weekend, and they'd all had a great time together at the Science Museum and zoo.

She finished her drink and gazed over at the cricket match where Lucas appeared to have just whacked the cricket ball straight into his father's nuts, to raucous cheers from David and Charlie. She burst out laughing as Hugh collapsed theatrically, demanding to be brought alcoholic sustenance immediately.

Yes, she thought to herself happily. Sports injuries aside, things had worked out pretty well for the Joneses.

Epilogue

Two months later Alicia was waving goodbye to Hugh and the children at St Pancras station and wheeling her case through to the Eurostar terminus. Hugh – unromantic, unimaginative house-brick Hugh – had surprised her the week before by presenting her with a return ticket to Paris. 'I've booked you into a really nice hotel,' he said, hardly able to contain his glee at her astonishment, 'and here are some euros for you to spend. Oh, and Emma sent me the guidebook she and David used when they were there the other month. She's marked up all the nicest bars and restaurants they found.'

Alicia could not believe it. Even now, sitting on the train as it began accelerating out of the station, she still could hardly believe it. Here she was, Alicia Jones, forty and five months, speeding through outer London with a packed itinerary ahead of her. Next stop: Paris!

The city was bustling with life when she alighted at the Gare du Nord, the station full of holidaymakers lugging along suitcases, tour groups consulting maps, and coffee stands that smelled heavenly. Clutching her bags close to her (pickpockets were rife here, according to Emma's guidebook), Alicia followed signs for the taxi rank and waited her turn. It was so exciting, simply being in a queue surrounded by real French people. She had no idea what they were saying to each other, but it sounded beautiful. She was finally here. She was in Paris!

The hotel was in the third arrondissement, on a quiet road just a short walk from the Musée Carnavalet. Once she'd checked in, rather haltingly, and found her room, she sat for a few moments on the edge of her double bed and laughed to herself. 'Oh my God,' she whispered, on the verge of hysteria. 'I actually made it.' She flopped backwards, gazing up at the ceiling and grinning like a halfwit. 'I'm here, in Paris, for the whole weekend. It's happening!'

After texting Hugh that she'd arrived and all was well (she resisted the urge to phone and talk to him and all the children at great length), she washed her face, combed her hair and put on some lipstick. Right! So . . . what next? First, she'd like to take a stroll around the area to soak up the atmosphere. And maybe after that she'd sit and have a coffee, one of those short, strong Parisian coffees that blew your head off, according to Emma. Maybe even a cheeky glass of wine too. And why ever not?

Oh, she thought, smiling happily at herself in the mirror, this was going to be *fun*.

Over the next two and a half days Alicia must have walked miles. She saw the Eiffel Tower, the Arc de Triomphe, the Louvre, Notre-Dame and Sacré-Coeur. She ogled gorgeous shoes in Pring, sampled bonbons in Jacques Genin and ate buttery pastries in the grassy square at the Place des Vosges. The architecture was stunning, the food divine, the city brimmed with history and vitality, and the Parisians looked every bit as chic and sexy and cool as she'd hoped. She felt sated.

She *must* come back here with Hugh, she vowed, as she regretfully packed up her belongings on her last morning and said a sad goodbye to the hotel room. Wonderful and exciting as it was to explore the city alone, there had been moments when she'd wanted to share the beauty with somebody else, to point out an incredible view, to giggle over a haughty *madame* almost tripping over a runaway poodle, to clink wine glasses with at the end of the day.

Ah well. *Bof!* as the French said. They would just have to come back together another year. Izzy had already offered to look after the children any time, or maybe even Emma and David would want to practise their parenting skills and step into the breach.

She lingered in the doorway of her room for a moment, then pulled the door shut behind her and wheeled her suitcase slowly to the lift. *Goodbye, hotel, goodbye. Thank you for looking after me and being so utterly splendid. Thank you for one of the greatest weekends of my life. It's been amazing.*

Down she went, smiling as she thought of seeing everyone again later that evening and telling them all about her trip. But as she emerged from the lift to the ground floor, she stopped dead in shock. For there, signing in at the reception desk, was none other than Hugh. What the . . . ?

She blinked, wondering if it was a mirage at first, some kind of delusion. Maybe, because she'd just been thinking about him, she was projecting, turning complete strangers into husband-lookalikes. She rubbed her eyes and stared. No. It really was him – her husband, in Paris.

'Ah, there you are,' he said amiably, waving as she approached. 'Thought I'd surprise you. You're actually staying here for one more night – with me, this time. I hope you don't mind.'

'Mind?' she said faintly, her mind still registering his words. Then her mouth fell open and she laughed out loud – a rich, happy laugh of delight. He had actually done this, come all the way here to surprise her. She abandoned her luggage and ran across to him, throwing her arms around him with joy. 'Of course I don't mind,' she cried happily. 'I was just thinking how much you'd love it here. Oh, Hugh, I can't believe this! So who's looking after the children?'

'Sandra,' he said. He looked incredibly proud of himself. 'We hatched a plot together. Thank you,' he said, as the receptionist handed over a key. He held it up and winked. 'Well, Mrs Jones,' he said. '*Ma chérie*. Shall we go and unpack?'

Lucy Diamond's
Breakfast Recipes

For me, one of the best things about staying at a bed and breakfast is the actual breakfast. The thread count of the sheets? I'm not interested. The monsoon shower? Whatever. The thing that gets my seal of approval is a proper delicious breakfast to start the day. I'd be very happy to tuck into any of the recipes below, especially if served with a cup of tea, a newspaper and preferably an amazing sea view...

Eggs Benedict

Here's a confession: I am not very good at poaching eggs, despite repeated attempts. Mine always resemble misshapen white ghosts in the pan rather than perfect rounded beauties. Hopefully you are more competent than me though, and can impress your friends and family with this breakfast classic.

Purists have their Eggs Benedict with bacon or ham, but my favourite variation is with smoked salmon. For a vegetarian alternative (Eggs Florentine), you can use 250g of spinach wilted in a little olive oil over a high heat instead.

Serves 2

4 large eggs
3 tbsp white wine vinegar
2 toasting muffins
4 slices smoked salmon (or ham, or bacon)

Hollandaise Sauce

2 large egg yolks
1 dessertspoon lemon juice
1 dessertspoon white wine vinegar
115g butter

1. Start by making the hollandaise sauce. Blend the egg yolks in a food processor or blender for about a minute.

2. Heat the lemon juice and white wine vinegar in a pan until it begins to bubble.
3. Add this mixture to the egg yolks in a slow stream, while the blender is running.
4. Melt the butter over a gentle heat. Once it starts foaming, pour it slowly into the egg mixture, again while the blender is switched on. Slow, steady pouring is the key here!
5. Leave the sauce to one side now while you poach the eggs. Fill a deep saucepan with water and add the vinegar. When boiling, swirl the water to create a vortex (trying not to scald yourself in the process).
6. Break an egg and tip it in, holding the shell as close to the surface as possible.
7. Cook for about 2 minutes and remove with a slotted spoon. (Or, of course, buy yourself an egg poacher and use that, which is what I really should do here.)
8. Repeat with the other eggs, one at a time. Meanwhile, split and toast the muffins, then butter them and add a slice of salmon to each.
9. Top each muffin-half with an egg and then pour over the warm hollandaise to taste.

Blueberry Pancakes

Who can resist a fat fluffy pancake in the morning? Even better, these ones have blueberries in them, making them officially healthy. Well, that's my excuse anyway.

Serves 4

80g butter
250g plain flour
½ tsp salt
3 tsp baking powder
4 tsp caster sugar
2 large eggs
300ml whole milk
A few handfuls of blueberries, plus some extra to serve
Greek yoghurt
Runny honey or maple syrup to serve

1. Melt the butter over a low heat.
2. Sift the flour, salt and baking powder into a bowl, add the sugar, then form a well in the centre.
3. Beat the eggs, mix with the milk and 2 tablespoons of the melted butter then gradually pour this mixture into the flour, stirring to form a thick batter.

470

4. Grease a non-stick frying pan with a little of the melted butter and put it on a moderate heat.
5. Fold the blueberries into the batter then spoon 4 separate tablespoons of batter into the pan, leaving space between them.
6. Cook for a minute or so until bubbles begin to appear on the surface, then flip over and cook the other side for another minute.
7. Stack on a plate until all the batter is used up, re-greasing the pan with melted butter between each batch.
8. Serve each pancake with a dollop of yoghurt and fresh blueberries, and drizzle over the honey or syrup to taste.

Save up to 70 %

We're passionate about hotels and offering the best short breaks across the UK.

We love what the UK has to offer and believe that every little break should be a great one, that's why we handpick the best UK short-break deals that we know will appeal and delight ~ all with loads of great value added extras.

Working with

"bespoke"
HOTELS

we are offering all readers
15% OFF*

Quote PANMAC

to take advantage of this great deal!

www.greatlittlebreaks.com
08448 488 488

Book and stay by 31st December 2015!
*Any Bespoke Hotel featured on Great Little Breaks